THE
MAHOUND

by Lance Horner

A FAWCETT GOLD MEDAL BOOK • NEW YORK

THE MAHOUND

Copyright © 1969 by Lance Horner

Published by Fawcett Gold Medal Books, a unit of CBS Publications, the Consumer Publishing Division of CBS Inc.

ISBN: 0-449-13605-1

Printed in the United States of America

29 28 27 26 25 24 23 22 21 20

To my *luk chai*

SOT SICAMUT

Bangkok, Thailand

CHAPTER I

RORY MAHOUND, HEREDITARY LAIRD OF KIL-
burnie and fifth Baron of Sax, stood by his father's open
grave and felt the water oozing through the holes in his
brogues. His ragged kilt was sodden with water, and
the rough, wet wool scraped against the insides of his
knees as he straightened up after throwing the first damp
clod of clay onto the poor pine box half-covered with mire
in the bottom of the grave. The titles that had become his
since the death of his father two days ago meant little to
him. Just now he would willingly exchange them for a
drink of old Jamie MacPherson's hot sugar water laced
with a goodly amount of whiskey.

He had shed no tears over his father, who undoubtedly
was better off in his muddy grave than he had ever been
struggling to keep himself alive in the bleak dampness of
Sax Castle, where only four or five of the forty rooms
were now habitable. For the last year, the old man had
been wracked with coughs and fevers and certainly nobody could have wished him back for more suffering;
especially not Rory, since the old laird had never spoken a
single word to him except through old Jamie as an inter-
mediary. Now, at his father's grave, Rory scarcely heark-
ened to the words of the Covenanting minister. He raised
his head to see the rain beating against the man, dribbling
in streaks down his face and soaking the white tabs of his
collar so that the starch ran down onto his black robe
which the years had turned a musty green. He was mum-
bling something about dust unto dust and Rory felt he
should be saying muck unto muck. Then he caught the
hasty "amen" and saw the minister turn and head back to
the kirk. The few mourners moved off; Rory took one last

7

look at the wet pine box and the oozing clay walls of the grave and walked away himself. With a good two miles to the castle and no horse to ride, Rory jammed his bonnet down over his head, tightened the sodden plaid around his neck, and started back alone through the coming dusk. Besides the titles of Laird of Kilburnie and Baron of Sax, his father had left him exactly three pounds, four shillings and sixpence, two cows, a sow with piglets, the crumbling and mostly roofless Castle of Sax, a silver cairngorm brooch that had belonged to his Danish mother, a few rickety chairs and tables, a Bible with some pages missing, and a strong, healthy body.

His crop of yellow hair, his fair skin, his dark blue eyes, and his big feet and hands were all a Viking legacy from his mother who had died, poor soul, after her frail body had expended all its energy giving him birth. Her death had occasioned his father's hatred, so that for twenty-two years the only mothering he had known had come from old Jamie MacPherson. His father had ignored him.

It was Jamie who had talked to him, told him stories, rubbed goose grease on his chest when he had caught cold, and taught him all that he knew. This, in fact, was considerable, for although Jamie was weak in ciphering and the classics, he was strong in languages and geography. For many years, as a seaman, he had sailed the middle passage from Africa to the West Indies, and he had lost his leg when the redcoats had tried to break up that adders' nest of rebellious colonials at Bunker Hill. He had been born in the village of Sax under the crumbling walls of the castle, and he had made his way back there, first to Glasgow and then, stomping on his peg leg, to Sax, and taken up the duties as man-of-all-work at the castle, nursing the ailing baroness in her late pregnancy, feeding her bowls of barley gruel to strengthen her, and then acting as midwife for the lusty, squalling babe that had come into the world and caused her departure. The old laird had taken one look at the brat and another at his dead wife and then, after naming the hapless offspring Roderick, had turned his back on him and pretended that he did not exist.

Jamie had taken over and raised the bairn, whom he

8

dubbed Rory. As the years went on, he had taught Rory all that he knew—and it was a strange curriculum, for Rory learned early to speak Arabic and Hausa and to know the ports of Africa, at least those between Conakry and Calabar as well as the northern ports of Mazagan, Tangier, and Tripoli. At the last place, Jamie had been held in slavery for three years before escaping to Malta.

Jamie told the boy about the fabulous city of Havana in Cuba; thriving Bridgetown in Barbados; Port-au-Prince in Haiti; the prim city of Newport in Rhode Island, and the gray-stone and red-brick barrenness of Puritan Boston in Massachusetts. With Jamie in front of a smoldering peat fire when the old laird had gone to bed, Rory visited the Canaries and Madeira and the Azores; and when the boy was older Jamie introduced him to the waterfront taverns of Bristol and Cardiff and Liverpool and the bawdyhouses of Port Royal and New Orleans—without the boy ever stepping out of the kitchen at Sax Castle. He taught him to fight with his fists until there was not a youth in Sax Village who could stand up against young Rory Mahound. He taught him to snare rabbits and kill birds with a slingshot to eke out the slim fare of the castle kitchen. And when Rory had passed his fifteenth birthday, it was old Jamie who told him what it was that the village lasses held so precious under their petticoats and the best way to blandish them so they would part with it. In all, Rory was an apt pupil, talking to Jamie in Arabic much to the laird's disgust, brawling his way amongst the boys of the village, and becoming particularly adept at lifting petticoats under dark hedgerows.

Now, on his way back from his father's burying, Rory considered another legacy from his father, albeit an indirect one. It was the letter from his father's brother in Liverpool which had been received over a week before the old laird died. That and the coach ticket from Glasgow to Liverpool which he had not been able to use, for who could leave a dying father even though he had always hated the man? But now he could. Aye, there was nothing to stop him now. Jamie MacPherson could go and live with his son, which he had been wanting to do for a long time now, and as far as Rory was concerned the rest of

9

the roofs of the castle could fall in and the castle itself collapse into rubble. He never wanted to see it again. Never!

He and Jamie had read the letter over so many times he could remember it by heart. It was the first and only letter he had ever received, so it was an important milestone in his life. Now it was going to be even more important. With the rain driving in his eyes and the water sloshing through his brogues, he mumbled aloud every word of the crabbed, slanting handwriting.

Liverpool
Mar. 2, 1803

DEAR NEPHEW RODERICK:

I have heard through Jamie MacPherson of your father's illness and although my brother and I have not spoken for years, I do not feel that I should allow this animosity to extend to you, his son and my nephew, with whom I have never had any quarrel.

According to my reckoning, you have reached your majority, and Sax is certainly no place for a lad of your probable capabilities. With the loss of the family monies through your father's stupid and obstinate upholding of Charles Edward Stuart, the Young Pretender, there can be little left of Sax.

Having given up all pretenses of being a gentleman and entered into trade, I find that being a merchant of affluence is far better than living as an impoverished aristocrat and would recommend this same course to you. I am now the senior partner of McCairn and Ogilsvy of this city with numerous prosperous ventures, not the least of which is the lucrative trade in slaves between Africa and the American West Indies.

If you would consider foregoing your father's threadbare peerage and entertain the idea of becoming, in time, a prosperous merchant, I suggest that you come to Liverpool by means of the enclosed coach ticket and start in this business. It would be necessary for you to begin at the bottom and work your way up entirely on your own merit, without relying on me to further your advancement except as you have earned it. I am no believer in nepotism and shall adopt the same tactics with my own sons when they are old enough to go into the business.

To this end I am reserving a berth for you as supercargo on the ship *Ariadne*, Captain Sparks commanding. Allowing a week for this letter to arrive in Sax, a week for you to make up your mind and a week for your journey to Liverpool, you should be here a week before sailing time, the 30th of March.

I would prefer that you did not call at my home, but rather that you present yourself at my office, where living arrangements can be made for you with the factory clerks. Knowing the condition of your financial resources, I shall take the liberty of placing a sea chest with necessities for the voyage aboard the *Ariadne*.

YOUR UNCLE,
Jabez Kilburnie McCairn.

P.S. As you will see, I have changed my name from Mahound to McCairn. It was my mother's name and owing to the unfortunate connotation of the name Mahound,* I would advise you to do likewise.

Rory was still thinking about the letter when he arrived back at Sax, cold, wet, and cursing himself and the world. He threaded his way through the vast halls open to the sky, with their tattered rags of rain-drenched tapestries still hanging to the stone walls, their clutter of broken and abandoned furniture, and the dead weeds that grew in the broken flagging, until he arrived, through a long covered passageway whose roof was so low he had to stoop to traverse it and whose walls were so narrow they scarcely accommodated his broad shoulders, in the kitchen, one of the few rooms still roofed and intact. The sparse light, filtering through the deep window slits and struggling through the peaty smoke, left the room almost in darkness; but Jamie MacPherson had a generous fire in

---

*Mahound was an ancient name for Mohammed, the Prophet of Islam, which arrived in Scotland with the returning Crusaders. It was the root for such names as Mahon, Mahoon, Mahane, Mahoney, and Mahony. Through association with Mohammed, Mahound had been adopted into the Scotch dialect as the word for Satan, the Devil, the Prince of Darkness.

11

the fireplace, a kettle was boiling on the hob, and a pot on the crane sent off puffs of aromatic steam with each thick "glob" of the contents.

"Aye, my laddie, my puir, puir laddie." Jamie stumped over to Rory and unwound the sodden plaid from his neck. "It's soaked to the skin you are and ready to catch your death." He led Rory over to the high-backed chair by the fire, pushed him down into it, pulled off the wet brogues, and lifted his wool-stockinged feet onto the fender. "Now, rest yourself there while old Jamie makes you a cup of tea and warms that belly of yours with some porridge."

"Tea, Jamie?" Rory stared at the old man open-mouthed. "Since when has there been tea in Castle Sax?"

"Sent over by Mrs. Shaughnessy to cheer you up after the funeral. She may be a Papist and Irish to boot, but the old trollop has a heart of gold and wanted you to have a cup of tea. And I put some bacon in the porridge so it'll stick to your ribs. Now, tell me about the burying."

"At least the old Mahound," Rory stressed the last word, "is six feet under." He stretched his toes nearer the fire, his wool socks steaming.

"He's dead and buried and we must not speak evil of the dead, must we?" Jamie shook a doleful head.

" 'Twas not evil I was speaking. He was the old Mahound and now I'm the young Mahound. Dead he is and I can't mourn him. Jamie, I'm leaving for England come the morrow."

"I was hoping you would." Jamie ladled the porridge onto a trencher and rummaged in the cupboard for a wooden spoon. "Going to your Uncle Jabez, I suppose. Aye, 'tis the best course, milord."

"But not to his elegant mansion house, Jamie. It 'pears I'm not good enough to mingle with his family. Now what's this 'milord' business, Jamie?"

"Well, ain't you? Ain't you now Sir Roderick Mahound, Baron of Sax and Laird of Kilburnie?"

"No. At least I do not intend to be. Sir Roderick with my big toe poking out of my stocking? Baron of Sax with three pounds in my sporran? Laird of Kilburnie, eating a plate of porridge with a wooden spoon and wondering

12

where the next plate is coming from? No, Jamie, I'm none of these, but I'll not change my name to McCairn. I was spawned by the devil. The Mahound I am and the Mahound I'll be. Now listen to me, Jamie."

The old man stood before him, his hands placed solidly on his hips. "Since when are you, whether you're Lucifer or the Archangel Michael himself, telling me to listen to the likes of you? Eat your porridge and let the vittles stop your blathering mouth. Brought you up, I did, and I'll listen to you when I'm ready. So you're off to Liverpool and away you go. And what's to become of puir old Jamie, I'd like to know!"

"Your feet have been itching these months past to go and live with your son. You know it. His cottage is more comfortable than this rookery and you'll not have to look after me."

"As if that was any trouble."

"And you haven't had a farthing all these years. Now Jamie, for this minute I'm the laird and you're listening. There's two milch cows and the sow's just farrowed. One cow's yours along with the sow and piglets. Take them to your son so's you'll not be dependent on him. I've got the clothes on my back and three pounds."

"With ten shillings more," Jamie added. "See," he took down a tin cup from the top shelf of the hutch and poured the contents into his hand. "They're yours. Sometimes I sold eggs or a flitch of bacon, stealing from the old laird and I've kept it all here. It's yours, take it!"

"Then you'll keep the animals?"

"That I will. I cannot see you arriving in Liverpool with a sow and a litter of pigs. When are you off?"

"Come morning. I talked with Davy Campbell before the burying and he's driving his cart into Doune tomorrow. Leaving at dawn he is, and I'm to meet him at the brig. I'll ride shank's mare from there into Glasgow." He had finished the porridge and stood up to put the trencher on the table.

The old man bowed his head in assent. He loved this boy. He had meant more to him than his own son, for he had mothered him since the day he took him away from his dying mother's breast. He regarded Rory, who was

13

now standing with the glow of the fire on him, and he raised his head to get the full glory of him and fill his eyes with him once more. Ah, he was a braw lad; a tall lad and a strong lad, and give him a couple more years and he'd be taller and stronger still.

The Viking blood that had come down through his mother was more apparent than his Scotch blood. He was taller by a head and shoulders than Jamie, even in his stocking feet, and his shadow from the firelight lengthened out over the floor and up the whitewashed wall like the shadow cast by a giant. His hair was the color of ripe corn, straight and long, curling inwards when it reached the nape of his neck to make a golden casque on his head. Dark brows that lifted on the ends like birds' wings over-shadowed blue eyes so deep they were almost violet, darkened by the sooty lashes that were such an unexpected contrast to his light hair. The nose was short, wide-bridged and straight, perhaps even overwide because the nostrils were large, but it added a measure of strength to his face which the lips—too curved, too broad, and too sensual—tended to weaken. The chin was square, cleft in the middle, and hairless, with no sign of a beard showing on the smooth skin. Although the ears were hidden by the hanging locks of hair, Jamie knew them to be small, set close to the head and quite out of proportion to the smooth white column of neck that disappeared into the ragged shirt collar. Under the shirt, Jamie knew the lad was firmly muscled with a barrel chest, a narrow waist and a hard, rigid belly. Below that he did not know, now that the lad was a grown man and no longer came out to the kitchen to dress before the fire, but he had heard gossip that the cotters' young daughters were all chasing after the lad, which proved that he was well enough endowed to satisfy any woman. Well, it would be a blessing and a curse to the lad—a blessing because he could please all women and a curse because they would never leave him alone.

"Tomorrow then?" Jamie asked as though it were the most natural thing in the world to start off for England in the morning. "I'll try to get you a good breakfast and I suppose that's the last I'll see of you."

"It may well be, Jamie, but I'll never forget you. You've coddled and spoiled me and slapped my arse when I needed it. You've taught me to fight and poach and, although you've never helped me do it, I've learned to tumble the lasses from what you've told me. You've done much for me, Jamie, and there's little enough that I can do for you. Take anything here you want. There's not much but the pots and pans and a chair or two, but take them."

"I'll help myself," Jamie nodded, "and there'll be no reason to lock the castle. There's nothing in it that the poorest cotter would want. But there's just one thing." He looked the question at Rory. "There's two cows and you told me to take but one of them. What about the other?"

Rory grinned sheepishly, the red mounting to his face.

"It's for Mary MacLeod."

"She with the belly so big she can't even get up to the loom? You planted it there, I'm a-thinking." Jamie chuckled, stamping his peg leg on the flagging.

"That I did," Rory boasted. "She'll be happy to raise up a little Sax. Pleaded that I marry her, she did, well knowing that I'd father no Mahound in any brat of hers. The cow will pay her, and if it's a boy, I hope he looks like me, Jamie."

"There's three toddlers in the village now, all with yellow hair and snub noses like your own. You know," Jamie slapped the palm of one hand with the fist of the other as though he had settled a momentous question, "it's your kilt what's to blame."

"This poor thing?" Rory flicked its ragged edge.

"That," Jamie nodded his head more vigorously. "When a man wears britches, he has to take time to undo all the buttons and straps and strings. But with a kilt, it's just h'ist it up, the work of a moment in a bedroom or behind a hedgerow. Yes, Rory lad, kilts have been the ruination of more Scotch lasses than the Mahound himself."

"Kilts or britches, Jamie, before the year is over there may be a couple or three more besides Mary MacLeod's. If Mary MacLernen and Mary MacDonald and Mary

15

Duncan all start swelling, you'll know why. The name Mary seems woven into my fate, Jamie."

"You're a rakehell and a libertine, Rory my lad." Jamie's words indicated more pride than censure. "I suppose there'll be a trail of towheads and flat noses all the way from here to Liverpool."

"Not unless the coach stops." Rory started to unbutton the worn silver buttons of his old green velvet jacket. "And now I'm for bed. I'll take a candle, to read over my uncle's letter once more. I'm just hoping I won't be too late. The *Ariadne* sails in about a week and I want to be on board."

Jamie's hand lingered on Rory's arm when he handed him the candlestick. "You're a good lad and a hot-blooded one, Rory, but the women could well be your ruination."

Rory laughed. "I'm going to Africa, Jamie, where the lasses are all black as coal; and I'll wager not one of them's named Mary, so you won't have to worry."

"Black or white, they'll be women and you're Rory Mahound and they'll be running after you."

Rory opened the door of the little bedroom off the kitchen, shivering as a cold blast of air hit him in the face. "Then let them run, Jamie. I hope they can run faster than I can. Good night."

Jamie stood still for a moment after Rory had closed the door, then sank to his knees with his elbows in the big chair. "Good God," he prayed, "keep the bairn safe."

CHAPTER II

MINOR ACCIDENTS AND DELAYS COST RORY three days on his journey. Davy Campbell was unable to go and Rory had to hike the whole distance from Sax to Glasgow, where he was too late to catch the daily diligence and had to remain until the next day. This loss of time was, however, one which turned out in the end to be far from irritating.

It was the first time he had ever been in a city, and he decided that grim, granite, and depressing as Glasgow was, it was an improvement over the desolate moors of Sax. At least there were people in the city and with them movement and bustle, something constantly going on. With no baggage to encumber him, he left the inn which served as a coach station determined not to spend any of his precious shillings merely to stretch his big frame out in a bed for a few hours. The weather had turned warm and sunny and he had noticed a straw stack in the inn yard. That would serve for his overnight accommodation and he would save himself some money. Until then he would indulge himself in the sights of the city. From a sidewalk vender he purchased a bowl of broth for a penny and, although it was only barley and hot water, it managed to ease his stomach. Then he strolled out on the town.

Wandering aimlessly about, with every prospect new and interesting, he came to the docks and for the first time saw sailing ships with tall masts and carved and painted figureheads. One like them was to be his next home, and although they looked monstrous large tied up at the docks, he wondered how they would seem in the middle of the ocean.

Late in the afternoon, with the effects of the barley broth wearing off and his always hearty appetite asserting itself, he started back from the docks, only to find that with the twisting and turnings of the streets he had lost his way. Picking at random a crooked street that seemed to lead back in the direction from which he had come, he walked along the narrow sidewalk, cursing the inhabitants for dumping their slops and offal onto the streets and gutters. Close to the houses, where it was somewhat cleaner, he loitered for a moment, watching a dancing bear on the opposite sidewalk.

It was a most comical sight. The bear was dressed in tattered red and green silks with a multitude of tinkling bells, and it slouched along at the end of a rope behind a gypsy in an equally fantastic rig. Now, Rory reasoned, he

17

could live at Sax Castle all his life and never see anything as outlandish or amusing as that. While he was staring goggle-eyed at this spectacle, he felt his bonnet snatched from his head. He whirled around; there was nobody nearby. Convinced for a second that he had imagined the whole thing, he put his hand to his head and sure enough, it was bare. He heard a derisive little laugh from above and snapped his head up. There in an open window, dangling his cap just out of his fingers' reach, a girl leaned on the sill, her white gown so brazenly opened that two tempting breasts were displayed almost in their entirety. They were milk-white, round and smooth, and he could even see the ruddy nipples, all of which held considerably more interest for him than the battered bonnet she held in her hand. He found them even more engrossing than the shuffling bear or the gaudy gypsy. With some difficulty he lifted his eyes to her face, perceiving that it was young, pert, and saucy, with ringlets of black hair escaping from under a white mob cap.

"What are you gawking at, Flaxpoll?" her fingers opened the gown a little further and cupped one of the tempting breasts. "At this? Pretty, ain't it?"

" 'Twould be hard to choose between them, lass." Rory bowed with all the grace of a Cavalier at St. James's. "If my life depended on it, I could not tell which of the two would be the prettier but, of course," he winked at her, "it would be necessary for me to make a most careful comparison. My eyes could deceive me but add my fingers to my eyes and I'm sure I could determine which one was the prettier or if they both have the same amount of beauty. However, whilst talking about such tempting objects, I'd like my bonnet back."

"Then why don't you come in and get it, and if you want, you can use your eyes and your fingers too. Stop lollygagging out there on the pavement and come inside."

"Would your name, lass, by any chance be Mary?" he grinned at her.

"And would you be the devil himself to know that it is? Yes, Mary Davis it is, but how you know it is something I can't get through my noggin."

"You're right, Mary Davis, I'm the Mahound himself—

Rory Mahound at your service and it's in I'm coming without any more lollygagging."

She pointed to the street door which stood ajar and ducked back into the window, closing the shutter tight. The door led into a dark entryway stinking of boiled tripe and mice, but almost immediately a door opened and he stepped into a warm room and into the girl's arms. She only reached to his chest but he lifted her bodily until her lips reached his, then sat her down again and spun her around until her back was to him and with both hands started to investigate that which he had only partially seen. He encountered no difficulties, for the robe she wore had neither buttons nor strings. For a long moment he satisfied himself, felt the hot itch of desire mounting, and knew that his kilt was standing straight before him. She turned around to face him, his poor worn bonnet in her hands.

"That'll be two shillings," she said.

"Two shillings for what?" He looked from the hard nipples of her breasts to the cap. "For my old bonnet? Why, lass, if I could afford two shillings I'd buy me a new one and throw that aged thing away. Besides, you've no right to steal my bonnet and charge me two shillings for it."

"It's not for the cap," she tossed it back to him, "such a miserable holey thing that it is. It's for what you're going to do to me now."

"And who said I'm going to do anything to you that would be worth two shillings to me?"

She pointed down to his threadbare kilt. "You ain't saying it but Old Harry's saying it for you."

He glanced down and grinned, but then his words became serious. "I've never paid for it yet, nor never will. 'Twould take all the pleasure out of it to think I was wasting two shillings on something I've found under every hedgerow." He plastered the cap securely on his head and started for the door.

But she was ahead of him and reached the door before he did, flinging her back against it. When he would have lifted the latch, her hand restrained him and he pressed the length of his body against hers. He felt her hand release his and reach under his kilt.

"Old Harry's right." She sucked in her breath. "He's the Mahound himself." She clutched at him frantically for a moment, then withdrew her hand and shot the bolt of the door, letting her robe fall to the floor.

"It won't cost you no two shillings, lad." She fumbled with the buttons of his jacket. "Your kilt may be ragged and your jupe patched; your bonnet's holey and your sporran's empty; but you've got something there that even a dockside trollop like Mary Davis has never seen the likes of before and never will again, I'm thinking. Such a bonny maypole it is, it's worth two shillings to Mary Davis for something to talk about the rest of her life. Change and change about: Mary Davis'll pay you two shillings herself. It'll be more of a sight to see than the bear you were goggling at."

Never before and never afterward would Rory earn two shillings more pleasantly. Her professional touches made it more exciting for him than the inept fumblings he had enjoyed with the Marys back home and he soon discovered that she was giving him more than his money's worth because her blandishments and her whispered endearments showed him that this was not just a two-shilling tilt. Unfortunately it was over far too soon, but even then she would not release him.

"I've got to go, Mary luv," he struggled to sit up but she pushed him back. "I'm catching the coach to England come morning and there's only one straw stack in the inn yard. I want to be the one who snuggles down in it tonight. Roaming the streets of Glasgow till dawn holds no pleasant prospects for me."

"A straw stack in the inn yard!" She pulled him back. "And what does a straw stack have that Mary Davis cannot offer?"

"Damned little!"

"Then you'll stay here, Rory Mahound, if that's your name, and a fitting name it is for you. We'll close the shutters tight and keep the door locked. Mary Davis can afford it this once in her life because 'twill never happen again. There's a leg of cold mutton in the meat safe and a

20

loaf of bread. I'll put the kettle on and we'll have a cup of hot tea with a drop of whiskey to finish it off. Then, with our bellies full, we'll all three have some sport."

"All three? You expecting somebody else?"

She nodded, shaking the black curls down over her face. "You and me and Old Harry," she pointed. "He's somebody all by himself. Poor fellow, he's resting now, but after we've had a nice cup of tea, he'll be standing up strong and hearty again. Just you wait and see."

"Aye, it's spoiling me you are, Mary Davis, and I love you for it."

Rory stretched back on the bed, his hands behind his head, watching her as she bustled about the small room. From a cupboard over the small fireplace, she took down a plate with a cold joint and a loaf of bread. She cut the meat in thick slices and then the bread. When the water was boiling, she poured it over the tea and let it steep. Going to the cupboard once again, she took down an earthenware bottle. The small deal table she pushed over to the bed, covering it with a piece of coarse white linen. With Rory sitting on the bed and Mary in the one chair she possessed, they had a cozy meal and Rory found it far better than the cold comfort of the haystack. Mary Davis was a pretty girl. It was evident that she had not been long at her profession and Rory could see that she was genuinely taken with him. Just like all the rest of the Marys.

After they had eaten, she pushed back the table and joined him in the bed. Just as she had predicted, Old Harry obliged them not only once but twice before he curled up for a rest. While he was resting, Rory and Mary Davis talked, not so much as lovers but as old friends. Through the crassness of her vulgarity, Rory caught glimpses of a very decent person, and although, as she was the first to admit, she was a strumpet and a two-shilling whore for women-hungry sailors just off the ships, Rory found her witty and engaging, and also (though in this he was not too much surprised) he discovered that she was madly in love with him.

"Why must you be off to England?" she pleaded, twisting his long yellow strands of hair in her fingers. "A

21

miserable place it is, I've heard. Whyn't you stay here with Mary Davis?"

"And what would we eat when the cold joint is gone?"

"I'd earn more."

"And I'd stay here flat on my back, letting you support me?"

"Nothing of the kind! Look you, Rory Mahound, I can't do two things at once. I can't stay here earning the shillings with one customer and be out on the docks lining up the next one. Some days I get five men and that's ten shillings; some days I'm lucky and get ten and that's a whole pound. But now if I had a likely lad a-pimping for me, I'd mayhap take on twenty and that's two pounds. I'd split with you. A pound for you and a pound for me. Think you that you can make such a princely salary as that in Liverpool? A whole pound a day? Why! 'Tis more than the Lord Mayor himself gets and I'll do all the work."

A pound a day! It was a tempting offer. Few men could earn as much. But Rory shook his head. "You tempt me, Mary Davis, but no matter how your words or your lovely white tits or the prospects of spending all my nights with you tempt me, I'm for Liverpool tomorrow. It's my uncle who's expecting me and I'm off on a ship to Africa. I may not earn a pound a day, Mary Davis, but I'll be seeing the world."

"You'll not see any as white and round as these in Africa." She cupped her hands under her breasts. "All you'll find will be black ones. I've nary seen but one blackamoor in my life but I hear that in Africa all men and all women are black. When you see those black sluts, you'll be wishing you were back with Mary Davis."

"That I will, and Old Harry too."

"Then stay, Rory," she pleaded with him. "The wee house here is mine, left to me by my father. Sarah McCrory who does her whorin' business in the room above can get out. She pays me only a shilling a day for her rent and you can have her rooms so's you'll have a place to stay when I'm working. I'm no daft and silly lass what's expecting you to marry me. Maybe you won't stay with me very long but while you do I'll have you, Rory, and no woman

22

could ask for more. Of all the men that's ever pawed me and gasped and gurgled over me, you're the only one I've ever wanted. Bide here with me."

"Nay, lass, tempt me no further." Rory tempered his answer with a kiss. "I'm beholden to my uncle who sent me the money for my coach fare to Liverpool, and it would be fair stealing if I didn't go. I keep my word, Mary Davis, if I do nothing else. But I'll promise you one thing. Some day I'll be coming back from Africa and when that day comes I'll hie me back to Glasgow to see you. Write down your street for me before I go so I'll know where to find you."

" 'Tis better than nothing," she sighed and snuggled closer to him, grasping him tightly. "At least it's something to look forward to. I'll be thinking of you, Rory, with every man that puts his dirty paws on me, and I'll be wishing that it was you, so strong and clean and fine with your shining hair."

"Then we'll go to sleep on it because I must get up early to catch the coach at seven o'clock, if I can find my way back to the inn."

"I'll come to wish you Godspeed. Don't worry, I'll not disgrace you. I've got decent clothes and I'm no bawd in public. So good night, Rory lad, and we'll wake up early, you and I and Old Harry himself."

"That we will, Mary Davis." He stretched out his arm as a pillow for her head and drew her close to him. The spent tallow dip guttered out, leaving only the dying embers of the peat fire to cast rosy shadows in the room. He was dozing off, contented, happy, and secure in the little room, when Mary Davis, who had not closed her eyes, not wishing to lose sight of him while there was still some light, placed her lips close to his ear and whispered.

"I've been thinking, Rory lad."

"Of what, Mary Davis?" He roused himself.

"I'd like something to remember you by."

"All I've got," he answered, "are the clothes on my back, and you know how poor they are. All told they're hardly worth the dustbin. If I left you my kilt I'd go to Liverpool naked; if my jupe, I'd freeze to death; and if my bonnet, I'd catch me a churchyard cough I'd never get

23

over. All the hair's worn off my sporran and my dirk is no
better than a kitchen knife, but I tell you what I'll do,
Mary Davis," he kissed her, "the one thing I have from
my mother whom I never saw is a cairngorm brooch that's
in my sporran, and if you'd like it, it's yours."

"I couldn't take it, it being your poor dead mother's.
I'm a decent girl even though I'm a whore. But I thank
you just the same."

"Then I'll send you a present from Africa, that I will.
It's a promise. So you watch out for it, Mary Davis, and
when it comes you'll remember me and Old Harry both if
you haven't forgotten us by that time."

"That I'll never do, Rory. Neither one of you."

CHAPTER III

WET, SORE, AND SHIVERING FROM LONG HOURS
perched on the roof of the coach, Rory Mahound arrived
at Liverpool late in the evening. He felt he had been fortunate in arriving on time because tomorrow was the day
the *Ariadne* was scheduled to sail. He eased himself down
from the company of the bales and bundles and stumbled
into the common room of the inn. The roaring fire was
welcome and he went to it to rub his chapped knees and
chafe his raw hands until he was shooed away by the bar-
maids who were waiting in line to fill mugs with hot water
for grogs and use the heated pokers for mulled ciders. Nobody paid any attention to him except to push him around
from place to place until at length one barmaid, who had
inventoried him with admiring eyes, spoke to him.

"Get out from under my feet, you overgrown lummox,
and sit yourself down at that table over there," she pointed to an empty table, then winked and smiled at him
which took away the churlishness of her words. "You cut

a sorry figure, my lad, and methinks a good hot drink of Barbados rum sweetened with treacle and greased with butter might warm your guts. You're shaking like a dog shitting on a briar bush." She straightened up on tiptoe to whisper to him, "And it won't cost you no thruppence either." She waited until he had found a place at the table and then brought his drink.

He smiled his thanks at her. "Would you know, lass, where Lively Court would be in this town? It's a business place and the firm's name is McCairn and Ogilsvy."

" 'Twould be closed by now. It's nigh onto ten o'clock and all the clerks and apprentices are locked in for the night. Poor boys, they have to be in at nine o'clock and they never have a bit of fun."

"Then which way to the docks, lass?"

"That's no place for a lad like you. You'll get crimped."

"Crimped?" he repeated blankly.

"Impressed, waylaid, shanghaied, seized, spirited away! It's hard to get seamen today, and ships' masters will go to any length to get a crew. The life's so hard and the masters so cruel, nobody wants to ship out." She laid a hand on his shoulder, squeezing the flesh under the fabric of his jacket. "I'll be here till the wee hours of the morning, else I'd ask you up to my rooms."

"And my thanks on it, lass, but you've no need to worry about me. I'm already signed up. Supercargo on the *Ariadne*."

"Then more's the need to worry about you. That's the slaver what's captained by Sparks, the scourge of the sea—handsome as hell but a black-hearted rascal if there ever was one. Better to get yourself crimped and carried aboard some other vessel."

"I can take care of myself, lass." He doubled up his arm so that she could feel the swelling of muscle under his sleeve.

"More's the pity I'm working tonight. Get back here 'round midnight and I'll see if I can get off early. 'Twill be warmer than roamin' the streets."

He nodded in agreement. "But I'd like seeing the docks and 'twill pass the time till midnight."

25

"Just you be careful." She gave him the directions and then, at an order barked from nearby, she was off. The hot drink warmed Rory all through and his spirit was renewed within him. Feeling topful again, he made his way into the wet streets, trying to remember the barmaid's directions. Such street lights as were lighted gave but a feeble illumination and gray tatters of fog streaked down around the guttering candles. He walked he knew not how long, but long enough for the effects of the hot rum to wear off. Nobody was abroad at this late hour on such a wretched night and the streets were deserted. Nary a light showed from the windows of the soot-stained gray stone buildings, and Rory wandered alone, hoping to meet some stray soul from whom he might ask directions. He felt he was nearing the water for the fog grew heavier and now, as he walked, he could see only a small circle around himself. It was always the same, oily wet black stones under his feet and gray granite walls at his side. Halfway down a block, he spied a street lantern bracketed to the corner of a building, its feeble beams making concentric circles in the fog. As he neared it he could see, albeit dimly, another person, who had stopped under the light and waited for Rory to come up.

"Aye, 'tis a bad night," the fellow said.

"'Tis that indeed," Rory answered. The sound of a human voice was reassuring and Rory stopped to appraise the stranger. Although shorter than Rory, he was strong and heavyset; an agreeable-looking young fellow with a sailor's leather hat and wide collar edged with white braid on his pea jacket. The hat did not entirely hide a shock of red hair, and Rory noticed a wide ring of gold pendent from one ear.

"Whereat bound, lad? Would be from Scotland, I take it with that kilt and bonnet. Well, I'm from Dublin and that makes both of us strangers here."

There was an air of friendliness to the stranger's words and Rory liked the looks of him. He had a broad, friendly grin and Rory welcomed even a short moment of companionship.

"Heading for the docks," Rory answered, "but I've lost my way."

"Well, you've a bit of a walk ahead of you for that's where I'm just coming from. There's nothing to see when you get there save ships and more ships, and it's getting away from ships I am. I'm Tim O'Toole, seaman, and here's my hand on it."

Rory stretched out his hand. "Rory Mahound, at your service."

"Well, then, matey, if you're at my service, whyn't join me? I was just figuring whether I'd walk to the right hand and get me a drink in the 'Isle of Jamaica' or to the left and take my grog in the 'Bight of Benin.' Your looks say you could do with a little warmth yourself, so, since you're at my service, join me. 'Tis no night to be wandering the streets of Liverpool alone."

"It's glad I'll be to go with you."

"And then, cock, after a couple of grogs under our belts, we'll head for old Mother Blood-and-Guts."

"Mother Blood-and-Guts?"

Tim combined his engaging grin with a slow wink. "Just a name we have for the old bawd. She's got a stable of whores what spreads their legs for sixpence for a quarter of an hour. They're not much good, even when a man's been to sea for three months, but at least they're women and that's the first thing a man wants when he gets ashore."

It suddenly occurred to Rory that he'd have no women when he went to sea. There'd be no Marys under the hedgerows or in snug little rooms in Glasgow. There'd be nobody like the barmaid who'd said she'd wait for him tonight.

"And how does a man get along at sea without a woman?"

Tim's finger nudged Rory in the ribs. "It's not easy, lad, not easy. There's them what marries themselves up with their right hand and there's them what don't. On the way out there's always an apprentice seaman or a cabin boy what'll bend over the apple barrel for a piece of plum duff and on the middle passage the hold's filled with black savages. Now I say there's nothing better than a nice black boy around fifteen with a tight arse—once you get him so he won't scream his bloody head off."

27

"That's not for me." Rory shook his head.

"Then you've never been to sea?" Tim took Rory's arm.

Rory shook his head. "Sixpence did you say, Tim?" Rory figured he could afford that, and with the barmaid awaiting him, he'd get all he could tonight.

"Yea, sixpence, cock, if you're talking about the frigging sows at Blood-and-Guts. A farthing would be too much but it's a place to go and something to do. Only thing is you've got to be careful. Some of them tarts is fireships."

"Fireships?"

"Yeah, burning up with the French disease. But what's the difference," Tim shrugged his shoulders, "it's no worse'n a bad cold and a man's not a man until he's had a bout. I remember a year ago on the old *Dundee Pride* every man jack on board was dripping like a leaky bucket. Two nights before we sailed from Havana, half the ship visited the Casa de las Delicias and the night before the other half. Well, cock, here we are at the 'Isle of Jamaica.' Shall we go in for a nip? The more you get under your belt, the prettier the blowsies at Mother Blood-and-Guts will look."

A guttering candle in a lantern lit up a weatherbeaten sign roughly shaped to resemble the map of the island, and a glazed door with a red curtain behind it invited them in. Inside, the fumes of tobacco were even thicker than the fog, but it was warm and a buxom barmaid smiled at them from behind the counter. They found a settle and table by the wall and sat down, Tim against the wall and Rory facing him. It was the first time he had had an opportunity to get a really good look at his companion and he decided that he liked Tim even better. He noticed the thick muscles under the wool jersey as Tim slipped off his pea jacket. He might be a few years older than Rory, and he gave the impression of immense strength. His green eyes were merry and his lips were curled in a continuous smile except when he grinned, which was often, when he displayed an even row of teeth.

"So your name's Rory Mahound," Tim reached across the table and laid his hand on Rory's.

28

"The Mahound himself," it was Rory's turn to grin.

"The saints preserve us." Tim crossed himself mechanically. "Old Harry himself. But you don't look like the devil, cock, with your yellow hair and that babe-in-the-cradle mug of yours. Aye, you're a handsome lad, Rory Mahound, and now how about a drink?"

"Good idea," Rory agreed. "And I've a shilling to pay for it with."

"Your money's no good with Tim O'Toole. I'm paying for everything, even your doxy. But what will it be—Jamaicy rum or Holland gin? Rum, I say, for it's more to my liking than gin. Once a man tastes rum in the Indies, he loses his taste for gin or whiskey."

"And I'll take rum," Rory agreed, "not that I've a tongue for it, seeing as how all the drinking I've done's been the good whiskey of Scotland."

A girl brought their drinks and both Tim and Rory downed them; Tim in one gulp but not so Rory. He sipped his; it was dark and aromatic and smelled good, but the first fiery taste warned him that he could not sling the glassful into his throat the way Tim did. It took him two or three tipples to finish it, and he felt he was burning up all the way from his mouth to his stomach, but when the fire settled down in him, it turned into a pleasant glow that permeated the marrow of his bones and made him warm and happy. The second drink was easier to get down, and when it came to the third, he was able to toss it off as quickly as his companion. And, following Tim's example, he wiped his mouth on his coatsleeve.

The rum evoked in Rory a feeling of friendship for this Tim O'Toole who sat opposite him. Surely nobody could have a franker, more open face than his good friend Tim who had brought him to this cozy, homelike place. Tim was the best friend he'd ever had. Even the prospects of the barmaid at the inn had receded and he was glad he was with Tim—good Tim, witty Tim, his bosom friend and companion. He leaned across the table.

"You're my friend, Tim O'Toole, and it's lucky I am to have come across you. I never thought I'd meet with a boon companion like you, me being all alone."

"All alone, you say?" Tim regarded Rory with new

29

interest. "Ain't you got no family—nobody to miss you if you stay out late?"

"Can stay out all night and nobody'll care and I don't mind staying out all night with you, Timmy my friend," Rory gazed at Tim with drunken affection.

"Then why don't we start for old Blood-and-Guts? We sailors have a saying that a friend becomes a bugginsickle buddy only after you've fuddled, fought, and fucked with him. We ain't going to do no fighting, Rory, but we've drunk together and now we'll spread our wenches together. The house's just down the street and we'll have another drink there before we tumble the sows."

Rory tried to stand up but found himself unsteady on his feet. With Tim helping him, he inched out from behind the table and, leaning on Tim, he managed to get to the door. The cold air revived him somewhat and he staggered along on Tim's arm. He felt in high spirits—drunk as a lord and happy as a king. When Tim O'Toole started to sing an Irish song, Rory joined in, not knowing the words, but making enough noise to cover up the lack. Arm in arm they roistered down the empty street until they reached another oasis of light, this one also from a tallow dip stuck in a glass lantern. They halted before a blank door and when Tim pushed it open, they stepped into a large, low-ceilinged room, brilliantly lighted.

Rory blinked his eyes, befogged with liquor as they were and he had to shake his head before he could focus them on the room. Several men, whom he took by their dress to be sailors, sat at a table in one corner and each man had a girl—if such mature and hard-faced drabs could be called girls—sitting on his knee. The sailors were singing and banging the table with their pewter mugs while the strumpets in tattered wrappers, which did nothing to restrain their hanging breasts, fondled the men and slobbered over their faces. Rory judged that not one of the women was under thirty, such haggard and shopworn creatures as they were, some fat with enormous melon breasts and some lank with flat, pendent dugs. Tim propelled Rory to an empty table and no sooner had they seated themselves than two blowsies came to keep them company. A greasy-haired hag, her face whitened as

30

though with flour, perched herself on Rory's lap while an enormous old beldame with a bulging belly and thighs like hams straddled Tim. Their hoarse voices whispered endearments and Rory felt his kilt lifted but despite the energy of the virago that was manipulating him, he did not respond. The sour sweat smell of her repelled him, but he couldn't go and leave his friend Tim in the lurch. Not with him and Tim being bosom buddies!

"Well, look who's coming to make us welcome," Tim shouted out. "Old Blood-and-Guts herself!"

Rory peered around the naked shoulder of the harridan on his lap and saw, much to his surprise, a woman decently dressed in black coming toward their table. Her iron-gray hair was skinned back from her forehead into such a tight bun that her eyes seemed to be popping out of her head. She was tall and emaciated and had, Rory decided, the hardest face he had ever seen on a human being. It was flinty in its harshness and her eyes, gray as marble, looked out from under lashless lids. Even her smile was a mere stretching of her lips, lacking in any warmth.

"Welcome, lads." She bit each word off as she spoke it. "Mother's glad to see her boys and lucky you are to have my two prettiest girls. Ain't they the lovelies? And the tricks they know! Now, before you take my pretties upstairs, be generous lads and buy each one of them a tot of gin so that they'll be in the mood to entertain you better; and have one for yourself so you'll enjoy it more."

"This one's like a dead eel," the one sitting on Rory's lap screamed out. "It'll take more than one tot of gin to put life in him."

Tim pushed the one on his lap to the floor while he stood up to get his poke out of his pocket. "This one's on me, Rory gossoon. And I'll stand for the wench too if you can stomach her." He picked the coins from the leather bag and handed them to the old woman, pointing to Rory. "The lad's had too much to drink, Mother. Fix him up with one of your special drinks so that he can get it up for your woman that's been trying so hard." He extracted another shilling and handed it to the woman. "Remember now, the special one for the lad—the extra special one."

31

She was soon back with three noggins of gin and a larger tumbler that she placed in front of Rory.

"You'll find it a wee bit bitter, lad, but it's a good stomach settler and it'll raise your rod so our bonnie Maggie will scream for mercy. Drink it down."

"Yes, drink it down, Rory," Tim urged, "though I doubt if anything less than a caber would make Maggie yell."

"And that's what it is," Rory raised his glass, "a heavy beam if there ever was one." He drank the glass. It was bitter and yet sweet at the same time, sticking to his throat like treacle.

"Now up with you, Rory," Tim dislodged Maggie who seemed loath to relinquish her hold. He got his hands under Rory's armpits and hoisted him up. "Timmy'll help you, Rory gossoon."

But Rory didn't hear him. He sank down through a mass of black cobwebs that brushed him all over with a soft bittersweet touch like the taste in his throat. He could feel Tim's arm under him, supporting him, but he sensed it only for a fleeting instant and then the blackness engulfed him and his sleep was dreamless, dark and void.

"Get him out of here," the woman in black commanded.

"I'll need help, Mother." Tim relinquished his hold on Rory and let him slip to the floor. "Is Big Hannah here?"

"She's busy at the moment but she'll be down in three shakes of a lamb's tail."

"Can she help me with him?"

"I'd rather she'd help you than for the catchpolls to find him here."

"Then tell her to slip on her shoes and a coat."

The old woman disappeared up the stairs. The one called Maggie came over to look at Rory, bent down, and let her fingers slide across his face.

" 'Twould have been like he said," she sighed, "a fair caber."

CHAPTER IV

RORY DRIFTED SLOWLY UPWARD THROUGH the clinging black cobwebs that engulfed him. A flash of consciousness would come to him momentarily, then he would sink once again into the confusing morass of semi-oblivion. As the instants of awareness grew longer and more frequent, he discovered that he was bracing himself to keep his body from swaying to one side and then the other. When he tried to shift his position, he experienced pain which, surviving from one lucid period to another, caused him to tentatively examine his head. His fingers encountered a lump the size of a plover's egg. Gradually, with longer periods of acute awareness, he felt such a splitting pain in his head that it entirely obliterated the cobwebs and brought him to a realization of himself and a wonder as to where he might be.

When he was able to open his eyes, the greasy unpainted boards at his head and side conveyed nothing to him. Slowly he turned to look in the other direction. In a murky twilight he gradually distinguished a tier of shelves that seemed strangely like the one he was lying on. As his eyes became accustomed to the uncertain light, he saw that on some of these shelves there were men sleeping. At least he was not alone. Suddenly the planks on which he was bedded shifted and he banged against the bulkhead, remaining there only a moment and then being tossed back again. He was saved from pitching onto the floor only by the guard board at his side.

If his head would stop splitting and shuttling, he felt he might be able to collect his thoughts; but one thing he did know for certain, he had never been in this particular place before. Then where was he? Ah yes, he was in

33

Liverpool. Of that he was certain. And he had met somebody. Somebody named Tim. Tim O'Toole! A sailor! They had had some drinks and then had gone to a bawdyhouse together. A woman—some desolate old drab—had been sitting on his knee. He must be still in the house. Yet if he was, why were there only men sleeping here, and why was the floor pitching and rolling?

The movement became even more violent, and he was catapulted from one side of his narrow coffin to the other. He turned onto his back and tried to sit up, but whacked his head against the low ceiling over him. It did nothing to help his headache, which increased in intensity and now combined with a feeling of nausea that knotted his stomach and sent a surge of sour vomit into his throat. He perceived that he was naked except for his shirt and realized that part of his discomfort was from the cold. Then, despite all he could do, the vomit frothed from his mouth and he cared not a whit that its hot vileness befouled his body. He was so entirely miserable, so distraught with the continuous movement, so cold, dry-mouthed, and bewildered that he longed for something that might end his sufferings, even if it sent him back again into the dark cobwebs from which he had emerged. Again he puked and this time he felt he had disgorged his very guts themselves. Too weak now to hang onto the side of his cage, he let his head roll back and forth, hitting first one side and then the other.

A light that momentarily illuminated the semidarkness was followed by the sound of footsteps—boots on planking—and Rory saw a shadow advancing toward him which by the moving legs he identified as a man. The shadow came closer and a hand, not too ungently, almost affectionately, grasped his shoulder and shook it to rouse him.

"Rory lad, 'tis your arm-in-arm cully, your rumbloke blowboy, Tim O'Toole. Tell me, how's the state of your health this morning?"

Tim O'Toole? Once again the name struggled for identification in Rory's consciousness. Tim O'Toole—the Irishman who had befriended him. He tried to inventory the features before him to see if they corresponded with the man he had met the night before. Yes, he remembered the shock of bright red hair, the green eyes, and the disarming grin.

"Tim O'Toole! My good friend from last night. But where am I now, Timmy? Tell me! Am I still in the whorehouse and if I am what's happened to it that it's a-reeling and a-rolling like a ship at sea?"

Tim untied his neckcloth, soaked it in a bucket of water on the floor, and wiped some of the vomit from Rory's body. "Well, lad, in a manner of speaking that's where you are."

"At old Mother Blood-and-Guts?"

"No, on a ship."

"On a ship? Tim, what's happened to me and where am I?"

"Well, you might say as how I'm your bloody savior, lad. Saved your life I did from the deepest of peril and danger. If it wan't for me, Rory, you'd be a-lying froze stiff in some gutter in Liverpool with the catchpolls dumping you in a grave in the potter's field."

"I'm mighty grateful, Tim."

"That's what an arm-in-arm cully's for, Rory me lad. Now it happened this-a-wise. You must have et something or it might be you were not used to the rum. It does happen sometime that rum works that way the first time a man downs it particularly if he's always been a whiskey drinker afore. Knocks the hell outa his stomach, it does. Well, I was just taking you upstairs at old Mother Blood-and-Guts with that fearsome-looking old sow you was determined to spoil yourself with. If ever there was a fireship, she was. Hated to see you do it, Rory me lad, but you was dead set on it and wanted me with you too. I got you to the top of the stairs and then you pegged out in a heap on the diddly-frigging floor. Hit your head enough to crack the skull open. You was out like a snuffed candle. All your decks was awash. So then, what to do with you? Old Mother Blood-and-Guts said I'd have to get you out of her place. But what to do with you? I managed to get you out in the street and stood you up against a wall. If I hadn't been a friend of yours I'd have left you in the gutter where you'd either catch your death or the

35

catchpolls would nab you. But I'd taken a liking to you, Rory lad, and I didn't want you to perish. I looked in your sporran, I did, and nary a farthing in there or I'd taken you to an inn and put you up for the night. Chanced that I didn't have a copper penny to my name after paying for the drinks and the whore you was dead set on having. So I slung you over my shoulder and brought you here to the ship. A heavy load you were, lad, but it wasn't too much to do for friendship's sake, was it?"

A surge of gratitude caused Rory to take Tim's hand and squeeze it. "You did me a good turn, Timmy, and it's glad I am to see a friendly face and now if you'll help me get my trogs on I'll be up and away and glad to get back on land after all this reeling and rolling. Who'd ever think a ship tied up at dockside would flounder so?"

"Oh, yes," Tim hesitated. "I forgot to tell you, Rory. We ain't dockside no more. Soon's we got on board, captain shouts that we're sailing on the morning tide and what with me being up in the shrouds to crack on sail, I plumb forgot about you till we was fair out in the bay. Then I thought of you lying here in my bunk down in the fo'c'sle and the first chance I got after everything's been squared away, I came down to rouse you. I've got you in a peck of trouble, Rory, but it was just my friendship for you what done it. Better to be here with me than tossed into an open grave in Liverpool. Tim O'Toole is one what looks out for his bosom-cully and I've already spoken to the Old Man about you. He says he can use an extra deckhand for the voyage so's I'm to bring you up to his cabin and he'll sign you on as an apprentice seaman."

Rory eased himself out of the bunk, hanging onto Tim to steady himself. He retched but there was nothing left in his stomach to vomit. With Tim's help he got his feet into his socks and brogues and the kilt buttoned around his waist. When he went to hang the sporran at his belt, he remembered something.

"You say there was not a farthing in my sporran?"

"No, I looked." Tim seemed disinclined to pursue the subject.

"I had three pounds and some shillings and a pin that belonged to my mother."

Tim's voice dripped a honeyed sympathy. "Aye, 'tis a shame. A pin that belonged to your sainted mother! 'Twas that slut what lifted it. I saw her hand up your kilt, lad. While she was trying to get you up with one hand, the other was fishing in your sporran. Never trust them strumpets. Many a sailor lands in port with his poke full and heads for a whorehouse only to come out later without a piece of copper to his name."

"I would have given my mother's brooch to a bonnier wench."

"Aye, 'tis a diddly-frigging shame, lad. Here, douse your face and comb your hair and button your jacket. Put on your bonnet, cully, and you'll look fair respectable. Let's roust and hie above decks. You can thank Tim O'Toole for getting the Old Man to sign you on, otherwise you'd be put in irons as a stowaway with naught but bread and water to fill your growler. But you've always got your arm-in-arm cully, Tim, who's forever looking out for you. Topside for you, lad."

Once up the ladder and out onto the clean white deck, with a splash of sun breaking through the clouds, the air fresh on his face and the gulls mewling, Rory felt better. Land was just a dim gray line on the horizon. He gulped deep of the air, straightened himself, and followed Tim across the deck, through a door, and down a narrow companionway, then up a flight of steep stairs, along another companionway to a white-painted door. Tim knocked and a voice from within bade them enter.

The contrast between the filth and grime of the dark fo'c'sle and the cheerful cabin that Rory entered made them seem like two different worlds. Wood paneling, painted white, reflected the light from a row of leaded glass stern windows in some of which were cages of singing birds and in others swinging baskets of flowering plants. Red Turkey carpets on the floor provided a vivid spot of color and the arm chairs bore signs of having been made by Mr. Sheraton. A polished brass brazier, swung by chains from a tripod, gave off an agreeable warmth; and the table beside it was covered in green baize that

37

reflected onto the face of the man bowed over it, giving him a strange pallor. He was reading a book and drinking from a china cup. Rory, piloted by Tim, stood before the desk, and it was a long minute before the man put down the book, carefully marked his place with a silk ribbon, and then looked up. He nodded at Tim and then studied Rory as carefully as Rory studied him.

If this was the captain he certainly was a young-looking man. He appeared to be not more than thirty years, although it was difficult to judge, because a peruke of fine white hair, arranged in pompadour style and tied behind with a black taffeta ribbon, completely hid his real hair. His face was tanned by the weather, but where the lace at his cuffs parted to show his wrists, Rory could see that his skin was milk-white. He would have been a handsome man were it not for two deep furrows that extended from his nose down around his mouth and hinted at cruelty, dissipation, or both. He was wearing a coat of black watered silk, braided with silver, and a lace-trimmed shirt with elaborate ruffles escaping under the wide turned-back cuffs of black velvet. The hands which still fondled the book terminated in slender, well-tended fingers, one of which sported an enormous diamond ring. When he spoke, his voice was low and well modulated, and his accent was that of a university man. He smiled as he regarded them, but it was not a pleasant smile—it was more of a sneer, Rory decided—and he addressed himself to Tim as though Rory were merely a piece of furniture that Tim had brought in.

"If you could but read, Timmy O'Toole, I'd recommend this book. It's droll indeed and tells about the adventures of a young lass named Fanny Hill who arrives in London fresh from the country. Ah, would that my life were as pleasant and exciting as Fanny's. Hers is the kind of life we should all be living, instead of this daily drudgery. And, when her own life did not provide enough excitement, the fair Fanny was not above peeping into the lives of others. It's a book that fair titillates a person, Timmy. But ah me, we are digressing, are we not, Timmy? This raw clod I take to be the new apprentice seaman

38

who has so kindly consented to grant us the benefit of his services."

His voice changed suddenly, becoming sharp and imperative as he pointed one finger at Rory. "Stand at attention, Johnny."

Automatically Rory straightened to his full height, his eyes meeting those of the captain.

"That's better, Johnny. The first thing to learn aboard ship is to know that you are nothing but the scum of the earth and that your captain stands next to God. Don't ever forget that."

"I'll try not to," Rory answered back.

"You'll *try*? You'll goddam *well* try. You'll not only try but you'll *do* it. And furthermore, you'll address me as 'Sir.'"

"Yessir."

"That's better! Do you know why I take the place of God here on this ship? Don't answer! It's because here I'm all-powerful. Here you do as I say. Did you know I could keep you in irons for the rest of the voyage? Did you know that I could abandon you at the first port of call, Funchal in Madeira? Did you know that if I wanted, I could have you lashed forty times for stowing away and have you sent to gaol on our return to England, if I could manage to keep you alive on bread and water during that time?"

The finger which had pointed so sternly at Rory now made lazy circles on the desk and the voice sank to a confidential whisper.

"But I'll do none of these things, Johnny. Tim O'Toole, who has been with me for four voyages and to whom I am indebted for the favor of speaking with you, tells me that you are a friend of his, so I'll do a favor for Timothy and sign you on, save your life, keep you from prison, and spare you the cat-o'-ninetails." He dipped a quill into a silver inkpot, scratched a few lines on a sheet of foolscap, and pushed it across the desk to Rory. "Your papers, Johnny, lacking only your name as a signature and if you cannot write, as I suppose you cannot, just make a cross, 'twill be enough."

"Sign it, lad," Tim prompted him with a nudge.

39

"I'll put my name to nothing until I know what I am signing." Rory stared straight at the captain.

"Then read it, if you can decipher the King's English." The captain flipped the paper with his finger. "You'll find it's in order. You're signing on as an apprentice seaman at twelve shillings a month, with one two-hundred-and-fiftieth of a share in the profits of the voyage."

"Then I should know where we are bound, what ship this is, and to whom I am talking."

"Your questions are in order, Johnny. I'll answer them. This is the ship *Ariadne,* owned by McCairn and Ogilsvy, factors of Liverpool, bound for the West Coast of Africa; and I, Johnny, am Captain Horatio Sparks, and if I can be excused for tooting my own horn, I'm the youngest captain in the slave trade and—I believe O'Toole will bear me out—the hardest and the strictest."

"That you are, Captain Sparks, sir," Tim bobbed his head in agreement.

Rory reached over, grabbed the sheet of paper, his eyes still on the captain, and deliberately tore it in half, fitted the two torn segments together, and tore them again and then again until they floated from his hand, a shower of white flakes, onto the captain's desk.

"I am pleased to meet you, Captain Sparks. But I'm no Johnny Raw. Permit me to introduce myself. I am Sir Roderick Mahound, Laird of Kilburnie and Baron of Sax, and nephew of Mr. Jabez McCairn of McCairn and Ogilsvy. As proof of this, if you would care to have one of your seamen investigate, he will find that a sea chest has been delivered to this ship for this same Rory Mahound who has temporarily decided to forego his peerage because he has no desire to rank higher than his uncle or his captain. Also, if you will jog your memory, Captain Sparks, you will recall that a berth has been assigned to this same Rory Mahound as supercargo of this ship. Said Rory Mahound, although grievously delayed in his journey from Glasgow to Liverpool, is now reporting for duty."

If Rory had thought to ruffle the superb composure of Captain Sparks, he was mistaken. Not a muscle changed in his face. He stood up and bowed slightly from the waist, his hand extended, the diamond on it sparkling.

"My apologies, Sir Roderick, and that will be the last time I shall address you as such. I have been laboring under a misapprehension. Your berth on this ship has already been filled owing to your nonarrival, but I shall make the present incumbent your assistant for the voyage. And now, if you will be seated, Mr. Mahound, we shall discuss matters of importance to both of us." He signaled to Tim. "You may go, Tim."

"But the gold guinea you promised me, Captain?"

" 'Twas for a seaman, not a supercargo."

"And I had all that work for nothing?"

"Nothing," the captain agreed.

Rory spun around to face Tim. "Then it was out-and-out crimping after all! All this soft sawder about your being my arm-in-arm cully and all that. 'Twas just to feed me your damned drink and get me on board."

"Well no, Rory. . . ." Tim hung his head. "Fact of the matter is, I liked you. Sure, I crimped you, but all the time I was doing it I was thinking we'd be good friends on this voyage. I like you, Rory, I do."

Rory disregarded him. "Have I your permission to fight this man, Captain Sparks?"

"Oh no," Sparks smiled, "he'd whip you, Mr. Mahound. Tim O'Toole is the best fighter on the ship."

"Maybe I'd beat him."

"Maybe you would." The captain appraised Rory's height and the width of his shoulders. "You look like no round-heeler to me, but I'll not have my officers indulge in any fisticuffs with my crew. We may be able to arrange something later, Mr. Mahound. We lack entertainment on a long voyage and I shall think of something. Make yourself scarce, Tim."

"I meant no offence, Rory," Tim stammered. "I liked you from the first moment I laid eyes on you."

"Mr. Mahound is a ship's officer and hereafter you will address him as such." Sparks pointed to the door. "Now get the hell out of here and if you linger another second, I'll have you strung up to the mast and let you savor ten strokes of the cat." He waited for the door to the cabin to close behind Tim, waved Rory to a chair, and tinkled a bell on the desk.

A door on the opposite side of the cabin opened and a girl entered. She was black as jet—a polished blackness that caused her skin to be highlighted by blue and shadowed by amethyst. Despite her color, Rory thought her one of the most beautiful girls he had ever seen. Girl? No. Regardless of what age she might have been she was a woman—all woman—a tall Junoesque statue of living black. Under the thin silk tissue of her robe her breasts showed, not round and white like those he had seen before, but elongated and pointed with dark nipples that seemed about to force their way through the thin silk that covered them. She was slender of waist and long of leg. Her face under the scintillating turban of iridescent silk was perfectly formed, though her lips and nostrils were slightly Negroid, which added a fillip of exoticism to her features. She walked slowly, her legs undulating under the thin robe, and approached Sparks, bowing low. But her obeisance was not humble. In it she lost none of her dignity, but rather conferred dignity upon Sparks, that such a person as herself would deign to bow to him.

Rory was glad that he was sitting down. Had he been standing, he knew that the effect of this strange creature and her magnetism over him would be all too apparent. He waited a long moment for her to speak, anxious to hear her voice, knowing before she spoke that it would affect him in the same way her physical movements had.

"What yore pleasure Captain Mongo?" Her voice had the deep tones of a bell and her words were strangely accented.

"Qarma, brew a cup of tea for Mr. Mahound and bring it here."

For the first time since she entered the room, she seemed to be aware of Rory's presence. Now she stared at him, the ghost of a smile on her lips and the slightest quiver in her nostrils. Although she looked at him for only a fleeting moment, Rory felt naked under her gaze and he knew from the momentary lingering of her eyes that she had discovered her ability to arouse him.

"A cup of tea for Mr. Mahound," she bowed slowly,

42

turning her back on the captain, but she did not bow so low that her eyes had to leave Rory's. Then, straightening up, she turned and walked back through the open door. Her walk was effortless, yet every muscle in her lithe body seemed to move. The thin silk was molded to her back and accentuated the sway of her buttocks. Barbaric silver ornaments tinkled with rows of little bells, and a strange perfume of musk remained behind her.

"My God! What a woman!" Rory let the words escape without being conscious that he had spoken. Any man who could master this she-devil must be a man indeed.

"Yes, Mr. Mahound." Sparks's words brought Rory back to reality. "I agree with you. Her name is Qarma. She is a Yoruba but I swear she must have some Jaloff blood because of the fineness of her features." He leaned forward across the table and took one of the quills from the penholder, then lightly rapped Rory's knuckles. "I don't think I need to mention, Mr. Mahound, that she is my property, bought and paid for."

"I understand. Indeed I do. Had I bought her myself I would feel the same as you do."

"At least you'll have something to think about on your voyage, Mr. Mahound." Sparks laughed. "Just thinking about her will make the voyage more interesting, what?"

Rory drew a long breath and shook his head.

"It may make the voyage more interesting, sir, but it will certainly make it more difficult."

"Perhaps the thoughts of Qarma will inspire you to reach Africa more quickly. You'll work harder but, alas, I must warn you. There are few in Africa like Qarma, so don't set your hopes too high."

"You're a lucky man, Captain Sparks." Rory took another long breath.

"On the other hand, Mr. Mahound, quite the opposite. Most of the time I am bored to death. I do try, however, to overcome my boredom and perhaps having you on board will help me to accomplish that."

CHAPTER V

CAPTAIN SPARKS'S ATTITUDE TOWARD RORY continued to be overcourteous, tinged even with a modicum of ironical respect, but Rory felt that under the suave urbanity of the man there lurked some strange inner hatred. In his first skirmish with Sparks, Rory had had the upper hand and Sparks had been forced to submit; but Rory knew that he would eventually assert his dominion and Rory would have to submit. Perhaps, and here Rory could proceed only on blind conjecture, the man might be jealous of him. Rory was younger, stronger, taller and, if the cracked mirror in his cabin did not lie, he was better looking, with a greater appeal to women. Or the fact that he was a baron might place him on a higher level than the captain of a mere slaver. Well, Sparks could forget that for all Rory cared. He felt no superiority from the worthless handle to his name which had never benefited him. He'd been a fool to make such a bragging stand before the captain anyway, shouting out that he was Baron of Sax for no reason at all except for the momentary satisfaction of taking the captain down a peg or two. Then again, it might be that Sparks resented him because his uncle was head of the company. If he only knew how little advantage that was. But perhaps, and here Rory felt he might be on the right track, Sparks had noticed the one brief look the girl Qarma had given him that first day in the captain's cabin and how he had stared at her buttocks undulating under the tightly stretched silk when she walked out to get his cup of tea. And it was barely possible that Sparks had noted Rory's immediate response to her blatant physicality. Whatever it was, Rory was certain that the captain hated him.

But for all these reasons, or none of them, or any one of them, Rory felt he could not trust the captain, although he could not, as yet, complain of the man's treatment of him. Although a supercargo did not rank with deck officers, Sparks nevertheless invited Rory to eat in the officers' mess; gave him a cabin of his own, minuscule though it was; addressed him as Mister, and demoted old Mr. Stoat who had been signed on as supercargo to the position of Rory's assistant.

At least there was no doubt in Rory's mind about Stoat's dislike for him. The old man was not able to conceal it under a cloak of polished good manners like Sparks did, but as Rory was perfectly willing to let Stoat do most of the work and even accept the credit for it if he wished, Rory saw no reason why the old man should be resentful. There was a lot of work to do—miserable, confining clerical work—which involved writing inventories into ledgers and a constant counting of the bales, crates, and boxes in the hold, along with checking and tallying and balancing. Rory worked away at it under Stoat's direction, but he knew he would never be able to keep the records in the precisely neat way the old man did and he also knew it was a job he would always dislike and shirk as much as possible. He could never be a drudge, filling dusty ledgers with rows of figures.

Another thing that he disliked about the work was that it kept him below decks in a dark little cubbyhole off the hold. Here he and old Stoat sat across from each other at a deal table. Their only light came from two tallow dips on gimbal stands that swayed with the ship and oftimes scattered hot tallow on Rory's fingers and the ledger pages. Stoat was a wizened-up leaf of a man with a dusty smell and a skin that looked as dry as the foolscap they wrote on. He had spent a lifetime poring over ledgers in counting houses and ships' holds, counting that day lucky when he could have a sausage for his supper. He could add up a column of figures before Rory had even started to do the sums on his fingers and, according to Stoat's own testimony, he had never made a mistake in his life. So be it! Rory knew that he himself had made plenty and would make a lot more. If fate had cast him in this dark hole

45

with Stoat, he would have to make the best of it. Stoat's conversation was limited to business and most of his time was spent carping at Rory for the slovenly way he kept his books and the errors he made.

The truth was that Rory was lonely not only for those Marys whom he had left behind, but for a companion of his own age, of which there were none on the ship—at least none on the quarterdeck. Johnny Day, the cook's boy, was about fourteen and Leazy Elphin, the cabin boy, some two years older. Inseparable off duty, they were too adolescent for Rory to associate with, although they were favorites with the crew. Captain Sparks of all the officers was the nearest to Rory's age, but even he must have been ten years the elder. The first, second, and third mates were all men in their thirties and forties. Yes, Rory was lonely, and he often looked across decks to the forecastle where he could see Tim O'Toole, usually surrounded by a group, which attested to his popularity. Now Rory regretted that he had provoked enmity between O'Toole and himself. Tim was a fellow one could laugh with over a smut-crack, bosom-bird around with, and be, as Tim had put it, an arm-in-arm cully.

Yet the fight between him and O'Toole had been openly declared by Rory himself and now, having put himself on record as wanting to fight Tim, Rory would have been glad to get it over with. He had certainly not had in mind staging any spectacular bout for the whole crew to watch. He and Tim would have slugged it out between themselves; winner would be winner and loser loser, and then they would have shaken hands and forgotten all about it. But Captain Sparks, with his high and mighty ways, had declared that they should settle their difficulties on deck under his supervision for all to see. As the days passed and Rory's anger cooled, he willingly would have foregone the battle. Perhaps if it had turned out otherwise and Rory had actually been shanghaied onto a strange ship, he would have held onto his resentment; but as it was, he was here on the *Ariadne,* so all that Tim had really done was to bring him aboard a bit roughly. No, he didn't hate Tim, and from the way Tim had looked at him the last time they had passed each other by chance, Tim didn't

46

appear to hate Rory. The whole truth of the matter was that Rory didn't want to fight him now. Perhaps, as long as Sparks had said nothing more about it, the whole matter would be forgotten. Rory hoped it would. He'd like Tim for a friend.

But far more than the thought of Tim in those dark nights when he braced his feet on the board at the foot of his bunk and tensed his body, he would think about the strangely compelling black woman who was separated from him by only a few partitions. The one glimpse he had had of her that first day aboard was still with him, and he wove fanciful dramas in his thoughts of what might be taking place between her and the captain. Then, in his fantasies, he would take the captain's place and feel his own hands roving over that sleek black skin and experience the strange taste of her lips on his own. She quite blotted out all his memories of other women, even Mary Davis in Glasgow. Qarma! Even her name fascinated him with its barbaric charm.

Qarma! He saw little of her but enough to keep her always present in his thoughts. Every evening she and Sparks made a circuit of the quarterdeck just after sunset. She affected a concealing costume of varicolored veils that covered her face but could not disguise her figure when the wind plastered the thin silk against every curve of her body. The upthrust breasts, the nipples pointing through the silk, the roundness of her belly, and the majestic outlines of her thighs were almost more than Rory could bear. He wondered sometimes if Sparks did not parade her merely to provoke envy in all the women-hungry men on board. Despite the fantasies he had conjured up about her the night before, each time Rory saw her there would be something about her to provoke new fantasies and more elaborate ones. Her eyes would stare at him over her veil; she would thrust her breasts toward him or let her hand glide over her sleek flanks. It became a torment to Rory, yet night after night he would find some reason for being on the quarterdeck just to see her pass and to breathe in a whiff of her perfume.

On those occasions, Sparks was always most courteous. "Good evening, Mr. Mahound," he would say and bend

47

slightly from the waist, continuing his walk, Qarma a half-step behind him. She never spoke although she always stared at Rory, lifting her head to look at him and then letting her eyes fall to inventory his whole body. It was not from modesty that she dropped her eyes. Far from it. Her glance was so provocative that he always responded to it and he was glad that the sartorial splendor of his new uniform had not been entirely wasted. The tight white pantaloons that he wore were the first trousers he had ever had and the short blue jacket added a fillip of smartness to his uniform. With the reassurance of Qarma's darting glance, he strutted a little more, confident of his own turgid virility and the effect it might have on her.

Yet Qarma's were not the only eyes that he met. There was Tim O'Toole on the nights he played his harp. Incongruous as it might seem, Tim performed on the Irish harp, a small instrument which he could hold on one knee while he strummed it. He played plaintive airs, and the quavering thin obbligato of the strings mingled with his rich baritone voice as he sat on one of the gratings over the hatches amidships. His music attracted most of the crew, and after Rory had caught his nightly glimpse of Qarma, he would descend from the quarterdeck to stand by the mast and listen. Often Rory could see by the turn of Tim's head that he was looking at him and one night when Tim had stopped singing and the other seamen had left, Tim walked over to where Rory was standing by the rail, looking down at the scudding waves.

"It's sorry I am, Rory, for what I done to you."

"It turned out all right, Tim. I've no sour-on."

Tim looked over his shoulder and, seeing the deck deserted he laid his hand beside Rory's on the rail.

"Can we shake hands on it, Rory, and forget what I did to you, trying to crimp you like I did?"

"That we can, Tim, and we can be friends, too." Rory took the proffered hand and shook it.

"But I'm scairt pissless that we've still got to rough it up, cock, and the truth is I don't want to fight you. When it comes to fighting, I've as much hair on my chest as the next one. Sure, I've a reputation as a buggering-buff, but I'm no namby-pamby. I'm a real dinging cove with my

48

fists. Ain't no man on this ship what can lick me either in a fair-and-square or a rough-and-tumble. If the day comes when I have to fight you, I'll clapper-claw you from here to hell and back 'cause I've got my reputation to live up to. But I'd rather not, Rory lad. I ain't got the wish to scrum you or spoil that pretty face of yours. I'd rather we be friends."

"We are, Tim." Rory could not bear the fellow any ill will. "Friends it is, but we'll have to keep it on the quiet side, me being on the quarterdeck and you in the fo'c'sle."

"We can do that, just that. We can be cronies but not bosom pals. You see, Rory, one reason why I wanted to crimp you was so's we could be together. Took a liking to you I did, and it warn't just for the guinea I crimped you, not knowing you'd turn out to be quarterdeck. Oil and water don't mix, neither do quarterdeck and fo'c'sle, but we ain't going to be on the ship all the time. In two days we'll get into Funchal. I been there many a time and there's a mountain behind the town with a road leading up to it. At one point on the road you can sit and look for miles, feeling like God Almighty Himself with the world spread afore you. 'Tis a nice walk and I'll have shore leave. We could meet off the dock, Rory, and then there'd be no quarterdeck or fo'c'sle."

"We could, Tim, and I'd like nothing better than to take that walk with you and stretch out on the good green grass with solid earth under me. But I know I'll not get ashore. Old Stoat goes to check the invoices at the wine cellar for the Madeira we're taking on and that means I'll have to check it as it comes on board. I'd like to, though."

" 'Twould be nice—you and me just a-lying under the trees with nothing to think about. But as long as you'd like to, that's the important thing to me, and if we can't do it here, we'll do it when we lay over at Rinktum Castle, though there there ain't no mountains to climb. Ain't nothing but a bloody, stinking river what's alive with crocs. We'll be there a week or more, though, and mayhap we'll find a place to go and be private-like. But mark my words, we'll be fighting before we gets there. You can be sure of that. Old Bastinado himself will see to that."

"Bastinado?"

"The blasted, bloody, diddly-damned old hell-raiser hisself! The Old Man! The captain! 'Tis a name they have for him in the fo'c'sle because he's the floggin'est captain in the slave trade. Likes it, he does. Gets a regular muck out of it. Likes to see the lashes fall and hear some poor bastard scream. Everyone's wondering who'll be the first this voyage. Been more'n a week and no cat yet, but it'll be coming, just wait and see. Sometimes he lets Big Stinger play the cat and other times he lays it on himself. But it's on the middle passage that he gets his real licks in. Has one of the poor niggers lashed every day and stands there watching it with the spit drooling down his chin and his britches a-standing straight out. 'Tis them that say he lashes that poor nigger wench of his every night and we're hoping it's so because it keeps him from stripping the meat off our backs."

"I've heard the screaming from his cabin." Rory was beginning to understand certain noises he had heard.

"There's them what gets their charge out of whopping, so I'm told. And Old Bastinado's one of them. So, let him get his from that nigger bitch if he wants. He took her on at Fernando Póo on the last voyage. Bought her from a pimping nigger what rented her out to him first, saying she was his own sister. Never let her off the ship in Havana nor Port-au-Prince nor Bridgetown, neither. Pssst! Try to get ashore in Madeira. Got to go now." Tim looked over his shoulder at an approaching shadow and slunk away. Rory turned, saw that it was Matthews, the first mate, and bade him good evening before he returned to spend another night, bracing his feet and clutching at his thin mattress. When he did sleep, Qarma ran after him, chasing him with a lash in her hands, and when he at last succumbed, panting in her arms, she metamorphosed into a Tim whose flesh instead of being hard and muscular was soft and smooth. He awoke, his body wet, gasping for breath. Then he slept soundly.

When they arrived in Funchal, just as Rory had anticipated, he was not allowed ashore except to walk the length of the dock. It seemed impossible that there could be such a change in climate from the cold fogs and chills of Liverpool to this balmy air, with the flowers all in blossom, the streets covered with violet petals from the jacaranda trees, and the soft mountains of malachite and amethyst that rose straight from the sea. It was hard to believe that only a few weeks before in Scotland he'd been as cold as a witch's tit.

He had his eye out for women, but the few that he saw in his brief sojourn were of little consequence, for they were shrouded in black from head to foot in the all-enveloping *capote-e-capella* which made them about as attractive as last year's haycock being blown along the street. Their faces were hidden and one could only guess from the voluminous black draperies whether they were young or old, slim or fat. That there were bagnios near the dock he had heard from the sailor's talk, but if their occupants were anything like the sows at Blood-and-Guts in Liverpool, he felt he was not missing much. He would have enjoyed going for the long tramp with Tim. It would be nice to have someone to talk to, and he'd like to feel once more the dirt crunch under his brogues; but he had to return on board to check the barrels and casks of wine.

When the last grunting stevedore had deposited the last cask on deck and the last unwilling seaman had lowered it down into the hold, Rory's job was over, but even then he could not go ashore. Most of the seamen had gone and Rory was the only officer left on board. His responsibilities were few, and there was really nothing for him to do but stand on deck, lean over the rail, and watch the hawkers of baskets and embroidery who, sensing that the ship was deserted, were already packing up their wares and departing. When they had left, he raised his eyes to the dim purple mountains and watched the glimmering stars of candles being lighted in the mountain homes.

Seeing these reminded him that he had not lighted the stern lantern, and he climbed the stairs to the quarterdeck. His tinderbox flaring up for one brilliant moment, he espied a movement that was at once swallowed up by the darkness. He lighted the tallow candle in the lantern, lowered the glass side, and stepped back out of the circle of light. Waiting for his eyes to adjust to the darkness, he again sensed motion—near the mizzenmast.

His cautious footsteps made no noise on the deck as he

51

crept toward the mast, his body tense and prepared for whatever he might encounter. Whatever it was that he was stalking did not move, and when he reached the mast and edged his way stealthily around it, his fingers touched the softness of flesh and he was aware of a strange perfume— the heavy scent of patchouli mingled with an almost over-powering odor of musk. The source of this fragrance still did not move, and as Rory's fingers continued their exploration they encountered the full breasts and the taut nipples of a woman, then slid down over her naked belly. Whoever it was, whether it was some strumpet from the town who had sneaked aboard or, more likely, Qarma, she was without a stitch of clothes, stripped to the buff. Then, while his own fingers explored, they were encouraged by the frantic seeking of the woman's fingers under his clothes, and he knew for a certainty it must be Qarma. Surely no other body could be as statuesque or as voluptuous as hers. While her fingers continued on their wanderings, she leaned against him, moaning and quivering, pressing his body against the mast. Entranced by this presence that was felt but not seen he forgot everything but her nearness and the fire of her moving fingers which seemed about to explode him into another world.

He gasped, forcing her fingers away, and in his exigency found only harsh words for her. "What goes on here? You—bare-arsed naked up here on deck?"

She released him, but whispered from a mouth pressed on his. "I tire of the little cabin where I spend so many days. I wish to feel the soft breeze on my skin, kissing it. The Mongo, he is away. I do as I please." She pulled her fingers from his restraining hand and renewed her efforts. Rory met them with a response which must have surprised even Qarma, and she continued even more frantically, holding his weight now in her strong arms. "You are young, white man with hair of gold, and you are very much a man. Qarma wants you and Qarma will have you now, here. Now!"

Rory sucked in his breath, clinging to her. "Damn it to hell, woman, I want you too and that should be as plain to you as the mast behind me, but you're Captain Sparks's wench and I'm damned if I'll be caught sniffing around his bitch."

"They call you Rory, yes?" She caught his underlip with her teeth.

"They do that, but what's it got to do with me tasting the cat if the captain comes back and finds us here?" He reached down to retrieve his breeches, which had fallen to his ankles. "You buff-naked and me nearly so!"

"But he comes not back tonight, Rory. The captain he is in Funchal and he is very happy there because he have new women to play with him. He say he not come back till morning and I think the captain he like Funchal very much because he always stay the night when we are here. He think he lock me in his cabin but Qarma smart. She get out. She have key that Mongo he thinks he lost once long time 'go. You come, Rory."

"Come where?"

"It better in captain's cabin, yes?" Her avid mouth teased him until his knees felt like water.

For the first time in his life, Rory was with a woman whom he did not have to bend his head to kiss, nor did she have to stand on tiptoe to reach his mouth. With the captain gone, why be cautious? His arms encircled her and now, his strength coming back to him, he seized her and crushed her to him. This time it was she who sought release from him. "You come, Rory? You let Qarma show you more?"

"Goddamn it, yes! I'll come wherever you say and do whatever you want to me to. I'm needing it badly."

"Then little Leazy or perhaps the red-haired Tim do not serve you too well?"

"What the hell do you mean? I'm no buggering gill and I'm not scuttling Leazy nor Tim neither."

"Then take me, Rory. Take me like I've never been taken before. Come!"

"Wait woman, till I do up my buttons. Then you go first, but I'm thinking my cabin would be better than the captain's."

"The captain's bed is soft and wide and yours is so narrow. Don't worry, he won't be back."

"Then off with you and I'll follow."

He waited, saw her move as a darker streak in the darkness, saw the door of the companionway open, saw her black silhouette gilded by the light as she stepped inside, and then, allowing her another few minutes to reach the cabin, he started after her. He knocked faintly on the white cabin door and heard her invitation to enter. Pushing the door open, he was met by a blaze of light that dazzled him. All the candles in the cabin were alight and Qarma was applying her tinderbox to the last unlighted one in the wall sconces.

"Why the bonfire?" He would have preferred the darkness that erased her black skin and made her like the women he had known.

"You do not want to see me?"

"Well yes, but it's better in the dark."

"But with Qarma, no. Qarma like light. She like to see her man. She like to see how he like what she do to him."

She ran to him, smothered him with kisses, stripping his sweat-plastered shirt from him, tugging at the wide leather belt with the big brass buckle, and when she had unfastened it, peeling the pantaloons from his legs. She stared, open-eyed, ki-yied like a bitch in heat, and then fell to her knees, clasping him around the waist and slavering his body with her lips. Looking down on her, he loosened the gaudy cloth which was wound, turban-wise, around her head, and was shocked to see when it was stripped off that her pate was cleanly shaven, as smooth as an egg. He was disappointed. His fingers had been itching to lose themselves in a woman's hair and now the shiny baldness repelled him. Involuntarily he drew away from her.

Evidently she sensed his reaction, for she pulled herself up to stand before him, belly pushed out, thighs apart.

"No hair," she grinned. "No hair on Qarma nowhere. It is the custom of my country and the captain he like it. He like this better though." She whirled quickly, her movements like a cat's, yanked open a drawer in the table, and drew out a whip. It was a delicate instrument of finely plaited silk, the end betasseled. Before Rory realized what she was doing, she had raised it and brought it down across his shoulders. The sting of it angered him, and when she raised her arm again he grabbed at it, only to

54

find that her oiled flesh was too slippery for him to hold. She faced him, only a few feet away from him, her nostrils quivering, a thin hair of saliva drooling from one corner of her red-painted lips. Her eyes never left him while he extended one hand slowly, letting his fingers tweak the hard painted tip of one nipple.

"Put that frigging whip down. I've heard your master likes whips. Did you teach him to like them?"

"Like I shall teach you. In my country we do not do silly things like white men and women do. We have better time. All you white people do is groan and grunt and heave and then it is all over. You are just like all white men. You satisfy yourself in two minutes and then you care not what happens to a woman. A woman likes pleasure too. It is pleasure for a woman to whip a man and to master him before he masters her."

"I can give you pleasure without your whipping me. I've never had any complaints before."

She backed away from him and once again, before he could stop her, she brought up her arm. This time the lash bit into his flesh, and before he could catch her in her elusive flight around the table, she had inflicted several more lashes on him until he, leaping up on the table, jumped down on her, wrenching the whip from her hands. He would have broken the silken toy in his hands but it was too flexible to break. She struggled to regain it, snarling, biting, and clawing at him. Her long nails raked his back and even his strength seemed no match for her. She was no longer a woman but an animal, feral, slippery and strong, entirely savage in her fury. While he wrestled with her, trying to keep her fingers from clawing at him—for in her present frenzy she would willingly have emasculated him— he managed to slip one knee behind her, pushed her, and felt her lose her balance and fall. Immediately he was on top of her, straddling her shoulders and managing to pinion her arms to the floor. Suddenly he felt her go limp under him and the vicious snarl disappeared from her face while the wild light faded from her eyes. Straining her head up as much as she could, her tongue darted out, red and pointed, touching him like a searing flame and causing his senses to reel until his grip on her was loosened by the very urgency of her appetite for him. He toppled over onto her, gasping on the floor beside her, spent, satiated, and limp.

She wriggled away from his sapped body and slithered up onto the bed where she held out her arms, her fingers fanning an invitation, beckoning to him. Although, at the moment, she repulsed him, he was hypnotized by her writhings. Slowly he sat up, staggered to the bed and abandoned himself to her caresses, completely passive under the violence of her attacks. Her mouth, like some red wet obscene flower, slavered over him; her darting tongue kindled new fires in his blood—fires which he did not think could ever be rekindled—her compulsive fingers grasped, caressed, and manipulated with a demoniacal fury; her arms and legs intertwined over him while her heavy breasts smothered him. His body, ravaged and devasted by the force of her onslaughts, responded to her even while his mind repudiated her frenzy. The fire continued to mount in him, but this time, instead of allowing her her will, he forced her, regardless of her struggles to elude him, and once having become the master he had his way with her, roughly and brutally. He could sense in her something that responded to his rape of her, and he battered her without mercy despite her pleas. With one last convulsive gasp he fell upon her, drained of his unwilling desire. After a moment, despite her entreaties for him to continue, her clutching hands and her slavering mouth, he quitted her.

She spat at him, a gobbet of her saliva trailing down his cheek.

"You call yourself a man. Bah! Get back to the fo'c'sle and let the sailors play with you for indeed you are not a man."

"I've proved that to you, not once but twice, nay even three times when you count what happened up on deck." He reached down to the floor for his clothes.

"Poof!" She sneered at his accomplishments. "A man does not weaken so easily. After the first time he does not falter; after the second he needs only a moment of rest; after the third he lies quietly for a little while; after the fourth he might need a little sleep if he is a weakling; after the fifth he sleeps the rest of the night to refresh himself

56

for the sixth and seventh in the morning. Bah! White men are not men. Only black men are real men and I thought when I first saw you you might be as good as a black man. White meat does not have the taste of black meat. I spit on you."

Her railings meant less than nothing to Rory. He was entirely spent. For him there was nothing more that he wanted from this she-devil. Not so much to exculpate himself as his race, he said lamely, "No man can do those things." He was getting all his buttons in the wrong holes.

She sat up cross-legged on the bed and pointed a derisive finger at him.

"In my country they do. You should see my brother. Ay, ay, ay! What a man! So handsome I cannot tell you about him. He has taken twenty women in one night and the last one screamed as loud as the first. When I was but a little girl and my brother was but fifteen, he could do better than you. Bah! I called you a man but I was wrong. Again I spit on you and all puny white men."

"Spit and be damned. When the captain returns tomorrow morning let him give you the sixth and the seventh if he can do it. I'm off. My God, how you stink. Don't come near me again, ever. I'll not face the chances of the captin's cat again for you, you black bitch."

He opened the door and peered out into the companionway. Seeing that it was all clear, he closed the door behind him, hearing her slipper as she flung it against the door. Out on deck the freshening breeze told him that the ship was moving, and he ran to the rail and peered over, seeing the white foam making lacy arabesques on the oily black water. Racing up the steps to the quarterdeck, he saw the second mate standing at the helm.

"We're under way, sir?" Rory could not hide his surprise.

"Aye, aye, Mr. Mahound, that's plain enough to see."

"But Captain Sparks? He was ashore for the night."

"Captain Sparks returned about two hours ago, Mr. Mahound, and gave orders for us to sail on the outgoing tide."

"But Captain Sparks is not aboard." Rory was certain

about that fact because he had just quitted Captain Sparks's bed.

"Captain Sparks *is* on board, Mr. Mahound, and I believe he is sleeping in his cabin."

There was nothing more that Rory could say. Either he had been dreaming or the mate was lying. Rory knew one thing. He had not been dreaming. The fact that his shirt was buttoned all wrong proved that. The devil had been at work that night and this particular devil's name was not Mahound. It was Old Harry himself. Rory felt he could almost smell burning brimstone, but he knew it was the trace of Qarma's perfume that had rubbed off on his body. Well, why should he complain? He'd had what he wanted and more than he wanted from that black bitch. For once, since being aboard this ship, he had not had to brace his feet on the footboard of his bunk and conjure up images of her. He breathed a sigh of relief. Wherever Sparks was, he had not come bursting into his cabin and found Rory wrestling with his doxy. He bade the second mate good-night and walked down amidships.

The thin silver notes of Tim's harp tinkled in the air. Rory would not seek Tim out tonight. Instead he'd go to his own little closet and sleep. No use in thinking what might have happened. It hadn't. But he was damn sure of one thing—he'd never jeopardize his safety again by playing around with that bald-headed whore. He shuddered. Even the reek of her disgusted him now.

CHAPTER VI

THE NEXT MORNING WHEN RORY WENT BELOW to the airless cubbyhole he shared with old Stoat, faced with a full day's labor of entering the new cargo of wine that had been taken on board at Madeira, he found Stoat slumped on the floor, loaded to the gunnels. He had dragged in one of the casks of Madeira and broached it. Part of the wine had spilled from the bunghole and made a puddle on the floor in which the old man was lying. It was probably the first time in his whole penny-pinching life that he had had all he wanted to drink. Rory upended the cask so that no more would spill out—not forgetting to help himself to a generous swig—straightened out Stoat's legs, placed a rolled-up sack under his head, and sat down at the table.

He never anticipated the day's work with pleasure, but today he dreaded it more than usual. Now, this morning, he wondered if he had dreamed it all. But no, there were the wales from her whip and the marks of her teeth on his body. Finally, after staring at the dusty calfbound ledgers for half an hour during which he relived the scenes in the captain's cabin all over again, he sighed and opened the ledgers, trimmed the wicks of the candles, and sharpened his quill. Could he have found further delaying tasks, he would have employed them, because he had no taste for the stifling cabin and even less for the monotonous task of scratching in the ledgers. Furthermore, he scarcely knew how to begin without Stoat's expert tutelage.

He need not have concerned himself. After the first dip of his quill in the inkwell and his first entry (which he was sure was incorrect), there was a rap on the door and Leazy the cabin boy entered. His babyish features were spoiled by a festering rash of acne and his pale blue eyes had dark circles under them, but he was blithe and happy as he slid his fat little bum up onto the corner of the table and stared at Stoat down on the floor.

"The old dosser's drunk, ain' he?" He pointed a derisive finger. "Got his mainbrace well spliced, didn' he, the old bastid? How about me helping myself to a swig of Madeiry seeing as how old Stoat's already broached the cask?"

"Go ahead." Rory could afford to be generous. "But don't get your sheets to the wind, Leazy. If you go staggering around with a full cargo aboard, they'll all want to know where you got it. As it is, I can mark it off as a broken cask and Captain Sparks will never be the wiser, but if you advertise it Stoat will get in trouble and so will I."

"I hates to tell you, but you're in trouble already, Mr. Mahound. That's why I'm here. Captain Sparks's compliments and all that shit and will Mista Supercargo Mahound kindly attend him in his cabin at once? Old Bastinado's breathing fire, although you'd never know it, him being so pernickety polite and all. When the old bastid's raising hell, you don't have to worry, but when he's cool and polite-like, he's got a marlinspike up his ass. He and that black doxy of his were screaming all night and she wan't able to serve him his breakfast this morning. Had to do it myself with all the other things I had to do. Now Old Bastinado sends for Tim O'Toole and you, Mista Mahound. What have you and Timmy been doing? You two been kissing off?" He leered down at Rory.

"None of your goddamned concern, you backdoor molly-O."

"Listen to the pot a-callin' the kittle black. Belike there's more to it than you and Timmy singing songs. Looks like Timmy's been playing with something more than the harp or the Old Man wouldn't of sent for the two of you. He don't mind if you keep it sort of quiet-like but . . ."

"If you weren't such a little blister, I'd flatten you out like I'd step on a cockroach." Rory laid the quill down regretfully. The prospect of a dull morning writing in the ledger seemed far more inviting than standing on the carpet in Sparks's cabin. Had Old Bastinado found out about last night? No, not unless Qarma had told him; but then, perhaps she had, if he'd whaled her enough. However, Leazy had said that Sparks wanted Tim to come also and certainly Tim had had nothing to do with the affair last night. Well, there was only one way to find out, and that was to face the music and trust to luck.

Nevertheless his hands were clammy with fear while he followed Leazy's bouncing buttocks up onto the deck and then down the white paneled companionway to the captain's door. Leazy knocked and the voice from within, much to Rory's surprise, did not sound particularly angry.

At least it was not that of a man whose mistress had just placed horns on his head.

"Come in." There was a semblance of anticipatory welcome in Sparks's voice.

The cabin looked entirely different this morning, with the sun streaming through the port windows. It was difficult to realize that it had been the setting for a sybaritic revel only last night. Now the caged birds were singing and the flowering plants gave the cabin such an air of domesticity that one might imagine himself in an English cottage. Streaming sunlight made a glowing spot of bright color on the Turkey carpet and a gilded aureole around the captain's glossy white wig. But despite the air of quiet comfort in the room, Rory's nose detected a lingering trace of Qarma's musk, although she was not there. Instead of her, Rory saw the dejected figure of Tim, his curly red head bowed and shoulders slumped, standing before the captain's green baize table.

Sparks looked up at Rory and the affability of his smile betokened bad news. Rory had learned that. Every member of the crew dreaded the captain's smile. And yet it was a charming smile, enhanced by his saturnine good looks, his poise and bearing and utter self-possession. His authority was unquestioned. He was supreme.

"Mr. Mahound," he nodded his head in acknowledgment of Rory's presence, "although I once said that I would hitherto address you only as plain 'mister,' I feel that this, being a rather special occasion, might permit me to dispense with the 'mister' for the nonce. Surrounded as I am by rogues and rascals, it is seldom that I have an opportunity to call a man 'sir.' So, Sir Roderick—with your permission of course—I desire to apologize for my negligence."

"I don't understand, sir." Rory was baffled. He tried to catch Tim's eye but Tim had not raised his head.

"Oh, you are much too modest, Sir Roderick. I know you have been blaming me, but you are of course far too polite to remind me of that in which I have been remiss. Ah yes, breeding always shows, Sir Roderick. A gentleman remains a gentleman even when he is only a supercargo. I am, of course, referring to your demand that morning after your most unfortunate arrival aboard—your demand for satisfaction from Able Seaman Tim O'Toole." Sparks leaned back in his chair, toying with a string of amber beads which he slipped through his fingers, clicking them one by one along a silken cord.

"That's past and gone, sir. I bear Tim no ill will for that." Rory extended a hand across the table to Tim which the latter made no move to accept. " 'Twas not really Tim's fault. 'Twas the whole goddamned system of crimping that's to blame, sir. Tim was but doing what you ordered him to do and his little plan backfired on him, seeing as how he got nothing out of it. After all, let us say he merely delivered me to the right place, even if it was through the back door."

"Oh, yes." Sparks smiled broadly and clicked three beads in rapid succession. "The back door is indeed a specialty of Tim's. However, one has to be broad-minded on a long voyage like this and close an eye to the breaking of His Majesty's law. Otherwise every man jack sooner or later would be hung from the yardarm and there'd be nary a seaman left to man Britannia's ships. But I digress. It comes back to the settling of the differences between you and Tim and, although I stand accused of absentmindedness, I have not forgotten. It is merely that it has posed a problem for me."

"We could forget the whole thing. Tim and I are friends now."

"So that's the way the wind blows!" Captain Sparks winked knowingly. So you've become Tim's mollyfellow, eh, or perhaps it's the other way 'round and he's yours? Well, that will make it even more interesting because you see, Sir Roderick, I've promised myself a little entertainment and anything that adds spice to it will make it even more interesting. So, if you and Tim are kissing it off, it will be more exciting. However, it's been a most perplexing problem, believe me."

"But I'm not fighting Tim," Rory affirmed with finality, then added a belated, "sir."

"Of course not," Captain Sparks was enjoying his cat-and-mouse game. "No officer of my ship engages in fisticuffs with a common seaman. Why, supposing he did!

And supposing the seaman proved a better fighter? He'd be king of the fo'c'sle and cock of the walk. And even more serious, he'd be breaking the law which says that if a seaman lays hand on an officer, that's mutiny. Nor does a Scottish baron fight with dockscum like our Timmy. True, he might do other things with him, but fight—never! That, you see, has been my problem, and I must admit, it's bothered me, even more so because I had a slight disappointment last night and I'm not the man to take disappointments lightly." Sparks stood up, selected a key from the chain fastened to his belt, unhooked it from the ring, and handed it to Tim.

"Seaman O'Toole, unlock the small cupboard over the arms chest and bring me what you find there."

Tim came out of his trance, reached out his hand, and took the key and walked to the other side of the cabin, following the direction of Sparks's pointing finger. He unlocked the small door in the wainscoting above the large chest with brass corners, but when he opened the door, he recoiled, turned and faced the captain, his face horror-strained.

"Not that, sir." Tim was as near to blubbering as he had ever been since a baby. "Not that, sir. That I cannot do. I cannot."

"Cannot?" Sparks's voice cracked back at him. "Nobody asked you what you can or cannot do and furthermore nobody gives a damn. Take out what you find there and bring it here and lay it on the table."

Slowly, his hands a-tremble, Tim reached up into the cupboard and took down two long braided lashes which were coiled and tied into thick circles. Handling them as gingerly as red-hot pieces of iron, he carried them to the table and laid them down on the green baize top. Sparks's finger pointed to the strands of rawhide which tied each one and Tim untied them, whereupon Sparks uncoiled one of the whips and snapped it out full length. It was about six feet long, tapering from a handle-grip half as round as a man's wrist to a thin end, little more than a cord in diameter. He snapped it again, this time with more force, making it crack like a pistol, and then threw it to the floor where it coiled itself like a snake.

63

"In Italy they call it the *duèllo con scodiscios*." The smile did not leave his face. "And 'tis a rare spectacle indeed. It must be a holdover from the days when gladiators fought in the circus." He turned his smile on Tim. "It's a rum sight, Timmy, isn't it?"

"I saw it," Tim let his eyes drop to the snakelike coil on the floor and shivered. "Aye, sir, I saw it two days out of Havana on the voyage home when Peebles and Martinez fought. But that was different. They was out to get each other and there was bad blood between them. Yes, sir, I saw it once and I never want to see the likes of it again. Peebles with one eye hanging out and Martinez lashing him to a bloody pulp. But there's no bad blood between Mr. Mahound and me, sir, just as he told you."

"Aye, but there will be, Tim, indeed there will be, because when you feel the first taste of Mr. Mahound's lash and he feels the first of yours, you'll both forget this new friendship of yours. Then it will be each man for himself, to kill or be killed, although"—he waved a deprecatory hand—"I will not allow it to go as far as killing. I must remember that Mr. Mahound is Mr. McCairn's nephew and I cannot report to him that his very own Sir Roderick was killed by an ordinary seaman. And as for you, Tim, I don't want you dead either. You're a good man and I need you.

"But it'll be entirely fitting and proper for you two to fight it out this way. Your fists, Timmy, will not touch an officer and Mr. Mahound will not have to touch you. So, it's all settled now; and believe me, it has been an interesting problem to work out. Tomorrow night at six bells, amidships. I'll have the bosum pipe all hands on deck after mess. And, as these instruments have not been used for some time, I'll give one to each of you now. The leather may be stiff and I suggest a greasing. Cook will oblige you with a bacon rind to grease them with, and I am not the one to object to a little practice with them when you're off duty. However, don't try to lose them overboard. 'Twill do you no good—I've got another pair. Pick up the whip and go, Timmy." He swung around in his chair and pointed to the door.

Rory stood still, waiting for Tim to leave, and when the door closed behind him, he faced Sparks defiantly.

"I refuse to fight Tim with one of these."

"Refuse and be damned," Sparks rose from his chair to face him, leaning across the table and looking directly into Rory's eyes. "You'll either fight with the whip or you'll marry the gunner's daughter yourself.* You've got a punishment coming to you, cock, and only you and I know what for."

"You mean ... ?" Rory began to suspect what was coming.

"I mean that Qarma was acting under my orders when she brought you down here last night. Aye, you thought I was really ashore, cock, and you were only too willing to play drake to Qarma's duck. Didn't take too much urging on her part to bring you down. I don't suppose you asked yourself whether the Old Man would care if you diddly-whacked his doxy. Oh, no! You only thought of what you were going to get and how goddamned easy you were getting it."

" 'Twas an unfair temptation. You knew how any man would react."

" 'Twas just that I wanted to find out, cock. You see, I took a tip from the charming Fanny in the book I was telling you about. She was a great hand for peeping, that one. You should read how she spied on one of the girls in the house and her Neapolitan lover. Oh, yes, and how she peeked in on the old madam and her upstanding young guardsman. Then she peeping-tommed it on the two bug-gering buckos that day at the inn. So I peeping-tommed it a bit myself. After all, a man gets tired of doing the same thing all the time and it's nice to see something different. Frankly I was a bit disappointed; it was an amateurish performance you put on."

"You were looking on?" The wind sagged from Rory's sails.

"Why not? But the fact that I peeping-tommed you does not excuse you. You were raring to put the horns on my head and you didn't give a billy-be-damned about me.

---

*To marry the gunner's daughter was to be tied to a gun and flogged.

I can't have you flogged for cuckolding me, cock, but I can see to it that you'll think twice before you lark with the captain's biddy on this or any other ship again. Not but what I'd have been disappointed if you hadn't, after all the plans I made; but take my advice. The next time you're ramstudious and boiling over, make sure all the lights are out and there's no peephole in the door." He pointed to a small round role in the door that led to Qarma's closet.

Rory's eyes followed the direction of the captain's finger and saw the hole in the door. It was something he'd never noticed last night, when he'd had other things on his mind.

"Now, Mr. Mahound"—Sparks picked up the second whip from the table and handed it to Rory—"it doesn't amount to a good goddamn whether you want to fight Tim or not; you're sure as hell going to and I'm going to enjoy every moment of it."

Rory grabbed the whip, half-minded to let the captain have it across the face; but he'd be keelhauled or hanged if he did. He turned to leave.

"And yet, Mr. Mahound," Sparks said as he made a formal little bow, "I want to tell you that I am greatly indebted to you. For a cod who's probably rogered nothing more lively than a heifer on a moor, you did remarkably well. The only thing you lack is a little finesse. Yet you did make the bitch scream for mercy. That's something I can't always do, because according to her there's nobody in the world can satisfy her but that black-rinded whango of a brother of hers in Africa. And by the way"— he held up a detaining hand—"if you have any idea of reporting this little episode of ours to your uncle in Liverpool, be assured that he'll believe my story before he does yours. That's all, cock; report back to your ledgers."

Tim was waiting for Rory below, hiding behind a pile of casks in the hold. Together they squatted in the darkness.

"We've got to go through with it, Rory."

"Looks like it, Tim. It's not that I hold any grudge against you and that's what makes it harder for me. To hit

66

a man in anger is one thing but to hit a man in cold blood is another."

"I'm not wanting to hit you either, Rory. But you be careful of one thing and so will I. Keep away from my eyes. Lay it on the shoulders and on the back, my arse if you want to or my legs, but don't mess up my face or blind me. And don't touch my pride-and-joy and I'll do the same for you."

"We'll do even better than that, Tim. You've seen one of these fights. How long does it last?"

"Till one man's down and the other lashes him so's he gives up."

"Then I tell you what. One of us will slip and the other will be the master. It'll be me if you want, I can take it."

"No, Rory, you're bigger'n I am. It's more natural for you to win. We'll stall for a while and then we'll get in a few good licks to make it seem right and even those are bound to cut us up pretty bad, even if we're careful. That lash cuts through flesh like a knife 'cause it's got thin steel wires in it. Then I'll back up and stumble over my own foot. You'll let me have it once or twice and I'll scream out that I'm licked and that'll end it. We'll try not to mess each other up too much, and remember, we'll keep away from the eyes and the rappers."

"I'll shake on it, Tim. Don't take it personal-like if I hurt you and I'll bear you no grudge if you do me. We'll put on a show for Old Bastinado because that's what he wants. Yell as loud as you can when I hit you and so will I. Who knows, Timmy boy, after it's all over we may be better friends than ever."

"That we will be, Rory. Regular arm-in-arm cullies. I'll not mind taking it from you." He half-turned and fished behind him, located what he was looking for and drew out a big pewter tankard. "It's prime Madeiry. Let's not go to work for a while, Rory. We'll sit here in the dark and drink. There's not enough to get roaring drunk on, but it'll help."

Rory reached for the tankard. "Here's to you, Tim. What was it Old Bastinado said? Oh, yes. Here's to you, my bugginsuckle!"

CHAPTER VII

THE SUN SANK SLOWLY INTO THE SEA, A LOP-sided ball of fire that touched the distant horizon and seemingly poised there for a long moment before it was swallowed up by the water. Green, mauve, and fuchsia clouds slowly faded into a nacreous gray and the blue water became lead-colored and metallic-looking. The ship's bell clanged out its six strokes and when it stopped the shrill notes of the bosun's pipe brought all hands on deck—a grimy, sweaty crew in dun and colorless garments. As if to offset their drabness, the rail of the quarterdeck suddenly blossomed into color as Captain Sparks appeared in a resplendent coat of red Genoese cut velvet all a-glitter with gold lace, breeches of white sarcenet, and white silk stockings. A black tricorne, from which floated an enormous yellow ostrich plume, sat on his white wig which was tied behind with a bow of black taffeta ribbon. He carried a brace of silver-mounted pistols in the blue sash girding his waist and a court sword hung at his side. Leazy followed him, lugging one of the armchairs from his cabin, and placed it behind the rail. When Sparks had accommodated himself to it, Matthews, the first mate, arrived to stand beside him. With a courtly gesture Sparks offered him his enameled snuffbox and then, snapping his fingers at Leazy, ordered a carafe of the new Madeira and glasses for himself and his first officer.

The scuttlebutt had already informed the crew of the duel, and there were no laggards as they swarmed up from the fo'c'sle and down from the ratlines to crowd the deck amidships. It was going to be a bloody good show—one that appealed to their primitive, sadistic impulses—and they didn't want to miss it. Didn't want to miss seeing

Timmy-boy get his pretty white ass striped with red; wanted to see Mahound get his deserts, which he surely would because Timmy was a fighting cove, the cock of the fo'c'sle. He'd won the position with his own fists and they all knew his capabilities. Rory was an unknown quantity, but even though he was a big fellow, their bets were all on Tim. Except for the second mate, the helmsman, and the lookout in the crow's nest, not a man jack of the crew was missing. Even old Stoat had slept off his drunk and was on hand, a little weak in the knees but able to navigate.

Rory, immaculately clad in clean white canvas pantaloons and his blue jacket, stepped from the companionway door of the quarterdeck and stood at attention. All eyes were on him until the crowd parted and Tim emerged from the fo'c'sle. He was greeted by loud cheers, which had certainly not attended Rory's appearance. Tim was the crew's own man. There was nobody but Sparks to cheer Rory, and the captain was not in the mood for cheering his supercargo.

The grating over the main hatch had been spread with sailcloth to make an elevated stage; a hempen cable was strung around it through temporary eyebar stanchions. The small forge from the smithy had been carried on deck—just why Rory could not understand—and two long rods were being kept red-hot in its coals. Spottswood and Stinger, two bearded giants who were in charge of the slave deck during the middle passage back to the Indies, stood at opposite corners of the roped hatch, grinning at the mob below them in anticipation of what they were about to see. Stinger beckoned for him to come up and when Rory jumped up onto the hatch, Stinger obsequiously lifted the rope for him to step under. Tim had to scramble under by himself. With Spottswood behind Tim and Stinger behind Rory, they stood there in awful isolation, listening to the comments of the crew. There were plenty of shouted encouragements for Tim, interspersed with catcalls and jeers for Rory. He was not unpopular, but he was an officer and this contest was not only between Rory and Tim but between quarterdeck and fo'c'sle. Sparks allowed them to cheer themselves hoarse until the sound finally died down and he rose and leaned indolently on the rail with one hand, his other twirling one of the pistols. His words came slowly, even diffidently; but as all the crew knew, the apparent unconcern was indicative of one of his most dangerous moods.

"My hearties," he began with a lackadaisical gesture toward them, "if ever I've seen a bigger bouquet of assholes or a more shifty-looking gaggle of plug-uglies than you are, I'd like to know where it might be except in the lower depths of hell. There's not one of you rum coves but what's cheating Jack Ketch, and I've no doubt that every man of you will end up wearing a hempen collar and dancing on thin air from the yardarm. It's what you all deserve. But you're now on the *Ariadne* heading for Africa and as long as I have this"—he brandished the pistol languidly—"and you have nothing but your filthy bare hands, I know that every one of you buggering cods fears me. You damn well may. I'll string you up by your thumbs and strip the dirty hide right off your backs if you so much as look at me out of the corner of your eyes. We've had no floggings so far on this voyage, more's the pity, but the first man that steps out of line gets spread-eagled on the grating for a taste of the cat. Do you understand, you buggering bastards?"

"Hurrah for the captain!" It was the kind of language they understood and liked.

Sparks hesitated a moment before continuing, surveying them all with a sardonic smile as he twirled the pistol.

"So now, you itching apes, we're going to settle a little grudge between two of my men. If it had been two of you bunghole-whangos, I'd have had you slog it out catch-as-catch-can and the devil take the hindmost. You could go at it tooth and nail, no holds barred, gouge out each other's eyes or chew off each other's balls. Still, one of these men is my supercargo. And though to my way of thinking a supercargo is nothing but a goddamned sniveler who should be put in irons and kept in the hold with only his ink to drink and his ledger to chew from one port to another, His Majesty, God bless him"—Sparks momentarily removed his hat with the gaudy plume—"says that he's a ship's officer, even if he is nothing but the tag end of a bitch's litter. Therefore Mr. Mahound," he gestured in

Rory's direction, "ranks as an officer of this ship. Now Tim O'Toole, whom I scraped out of a Cardiff cesspool, is an able seaman. You all know Timmy as a bugginsuckle blowboy, but he's one of the best seaman I've got and a buffing boxer besides. However, if Tim O'Toole swings his fist into Mr. Mahound's face, that's mutiny—a scummy seaman striking an anointed officer—and for that I'd have to have our Timmy hung. So I've made sure Tim's fist will never touch Mr. Mahound. For your entertainment, you bloody rum coves, we're going to have a duel with whips. And"—he cocked the pistol—"if either man refuses, he'll get a ball through the head or buggered with a red-hot poker. Spottswood, Stinger, shake your arses; get the men ready."

Stinger persisted in his attitude of deference toward Rory. "If you'll give me your jacket, Mr. Mahound, I'll see that no harm comes to it." He waited while Rory removed his jacket and handed it to him. "And now your shirt, Mr. Mahound."

"My shirt?" Rory asked. "That too?"

"Aye, aye, sir," Stinger was properly obsequious, " 'tis better that way. The lash cuts through the cloth and leaves thread and lint in the wales. Makes them harder to heal, sir. Besides, it's cap'n's orders."

Rory stripped himself of his shirt and handed it to Stinger, who hung it over his arm with the jacket. Tim had already removed his jersey.

"And now the pantaloons." Stinger held out his arm.

"But I've no smallclothes on under these."

"Then the less for you to take off, Mr. Mahound. And neither has Tim." Stinger jerked a thumb to where Tim was standing buff-naked.

"I'll not strip myself. . . ."

"Oh, yes you will, Mr. Mahound, or you'll have a lead ball through your ear." Rory turned and looked up at the quarterdeck to see Captain Sparks aiming his pistol at him. He stripped off his pantaloons. As he handed them to Stinger, he could not resist the temptation to say to Sparks, "Aye, aye, sir, and why not? I've nothing to be ashamed of."

"That he ain't!" A voice from the ratlines rose over

other ribald remarks of derision from the crew. But these were also mingled with some words of praise.

"Regular banger stud, ain't he!"

"Take a good look, Timmy lad, and see what a real man looks like."

"Something for you to aim for, Timmy. Slice them danglers off."

"Ain't he white and lovely tho' with all that yellow hair!"

"And a pretty pink ass like a spanked baby's."

Rory forced a grin on his face and waved up to the shrouds and down to the deck while Stinger hung Rory's clothes over the rope and fished in his pocket, drawing out a length of tarred line. Holding Rory's left hand behind his back, he secured his wrist, brought the cord around Rory's body again and knotted it tightly so that Rory's hand was securely immobilized in the small of his back. In his free right hand, Stinger placed the handle of the whip, its length glistening with oil.

"You starts when the cap'n counts three," Stinger whispered. "Don't try to show him no mercy, Mister Mahound. Cap'n's wise to all that. In the mood Old Bastinado's in he'll shoot first and think afterwards, and if he thinks you're azzling out, he'll make me prod you with a red-hot iron. Scuttlebutt is that someone raped his doxy last night and he's fair frothing. Aim for Tim's head, Mr. Mahound. Get his eyes first if you can. It's the only way you'll ever win. I'm all for you, Mr. Mahound. Not that I've got naught against Timmy, but I'm seconding you."

Rory stepped out and faced Tim across the white sailcloth. Tim was trussed up like himself, his right hand free and the whip in it. Rory was astonished at Tim's obvious strength. He had never suspected Tim was such a hefty ape. Although he was a few inches shorter than Rory, he was a compact mass of muscles that flowed and bunched under his skin. His bull-like neck disappeared into wide, heavily padded shoulders. His belly was flat and muscle-ribbed, and his sturdy feet, planted firmly on the deck, bore the weight of hefty leg columns. Tim, without his clothes, was a far more formidable opponent than Rory had ever imagined.

The light still held and with the sun gone, there was nothing to blind Rory's eyes while he waited, tense, his eyes on Tim. Tim stared back at him just as intently and each man circled warily. He heard the captain's measured "One, two, three" and the shrill note of the bosun's pipe.

It had started now.

Although Rory felt nothing but friendship for Tim himself, he realized that this man facing him was no longer the Tim he knew. He had suddenly become an enemy who was out to kill or mutilate him and Rory was fully aware that he would have to fight back to protect himself. He couldn't show any mercy to Tim and he expected Tim to show him none either. The only thing he remembered was Tim's promise to keep away from his eyes and not to emasculate him. Yes, it was started now, although so far neither had raised his hand against the other. They continued to circle, each eyeing the other, neither wanting to inaugurate the attack.

"Get started, you cowardly coves," Sparks shouted, "or I'll have Stinger goose you with a red-hot iron." He was standing now, his eyes on them. Although Rory did not dare to take his attention from Tim for a second, he could feel the expectancy in the captain's voice.

Suddenly Tim's arm jerked up and the whip snaked out. Rory sidestepped while he aimed his own blow, anticipating Tim's step to the left. The whip landed on Tim's right shoulder, curled around his neck, and bit into the white flesh, leaving a scarlet brand. But the one moment of inaction that Rory had taken to observe the efficacy of his blow proved his undoing, for Tim's whip lashed out and caught him on the thighs, just under the buttocks, with a searing flame that penetrated his whole body. Now the fight was on and there was no respite for either of them. It was lash out and move, lash out and move, each trying to judge the other's next step by the glance of his eyes to right or left. Rory's whip caught Tim on the ear and the blood that spurted told him he had ripped part of Tim's ear off. Then again, Tim caught him, this time across the chest with a backhand lash that cut through the skin, causing first an ooze of blood and then an outpouring that encarmined Rory's body.

73

Rory could find no refuge where the stinging lash did not seek him out and he was all too conscious of his own pain to realize that he was inflicting pain himself. Now he was happy to see the red welts criss-crossing themselves on Tim's body. Each effective whirl of the whip delighted him until he felt the pain that came from the one he received in return. The creature opposite him was no longer Tim—no longer a human being; it was merely something which he must conquer before he, himself was conquered.

His tightly manacled hand made it difficult for him to maintain his balance when he put his full strength behind the lash; twice he nearly fell. After what seemed hours of swinging the whip—in actuality only a few minutes—he was aware that he was developing a certain technique: an overhead stroke that brought the whip high into the air and straightened it out like a rod until it fell on Tim's body, where it then curled like a living thing around the lacerated flesh.

"Ky-yi! Mother of God!" Tim kept yelling as the lash continued to search him out.

Rory did not waste his breath in shouting. He had only one thought. Preserve his strength, outlast Tim.

One of Tim's strokes laced around his belly and there followed almost immediately another around his calves that almost brought him to his knees, so intense was the pain. Something functioned automatically in Rory's mind. Tim's legs! That was the thing to aim for. Ducking his shoulders now and keeping his head low, Rory changed from the overhead stroke which he had almost perfected to a wide lateral one that brought the lash time and time again around Tim's legs until they were entirely ensanguined and the once-white canvas was blood-slippery under their feet. The light was fast fading and a badly aimed flick by Tim had cut Rory's scalp so that his eyes were flooded with gore and it became almost impossible for him to see. His long blood- and sweat-soaked hair swished in his eyes and he cursed the fact that he had not used shears on it before he started in on this game of murder.

Slap! The lash again cut into Tim's legs. Smack! It bit into Rory's right shoulder but he could sense that Tim's blows lacked the fire they had had at first. The cuts he had inflicted on Tim's arms were beginning to take effect. Now he concentrated entirely on Tim's legs, cutting into them time after time, no longer making wide swings but short, snappy cuts that bit deep into the flesh. Tim was stumbling, his legs no longer able to hold him up, and at length he sank down, almost at Rory's feet. He tried—and Rory sensed that he was not out but only shamming—to lift himself up but he could not make it and sank down again. Rory advanced to stand, spraddle-legged above him, a foot planted firmly on either side of Tim's chest, listening to Tim's blood-strangled cries of "Enough, enough!" He looked up to where Sparks was standing and suddenly a roar went up from the crowd.

"What are you stopping for, Mr. Mahound?" Sparks's voice cut through the cheers of the men.

"I'm no murderer, sir," Rory had to clear his throat of bloody phlegm before he spoke. "Let me remind you that our fight was not to the death. I've beaten him. He's given up. The fight is finished."

"There's plenty of fight left in Tim. He's not finished until I say so." Sparks was standing up and Rory could see, even with his blood-blinded eyes, Sparks's contorted face and the maniacal look in his eyes.

"Finished it is," someone on the deck shouted.

"Tim put up a good fight!"

"He's beat and he says so."

"Lift up Mista Mahound's arm," a voice came down from the ratlines. "He's won fair and square."

"Lift his arm! Lift his arm, lift his arm!" The crew took up the chant from deck to shrouds.

The demoniacal look faded from Sparks's face and he held up a hand to quiet them but they were beyond his control. He was only one man and two pistols against many. It was a dangerous moment, with Sparks sitting on the powder keg and the crew holding a lighted match. Better to prove his magnanimity and hold his popularity than to defy such odds.

He held up his hand, waiting for the chant to die down.

"Lift his arm, Stinger," he shouted. "We proclaim Mr. Mahound the victor."

Stinger walked out onto the slippery canvas and raised Rory's arm high. For a long moment he held it there, triumphant over the supine Tim while the crew cheered themselves hoarse. They were all for Rory now. Their favorite was forgotten.

"Cut me loose, Stinger!" Rory struggled to free his hand and welcomed the knife with which Stinger slashed the cord. Grabbing the knife from Stinger's hand, he knelt down to where Tim still lay on the canvas. There was a hush and a gasp of breath from the onlookers. Many thought, despite his words, that Rory was going to finish Tim off; but he sliced through the cord, pulled Tim's arm from behind him, and lifted him to his feet.

"Stand up, Tim," he encouraged. "You put up a good fight. Everyone's satisfied and we can both see, thank God." On a sudden impulse, he lifted Tim's hand high in the air and a cheer broke out from the crew.

Tim leaned heavily on Rory.

"We'll shake hands on it, Rory lad," he whimpered.

"That we shall," Rory clasped Tim's hand.

Supporting Tim and accompanied by the cheers of the crew, Rory hobbled across the canvas, ducked under the rope which Stinger held up for him, and then stumbled down onto the deck to reach up and help Tim down. The crew parted, making a lane for them to the fo'c'sle; slowly and painfully they limped along, leaving bloody footprints on the scoured white deck.

Spottswood and Stinger followed them.

"Lie down on the deck, Mr. Mahound, and you too, Tim," Spottswood spoke roughly but with a certain kindness in his voice. "Sea water's best to wash them wales."

Willing hands supported Rory and Tim as they fell to the deck, and willing hands trailed a bucket over the side, bringing it up time after time to slosh their bodies with the cool brine. Someone dragged out two thin straw mattresses from the fo'c'sle and placed them on the deck while others wrung out old shirts and cloths and applied them in compresses over their bodies.

For a long time they both stretched out on the mattresses, unable to move. The cold compresses turned warm on their bodies and darkness overtook them. Some of the

76

crew were chanting, others were running up the ratlines to reef the sails because there was a blow coming up. The scudding clouds hid the stars.

Rory found enough strength to raise his head and reach over to touch Tim.

"No hard feelings, Tim?" he asked.

"Yes, Rory Mahound." Tim had difficulty in speaking. "I've hard feelings in my heart but not for you. Only for myself. Never again will I crimp a man for a filthy golden guinea. Never again. But no matter how hard I feel toward myself, Rory Mahound, I cannot help but be glad that I brought you to this ship. Bad as it is, I'm happy you're here." He managed to squeeze Rory's hand.

Rory returned the pressure. "Belay that, Tim, we're friends. Look, cully, it's getting cold. Better we get below. Can you walk?"

"That I can, even though my legs are raw beef."

"I'm sorry."

"Don't be. We've got our eyes and our pride-and-joys. The rest will heal."

They helped each other up and then separated, Rory going to the quarterdeck and Tim below to the fo'c'sle. Once in his tiny cabin, Rory threw himself down on his bunk. He could not lie in any comfort. Every muscle ached, every laceration of his flesh jumped with pain like a toothache. All he could do was lie there, counting the ship's bells. At eleven bells, the door of his cabin opened. It was the captain, and his lighted candle showed he was holding a glass in his hand.

"Drink this," he proffered the glass to Rory.

"Are you trying to poison me now?" Rory refused the glass.

"Aye, cock, you've a bad opinion of me. I've no evil designs on you. I've had my fun, thanks to you. First you and Qarma and now you beating Tim. This is nothing but an opium pill dissolved in wine. After all, I do owe you something. You've released me from two nights of boredom, and boredom is my greatest enemy. So, Sir Roderick, I'm indebted to you. Nay, more than that, I really like you, cock. I really do. You see, I'm fed up with the

77

commonplace, the everyday, the banal, and the usual. You're different. I like you."

"You've a hell of a way of showing it." Rory took the glass and gulped the contents.

"I'll make it up to you, Sir Roderick. I'm indebted to you and I'm not a man to be ungrateful." Sparks closed the door behind him.

Despite his wounds and his pain, Rory slept.

CHAPTER VIII

THE ONE SMALL PORTHOLE IN RORY'S CABIN allowed only a pale, aqueous light to creep in, which dappled the white walls and ceiling with moving reflections from the sun on the water below. This light, replacing the long darkness, awakened Rory from his drugged sleep. He felt such a soreness in his whole body that he was unable to find any position in which he could rest with even a degree of comfort. His questing fingers wandered over his bare chest and encountered blood-encrusted welts as thick and ropy as his fingers themselves. These welts were not confined to his chest; his thighs and legs were corded with wales, one shoulder was laid open, and his hair was blood-matted.

A sudden fear gripped him. Had he been hurt in his most vital spot? For a long second his hand trembled in indecision. He must know, but he could not summon the courage to find out. From the various aches of his body, he tried to ascertain if there was any particular pain in that area. No, he could not sort out one bodily pain from another, but encouraged by the fact that he felt no definite agony in that area, his hand became exploratory. Everything that should have been there was there. He grunted in satisfaction. Tim had kept his promise, and he found satisfaction in the thought that so had he.

Judging by the light and the sounds on deck, it must have been midmorning; but nobody had come near him and it was certain, in his present condition, he could go nowhere. Once he tried to swing his legs over the edge of the bunk but found he could not bear the pain, so he fell back, punching the thin pillow behind his head to give him some support, and allowed himself a session of self-pity, interspersed with rounds of cursing Sparks, his uncle in Liverpool, his father, and, most of all, Qarma who, he believed, was responsible for everything. Why hadn't he left the bitch alone? But no! In spite of everything that had happened, he was glad that he had had her, even though he had been putting on a raree show for that bastard Sparks. At least he had something to think about now to help him get through the womanless weeks ahead. He'd given that black bitch more than she'd bargained for and he bet it was more than she'd ever had in her life. All that bragging about that brother of hers—lies, nothing but lies. No man could ever do what she claimed that black bastard could do. Never!

His anger and his thoughts about Qarma had temporarily taken his mind off his discomfort; now, because he could no longer sustain that anger, his body started to pain him again. Strangely enough, he discovered that in spite of his discomfort he was hungry. Goddamn Sparks and his whole back-scuttling crew! Were they going to let him starve? At least Tim, down in that stinking fo'c'sle, would have someone to bring him a bowl of hot porridge. That set him to thinking about Tim and wondering how he was. As Sparks said, Tim was the scrapings of the gutter, and yet he was a rum cove, a friend. Sure, Tim was a fighter and a good one. He could knock any man down that ballyragged him, and yet the fact that Rory could see the dancing lights on the ceiling this morning attested to Tim's goodness, for he could have whipped out both of Rory's eyes and saved himself a lot of punishment. True, he could have done the same with Tim.

He wished Tim were right here now. They'd be company for each other in their misery. Well, Tim liked him and even that bastard Sparks had said that *he* liked him. Stinger did too! And the crew had cheered him. So what the hell? He had no enemies and his back was beginning to feel better. By shifting, he finally found a position where he could rest with a modicum of pain. He drifted off into that borderline realm between sleeping and waking where he was oblivious to both his pain and his thoughts.

The sound of the door opening awakened him from his half-slumber; squinting through his lashes, he saw Sparks in the doorway, the white hair of his wig catching the dancing spots of light. He lay without moving, conscious of Sparks's appraisal of his body. Sparks looked him over, then closed the door. A few minutes later there was a loud rap and Leazy entered. He carried a bowl of steaming porridge in one hand, a jug of water in the other, and a small wooden firkin under one arm.

"Cap'n says you mought be hankering for something for your belly." Leazy set the jug of water on the floor, eased the firkin down beside it, and put the wooden bowl of porridge in Rory's hands. "Look, Mista Mahound, cook put butter on it and bacon too. Eat it up, sir. Make you feel better to have something inside you."

"Well, what's the scuttlebutt this morning, Leazy?" Rory managed to get a spoonful of the porridge up to his mouth. It was hot and cook had not been stingy with either the butter or bacon. It found a welcome place in his stomach, warming him all the way through.

"Whole ship's a-talking about you, Mista Mahound. Saying as how you whipped Tim clean and proper and didn't blind him nor maim him. Regular toff you are, a-holding up his hand. They're all saying as to how you're a proper rum cove, Mista Mahound, and as how Old Bastinado is a mucking mudsill. Him and his Hottentot slash of gash! Ain't no secrets on this ship, Mista Mahound. Too many eyes and ears all around. Everybody knows that Old Bastinado sneaked aboard and got that black bitch to take you down to his cabin. He likes to watch another man plugging his wench, he does. Last voyage in Havana he got one of them Cuban half-breeds on board and had him slip it to her whilst he peeked through the hole in the door. Poor bastid left the ship all cut up and bleeding like a stuck pig. Peeking in on a raree show ain't nothing new for cap'n. Got queer ideas, Old Bastinado has."

"Seems to me everyone on this ship has." Rory scooped up the last spoonful of porridge. "Even you, Leazy."

"A boy has got to live, Mista Mahound. Being cabin boy ain't always an easy job. Have to please all those fo'c'sle gulpins. But whatever it is it's better'n that orphan home I was in. I get to eat here."

"What's in the firkin?" Rory pointed to the floor.

"Taller. Cook says there ain't nothing better'n taller for cuts and bruises. He always keeps some on hand for treating the fellows that Old Bastinado cats. Says for me to rub it on. Want me to, Mr. Mahound? I'd sure admire to do it and I'll be careful not to hurt you."

The tallow stank like a dead sheep but Rory turned over and let Leazy rub it in. He winced as the boy touched him but, true to his word, Leazy was gentle as his hands slithered over Rory's body. When he had finished and Rory was greased up like a pig at a village fair, he settled back, feeling more comfortable.

"Ask cook if he's got any more of that for Tim."

"Tim's all greased up," Leazy grinned. "Tended to him first, I did, begging your pardon. Tim's in worse shape than you, Mista Mahound. His left leg's cut to the bone. Can fair see the white of it."

"I'm sorry. Tell Tim that, will you?"

"Tim knows. Tim don't bear you no grudge, Mista Mahound. He's got no sour-on for you." He pointed to the jug on the floor. "Water, Mr. Mahound. Can you reach it?" Leazy reached under his shirt and drew out a book bound in calfskin. "Cap'n sent this to you."

Rory took the book, almost nauseated by the sour smell of Leazy's armpits.

"I'll be back with your dinner." Leazy took a long look at Rory. "Sure there ain't nothing more I can do for you, Mista Mahound? All you got to do is ask."

Rory shook his head and Leazy edged slowly out the door, closing it behind him. The book that Sparks had sent was the same one he had been reading the day Rory came aboard—the one about the girl called Fanny Hill.

81

Rory opened it, intrigued by illustrations that left nothing to his imagination about the character of the heroine and whetted Rory's appetite for the text. He soon became engrossed in the story; but, as he was a slow reader and had to stop to examine each picture in all its minute details, he did not get very far before he fell asleep.

For two days and two nights he kept to his bed, waited on by Leazy, greased up daily with mutton tallow, while he followed the peregrinations of the fair Fanny. He slept a lot, half-drunk from the wine that Sparks continued to send him. The pains subsided and the soreness became almost bearable. Thanks to Fanny's escapades, the wine and the little extra tasty touches which cook added to his meals, these few days were a peaceful interlude in Rory's life. The pictures, however, and the lurid descriptions in the text applied the match to a train of thought that wove strange fantasies in his mind. He was almost tempted to delay Leazy on one of his visits when he brought food, but the boy's stench and acne-spotted face repulsed him.

On the second day of his confinement, he heard frenzied screams, and when Leazy brought his supper, he told Rory that on Sparks's orders two men had been flogged that afternoon. What for? Well, one had been caught asleep on watch and the other had not polished the bright work entirely to Sparks's satisfaction. But, Leazy hastened to inform him, this was a proper rum voyage because usually Sparks flogged every day. Yes, Leazy admitted, he liked to watch; it sure charged him while it was going on but he felt sorry for the poor bastards afterwards. He was glad there had been so little flogging on this voyage. Maybe Old Bastinado was getting rid of some of his feelings on that black wench of his.

On the third day, with Leazy's help, Rory managed to get dressed and step out on deck. The first person he encountered was Sparks, who greeted him affably as though nothing had ever happened, albeit he held his nose as Rory came close to him.

" 'Od's blood, Mr. Mahound, you smell like an over-done saddle of mutton. Cook's been fixing you up, I suppose. He thinks tallow will cure anything—even the

82

French pox. Tell me! How did you enjoy Fanny?" He closed one eye slowly in a meaningful wink.

"One could not ask for a better companion, sir, during an indisposition. Most thoughtful of you to provide her."

"Really, Mr. Mahound, you must come to realize that I am not such a bad sort after all. Mostly bored. There are limitations to the amusement one may find aboard ship, entirely surrounded by men."

Rory looked a question at him.

"Qarma? She's not a woman, Mr. Mahound. She's nothing but an animal. She's better than a bitch, of course, because she can talk and, I suppose, think. But don't make the mistake of confusing niggers with human beings. They're not. If you get to thinking of them as humans, you'll have no stomach for this bloody business. They're nothing but two-legged animals and that's that. We buy them; we sell them; and in the Indies they work them. They're so much flesh at so much a pound, on the hoof.

"You'll come to understand that a nigger has only the most primitive, bestial instincts. When he's hungry, he eats; when he's tired, he sleeps; and when his blood gets hot, he ruts. If he can't get a woman, he takes a man or beast. I've heard they screw crocodiles in Africa and I don't doubt it. Waste no sympathy on them, or on Qarma either. All she wants is a man and there's never been one yet who could satisfy her, unless it's that goddamned brother she's always talking about. I'm sick of her. I plan to sell her off on this voyage. She'll bring a good price in Havana or Port-au-Prince," Sparks sighed and shrugged his shoulders as though to dispose of the whole matter. "I trust you bear me no ill will, Mr. Mahound."

Rory was politic. Once he could have killed this smiling rascal. Now he rather admired him for his patent villainy.

"No ill will, sir." He even smiled as he said it.

Sparks slid a finger up under his peruke and scratched his head.

"Do you play any musical instrument, Mr. Mahound? If it's bagpipes, don't mention them because I do not consider them music."

Rory was entirely confused by the abrupt change of

83

subject. He knew nothing about music, although he did not agree with Sparks about the bagpipes. He rather liked to hear their skirling. He shook his head in reply, wondering if some diabolical idea of Sparks was already hatching.

"I merely asked because Tim O'Toole is laid up and unable to play his harp. I thought of having a bull dance on deck tonight. Helps the men to ease off a bit of steam, but without Tim I guess I'll have to forget it."

"How is Tim?" Rory asked.

"Not too good, I regret to say. His right leg is not healing and he's confined to his bunk. Tim's a good man but I'm afraid he's going to lose his leg."

"Permission granted to visit him, sir?"

"Why, of course, Mr. Mahound. And convey my sympathy to Tim. Tell him if it becomes necessary to amputate his leg, I'll oblige him by doing the job myself. Not that I've had any experience as a surgeon, you understand, but I'd at least be able to saw it off with a little more comprehension than anyone else."

"Of that I am sure," Rory could not tell whether the man was genuinely concerned over Tim or not. One could never know whether Sparks's words were uttered in sincerity or sarcasm. "I'll deliver your message, sir." He started to walk away.

"But one minute, Mr. Mahound," Sparks held up his hand. "I quite forgot. Tell me! Of the various pictures in the book, which one intrigued you the most? It will be interesting to see if our taste coincides."

"I believe, sir," Rory answered slowly, looking Sparks directly in the eye, "the one where Fanny peeks through the hole and sees the other girl entertaining her Neapolitan friend."

"*Touché.*" Sparks laughed and raised his right jand as though to clap Rory on the back and then thought better of it. "Permit me to say, however, that Fanny herself had no more exciting spectacle than the one I witnessed. That Neapolitan could not exceed you in prowess, Mr. Mahound."

"Thank you, sir. I'm glad I gave satisfaction. Had I

known, of course, that you were watching, I might have done even better."

"No, you'd have been all too conscious of my watching you; but you've rather disappointed me these last few days. I had in mind a repetition of that incident that Fanny describes when she stood on the chair in the inn and peeked through the partition to see the two young laddy bucks on the other side. I figured after reading Fanny, you might find Leazy of interest but, alas, my moments at the keyhole were wasted."

"I'd have to be at sea a long time before I'd want to tackle Leazy!"

"Can't say that I blame you. He was rather a Ganymede when I signed him on for the last voyage but, alas, he's changed. But then, cock, don't judge me too harshly. When a man's bored, he'll do most anything. You're excused from work and watches until your wounds heal. Go and see Tim and tell him I hope his leg turns out all right. And here"—Sparks reached in his pocket and drew out a shiny gold guinea—"give this to Tim. He really earned it after all."

Rory took the coin and his dismissal. Surely the man must be daft. Or perhaps, as he said, he was merely bored with life. He was a good captain, if one took into consideration only the immaculate cleanliness of the ship, the discipline of the crew, and the man's expert knowledge of navigation. But he was unpredictable. One moment he would be charmingly polished and urbane; the next he would be cruel, sadistic, and without mercy. Oh well! There was little that Rory could do about it except, if possible, keep in the man's good graces. But he'd forget about him and go and see Tim.

He crossed the deck and descended into the fetid fo'c'sle. This was one part of the ship where Sparks' spit-and-polish housekeeping had never penetrated. It belonged to the crew and they were permitted to keep it the way they wished; few captains dared enforce their discipline on that part of the ship. Occasionally some sailor with a passion for neatness would keep his own bunk in order—the mattress clean, the blanket folded, and his clothes hung in some sort of order—but in most cases the

85

mattresses were filthy, the blankets tumbled in a heap among a welter of dirty clothes, and the man himself stinking, unwashed, uncombed, and lousy.

Rory picked his way through the gummy woolen socks on the floor, the torn jerseys, and the paint-stiff pantaloons, until he came to Tim's bunk.

Tim, stretched out naked and moaning, did not hear him and did not open his eyes until Rory shook his shoulder.

"I'm sorry things are going bad with you, Tim."

Tim's green eyes were clouded with pain. "No need, matey. How are you?"

"Getting along fine, Tim. They tell me your leg still troubles you."

"That it does, Rory. Pains something terrible, it does."

Rory found a stub of a candle and lighted it, then knelt down on the floor to examine Tim's leg. There was a long gash, pus-filled and badly swollen, the flesh a strange dead white bordered by dark angry red. The whole leg was puffed up, the skin stretched and shiny. It felt hot to Rory's touch.

"How does it look?" Tim spoke softly as though he dreaded the inevitable answer.

"Well, I could say it looked fine, Tim, and I'd be lying to you. It's bad, Tim, but it not so bad but what we can't do something about it. There's a medicine chest in Sparks's cabin and I'm going to get it. I know little about how to treat wounds, but I know at least that you should be clean and out of this stinking hole.

"Proud flesh, that's what they call it. 'Tis not uncommon in a wound. We've got to draw out the poison. My old Jamie fell and cut a nasty gash in his arm and it swelled up like your leg. 'Proud flesh,' Goodwife MacLaren, who knew all about herbs and simples, said, and she made up a poultice of bread and milk and put on it. That cured it. But wait you now a minute, Tim. I'm leaving but I'll be back. Don't worry, I'm going to look after you."

Rory went up the stairs and out onto the deck. He spied the captain on the quarterdeck and raced up the stairs to him as fast as he could.

"Well, well, Mr. Mahound." Sparks's diamond flashed in the sun as he waved to Rory. "It would seem that you like my company in that you seek it again so quickly."

"Your permission, sir, to doctor Tim. The way his leg looks, I don't think he'll last much longer unless something's done. He's in a bad state. I'd like to see what I can do for him."

"Turning yourself into a bloody nursemaid, are you? Just to save Timmy from losing his leg? Well, now, 'twould seem that we have Faith, Hope, and Charity and all the other Christian virtues aboard ship, with you acting as Granny Fingersmith for Tim. Yes, save Tim's leg if you can. He's no good to me with only one shank. I've said you need not report for duty. Do as you damn please."

"Then I'd like to move Tim to the little cabin next to mine that's empty, sir. There's not much I can do for him in the filth of the fo'c'sle."

"Belay there, Mr. Mahound! That's a horse of a different color. A seaman in officers' quarters. I hardly think . . ."

"Tim's a good seaman. You said so yourself. He's no good to you with one leg, so it seems to me he's worth saving—especially when you have to resort to crimping to get a man."

"Well now, you may have something there, Mr. Mahound. I do believe you're right."

"I'd like to get Tim back on his two feet."

"And you'd like to play house with Timmy in the cabin next to yours. Laugh, Mr. Mahound. That's a jest. Have you no sense of humor? Must you always be so serious?"

" 'Tis a serious matter, sir. Would there be any laudanum in your medicine chest?"

"I'll see that a bottle is sent to your cabin. I've never had a seaman on the quarterdeck, and I'll not have one now; but if you were to move Tim there and I did not know it, 'twould make damned little difference. I will know nothing about it, understand?"

"Then I'll not be thanking you, sir." Rory left and went to the galley as fast as his own poor legs would carry him. The cook shook his head when Rory asked about white bread, but when he found out what Rory had in mind, he nodded his head sagely.

"Oatmeal porridge will do as well, Mr. Mahound. Flaxseed might be better, but a good poultice of oatmeal will bring the core right out of a carbuncle and if it'll do that it's good for drawing poison out of a wound. I'll stir up a kettle full and keep it on the back of the galley so's you can change it when it's needed."

"And some hot water, cookie. Tim needs washing."

"Aye, aye, sir, a boilerful will start heating, Mr. Mahound. You're a rum toff, sir. We all like Tim and we'll be grateful to you."

In an hour, Rory had Tim moved, scrubbed clean, his hair combed, a pillow at his back and stretched out in some degree of comfort, chewing on that greatest of all delicacies, a fresh pineapple which cook had purchased in Madeira and delivered especially to Tim by Leazy. A cloth bag filled with hot oatmeal was tied with strips of rags around the wound in his leg. He looked up at Rory and smiled. It was a wan smile but there was no longer fear in Tim's eyes.

"Feels better already," he said. "What are you going to do now, Rory?"

Rory sat down at the foot of the bunk and opened the captain's book.

"I'm going to read to you, Tim. 'Twill take your mind off your leg when you hear about this wench Fanny and what happened to her when she came to London. Her adventures are enough to work any man into a lather. I'll show you the pictures too. Aye, wait till you hear about Fanny. You'll be standing up straight as a soldier, Tim, and you'll not need two good legs to stand on neither."

CHAPTER IX

DURING THE NEXT WEEK, RORY'S WOUNDS healed. He did not know whether he had the mutton tallow to thank for it or not, but the wounds left no scars, for which he was grateful. Tim was not so fortunate. The swelling went down from his leg and he was able to bear his weight on it, but the sore did not heal and still caused him pain. Rory went back to his gray dungeon with old Stoat and Tim reluctantly moved his gear back from the quarterdeck to the fo'c'sle.

Then one morning when Rory awoke his bed was stationary for the first time in many weeks. It was a strange and almost forgotten sensation. He felt neither pitching nor rolling and, except for a gentle swell which caused the vessel to rock slowly and almost imperceptibly, Rory might have been back in Sax Castle. But there was one other difference—the damnable heat! It filled the cabin like a wet solid thing that pressed down on him like layers and layers of damp wool. There was no escape from it. No relief. Even the feeble breeze that penetrated his porthole was hot. The heat clung to him like an incubus made of wrung-out rags; at the same time, it was like a searing flame.

His slightest efforts required superhuman strength, but he finally managed to accumulate enough ambition to roll from the wet mattress and hoist his long legs over the edge of his bunk. Having accomplished that monumental task, he got to his feet. Rivulets of sweat channeled down his back, and his groin itched with an itch that scratching would not assuage. His very eyeballs seemed glued in his head, immobile, and stagnant. Slipping on his shirt and pantaloons, still soggy from yesterday's sweat, he stumbled out on deck to find the rails amidships lined with seamen, all staring down intently into the smooth, oily, dark water.

Rory deserted the quarterdeck and came down to where Tim had propped himself against the rail. Tim made a place for him and Rory leaned over. Alongside he spied a welter of dugout canoes, each jockeying for a position near the ship. Black men, naked except for flimsy loincloths which, soaking wet, outlined rather than concealed what they were supposed to hide, balanced themselves precariously in the narrow canoes. These, Tim explained, were the famous Krumen of the Slave Coast—free Negroes because of their prowess on the water and their necessity to the white traders. Some were standing in their canoes, holding up fruits of strange shapes and colors which Rory had never seen before. The sight of fresh fruit, regardless of what it might be, was so tempting that he inquired of Tim how he might get some. That was easy, Tim informed him. All he had to do was catch the eye of one of the howling Kru boys, hold up a copper penny, and then throw it. No matter whether it was caught or not, it would be retrieved. Rory followed Tim's instructions, gained the attention of a coal-black fellow whose immense white teeth grinned back at him, and then tossed the penny. It was poorly aimed and fell short of the canoe but the boy was over the side in a flash of black limbs and pink soles, disappearing into the water only to surface, grinning as broadly as ever and holding up the penny in his fingers. He threw a thin line to Rory and when Rory caught it, he tied the other end to a basket made of plaited palm fronds and Rory hauled it up the side of the ship.

The strange phallic-looking yellow fruits were new to Rory, but Tim had eaten them before. "Bananas," he named them. They must be peeled before eating. Tim demonstrated by pulling off the thick yellow skin and handing Rory the creamy white, pulpy inside. Rory found them delicious. After a steady diet of porridge, salt beef, and hardtack, anything fresh would have tasted good. Rory found a subtle flavor in the bananas that he had never encountered before. The round yellow oranges he had heard about but never tasted, and these, he discovered, were even more refreshing than the bananas. The green limes were too tart and puckered his mouth, but after he ate one he felt refreshed. Between Tim and himself they finished the basket.

Beyond the shouting, churning maelstrom of canoes in the water below, Rory looked out to see a low, flat strip of green trees, apparently growing out of the water on stilt-like roots. Between them, narrow openings in the greenery disclosed channels of darker water and at some distance beyond the tops of the trees, he could see a white tower from which floated the house flag of McCairn and Ogilsvy. While he continued to scan this unreal and improbable landscape, a boat emerged from the lush greenery of the shore. It was a ship's boat, manned by half a dozen blacks whose oars rose and fell with mechanical precision to the beat of a drum. On the raised dais at the stern, a black plied the tiller, while under a red-and-white awning two passengers sat in the body of the boat. As Rory watched this almost regal progress, he heard his name being called from the quarterdeck and went up to find Captain Sparks beckoning to him.

"Mr. Mahound," Sparks's voice had a peevish whine to it, "it would be appreciated if you remained here on the quarterdeck. It hardly seems necessary for me to yell my head off to attract your attention while you lollygag amidships with a seaman."

"At your service, sir." Rory hoped he could end the voyage without coming to blows with the captain who seemed to alternate between making definite attempts to be disagreeable and then negating them by some unexpected pleasantness.

"That son of a drabble-tailed monkey," Sparks whirled sharply and pointed to the boat which was coming nearer, "calls himself Dom Pedro da Souza and styles himself as the *senhor* of Rinktum Castle. He is the goddamndest oiliest, slipperiest, slimiest bastard that ever drew a breath of air and I'd trust him no further than I would a Tyburn jock-gagger. But we are dependent on the bastard. He's in charge of collecting slaves here for the company, and if we're lucky we can fill our holds here without having to go to Badagry or Calabar and pay higher prices.

"He's here to get slaves for us, and as we support this place, we get them cheaper; but I think the fly-by-night

91

two-timer is double-crossing us. We get mostly a poor lot from him—flat-faced Yorubas, Soosoos, and only an occasional Ibo or Dahomey. It's the Fans, the Jaloffs, the Hausas, the Mandingos and the Sudanese that bring the money today. I think this goddamned Souza gets them and sells them for big prices to other factories or vessels, then takes the money and buys poor stuff with it while he pockets the profits. Once in a while he surprises us with a few prime specimens, just enough to keep us satisfied; and these, he says, come from some fiddle-faddle young Arab princeling who brings a twice-yearly caravan to the coast."

"Yes sir," Rory agreed although he did not know why he should be singled out for this conversation or for this information.

"Now you, Mr. Mahound, don't know a goddamned thing about niggers." Sparks continued to watch the progress of the longboat while he talked to Rory. "But I do. Souza and I don't get along and the last time I was here, I nearly shaved off his beard with my cutlass. By the way, he's got someone in the boat with him. Wonder who that might be."

"I'm sure I don't know," Rory answered.

"As I damn well know you don't. But, as I was saying, I'm going to send you ashore with Souza and you'll stay at Rinktum Castle while we're here. You're going, not as Rory Mahound, the most worthless supercargo a ship ever had, but as Baron of Sax, the nephew of Mr. McCairn himself. I want you to scout around and see what Souza's got in his barracoons. Use your wits, if you have any. You may not be able to tell a Jaloff from a pigmy, but you can at least recognize strong, healthy-looking nigger bucks if you see them. That's what we're looking for and we'd like to get three hundred if we can. I'd also take about fifty wenches if I could get them. They don't fetch as much as bucks but they're used for house servants in Barbados and white men on the island are developing a taste for nigger flesh for bedmates."

"Yes, sir." Rory welcomed the chance to go ashore. He was also glad to be relieved of the arduous task of check-

92

ing out the cargo and being cooped up with old Stoat. It was hotter than the hinges of hell below decks.

Sparks regarded him appraisingly. "If you're going to be a high cockalorum, you'd better dress the part, too. Come to my cabin and I'll fit you out in some of my clothes. It'll take some time for Souza to get here. You're a bit bigger than I, but my clothes will fit you well enough and you'll look like something in them. You'll need a servant too. Whom do you want to take along with you?"

"I'd prefer Tim to anyone else."

"I'll have Stoat open the slop chest and fit him out in new trogs. How's his leg? Can he walk on it?"

"It pains him still and the wound's not closed, but he can get around."

"Should have been cauterized. Never mind now. Got to get you dressed up so you'll look like something. Qarma'll help you but don't get your mind set on humping her again. No time for it. Besides, Souza'll furnish you with a black wench tonight if you can stand her musk. It's as much a part of African hospitality as serving you dinner. Come!"

Once in the cabin, Sparks tumbled out an array of clothing from his wardrobe. Rory hastily selected a garnet velvet coat laced with gold, white satin breeches, white silk stockings and black buckled shoes. Yelling for Qarma, Sparks had her search for a frilled shirt, a black stock and a cocked tricorne edged with white marabout.

From a carved camphorwood chest, he pulled out several white linen suits, tailored more or less in naval uniform style, and threw them with a pile of shirts and underclothes.

"Velvet's too hot for this climate but today it'll make a good impression on Souza. Wear the white clothes after you get ashore but be the high-mightiest snob you know how to be. I'll be coming ashore tonight or tomorrow. See if you can get some information for me by that time. There'll be a ship's boat at Rinktum dock for you at all times in case you want to use it. If Souza's got any herd at all, we'll be here several days loading and unloading. I've heard rumors that he has a secret stockade up the river where he keeps his private stock. If you can forewarn me that he has a reserve, I'll have the upper hand over him. Get dressed now. He must be coming aboard; I just heard the ladder dropping. Qarma will help you dress. Hurry!"

Qarma hindered his dressing more than helped it. He had to struggle to get into his clothes while she knelt before him, her arms around his waist. He slipped on his shirt and coat with difficulty for her wanton slaverings tempted him to yield to her. It took willpower for him to push her away in order to draw his breeches on, but once away from her darting tongue, the very musk of her body nauseated him. He wondered, in some part of his mind which was detached from the business of getting dressed and the necessity for warding her off, if he'd always feel this way about dark flesh. Reproachfully, she stared at him with eyes quick-darting from his own eyes to his body while he finished dressing and tying his cravat. Then, just as he was about to leave, she flung herself at him again, ripping open the buttons he had so carefully buttoned.

"Nobody watching. Quick, man. Let me have you. Will only take a minute in the state you are in."

He twisted away from her, pushing to free himself, and struggled toward the door, pulling her weight with every step and trying in vain to redo the buttons which she had unfastened. With the door open, he unlaced her fingers, flung her back into the room and before she could regain her balance he had closed the door, locking it with the key Sparks had left on the outside. It took him a moment to catch his breath and to arrange his clothes so that his encounter with her would not be too conspicuous. When he got up on deck, he found that Souza was just arriving. The bosun was standing at the rail, ready to pipe him on board.

Tim, still limping painfully, appeared in new, creased white pantaloons, blue jacket and leather hat, his pigtail stiffly tarred. Sparks, standing at the head of the stairs that led to the quarterdeck, was fully accoutered with dress sword and a clutch of enamelled medals and stars on his chest which Rory knew he had never officially earned. Nevertheless he cut a handsome figure and Rory beside him, his gut sucked in so he would not split the seams of

Sparks's breeches, was, despite himself, peacock-proud of his own elegance.

A yellow hand appeared first on the rope ladder, then slowly the man himself came up to be helped over the rail and onto the deck. Souza was a tiny man; had he been a few inches shorter he would have been a dwarf, but there was nothing grotesque about him, for he was perfectly formed and delicately made. Coffee with only a little cream might have described his muddy color, and Rory, in his ignorance, laid this to the fact that he was a Portuguese; he was later to find that the man was a mulatto whose wandering father had sired him on a Soosoo wench. He might have been fifty because his hair was white and his face sagging with wrinkles.

Souza was followed by a huge young Negro who, Rory considered, was the most impressive male specimen he had ever seen. The contrast between Souza's diminutive size and this dark Hercules was all the more apparent as they stood beside each other on the deck, waiting for Sparks and Rory to descend to greet them. Souza could have walked under the Negro's upraised arm with a head to spare. The Portuguese was elaborately dressed in European clothing which, had it been clean, might have rivalled that of either Sparks's or Rory's own, but the sheer magnificence of the young Negro's raiment put them all to shame. He was dressed in a sky-blue garment of fine wool with wide flowing sleeves, and the garment was purposely unfastened to disclose an underdress of heavy white silk, embroidered all over in blue and green and heavily encrusted with pearls. His head was wound with a bright green turban from which sprouted a spray of white ostrich plumes, anchored in place with a huge ruby. Yet, with all this feminine frippery, there was a compelling masculinity about the fellow.

As he approached the two men, walking a few steps behind Sparks, Rory could see that the fellow was not as dark as he had at first imagined. He was somewhere between a soft brown and tan—a tawny, leonine topaz with highlights and dark shadows like the gem itself. Eyes, dark and doelike, looked out from under finely penciled brows with an upsweep like a bird's wing. The nose was short, broad-bridged, and slightly flattened, but the flaring nostrils were sensitive. His lips were wide, far thicker than a white man's, moist and grape-colored, and the chin was strong, deeply clefted, and so smooth it appeared as though he had never shaved. A vein pulsed in the wide, smooth neck column and even under the voluminous gowns there was a suggestion of the wide, barreled chest which sank into slender hips. Rory, to whom masculine magnificence and comeliness had never been worth a second glance, found himself impressed by the savage beauty of the young Negro who, despite the small steps he took to keep pace with Souza's short treads, moved with the grace of a leopard. Suddenly Rory felt he was face to face with Africa—the real Africa.

Souza came forward to shake Sparks's hand and even before he relinquished the captain's grip, he was introducing the Negro.

"His Exalted Highness, Baba-il-Kadir ben Idris, the Shango of Sa'aqs, son and heir to that great lord, the Sultan of Sa'aqs."

Sparks stepped forward with a wide smile.

"The Shango of Sa'aqs! We are honored, your Highness. Please forgive my ignorance of your arrival. Had I known, I would have fired a salute—a salute of twenty-one guns." He signaled to his first officer to come down to the main deck and in a few whispered words ordered him to go to the arsenal and, together with the second and third officer, procure and load hand arms for the necessary round of firing. Then he greeted the shango with a low bow and a sweep of his plumed hat.

"Sa'aqs!" he exclaimed loudly, his eyes on the shango. "And Sax." He turned partially to Rory who was behind him, motioning frantically for him to come nearer. "Allow me, Your Exalted Highness, to present one of the most important men in my country, the Baron of Sax"—he gave particular emphasis to the name—"Sir Roderick Mahound, who is the nephew of the great McCairn himself who owns this ship and this factory. Sir Roderick, the Prince of Sa'aqs." And then, as Rory stepped up, he whispered, "Luck smiles on us, cock."

Rory offered his hand but it was ignored by the shango.

Instead the fellow snapped his fingers and, with one hand over his heart, he bowed, transferring his hand to touch his forehead. In the course of his greeting, the plumes on his turban brushed Rory's face and when the big fellow saw what had happened, he grinned, then laughed aloud, considering it an immense joke, yet nodding an apology. Rory shared in the joke, pointing to the tall feathers and then to his own face, shivering to show how the feathers had tickled, and then joining the shango's laughter.

Chuckling, the African snapped his fingers again to summon one of the Negroes standing at the rail. The man called fell flat on his face, edging along on the deck by lifting his body with his elbows, until he came within a few feet of the Shango. He lifted his head but kept his eyes averted from the presence of the other. The shango spoke to him in Arabic, and although it had been a long time since Rory had sat by the peat fire at Castle Sax and talked with old Jamie in Arabic, he found he could understand the man's words.

"Who is this yellow-haired N'zrani that he should have the same name as mine? I believe it to be some trick and yet the fellow looks honest enough and his looks please me. I like him and yet you need not tell him so."

Although not sure of whether he was doing the right thing, as prescribed by etiquette, Rory laid his hand on the Shango's arm and spoke to him in Arabic.

"Peace be unto you, my lord Shango, and to your household. May you live for many years and beget many sons. It is indeed strange that we should answer to the same name, but the fact that my father was a great lord in Scotland"—might as well lay it on thick while he was doing it, he decided—"and yours a great lord in Africa proclaims that the name is indeed a noble one. There is no trick, my lord Shango. The name of Sax has been in my family for many hundreds of years. I rejoice that it is also your name, which would seem to make us brothers—and, by the three sacred hairs of Mohammed's beard in Mecca, I can think of no man I had rather call brother than yourself."

The firing of the pistols interrupted Rory and he could see the shango counting them off on his fingers and the

97

look of pleasured importance come over his face when the shots mounted up to twenty-one. Then in open-mouthed wonderment he stared at Rory.

"You speak to me in the words of a True Believer, my lord of Sax. Perhaps then you are not a N'zrani but a follower of the Prophet, may he rest throughout all eternity in Paradise."

Rory saw a chance to ingratiate himself with the young man. Why he should want to do so, he could not explain to himself, but since first seeing him, he had desired him for a friend. His own religion had meant little to him. It was rare that he had attended the kirk at Sax and, whereas Jamie had been able to teach him much of the world, he had not instructed him overmuch in theology except for the stock phrases in Arabic which the followers of Islam mutter perfunctorily. Rory had accepted the fact that there might be some faraway God (who certainly was not interested in him), but beyond that he had little thought about the matter. Now, confronted by a direct question as to his leanings, he did not hesitate to lie, particularly as he could sense the shango's unspoken desire for him to be converted or at least interested.

"One of my reasons for coming to Africa, my lord Shango," the words came easily to him, "is to find out more about your Prophet; my other name, Mahound, is the name of your Prophet in my language. I could find nobody in Scotland or England who could instruct me and I am indeed thirsty for knowledge."

The toe of the shango's yellow slipper caught the prostrate interpreter under the throat and lifted him up, then kicked him so that he rolled away, whereupon the shango opened his arms wide and embraced Rory. The huge arms encircled him and Rory felt his head pressed against the other man's cheek. There was a clean odor from the immaculate garments with a faint suggestion of some spice, but there was none of the musk that he had smelled on Qarma's body.

"This man is indeed my brother because he has the same name as mine." The shango released Rory and fumbled with the clasp that held the ruby in his turban. He unfastened it and pinned it to the lapel of Rory's coat.

98

"And you," he pointed to the interpreter, "you son of several she-camels, will so inform all my men. While I am here he will be my guest, and you will accord him the same honor you do me. Furthermore, I am going to take him home to Sa'aqs with me. Look, see his hair, the color of saffron. My mother's prophecy is already fulfilled."

The interpreter, who had just managed to catch his breath after being kicked in the windpipe, inched back over the deck and kissed Rory's shoe. The shango seemed satisfied and pointed to Tim who had come to stand behind Rory. "And who is this man with hair the color of bright copper whereas yours is the color of bright gold?"

"First, my thanks for your gift . . ." Rory began.

The shango waved the thanks aside in depreciation of the value of the ruby. "It is a mere trifle, but this man . . . ?"

"My servant, my lord Shango."

"Then why does he not kiss my babouche? My servant humbled himself before you."

"Because he is a N'zrani, my lord, and as such it would not be fitting for him to touch your person." Rory had no intention of humiliating Tim by making him crawl on deck.

The shango seemed content with Rory's answer, but hesitated a moment before he answered. "Of course. We do not welcome N'zranis at Sa'aqs, but he will be permitted to come with you. Come! We leave. You are my guest."

"My lord Shango. . . ." Once again Rory started to speak, but Sparks, who had witnessed the whole proceeding with unfeigned surprise, and had just received a brief explanation from the interpreter, finally found his tongue. He had, of course, no idea that Rory could speak Arabic.

"My lord," he began and then, arrested by the haughty look in the shango's eyes, bowed low. "My lord of Sax is, I am certain, most grateful for your invitation. Will you permit him a few moments to gather his personal belongings and allow me to take leave of him for, as the nephew of the great McCairn, he undoubtedly has some instructions to give me?"

The expression on the shango's face did not change

until the interpreter, whose knowledge of English seemed to be adequate, spoke to him in Arabic. Rory was able to understand the subtle changes which the interpreter made in Sparks's speech, in that he changed Sparks's words into those of utter humility and begging. The shango listened and then nodded curtly in acceptance, ignoring Sparks and addressing himself to Rory.

"I shall be happy to await my brother."

He turned and without a word to Sparks or Souza, walked over to the rail where the ladder hung. Sparks signaled for the Portuguese to wait and led Rory to his cabin. Qarma was making the bed and she glanced up at Rory as they entered but he disregarded her and Sparks dismissed her. Waving to a chair on the opposite side of the table, he indicated that Rory was to be seated.

"Indeed you are a continuous surprise, Rory Mahound. Do you never follow a fixed pattern like that of other people? You appear on my ship, reeking of sour vomit as if you had been spewed out of hell. You, looking like a fucked-up mudlark, turn out to be Milord of Sax and the nephew of old McCairn. You rape my slave and provide me with an evening's entertainment such as I've never seen before. You whip one of my men to ribbons and then nurse him back to health. Now, in five minutes, you have been proclaimed brother by a fleabite nigger princeling who thinks he's hell on stilts and actually is, as far as we are concerned, because he controls the finest slaves in Africa. Then you talk with him in Arabic and he flings his black arms around you and presents you with a ruby worth more than this whole ship. Keep it up, Rory Mahound! My greatest enemy is boredom and I'll never fear it as long as you're around."

Rory shrugged his shoulders. He still could not decide whether he liked this man or not. If he could only be sure that he was sincere—but, he realized, one could never be sure of anything where Sparks was concerned. Just now he wanted to believe in him. Strange, how he could believe in that gaudy black fellow out on deck at first meeting, yet could not believe in the captain, regardless of his seeming good will of the moment.

Sparks must have sensed his feelings. He extended his

diamond-glittering hand across the table with an open-hearted gesture of friendliness.

"Come, my lord Baron, Sir Roderick, Rory! Let there be no more bad blood between us. You've no cause for any hell of a yen for me because I've not pampered you on this voyage, but let us part friends."

"We are parting then?"

" 'Od's blood, let us hope so before we start boring one another. Look! I'll be brief. This is the bloody cove I was telling you about. The pappy of this nigger Apollodollo is one of the most important slave dealers in Africa. The Sultan of Sa'aqs! His caravans contain the finest specimens —Hausas, Mandingos, Jaloffs, Senegalese, Somalis, even an occasional Sudanese. He has vassals by the hundreds who pay their taxes to him in slaves; he leads his own slave expeditions to capture more; and he has agents scouring Africa to get the finest specimens. Slaves from the Sa'aqs caravans bring the highest prices in Cuba, Barbados, Haiti, and the United States. He never deals in cheap stuff like Yorubas, Soosoos, Dahomeys, Ibos, or the riff-raff of plundered villages near the coast. Not for him. He gets fine specimens, keeps them fine, and delivers them fine. Most slave captains will jump out of their skins just to get a few Fantis, but old Sa'aqs doesn't think even Fantis are good enough for him."

"Then why don't we buy from him?" The answer seemed simple to Rory.

"Because once, a few years ago, when he did come to Rinktum Castle with some slaves for us, that goddamned little wharf rat, Souza, neglected to fire off the salute of twenty-one guns which royalty here expects. So old Sa'aqs left in a huff and hikes his ass over to Erickson of Castle Frederick. Now we never see a Sa'aqs caravan unless this billy-be-damned prince has a few left over that Erickson either doesn't want or doesn't have room for. McCairn and Ogilsvy would both give their balls to get the Sa'aqs caravan first. Now you, cock, seem to have your big foot in the door just because this prince has taken a liking to your yellow hair. So, cock, it's up to you. Go with the shango. The billy-boy's a nigger but he's the sultan's favorite son and the only one of about sixty that the old

101

sultan has spawned who has the title 'shango' which means he's heir apparent."

"So . . . ?"

"Butter the black bastard up; make a friend of him; polish him up; flatter him; become a convert to Islam; even sleep with the bastard if you have to—but get his slaves for us here at Rinktum and your uncle will give you the whole frigging business. You'll make your fortune and we'll make ours. It all depends on you, cock, and that pretty nigger boy out on deck."

Rory considered the matter. This time he knew that Sparks was serious. There was a certain amount of sound business acumen in his words, yet, for some reason, Rory was unwilling to hornswoggle the young fellow who had embraced him up on deck. He did not know him; he had no particular reason to like him and, as Sparks said, the fellow really was a nigger; yet there was something about him which made Rory feel that their paths had come together for a very particular reason. Already there seemed to be some sort of tie between them. It must be something more than the similarity of names, but whatever it was, he felt closer to this Shango-lad than he had ever felt to any other man save possibly Jamie.

He nodded his head slowly. "All right! I'll do as you say. I'll be friendly to him but I'll not lie to him and I'll not cheat him. I guess now I really meant what I said when I told him I wanted to know more about his Prophet. I do. I'll not force myself on him, but I'll go wherever he invites me. If the black flesh he peddles is valuable to us, I'll try to get it, but I'll not play ducks and drakes with him and I'm goddamned sure I'll not sleep with him. I like him and for some strange reason I trust him, even if he is a black savage."

"He's no black savage, that billy-boy. He's a handsome brute even if he is a nigger. He is royalty too, even if it is only mud-palace royalty. Sa'aqs is an important sultanate. Strange that I never thought of the similarity of names till today. Sax and Sa'aqs! Sound the same, don't they? There's a port in Tunisia called Sax but I don't suppose it has any connection with this handsome ape. And I can't see how any castle in Scotland could connect up with him either. There are Saxes in Germany too. But I'm sure none of these places have any connection with this fellow, whose father is a secondary sultan under the Sultan of Morocco. Anyway, your name made an impression on him and he's opened up his arms and taken you to his bosom, so to speak."

"If I'm going to traipse all over Africa with this Shango lad, when do I get back to England?"

"I'll be returning to Rinktum Castle in another six months. That will give you time to get to Sa'aqs, get yourself in good with him and his pappy, get as many of his slaves as you can, and get them back here at Rinktum in time to meet me. Take Tim along with you. You'll be glad to have someone to speak English with. I'll explain matters to your uncle and, who knows, Old George himself may even pin a Garter on you. He's got stock in the company, so they say."

Rory put his hands into the pockets of the pair of Sparks's breeches he was wearing and turned them inside out. "You're glib about my going off into the wilds of Africa, but after the build-up you give me, making me such a rinky-dink cove and all, hadn't I better have something in my pocket?"

"To be sure." Sparks extracted a key from his pocket and unlocked one of the drawers under his bed. From a leather pouch he counted out a quantity of gold and silver and transferred it to a smaller pouch which he handed to Rory. "Here's a hundred pounds. Old George's profile is recognized here in Africa and you'll find it acceptable anywhere. I'll even do more for you. I'll dash the shango with the best dash he's ever had. I'll choose it myself from the cargo. We've got some silver inlaid guns, some velvets from Lyons, some lace from Brussels, a couple of silver-gilt crowns from Birmingham, and I'll throw in all the Madeira he can drink. Arabs don't hold with drinking except for their stomachs' sake, but you'd be surprised how many of them develop the pip when they see a glass of wine. I'll see you again when I come on shore. Now, out on deck with you. If you need anything before I return, squeeze it out of that damned Souza. He's a weasely sort but he's duty-bound to give you what you want.

Do the best you can for us all, cock. I'm depending on you. You know something? We're parting good friends." He offered his hand to Rory.

Rory took it with some misgivings and then shook it heartily. "You know, sir, you're a queer cove. One day you're the spawn of Old Harry himself and the next day I almost like you. Sure I'll shake with you, and we'll be friends but goddamn it, I'll never trust you. Yet I'll even forget the raree show I put on for you with Qarma."

"Don't! 'Twas the best bit of raree I've ever seen. She had to confess afterwards that you're hung better than that brother of hers; regular stud stallion she said. 'Course, I hoped she'd tickle you up a bit more with the whip, but the swiving you gave her was the best I've ever seen. Imagine that bitch screaming for mercy. So why forget it, cock? I intend to remember it."

"After her I'm not much for nigger wenches from now on."

Sparks held up a warning hand. "Don't speak too hastily, cock. That's all the gash you'll get from now on, with perhaps a little Arab thrown in to change the monotony. You'll get to like them, too. There's nothing better than a nigger wench, and in the dark what does it matter what color her skin is? Good luck to you, Rory. I'm letting the Mahound himself loose in Africa, but if you can get Sa'aqs's black meat away from Erickson, it'll be worth it. Good luck."

"Mayhap I'll need it." Rory, conscious of his new role, did not stand back for Sparks to precede him through the door. Instead he went first, not even bothering to hold the door open for the captain.

CHAPTER X

THE SHANGO OF SA'AQS, IN ALL THE GLORY OF his youth, height, good looks, and magnificent robes, had entirely stolen the show away from Dom Pedro da Souza. Souza had suddenly become such a nonentity that it was not until they were over the side of the ship and into the longboat that Rory had a chance to appraise the little man. He found him to be exactly as Sparks had described him—an oily, fawning little weasel. He seemed properly impressed with Rory's introduction as a nephew of the great McCairn and a peer in his own right. Rory instinctively knew the man was not to be trusted. Despite Souza's toadying compatibility, Rory sensed that the man did not like him and laid the reason to jealousy on Souza's part. He was right; Souza was jealous not only of Rory's youth and position but even more of the fact that he was white. The touch of the tarbrush had overshadowed his life. He always had to take second place.

Owing to the narrowness of the boat, they were seated in tandem, with a sturdy Kru boy oarsman between each of them. The shango's interpreter sat unhappily in the bow where he received the maximum spray from the sea. Next came Tim, who got a secondary splashing, and Souza who got what escaped Tim. Then, behind a Kru boy and under the canopy, came the shango who got almost none at all; and behind another Kru boy, Rory, who, like the Israelites of old crossing the Red Sea, came through the journey dry shod. As they neared the shore the blue water gave way to a dirty green-brown current, which flowed out from the seemingly impenetrable shore of mangrove trees, whose stiltlike roots supported a canopy of greenery.

It was a new world to Rory—a world of incandescent

sun; the smell of decaying vegetation; the glimmer of brilliant bird wings; the drifting logs which belied their appearance and disclosed two black beady eyes and the saurian snouts of crocodiles; and the sweat-shining black skins of the Kru boys. Over all he could sense, despite the brilliant sun, a strange brooding atmosphere which fascinated as it menaced.

They proceeded up the river a short distance until, around a bend concealed by a thick grove of mangroves, they came to a widening place in the stream where the current slowed to form a slick lagoon. On one side, on higher ground than the surrounding mangrove swamps, there was solid land, and here were the factories, the barracoons, the Mongo's house and store, and the big storage sheds that comprised Rinktum Castle—McCairn and Ogilsvy's African outpost on the delta of the River Niger. Its designation as "castle" had led Rory to imagine something along the lines of his home at Sax. He had pictured in his mind an establishment of stone walls, crenellated battlements, towers, and other accoutrements of defense. Instead he saw a shabby construction of wood palisades, bamboo huts, and palm-thatched roofs. Rinktum Castle, however, had no need of any defense. It was built to keep people in, not to keep people out. The whole settlement appeared extremely vulnerable, as though it could be captured by a band of children playing at Robin Hood. Perhaps it could be, but it served its purpose of collecting and keeping the slaves that would eventually be loaded on the McCairn and Ogilsvy ships.

The yells of the Kru boys in the boat were met by answering hails from the bank. With a deal of expert oar-handling and confused shouting, they came up to the sagging bamboo pier that ran out into the turgid water. Pink-palmed black hands reached out to help the passengers onto the jerry-built wharf which sagged and shook under the excess weight. A well-beaten path led almost perpendicularly up to an opening in a high stockade—a gate which was guarded by a heavy pair of iron-embossed plank gates. It was here that they entered and halted to get their breath after the steep climb from the pier.

Inside, Rory saw a hard-packed compound as large as a

parade ground, from which, in the center, the masonry tower flew the McCairn and Ogilsvy house flag. On the right a long line of white-washed wooden buildings, one story in height, sported a continuous verandah, upheld by palm trunk pillars. Facing this across the compound was another row of more substantial buildings that were partly of wood and partly of masonry, and here some attempt had been made at simulating European construction, for there were shutters on some of the windows and the pillars that supported the long verandahs were of stone, roughly squared, instead of palm trunks. All this was surrounded by the stockade, some fifteen feet in height, with the upper ends of the logs terminating in sharp points. At intervals there were sentry boxes atop the walls and Rory could see black men with muskets standing in them, for all the world like black crows in crude bird cages.

While they were waiting, three young men, whose slight build, pale olive skin and regular features gave them an almost Latin appearance, ran out from the protective shade of the verandah to meet them. One was encumbered with a huge umbrella of purple silk and gold bullion which seemed too large and awkward for him to handle; another had an instrument which looked like a cow's tail mounted on an ornate gold and ivory handle, while the third carried a large goatskin waterbag that boasted an accompaniment of brightly polished brass cups hung by chains around his neck. They circled the shango, bowing low and snapping their fingers and keening in high-pitched voices while they took up their positions. One stood behind him, tilting the awkward umbrella so that it shielded his face; the second started whisking the flies away from him with the cow's tail; and the third knelt before him, offering him water from the goatskin. At a word from the shango they became quiet and froze in their positions. Instead of moving on, the shango beckoned to Rory to come and stand beside him under the shade of the umbrella. Although Rory had only a rudimentary knowledge of Hausa, culled from Jamie's vast store of knowledge, he could recognize that this was the language the shango was speaking and was able to understand a few words. He gathered that the shango was sending the boy with the fly whisk off on an errand and was not surprised when the boy handed the whisk to he who toted the goatskin, hoisted up his long white skirts above his bare brown knees, and sped down the steep path as though he were being chased by seven devils.

Without any explanation as to why their little procession had been halted, the shango, with a glance at the sun, faced himself in a north-by-east direction and, standing erect with head bowed and hands on chest, he intoned a prayer to Allah which Rory was able to understand. Then he knelt on the carpet which the boy with the waterskin had been carrying and abased himself so that his head touched the ground and continued on with his prayer.

"We'll have to wait until he finishes with his prayers," Souza said in English to Rory, the sweat running down his face from under his hat. Rory decided that he, too, would kneel beside the shango and got down on his knees on the dirt of the compound, but the Negro, without looking at him, beckoned for him to come closer to him so that they might both kneel on the prayer rug.

Although Rory did not know the words of the prayer, he did accompany the shango in his various motions of obeisance, but while the other's eyes were closed, Rory took a further opportunity to look around the sun-glaring compound. He could see that some attempt had been made to landscape its barrenness. Great magenta swags of bougainvillea were draped over some of the buildings. A tree with a carpet of fallen yellow blossoms added an island of shade to one corner, and there were several exotic-looking plants or trees, Rory did not know which; but he recognized them as bananas, for among their huge lacquered-green leaves they bore pendent bunches of the phallic-looking fruits he had eaten that morning.

Rory stood up when the shango rose from his prayers and turned toward the gate to which the shango was pointing. The boy he had sent on the errand was returning, accompanied by three more boys. One of these carried an equally elaborate umbrella—this one of vivid scarlet—under his brass chains and cups. Once again they formed a procession. The shango led with his purple umbrella, his fly whisker on one side, and his water bearer on the other,

108

followed by Rory under the scarlet umbrella, complete with fly whisker and water carrier also. Souza, unprotected from the sun, at the mercy of the iridescent green flies and without benefit of drinking water, followed them, and after him poor Tim limped along as best he could.

As they neared the largest building at the far end of the compound, a number of slaves who had congregated there all abased themselves flat on the ground as Rory and the shango, safe now under the protecting roof of the verandah, abandoning their umbrellas but still accompanied by their fly whiskers and water bearers, passed into the cool shade of the building. Here, within the masonry walls, the narrow windows kept out most of the sun but none of the flies, so that Rory was grateful for the boy with the whisk, and although the water from the goatskin was slightly greenish and tasted of warm tallow, it was at least something with which to wet his throat. Souza clapped his hands in a nervous pit-a-pat which brought out a shaven-polled slattern of a black girl with a tray of wine glasses and bottles of port and Madeira. Souza looked a question at the shango who languidly raised his finger in assent.

"As medicine only," he smiled. "Being a True Believer, I cannot accept wine as a beverage, but. . . ." He allowed his words to trail off; refusing the wine glass that Souza offered him, he signaled to his cupbearer to hold out one of the brass cups to be filled.

Rory did the same, downed the wine, and had his bearer present the cup for a second filling. His eyes had become accustomed to the dim light in the room and he noted that it was elaborately furnished with fusty ornate French furniture from which the brocaded upholstery was hanging in tatters. It was an utter incongruity in contrast with the braided grass rugs and the dirt floors.

"Would Your Excellency care to repair to your quarters?" Souza half-rose from his chair. "They are those which I had readied for Captain Sparks, but if you will accept his accommodations I shall be honored." Though he was addressing Rory, he was speaking Arabic in order not to alienate the shango.

The shango gave Rory no chance to answer. "My brother, the Lord of Sax, is not sleeping in your stinking

109

rooms, Souza. He has no desire to be bedded down with cockroaches and centipedes, gnawed at by rats, and overrun with bedbugs and lizards. Your rooms are not a fit habitation even for a N'zrani dog and I do not consider that, as my Lord of Sax carries the same name as my own, he is a true N'zrani. Therefore I extend to him the hospitality of my own tent where he will be comfortable. Nor does he care for one of your greasy black sluts who have spread their legs to take every slave trader from Dakar to Calabar. The Lord of Sax, who is the brother of the Shango of Sa'aqs, resides in my tent and he will be expertly served by one of the women of my hareem."

"That is a great honor, my lord Shango." Rory did not know whether he might be jumping from the frying pan into the fire, but he was encouraged by one thing: the shango's robes, as well as those of all his attendants, were immaculately clean, whereas Souza's clothes were soiled and grease-stained. This he felt to be a good omen. There was something about Rinktum Castle that depressed him and now he realized it was more than the filth and sloppy housekeeping. After the spit-and-polish cleanliness of the *Ariadne,* the dirt of Rinktum Castle was all the more appalling, but that was not all. From behind the stockade he had been conscious of the doleful wail which continued in a varying pitch, rising and falling but never completely dying out. It was the soul of man, weeping in misery, longing to return to his home, fearing the morrow. Sometimes it welled up in a combination of a hundred or more voices of the hapless wretches behind the far stockade, then it would die down to only a few voices; but it was always present. Its hopeless anguish penetrated Rory and he wanted to run away from its awful impact on his feelings.

"We go, Souza." The shango put down his wine glass and clucked to his entourage and Rory's. "Come, my brother." He indicated for Rory to follow him.

Once outside, there was a scramble among the umbrella bearers to get their umbrellas over the proper heads. With the shango leading, they crossed the compound, passed out the gate, skirted one end of the palisades, and took a path leading upriver. They did not have far to go. About a hundred yards from the palisade, but hidden from it by a grove of tall palms, they came upon the tents of the shango, a small village in themselves. The tents were of black goathair, and one huge tent, with a side open toward the breeze from the river, dominated the others. From it waved a long black pennant inscribed in white Arabic letters.

"May you enter in peace, my brother." The shango led the way to the large tent and stepped inside. "I am aware that you are as yet an unbeliever and I should not, according to the law of Islam, share my tent with you. Yet I do have authority for so acting because, on the other hand, the Prophet enjoins hospitality upon us. Therefore I obey the law of hospitality and welcome you. This, my Lord of Sax, is now your home—the tents of Sa'aqs, poor as they may be."

Rory entered under the open tent flap.

"Many miles across the sea in the highlands of Scotland, my castle of Sax becomes your home, my lord Shango." Rory realized that the roofless castle was a poor substitute, but he knew he would never have to entertain the shango there. However, were the ruined castle of Sax as magnificent as George's Whitehall, he would have made the same offer.

"Now that you are here, my Lord of Sax," the shango started to remove his turban, unwinding the yards of green muslin himself and handing it to one of the boys who had followed him into the tent, "and as we are, as we have both agreed, brothers with the same name, it would seem that we might dispense with titles and formalities. I am familiarly called Baba by my father and certain of my brothers and even by my mother, although not by my wives."

"I am Rory." He reached out his hand. "In my country when two men are brothers, they shake hands."

Baba disregarded Rory's hand. "It seems a stupid custom, Rory. 'Tis a mere touching of each other's fingers. In my country they do not do such a paltry thing. They embrace instead." He threw his arms around Rory, enveloping him in a vigorous hug and clapping him on the back. "Now that we know each other better, let me say it

111

is impossible for any man to exist here in these horrible garments. They are beautiful," his fingers lingered on the velvet of Rory's coat, "but they are hotter than the desert at midday. Would you, my brother, deign to wear my clothes?"

"And why not?" Rory gazed straight at Baba, holding his eyes with his own.

Baba hesitated. "Because . . . yes, I shall say it. My skin is black; yours is white. White men do not consider black men their equals. My father is a sultan, yet white men treat me ofttimes with no respect and when they do show me respect, I have the feeling they are doing it merely because they want something from me. To a white man I am like a black savage running through the jungle with a stick in my nose, little better than an animal."

Rory smiled and reached out for Baba's hand. "In truth, Baba, you are the first dark man I have ever spoken with. Yes, your skin may be darker than mine"—he relinquished his hard grip on the other's hand but retained it in his own—"and yet this is a fine hand. It is strong and capable of good. I have never talked this way with another man, but I want to tell you that you are a fine-looking fellow and I have an idea you are a fine person. If you have no objection to your clothes touching a white skin, I would have no objection to wearing them. Let us never mention this matter of color again. The color of our skin matters no more than the color of our hair or eyes."

Baba's hand closed over Rory's. "We shall never mention the color of our skins again." Slowly he released Rory's hand.

Rory looked around the interior of the tent and he found it a far cry from the fustiness of Rinktum Castle. Its spacious airiness was cool and inviting. Thick carpets of colorful wool were soft underfoot, cushioned by the sand beneath them. The walls glowed with the dim iridescence of hangings shot with silver and gold. There was no furniture except for the big divans which lined the walls, covered with a variety of stuffs. Poufs of pillows made the divans more inviting. A few low tables gleamed with the nacreous reflections of inlaid mother-of-pearl, and on one a pierced brass burner wafted a plume of blue smoke, heavy with the odor of sandalwood. The perfume seemed to repel insects, for there were none of the bothersome flies or mosquitoes which swarmed in Souza's house.

"All here is yours, Rory." Baba's encircling gesture included the tent and everything in it. He clapped his hands and a young man emerged from the dark shadows of the tent. "This is Abdullah, who is yours to command." And to the servant he said, "Behold your other master whom you will obey as you do me. . . . And now, boy, open the chests. Let my brother choose his raiment. The only things of mine he cannot wear are the green turbans for he is not a Hadji because he has never made the pilgrimage to Mecca. Hold up the robes for him to choose, Abdullah."

The boy opened the chests, holding up one silk kaftan after another. For the second time that day, Rory was confronted with the problem of choosing clothes that did not belong to him; but Baba's clothes were so much more splendid than Sparks's that Rory was overcome by their magnificence. In his bewilderment he pointed to a robe of azure silk, its front a mass of silver embroidery pointed with seed pearls. Then, in rapid succession, Abdullah with Baba's approval presented Rory with a hooded djellabah of fine white wool, a pair of yellow slippers like those of Baba's, and a length of silver-shot muslin for a turban.

Baba motioned for the boy to put the robes on one of the divans and said, "Send in the red-haired man who is servant to my lord of Sax and do not return yourself. Nor will you permit anyone else inside the tent." He turned to Rory, the worried look making a triple crease in his forehead.

"Before changing our clothes we shall bathe in the river. We of Islam believe in cleanliness. We are not like the N'zranis who never bathe. Even those in the desert who cannot bathe with water cleanse their bodies with fine sand. Besides, the water is cool and it will refresh us. My slaves will beat the water so you need have no fear of crocodiles. You, my brother, shall wear cotton drawers while bathing and nobody but your red-haired slave shall attend you. It is not fitting that you should attend yourself, but on the other hand it is not fitting that my slave

113

should see you without clothes. Slaves gossip amongst themselves, you know, and it is none of their business that you were born a N'zrani. I prefer them to remain in ignorance."

Rory understood Baba's words, but they held little sense for him. Why was he taking such precautions that nobody should see Rory's body when apparently he had no fear that his slaves would see his own? His look of puzzlement betrayed his inability to understand.

"A naked man proclaims his belief instantly." Baba covered his embarrassment with a smile.

Rory shook his head, baffled.

Baba hung his head, not looking at Rory. He waited a long moment and one could almost see the struggle in his mind. When he finally spoke, he did so slowly, trying to find the right words that would save him embarrassment.

"I mean, my friend and brother, that there is one sure way to tell a follower of the Prophet from a N'zrani. It is not so easy to tell a True Believer from a Hebrew, because we of Islam follow a certain custom of the Hebrews. We believe that a man should dispense with a certain inch or so of useless skin. It becomes a sign of his manhood and a sign of his allegiance to Islam. One might think it a sacrifice, but the little pain he suffers in this operation is as nothing compared with the increased pleasure he will receive. Our women prefer it. It has been one thing that has bothered me about you."

Now Rory understood. He started to laugh and his laughter was so contagious that Baba lifted his head and smiled back at him.

"Why have you been beating around the bush, my brother? You mean that Arabs like Jews are circumcized and that a man, standing naked, can be judged as to his beliefs by whether he is hooded or not."

"That is what I was trying to say. When I know you better I shall not be ashamed to speak of such private matters with you."

"Then think no more about it. 'Tis true, the knife has never touched me. Such operations are not performed in Scotland where we have a contrary belief to yours. We think that the hood of skin gives a man even greater

114

pleasure and *our* women like it. But, although the knife has never touched me, Baba, fate must have intended me to be a True Believer. Look!" Rory peeled off his sweaty trousers and stood naked before Baba. "Regard me, Baba, and see how well I can qualify. When I was a young boy I started to outgrow my own skin. Nature removed the hood, for there was not enough skin left to cover me. Indeed, it was a matter of curiosity to all the other boys when we went swimming in the river. I was the only one among them unhooded, and I was sensitive about it. The other lads used to joke about me and call me 'Jock o' the bald pate.' But the lasses all seemed to like it even better than had it been fully clothed. Now I can be doubly glad that nature—or perhaps it was fate—took care of me." He walked a couple of steps nearer to Baba and arched his body. "Look, my friend and brother."

Baba stared, nodding his head in approval. *"Qismah!"* Baba slapped Rory's white shoulder. "No chirurgeon in Cairo could have done a better job. Allah be praised! We need have no fear that anyone will ever know. You are, to all appearances, one of us." He clapped his hands and yelled out for Abdullah, whispered to him a moment, then dismissed him a second time.

"We shall not need the services of your red-headed slave, Rory. Nor shall we use the services of the boy Abdullah. You shall be much better attended. In my home I have four wives, which is the total amount allotted to me by the Prophet. These wives are the mothers of my sons and one does not take one's wives on a journey lest they be seen by another man. Instead one takes one's slaves to satisfy the natural demands of one's body. Just as a man must eat and drink to keep alive, just as he must sleep to wake, so he needs the use of a woman to drain his body and keep him in good health. So, I shall present you with one of my slaves. Her name is Almera and I part with her with some regret, for she is well trained in satisfying a man's need."

"Then I cannot accept such a gift." Rory felt a swelling in his groin over the very prospects of such ministrations. It had been so long since he had had a woman, he had

115

even been anticipating the slattern that Souza was to have offered.

"But you must," Baba insisted. "Were I to give you something that was worthless to me, like these clothes, it would not be a real gift. Alas, I cannot claim that she is a virgin. She was when I purchased her, and it was I who despoiled her, but at least I can say that no man has ever looked on her face but myself. I am the only man who has ever entered her. When we arrive at Sa'aqs, you shall have as many virgins as you fancy, but until then, Almera is the best that I can offer you and I do so with apologies. Lo, she comes." Baba lowered his eyes, and then laughed, loudly and boisterously. "And, I think, not too soon, my Rory, for by all appearances you stand in dire need of her."

A girl glided through the curtains of the tent and although she pretended not to look at Rory, he knew that her sidewise glance appraised him. For a fleeting second, he saw her eyes widen and he felt that, under the veil, she had smiled; but now, demurely turning her back on him, she stood before Baba.

"Turn around, girl, and drop your veil." Baba gave her a gentle shove. "Behold your new master. You will serve him as well as you have served me. He is a lord of Sax, the same as myself. Go to him."

Rory was aware of dark hair that fell to her shoulders in a cloud of black smoke. She yanked the veil from her face and now, he could see more than the black eyes that blazed like coals. He could see skin of a light amber, lips that were full and red, and little ears that nestled like shells under the cloud of hair. She came toward him and knelt, taking one of his hands in her own and kissing it, her head bowed in submission. He reached down and lifted her up, feeling the warmth of her skin through the thin veils that separated her body from his.

"The Shango of Sa'aqs is a generous man to part with such a prized possession." Rory cupped her chin in his hands, wishing that for this one moment his friend might leave the tent so that he could be alone with this girl.

"He is indeed," she answered, her hennaed fingers stroking his naked body. "He has been most generous to
116

me, too, and Allah has been most generous to you, my lord of Sax. The hennaed fingers, all unembarrassed by the presence of Baba, continued their questing. "It will be a pleasure to serve you."

Baba's grin turned into a laugh.

"She doesn't seem to regret the fact that I am no longer her master. Have you no word for me, Almera?"

"Only to say that you are the best master a girl could have."

"Come girl, quit him now. We have other things to do and if you continue to tempt him, he'll have no mind for doing anything else but what you force him to do. Night comes, Almera, and your new lord will be here with me in this tent." He pointed to one of the divans. "It seems we have all been most generous with each other." Still laughing, he slipped out of his robes and girded himself with a soft white towel.

Rory extricated himself from Almera's embrace.

"It has been many weeks since I have had a woman," he smiled an apology at Baba.

"From now on you'll have no need to complain," Baba assured him. "Come, we will bathe. The water will cool you off."

CHAPTER XI

RORY OPENED HIS EYES UNWILLINGLY, ONLY to close them again to blot out the shaft of brilliantly moted sunshine which streamed through the opened side of the tent. After the strenuous night he had spent, he did not want to return to the reality of daylight. He turned on his side to look across the tent at the divan that Baba occupied. The black giant was awake, the sunlight picking out topaz highlights on his naked torso. He was propped up with a multitude of pillows behind him, sipping coffee from a tiny porcelain cup in a filigreed brass holder. Abdullah, the Moorish boy, was serving him, and there was no trace of either Almera or of Zayah, the other slave from Baba's hareem who had shared Baba's bed as Almera had shared Rory's. No, Rory thought, there was no trace of Almera, not even a lingering ghost of her perfume. No trace of her except for the small purple bruises on his body which her mouth had inflicted. He regarded them—souvenirs of delight—then stretched his arms up over his head, yawned and turned over to face Baba, pulling up the rumpled linen sheet to cover his nakedness before Baba and the boy.

"You are finally awake, Rory?" Baba pointed to the coffee pot and spoke quickly to Abdullah. "It is high time. I was waiting to finish my coffee and had been debating whether I would awaken you slowly by having Abdullah tickle you with a peacock feather or have him bring you to life quickly by dousing you with a bucket of water. But you have solved the problem for me. Look! The sun is shining and I have finished my morning prayers. I have dispatched my boys to the river to beat off the crocodiles and now we shall bathe and dress and attend to our business with that greasy son of a she-camel, Souza." He waited until Abdullah had poured the coffee for Rory and adjusted the pillows so Rory could sit up. "And now tell me, how did you sleep last night?"

"Sleep?" Rory grinned back sheepishly. "You did not truly intend that I should sleep, did you, Baba? Was that the silly purpose for which I went to bed? Alas, no! Sleep did not come to my eyes until the tent began to grow light. Then, when it did, I lost my companion. She departed along with your bedmate. Ah, if she were only here now." His hands sought the hardness of himself under the sheet.

"There will always be another night, my brother," Baba wagged a finger at him. "I sent them both away for a very good reason. A woman is too enervating in the morning and can only make a man feel drained all day. The erection that a man awakes with is not one of passion; merely an indication that his bladder is full. Two things

118

are needed to put an end to a stiff yard. At night a man
ejaculates his semen and he goes limp; in the morning he
pisses and it brings about the same result. All of which
proves that the morning erection is not the same as that of
the night. No matter how often one has recourse to the
chamber pot at night, he remains as hard as iron. But let
Abdullah hold the chamber pot for you now and you will
see that I am right. The morning hardness becomes limp
immediately."

Baba's words proved right as Rory knew they would,
although he had never considered such an interpretation
of his morning erection before. With the towel that Abdullah handed him, Rory stood up, wrapped it around his
loins and joined Baba before the tent. Together they made
their way down the steep bank to the water where a
semicircle of male slaves beat the water with palm branches and staves. Although they succeeded in keeping the
crocodiles away, they roiled up the water; but it was cool
and the soap that Baba provided was French—hard-milled
and smelling of lilacs. It was a joy to lather away the
sweat of the night, feel the cool water on his body. Baba,
who at most times was a serious young man, taking his
role of Shango as one that did not mix well with levity,
had shed his seriousness along with his robes and now
sported in the water like a carefree whale. He swam
underwater, grabbing Rory's legs, and Rory retaliated by
upsetting him. They wrestled, waist deep in the water,
raced, sported, and played until at length they stepped out
on the bank to be enveloped in long, soft white towels.
Baba's close skullcap of wiry black hair dried in an instant but it took a lot of rubbing and shaking to get Rory's
long locks dry.

While Abdullah was applying the towel to Baba, a new
boy—one of those who had been beating the water—was
rubbing Rory dry. He was a whit darker than Baba but
had the finely chiseled features of an Arab. Beads of water
dripped from his nakedness as he wielded the towel. There
was something startling about him that attracted Rory's
attention. Although the boy was adolescent, adder-slim
and reaching only to Rory's shoulder, he sported the

119

equipment of a giant. Rory could not keep his eyes away from it and even Baba noticed his concentrated staring.

"You like Fayal?" Baba pointed to the boy and even more particularly to the appendage that Rory was staring at. His voice was amused, even a faint suspicion of incredulity lurked in it. "He is a half-brother of mine, sired by my father, but he is slave-born and therefore a slave himself. His mother was a Senegalese and there are those who say that the people from Senegal equal those from the Sudan; but I do not believe it because my mother was from the Sudan and I like to think that the Sudanese are superior to all other tribes."

"Aye, but he is a handsome lad too," Rory shifted his gaze to the lad's face. "I had no idea that you were aware of what I was looking at, but it is true—I was staring at it. What a phenomenon!"

"Have you ever looked in a full-length mirror, Rory?"

"But when I was his age, my mirror would not have shown me what he sees in his."

"The Senegalese are noted for being stallions, although the Sudanese have an even greater reputation. Come, Rory, I did not know that you were interested in boys." Baba did not seem in the least disturbed over what he thought might be Rory's preference. "If you prefer him to Almera, take him, he's yours. He'll serve you as well as Almera and there are many who say even better."

Rory shook his head in vigorous denial. "This preference for boys is something I could never understand, Baba, and something in which I could never be interested. Many sailors are that way. We had a cabin boy on the ship who served many of the crew. I do not condemn them but it is something that would never appeal to me. My interest in this lad was at first mere curiosity and then I got to thinking of a girl I left behind me in Scotland. She was loath to part with me, my brother, because she said that never in her life before had she met a man who could satisfy her and she never expected to again. I was thinking about her when I saw this lad; thinking he would be a worthy substitute for me."

Baba questioned Rory with his eyes, shaking his head in incomprehension. "I do not understand your way with women. Is this woman you speak of a slave, that you would share her with another slave? We do not share our women here. Of course in a large hareem we keep eunuchs to keep the women happy but we never allow them to see a real man. To be sure, I have shared Almera with you, but that was not really sharing because I gave her to you. Would you be willing to let this woman you speak of enjoy herself with this boy?"

"She is a girl of the streets, Baba. I had her for one night only. The night before me she had another man and the night after still another. Yet she was a good girl. Although she was a street doxy she was generous, good and kind and loving. She took me in off the cold streets of Glasgow, fed me, warmed me, loved me, and wished me Godspeed in the morning. I promised her that I would send her a wee gift from Africa."

"She would be like the girls of the Ouled Nails then. They go to the cities to sell their bodies and then they return to their villages to marry, giving their husbands the money they have earned. I take it that this woman sold her body for money, eh?"

"Yes, but not to me. What she sold to others she gave me freely. But let us not discuss the matter further, Baba, for she is many miles away and I had forgotten her until I saw this young Fayal strutting around for all the world like a jackass."

"Ah, but we must discuss the matter, Rory. If it would make your life happy to send this lad to her, he is yours. It can be arranged. He can leave on your ship and I will see to it that he is well treated on the voyage and that he will not be sold. Your captain will not dare to disobey me, particularly if I cover his hand with gold. Then, when the ship arrives back in England again, he can send the boy to the woman you speak of."

The idea appealed to Rory. Imagine Mary Davis in gray Glasgow a-sporting her own Negro slave. How Mary would enjoy the lad, too! If she had enjoyed Rory, as she most patently had, how much more would she welcome Fayal. At least twice as much, Rory considered. Her own blackamoor! She would be the talk of the town. The only Glasgow whore to have such a distinction. He looked at

121

the boy, appraising him again with the same wonderment he had had the first time. There were tears in the limpid brown eyes now. Why should he change the boy's whole life on the impulse of a moment? Why send him from the sun and luxury of Baba's tents to the cold and squalor of Mary's house? He did not reckon with Baba, however.

"Why do you weep, young Fayal?" Baba seemed to have little empathy for the boy's feelings. "It is true that the great white lord wishes to send you as a present to his woman across the seas but it is only because you are superior to all other boys. You should be proud that Allah in all his wisdom has seen fit to equip you so that all men will envy you and all women desire you. You will be able to satisfy this woman who is a friend of the great white lord and she in turn will tell all her friends about you. You will have a larger hareem than a sultan and it will cost you nothing. It is a great honor for you and a great opportunity."

"It is the will of Allah." The boy bowed his head. *"Inshallah!* But alas I shall never see my mother again and I am not happy about leaving you, my lord Shango."

"You are too old now to go into the hareem, so you will never see your mother again anyway. You will find happiness in knowing that you serve me better when you do that which I ask." Baba turned to Rory. "The boy is yours, my brother. I will make the arrangements for his transportation to England, and you can write a letter for him to deliver to the woman who was, you say, so good and kind to you. It is little enough for you to do to repay her."

"My thanks, Baba. But I shall take care in the future not to admire any of your possessions for, whatever it be, be it robe, bed companion, or boy, you give it to me."

"As you would do for me, Rory." Baba slapped Fayal's bare rump and told him to go and dress himself and report to Souza's house. He and Rory walked back to the tent. Baba was deep in concentration. Finally he turned to Rory. "Why shouldn't I give what I have to you, Rory? All that I have belongs to you. I do not say this idly. Here in Africa we are men of quick impulses. We love quickly and we hate just as quickly. From the moment I saw you,

122

I liked you, but I must confess there is more to it than that. Before I left Sa'aqs my mother told me I would meet you. Although she was converted to being a True Believer, she was not born a follower of the Prophet. As an infidel, she believed in the gods of the Sudan. The Sudanese are a very old people with very old gods. Of course," he shrugged his shoulders, "there is only one God and that is Allah but . . ."

"But who knows," Rory tried to put him at ease, "perhaps there are older gods than Allah."

"Just so." Baba was now justified. "And, of course, the Sudanese are a very old people with very old gods. They are the oldest, the strongest, and the handsomest people in all Africa, and I say this with pride because I am half Sudanese and it is true."

"If you are a specimen of the Sudanese, I agree with you."

Baba nodded his head in acceptance of the compliment. "And so my mother, even today, although she is a faithful follower of the Prophet, sometimes consults with the old gods of the Sudan and speaks with the spirits of her ancestors. Just before I left, she did this to assure me of a safe journey and she informed me that her gods had told her that a strange prince, bearing my name but with hair of gold, would come to me and that I must take him as my brother. Therefore you but bear out the prophecy of my mother's gods, Rory. But come! The little Souza and your captain await us for breakfast in Rinktum Castle. I go, but I shall not eat his food. My own cooks will prepare my breakfast and carry it there. Neither shall I eat at the same table with Souza and your captain. You may choose whether you sit with them or with me; whether you eat their food or mine; whether you dress in their clothes or mine. You are free to choose."

"Would it please you if I sat with you?" Rory asked. He had never met anyone in his life who had offered him so much, including friendship, as Baba had, and he was anxious to do something in return. This would not be difficult because he liked the big brown fellow. "Then I shall eat with you, oh my brother! I shall sit with you and eat your food and drink your drinks and wear your

123

clothes. These men are not friends of mine. The welts you see on my back were caused by the captain and the wounding of my man's leg was also his fault. As for the Portuguese, he reminds me of something one might find crawling under a stone, and I do not trust him. I do trust you, Baba. I've had neither brother nor close friend in my life. Now that our paths have crossed I pledge you my friendship and with it my life."

"Ah, but I want more than that." Baba rummaged in one of the chests and brought out two robes, barbaric with gold threads and primitive designs. They were not like the Arab robes that he and Rory had worn the day before. He tossed one to Rory.

"Yesterday I honored my father in my dress. Today I honor my mother and attire myself as a Sudanese and so do you although it's the first time the world has ever seen a yellow-haired Sudanese. But, as I said, Rory, I want more than your friendship and your life. If we are to be true brothers, I want your soul."

"How can I give that to you?"

"Very simply, just repeat these words after me."

"Begin!"

"There is no God but Allah. . . ." There was an earnestness in Baba's words which had not been apparent before.

"There is no god but Allah," Rory repeated.

"And Mohammed is his prophet."

"And Mohammed is his prophet."

"That is all." Baba took the robe from Rory and draped it over him, leaving one shoulder bare. He placed a small cap on Rory's head, a pill box of white velvet embroidered with gold. He then dressed himself and as they stepped out of the tent, where their umbrella bearers were waiting, Baba grinned. "You know what you are, Rory?"

"I'm something of a cross between a Scottish baron, a Sudanese prince, and an Arabian shango."

Once again Baba's face became serious. "You're more than that. You're a Mussulman, a True Believer. The words you just spoke made you that. It is the will of Allah that you should no longer be a N'zrani. Think, man, and rejoice. We don't even have to call the barber in to have

124

him take off a snip of your foreskin. You were born to Islam."

"*Inshallah*," Rory answered. It seemed the most appropriate thing to say.

CHAPTER XII

AFTER THE SUN-DAPPLED, SANDALWOOD-scented freshness of Baba's tent, the interior of Souza's house stank of mold and vermin. It smelled as though the thatch of the roof and even the walls themselves were peopled with putrefied lizards, insects, and other dead things that once crawled. The breakfast table, however, was set up with a certain decayed elegance—a magnificent lace tablecloth, torn, stained and greasy; tarnished silver and cracked china. Sparks and Souza were already seated when Rory and Baba entered. They both rose respectfully. Souza, with a low obeisance to Baba, indicated the two empty places at the table, but Baba, who surprised Rory by unexpectedly uttering the two English words "thank you," clapped his hands. His retinue entered, with Tim bringing up the rear. They placed cushions on the floor after sweeping it with small brooms, and then placed low tables before them. Momentarily they left the room to return with dishes covered with high, conical bamboo covers. Baba seated himself, indicating Rory's place beside him, while Tim stood behind Rory alongside Baba's major-domo, an elderly Arab with white-pointed beard and the green turban of a Hadji.

Sparks stared, slack-mouthed and open-eyed, and then turned to Rory. "Well, you're a proper cully, rigged out exactly like a billy-be-damned nigger. Regular ass-wiper to his royal black cock-and-balls, ain't you? Sitting beside the bastard so you can hold hands?"

125

Rory was aware that Baba could not understand Sparks's words, but he knew that he could sense the sarcasm in Sparks's voice.

"Isn't that what you wanted?" Rory's words had an edge of anger. "Weren't those your instructions? And so, if His Highness, the shango,"—Rory bowed to Baba—"invited me to sit with him, should I not accept, particularly if I prefer sitting beside him to being beside you? So, goddamn it, hold your horses."

"Excellent, excellent." Sparks rubbed his hands together and beamed at Rory. "Now, before we finish breakfast, ask your nigger much-a-much why in hell he delivers all his best slaves to Erickson and leaves us only the rag, tag, and bobtail of his caravan. Souza tells me he brought only fifteen this time and although they were better than anything we had, they don't hold a candle to those he left up at Erickson's."

Rory nodded in agreement.

"And while we're about it, now that you and your nigger cully are leaving on your honeymoon, never you mind about spying on Souza here. I'll be here long enough to handle him and if you can persuade your tin-pot sultan cove to deliver here in the future, Souza won't sell any off for himself because he'll know you will know how many niggers are delivered here. His hands will be tied. Thank God neither of these buckos can speak English."

Again Rory nodded, but he did not propound any question to Baba. He felt that there should be at least some amenities before the matter of business was brought up and he proceeded to eat his meal. Tim, standing behind him, followed as well as his clumsy hands could perform the tasks. He peeled the oranges, although not as deftly as Baba's old Saleem. He poured the thick black coffee into the cup. He broke the crusty white bread and spread it with honey, passing all the comestibles to Rory after first testing them as he observed Saleem doing. He even wiped Rory's hands on the napkin which he carried over his arm like Saleem. Sparks, observing all this, had a difficult time to keep from laughing aloud at poor Tim's pretensions to lackeyship, but he took pains not to offend the Shango.

126

The conversation was desultory. The absence of rain was spoken of and translated by Rory to Baba who replied that the rainy season would soon offset the drought. Other unimportant matters were discussed and dismissed. Finally Sparks adroitly led the conversation to the subject of slaves, whereupon Rory noticed Baba stiffen. What little formal graciousness he had displayed toward Sparks and Souza disappeared.

"It is not my pleasure to discuss business today." His words had a finality that precluded argument. "Except possibly in regard to one small matter." He clapped his hands and Abdullah entered with the boy Fayal, dressed in a fine white djellabah. "This boy," Baba spoke slowly so that Souza could interpret into his hissing Portuguese for Sparks, "will be transported to England on your ship." He carelessly tossed a bag of gold toward Sparks. "He will go as a passenger and not in the slave hold. He will not be fettered or manacled and shall have decent food to eat. You will treat him with every courtesy because he is my brother and if he is not accorded that distinction or if anything happens to him, there will never be another slave from Sa'aqs delivered to Rinktum Castle. My lord Sax will give you further instructions for the lad." He signaled to Rory.

"From Liverpool," Rory continued, "you will send him with one of the sailors from your ship whom you can trust to Glasgow and see that he is delivered to one Mary Davis who lives in Skaggs Lane, in the third house from the corner, across from the fishmonger's shop."

Sparks tried hard to control himself but lost the struggle and broke forth into howls of laughter.

"Skaggs Lane in Glasgow? What know you about Skaggs Lane, Rory lad? 'Tis the haunt of the worst old bags in Glasgow—Skaggs' Bags, we call them, and a more frightening, gallows-cheating lot of doxies exists nowhere else in the world. Here's a likely lad that would bring fifty guineas anywhere in the world and you're sending him to Skaggs Lane. For shame, lad; 'tis a waste of good nigger flesh."

"It's there he goes and he'd better be delivered there

safely. Have pen and paper brought to me. I wish to write a letter."

Sparks spoke to Souza, who in turn called a servant who ducked out and returned in a moment with a small box desk which he opened and placed before Rory. In it were paper, ink, and a quill. Begging Baba's pardon, he wrote:

MARY DAVIS:

Do you remember the raw lad—the Mahound himself —along with Old Harry—that you took in one night, and the cold joint and the warm bed you shared with him? Well, 'tis he, Mary Davis, writing you from Africa and sending the present he promised you. It's warm flesh and blood I'm sending you. He'll be bringing Old Harry back with him. The laddie-buck's name is Fayal and, although he's your bondsman for life, he's well born, for his father's a sultan no less. Strip off his clothes, Mary Davis, and you'll get the surprise of your life. You'll discover that he's properly equipped to take my place. Treat him well, Mary Davis, and teach him to speak the King's English. Other things you'll not need to teach him. Send this letter back by the man who delivers it to you, and write me something only you and I know, such as the location of the cupboard where you kept the cold joint, so I'll know 'tis you that have the boy. You're a fine lass, Mary Davis, and I sometimes wonder if I shouldn't have stayed alongside you and earned the pound a day you promised me. Methinks you'll be the only one in Skaggs Lane to have her own black cockalorum. My love to you, Mary Davis, and don't forget . . .

Rory Mahound and Old Harry

He sprinkled sand over the leter, read it and then translated it loosely for Baba, who nodded his agreement. Rory folded it, lit the little taper in the desk and sealed the paper with a blob of wax, begging a curiously carved ring of heavy gold from Baba to make the impression on the

128

seal. This done, he handed the letter to Fayal. The boy was apparently reconciled to going to England because he displayed a nervous anxiety to get started and there were no traces of the tears of the morning.

Baba instructed the boy that he must guard the letter with his life and deliver it to the woman to whom Rory was sending him. He must, so Baba told him, do anything and everything that this strange woman wanted and in return the woman would be good to him. When Baba had finished his instructions, Rory spoke to Sparks and informed him that unless the letter were returned to him on Sparks's next voyage, he could expect no slaves from Baba in the future.

"You mean to say that the whole frigging business depends on our delivering this nigger sprat to a Skaggs Lane whore in Glasgow? Well I'll be damned and double damned! Can't you get His Toploftiness to make some commitment as to what he's going to do for us?" He turned and spoke to Souza in Portuguese and the little man nodded his head, peering shyly under his eyelashes at Baba.

"I know how to handle these bastards," Souza whined. "Show him a copper kettle full of bugle beads as a starter and he'll be willing to talk business. These savages would sell their own mothers for a bit of dash." He bowed low in Baba's direction and switched to Arabic. "His Excellency, the captain, is willing to pay you well if he can expect some of your best slaves on your next caravan to the coast, Your Most Illustrious Highness."

Baba regarded the man scornfully, his lip curling, his whole expression denoting his distaste.

"I told you I did not care to discuss business today, and usually I mean what I say. I have nothing to discuss with either your or the captain. Why should I? My lord of Sax is a person of more importance than either of you and any business matters I can discuss with him at my leisure. Besides, we have no time. My lord of Sax and I leave in the morning. He will be my guest in Sa'aqs until I take my next caravan to the coast. Now we return to our tents for rest and to become better acquainted with each other. My

129

lord of Sax will bid you farewell now as we shall not be seeing you again."

Souza quickly translated to Sparks, who jumped to his feet, ignoring Baba and addressing his question to Rory. "So, it's certain that you are going with him!"

"It would seem so. I'm only too happy to go."

Sparks shook his head in utter incredulity.

"I'll have to hand it to you, Rory Mahound. You don't let the grass grow under your feet. I don't know what hold you have over the black bastard, but you've done something to make him eat out of your hand. Keep on, lad, and we'll all be rich. Tell him that our gifts to him will be delivered to his tent this afternoon. Rest assured, you need not be ashamed of the dash we're giving him. It's ten times better than we ever gave a nigger before, but we expect to get ten times as much in return. I'll see to it personally that the nigger Jacky gets delivered to your doxy in Glasgow and I'll even treat him like my own son on the voyage home."

"Then keep him out of Qarma's way and don't have her stage any raree shows for you with him."

"Now, Rory lad, 'tis reading my mind you are. You wouldn't deny me a little fun on the way back, would you? He's only a stripling, but he'd team up well with Qarma."

"With a hold full of blackamoors, you've got plenty to choose from. Leave Fayal alone. I don't want him arriving in London with wales from Qarma's whip on his back."

"Oh, well, if you say so. But aren't you denying the lad the fun he ought to have? Yet it's as you say. I'll treat him as a guest of honor. I'll do anything I can for him if I can be sure that when I return in six months I'll see the barracoons of Rinktum Castle filled with prime niggers from Sa'aqs."

"You will," Rory agreed, "but it's understood right here and now, there'll be no double dealing with my friend the Shango."

"Agreed! Then we'll meet in six months, Rory Mahound."

"My lord of Sax," Rory prompted him.

"My lord of Sax and my erstwhile supercargo." Sparks smiled his peculiarly sardonic smile as he stood up and bowed low to Rory and then to Baba. "And my lord of Sa'aqs." He made an even deeper bow. "May you both have a pleasant journey."

"Inshallah," Rory answered. He found the word to be most convenient. "As God wills!" It was either God or Satan who had brought him so far and for a penniless Scot he was doing pretty goddamned well. He'd made the voyage; he had acquired a devoted servant in Tim; he had a friend in Baba; he'd sent his present to Mary Davis; and he had pounds in his pocket where before he had nothing. Not bad—not bad at all.

"Inshallah," Baba repeated as he left without a backward glance. Rory followed him, throwing the corner of the gold-flecked robe over his shoulder in the same careless manner that Baba had used. One by one Baba's retinue followed him out, Tim among them.

CHAPTER XIII

THE MIST, RISING FROM THE RIVER, OBSCURED everything in wreathing tatters of gray vapor. Were it not for the steamy heat, Rory might well have thought himself back on some fogridden moor in Scotland. Everything dripped with the moisture—the trees, the shrubs, even the tent itself; and inside, the tent poles channeled miniature rivulets down their polished surface. At this early hour of the morning the heat was already unbearable. The air, like damp cotton wool, plugged the nostrils. Almera's body, beside Rory, slithered like a wet snake as she endeavored to extricate herself from his tightly enfolding arms. It was time for her to quit his bed; Rory, loath to relinquish the warmth of her body, pulled her back, but the slipperiness

131

of her flesh enabled her to escape from him. She gestured across the tent, where Baba's slave girl beckoned to her.

"It is not that I want to go," Almera whispered. "I know that my lord would willingly have me dally here with him, but it is the order of my most illustrious lord, the shango. He said that we must leave early this morning and so I go, but I shall assuage your need for me tonight."

Rory released her unwillingly and watched her through half-closed eyes as she slipped on the enveloping robes and veil and joined Baba's girl who waited for her outside the raised tent flap. He saw Baba kick off the sodden sheet and swing his long legs over the side of the divan. Slowly, as if reluctant to waken, Baba stood up, stretched, his arms high over his head. In the dim light of the tent, he looked like a living bronze statue. Stepping noiselessly across the thick rugs, he reached down a hand to shake Rory awake, only to see that Rory's eyes were open.

"Ah, my brother," Baba grinned, his teeth a slash of white across his face, "last night you slept; I heard you snoring. Tell me, did Almera satisfy you? If not, if you have any complaints about her, I shall have her punished. She has only one reason for living—to satisfy you. The night before you slept not at all but last night . . ."

"I slept, Baba. Truly I slept. I'm no rutting athlete who could continue on with my record of the first night."

"Alas, Rory, you do not know how to take real pleasure out of a woman. You spend yourself too soon. Then you are over and done with. I'll have to teach you the value of kif." He pointed to the long slender pipe on the tabouret beside his bed. "With a pipeful of kif one can delay that final plunge into ecstasy which drains one of all desire." He sat down on the edge of Rory's couch. "Time enough to initiate you into the sublimity of kif some other night. Just now we must prepare to leave. I want to put as many miles between us and Rinktum Castle as possible by nightfall."

To this Rory readily agreed. He was oppressed by Rinktum Castle and all that it stood for. The ceaseless keening of the slaves in the barracoons depressed him. Of course, according to Sparks and Souza, they were only animals; but even as animals they merited better treatment

132

than they received. Animals? Rory regarded Baba. Although Baba's color was distinctly lighter than that of those unfortunates in the barracoons, he was still a Negro. His mother was pure Sudanese and although his father was nominally accounted a Moor, he too had probably been tarred with the same brush of blackness. Well, black he might be, Rory thought, but Baba was no animal, unless one might consider him a splendid male animal and that in a truly complimentary sense. Yes, that he might be but he was certainly human and definitely not savage. Rory contrasted the beauty of the rugs, furniture, and clothing in the tent with the bleak poverty of Sax Castle. Had conditions been reversed and had Rory been entertaining Baba at Sax, Baba could well have thought of him as a savage and a damn miserable one at that.

Disposing of the services of the beaters this morning, they bathed in the river, taking care not to venture beyond the shallows of the stream. Afterwards they ate a hearty breakfast under the trees—coffee, fruit, and bread. By the time they had finished, the tents had been struck, everything packed into chests and boxes, and much of it already loaded on the long canoes drawn up to the bamboo wharf. They were, so Baba informed Rory, to spend several days of their journey upriver in the Kru canoes. They were to meet Baba's caravan at a predetermined rendezvous where it had been awaiting him during his delivery of the slaves to Frederick and to Rinktum.

Once back with his caravan, Baba assured Rory, they would live in more comfort, in a better tent, with more servants to wait upon them. And, he winked at Rory, if by that time he had tired of Almera, he could pick another slave girl to serve him. However she would not be as white as Almera. No, she would be black but not necessarily ugly. Would Rory object to a black girl? No! But had he ever had one before? Only once? Then Rory had a surprise in store.

Although, Baba explained, it was considered a mark of distinction to have white and Moorish girls in one's hareem, they were more or less decorative, nothing else. For real satisfaction, there was nothing to compare with a black girl, and of all black girls, those from the little

133

kingdom of Ankole in Uganda were the best. They were born with the blood boiling in their veins. To be sure, they were hard to come by and commanded the highest prices, but once a man found one, he never begrudged the price he paid for her. Baba's breath whistled through his pursed lips. There were two awaiting for him with the caravan. Especially trained too. Just another reason why they should get started because the sooner they got there, the sooner Rory would understand what Baba meant. Of course, one was for him. Naturally! It was share and share alike from now on. According to Baba's mother, Rory was to have a profound effect for good on Baba's whole life. Sharing an Ankolan girl with Rory was nothing compared to what Rory was going to do for Baba. Nothing!

Tim was awaiting them at the pier and when he saw Rory and Baba approaching, he limped painfully up the path to meet them.

Rory regarded Tim's leg. "How are you feeling, Timmy lad?"

"Fit as a coring-mush, I am, ready to fight at the drop of a hat. You're taking me with you, matey?"

"With you dragging that leg, Tim? It's a long journey. Better that you stay here and rest it up."

"Fer Christ's sake, matey, don't leave me here in this hellhole," Tim pleaded. "I'm no good to Old Bastinado now. This leg will never carry me aloft in the ratlines and he'll not ship me out. In this bloody hole I'd die in a week. On, come on, lad, take me with you. The time'll come when you'll be glad of a few words of the King's English after all this heathen talk."

"God knows where we're going, Tim. I understand it's about fourteen days of traveling from here to Sa'aqs and only the first few days by canoe. Can you stand the trip? If you can, I'd like to have you along."

"That I can, matey. You'll take care of me. I'll be grand with you, Rory, but if you leave me here with that stinking Portugee, anything can happen to me. I'll probably end up in a bush peghouse taking on all comers at a penny a throw. Don't leave me here, Rory," Tim was blubbering.

134

"I could pay your board here." Rory recalled the pounds that Sparks had given him.

"And me a-going down to the pier every day to look upriver to see if you was coming back. Worry about me if you must, matey, but how about *me* worrying if *you* didn't ever come back? For the love of God, take me, Rory Mahound. You'll get sick of jabbering to these Ay-rabs and to your coffee-colored Jacky. Grimey, ain't he the handsome one though! Never thought I'd be saying that about a blasted nigger but he's even handsomer than them two naked stone men what holds up the doors of the bank in Liverpool."

Rory considered Tim's plea. Yes, it would be good to have one person from home along. He would get lonely for someone to speak English with. He nodded his head in approval.

"I'll do it, Tim, if you think you can stand the trip. I'll be glad of your company."

The long line of canoes was now loaded and they departed up the river, one by one, each canoe manned by ten Kru boys whose rhythmically flashing paddles propelled the canoes through the water with a piston-like regularity. Baba occupied the first canoe alone, where he reclined amidships under a tasseled canopy of black goathair. The next canoe, fitted up in similar luxury for Rory, was at his insistence shared by Tim. At first Baba had been averse to having Tim travel in the same canoe with Rory, but when Rory explained that Tim was a friend as well as a servant, Baba reluctantly agreed, although the expression on his face plainly betokened that a person could hardly be both a friend and a servant. However, he accepted the explanation, so now Tim reclined on a divan mattress and cushions under the canopy alongside Rory.

On the first stages of their journey, any shield from the sun seemed unnecessary, for the rank tropical growth of the trees, arching over the narrowing river, completely overshadowed them, forming a dim tunnel of verdure. Cranes stood one-legged on the shores and thousands of small birds, jewel-colored, flashed through the branches. The half-submerged logs turned into crocodiles, and curving

135

ripples marked the paths of water snakes. During the daytime Africa seemed a world of saurian monsters that ranged from the ponderous crocodiles to the tiny lizards, down through the snakes, frogs, and assorted reptiles. It was a world of teeming life, burgeoning from the ooze and slime of the river. Giant lianas festooned the trees and occasionally one of these would move, glide away with scintillations of light on its scaly sides, and disappear into the green twilight with ophidian grace. But apart from the reptiles of the water and the birds of the air, there was still another world—vicious, buzzing, pestilential, and overwhelming—which flew, alighted, bit, and poisoned. Huge iridiscent green flies anchored themselves to the flesh, and as soon as one pest had alighted, it was the signal for more to come. Mosquitoes hummed through the air and pierced one with steel needles which penetrated clothing and freckled it with spots of blood. However, the heavy wool burnooses which had seemed so stifling to Rory at first now proved their worth, for the mosquitoes could not easily penetrate their coarse fibers. Liberal applications of vinegar kept some of the pests from hands and faces and now Rory fully appreciated the fly whisk that Baba had given him. Its constant motion at least discouraged the pests momentarily. Strangely enough the Kru boys, although naked except for a sodden loincloth, did not seem to be bothered. The flies covered their bodies with a green incrustation and the mosquitoes buzzed around them, but they did not take the trouble to brush them off. Rory was later to learn of the immunity their black skin had built up over the many generations of Krumen who had paddled the river.

The canoes that followed were laden with the tents and their furnishings and all the attendants that Baba had brought with him. Soon, Baba had said, they would be joining the main caravan which had been encamped above the marshy ground of the delta, awaiting his return. Here they would have more comfortable accommodations than the crude ones he had been able to offer Rory at Rinktum. There would be horses for them to ride and the journey to Sa'aqs from then on would be overland. Most nights they would be guests of the local chiefs, kings, emirs, or whatever fanciful name the heads of various tribes wished to call themselves. All of these local potentates were sources of Baba's supply and they awaited his semi-annual trips to the coast with the pick of their slaves, for they knew he would accept nothing but the finest.

When the sun had reached its meridian, they stopped on a fly-infested sand spit which was made further uncomfortable by hordes of sand fleas. There they ate a hurried meal—greasy couscous which had been cooked the night before—a mass of tallowy semolina which was difficult to swallow unless washed down with the tepid water from the goatskins. Then they were on their way again. Rory marveled at the endurance of the Kru boys who never rested but kept up the steady rhythm of their paddling hour after hour. When dusk had filtered down through the trees to mingle with the green-black twilight of daytime, they stopped again, this time in a little grassy meadow that came down to the water's edge. Evidently it had been a regular stopping place, for there were rude, thatched lean-tos and a stone fireplace. Their evening meal was a warm one, and with it they had minted tea, hot and pungent from a bed of mint which some traveler had thoughtfully planted. Without undressing, they sought the shelter of the huts and slept until the bright sun of morning woke them.

The next day on the river proved the efficiency of the awnings, for soon they passed from the arboreal shelter into open country where the sun beat down upon them unmercifully. Now the trees parted overhead to let in the light and as they progressed up the river, the vegetation lost its jungle superabundance and became sparser. They passed native villages, perched precariously on stilts out over the water. Children and slack-dugged women waved to them but they saw few men. Rory was later to learn that the men spent most of their time in the big council huts out of the heat, leaving the work for the women. The men were warriors and their only reason for being was to protect their own village and raid other villages for slaves. Enmity between the tribes and even between villages of the same tribe was encouraged by the local potentates. All black flesh was grist for the slave mill and the petty chiefs

137

were not above filling their quotas even with unwanted members of their own families from time to time when their raids had not netted sufficient prime specimens to meet either their own cupidity or the slave dealers' demands.

After a long day of paddling, they passed another night in an established camp similar to that of the night before. In the middle of the night, Rory awakened to a series of chilling screams that jackknifed him out of the hut and down to where the dying fire illuminated two men struggling. As he came nearer, he recognized two of the Kru boys fighting with their paddles. These, made of the iron-hard assegai wood, were formidable weapons. Both men were screaming scurrilous insults at each other and Rory was somewhat surprised that Baba, who had evidently preceded him at the scene of conflict, made no effort to stop the fight.

"It is a matter of honor," Baba explained to Rory. "They fight over another boy and it will be a fight to the death. These Kru boys all have wives and children at Rinktum Castle but they also have *wives* among the other and younger canoe boys. Actually these marriages are even more binding on them than the ones they have with the women at the Castle, for they spend more time away from home than they do there. From what they are screaming at each other, it seems that one awoke tonight to find his boy-wife gone. When he started to prowl around the camp, he discovered his boy sleeping with another man. See! They fight without mercy. Ah, the fight is over and the winner has won his wife back."

While he was speaking, Rory had seen the swipe of the thin-edged paddle nearly sever the other man's neck. Wielded with all the brute strength behind the sturdy arm and shoulders of the canoe man, the paddle was as effective as a cutlass. The victim dropped and the victor, reaching down with a sudden movement, half twisting and half plucking, wrenched off the dying man's genitals and tossed them to the boy, who had been watching. The man's words were unintelligible to Rory but he needed no translator to tell what the fellow was saying. "Here, if you want him so much take him." Then, after words of anger

138

and recrimination on one side and entreaty and a begging for forgiveness on the other, they both grabbed the dead man's heels and trundled him off into the darkness.

"We'll be one canoe boy short." Baba shrugged his shoulders and accompanied Rory back to the hut. "But it won't matter. The man who won his boy back tonight will work twice as hard tomorrow. He'll want to impress the boy with his strength and stamina. On one trip a couple of years ago, I lost four Kru boys. They were all after the headman's boy, a simpering lad who flirted continuously with the other men. But the canoes went ahead just the same and when we landed at Rinktum, the headman bought so many strings of beads for his boy, the lad could hardly walk under the weight of them. Come, let's get some sleep."

The next morning Rory and Tim took a walk from the camp to relieve themselves in the bushes. Nearby they noticed a roughly conical mound of earth, about the height of a man, with the body of the dead Kru man sprawled upon it. His corpse was a corruscating mass of shiny black ants which had already eaten the flesh from his legs, exposing the white bones.

By midafternoon of that day, they reached a broad savannah of high grass studded with unearthly looking baobab trees. The huge cylindrical trunks seemed too big for the meager branches, and they looked as though they had been pulled up from the earth, their branches buried and only the roots in the air. After the lushness of the river, it was clean and light. Hosts of brilliant butterflies reflected a scintillation of light around the low, flowering shrubs, and there was even the suggestion of a breeze which fanned their faces. Under the shade of the trees, they came upon a tent city, larger and more elaborate than the one Baba had had at Rinktum Castle.

Some hundred men, varying in color from light cream to ebon black, awaited them on the sand spit where the canoes landed; their vociferous shouts of welcome, punctuated by volleys from their long slender muskets, set the tethered line of horses to dancing and neighing. The canoes deposited them as near the sandpit as possible and willing hands lifted Baba ashore to return, at his bidding, to carry Rory. They were finished now with the canoes and the sight of horses started Rory's worries about Tim. Lying at length on a mattress in the bottom of a canoe, he had not suffered overmuch, but Rory feared it would be different on horseback because he was sure Tim had never had even a speaking acquaintance with a horse.

Baba had waited for Rory to get ashore and now came to walk with him. A gesture of his hand encompassed the city of tents.

"Well, my brother, here you may have a tent of your own and you will not have to share mine." Baba pointed to a black tent only a little smaller than the one that flew his pennant. But, as he spoke the words, Rory noted a fleeting expression of sadness on his face.

"You'll be more comfortable alone, I suppose." Rory also felt a little sad at being separated from Baba. He had enjoyed the feeling of proximity when they had shared the same tent and, he had to confess to himself, he had enjoyed Almera more when he could hear Baba's all-too-audible enjoyment of his own woman.

"It is not of my comfort I think, my brother. It is of yours. As for me, I welcome your presence. It adds to my pleasure to hear the little sounds of your happiness. When I hear your gaspings for breath and the pleading moans and entreaties of Almera it spurs me on to greater joys, knowing that you are happy, too. Yes, I shall feel lonely in my tent now even though I shall have the choice of four slave girls instead of two."

"And I too shall feel lonely, Baba, because if you have enjoyed my sounds, I have taken pleasure in yours. Then too, I feel happier when I am near you. You are all that I have in Africa and Africa is a strange place. At times it frightens me, but when you are nearby, I have assurance. The time will come when we shall be separated. My path will go one way and yours another. When that day comes we shall long for one another's company. So, unless you insist on kicking me out, I prefer to stay with you."

"Allah be praised! You really mean it, Rory. You are not just trying to be polite?"

"I mean it, Baba."

Baba shook his head. "It is rather difficult for me to

140

credit your words although I know they are sincere. I have had many dealings with white men and although they pay me lip service, call me 'Your Highness,' give me a salute of guns when I arrive, choose things for my dash that they think will impress me, and even sit down with me at the same table, Rory, I know all the time what they are thinking."

"And what is that, Baba?"

"They're thinking, here's this black fellow who believes he's something special. Oh well, we'll humor him and let him think so if he wants. But we know he's only a black nigger, yet as long as he's got something we want, we'll pretend that he's important. We'll salaam to him and treat him as an equal. We'll give him a few yards of Manchester cotton printed in bright colors because that's what the niggers like. We'll load him up with cheap iron pots and German looking glasses. We'll give him some bugle beads to string in his hair and a brass ring for his nose. We'll butter him up with some tawdry jewels and old castoffs. Then we'll palaver over him and allow him to eat with us but all the time we'll know we are better than he is because our skins are white and his is brown. That's what they are thinking, Rory, and I hate them for it. Probably I would have hated you, too, if your name had not been the same as mine and if some ancient gods of Africa had not predicted your coming."

Rory stretched out his hand beside that of Baba's, comparing them.

"I see two hands, Baba," he said slowly. "Each one has five fingers and each finger has a nail. The same muscles and tendons control them. They are both strong hands when they grasp a sword but tender hands when they stroke the soft skin of a woman. These hands can guide a horse; they can tie a knot; they can shoot a gun; they can discover the most secret places of a woman's body. I can see only one difference in them."

"Their color?" Baba's eyes were now on his hand and Rory's.

"Yes, the color. The skin of my hand is white and that of yours is brown. Who is to say which is the most beautiful—a statue of marble or one of bronze? The

141

ancient Greeks chiseled their statues of white marble but they also cast them in black bronze and one was as beautiful as the other. Therefore I do not see that the brown hand suffers by comparison with the white hand any more than the bronze hand with the marble hand. They are both the hands of men. So, my lord of Sa'aqs, let us do as they do in my country. See, my hand seeks yours and clasps it. I grasp your hand and you grasp mine in return." He reached for Baba's hand and shook it vigorously. "It is an old custom and its origin is lost in history, but when one man shakes another's hand, it is a sign of good faith. It can also be a vow of friendship. It can betoken infinite trust. It is not a white hand shaking a black hand, Baba; it is my hand shaking yours."

Baba's hand grasped Rory's. "Thank you, my brother."

Rory was surprised to see tears in Baba's eyes.

"These cursed midges," Baba wiped his eyes, "they get right into a man's eyes."

CHAPTER XIV

ALTHOUGH AS USUAL, WHEN THEY WERE ready for bed, Almera was present to serve Rory this night—their first in the caravan camp—two other girls appeared along with Almera and Zayah, Baba's Moorish slave girl. Both of the new girls were as black as polished jet, yet there could be no comparison between these two exotic jungle orchids and the average shaven-polled, flat-dugged females Rory had seen on his passage up the river. These new girls were sleek-flanked and oval-bellied with upthrust pointed breasts on which the nipples, painted with vermillion, blossomed like strange parasitic flowers that fed on the blood beneath them. Their features were more Hamitic than Negroid—finely chiseled noses and

142

curved, not overfull lips that were sensually moist and inviting. Their hair covered their heads in close-cropped caps of black velours that were far from the ugly black peppercorns of wool Rory had seen. Although they were black—the sable black of darkest Africa—their limbs shone like polished gunmetal, catching and reflecting the dancing flames of the lamps with their every movement. Both of them exuded a fragrance of sandalwood and musk and there was something about the studied grace of their movements that reminded Rory of the fine Arabian horses he had seen when they landed. Both girls were naked except for a curiously woven girdle of multicolored beads around their waists, while their legs and buttocks were stenciled with vermilion and white arabesques. They followed silently behind Almera and Zayah with fluid steps, as though their feet did not touch the ground.

"I promised you a change, my brother." Baba winked at Rory and beckoned the girls to him. They came and stood before him while he ran his big hands over the sleekness of their thighs, then turned them around to let his fingers stray over the silken curves of their buttocks. He shook his head in mock derision of their charms.

"These two are indeed black, Rory, blacker than the heart of Shaitan himself. But do not let the color of their skin influence you. They have been delicately reared and trained in the arts of love since they were able to toddle. They come from far away Ankole where the most promising and the handsomest boys and girls are chosen when they are very young. Then they are dispatched to Khartoum to be trained to satisfy the demands of the princes of Arabia. The boys are all castrated and turned into compliant eunuchs, while the girls are forced to undergo a curious operation which makes them well-nigh insatiable. 'Tis said that one of these girls can take on fifty men in one night and that she will enjoy the fiftieth as much as the first. I passed through Khartoum on my first pilgrimage to Mecca and I left orders with Mohammed Laazib, the slave merchant of Khartoum, that he was to pick out two of his finest girls every year and send them to me. I also stipulated that they should be trained by old Miriam, the Jewess, who, 'tis said, knows more ways of pleasing a man

143

than any other woman in the world although she is now nearly a hundred years old. She has the rare ability of teaching a girl how to bring a man to the point of ecstasy and hold him there for minutes instead of seconds and to repeat this over and over again without him spending himself. It becomes an exquisite madness and will make you scream for mercy.

"These girls arrived during my absence and my father, may Allah bless every hair in his beard, knowing that I would be anxious to try them out, sent them down to me. They arrived by a special caravan three days ago and have been preparing for my coming ever since. How fortunate that there are two of them. And so now, do you, my brother, pick out the one that appeals to you."

Rory inventoried them both and they, noticing his appraisal of them, arched their bodies and fondled their breasts for his approval. He shook his head. It was impossible to determine which one was the more attractive.

"As always, my brother, you are unselfish, but as they are yours and as you have been anticipating their arrival for so long, make your own choice first."

"Bah! They are much alike." Baba compared one with the other. "I see no difference except that one might be a finger-breadth shorter, while the other has breasts that are a trifle rounder. Yet there is no law which says either of us has to make a choice. Our divans are so near together they can skip back and forth. That is, if you are willing."

"Of course. But Almera?" Rory had developed a deep fondness for the girl who had been with him.

"Almera? What has she to do with it? She is only a woman and a slave woman at that. Rory, she is less than nothing. Her only reason for existing is to live for her master and you are her master. Therefore whatever pleases you must make her happy. She is nothing but the clay pot into which you can pour your fluids. Sometimes, in truth, I do not understand you, Rory. A horse is a horse and a woman is a woman and a man rides them both because he is a man." He turned to Almera and crooked his finger for her to approach to him.

She came and threw herself at Baba's feet, and although Rory could see a suspicion of tears in her eyes, she denied

144

that she would be envious of any attentions Rory might pay to the new girl. The sidelong glance she stole at Rory from under lowered lashes belied the truth of her words, but Baba had taken them at face value and while he nudged her away with the toe of his babouche, he pulled one of the black girls he was fondling down into his lap and dispatched the other to Rory's divan. She moved toward Rory with the grace and coquetry of a black kitten and curled herself demurely at his feet.

"I am called Chatsubah," she purred in Arabic. "In my language that means one who can place her lord in the seventh heaven. I shall make you very happy." Her slender fingers coiled around his babouches and she removed them slowly as if it were a rite she was performing. Her fingers strayed to his ankles, then slowly upwards circling and caressing the calves of his legs. Her fingers were soft and cool to his flesh, yet despite their coolness, they kindled tiny fires wherever they touched. Without relinquishing the contact of her fingers, she uncoiled herself and rose to her knees, her hardened nipples pressing against him. Slowly her deft hands undid the fastenings of his burnous. Her every movement was slow, studied and provocative—a part of a ceremony which she had studied and practiced since she could remember. After each fastening of his clothing was undone, she delayed before going on to the next, kissing and stroking that part of his body which she had exposed. At length every button was undone, every string untied, every frog opened. Lifting her hand, admonishing him not to move, she sat back on her heels staring up at him while Almera and Zayah busied themselves in the tent, filling basins with perfumed water, placing fleecy white towels beside the couches, adding aromatic sticks of incense to the braziers and then retiring, but not before lowering the flap of the tent that opened to the camp and raising the other flap which looked out onto the star-studded darkness.

When their soft footsteps had died away, Chatsubah spoke to Rory. "Now, if my lord will stand up. . . ." She rose and disengaged Rory's robes so that they slid to the ground. Now that he stood naked before her, she seemed

145

convulsed with fright; her eyes widened, her lips trembled, and she retreated a step to kneel before him.

"Forgive me, my lord, forgive me. I have never seen a man before. Indeed not, for we always practiced on wooden dummies. But now I am afraid. I am such a small thing to accommodate such magnificence. I tremble, my lord."

Rory reached down a hand to reassure her but she would not lift her eyes to meet his. His glance strayed across the tent to where Baba was receiving like ministrations and he heard the girl at his feet repeating the same words and then he understood that they were spoken merely to make him glory in his own manliness. He patted her on the shoulder and she lifted her head to smile at him.

With the towel wrung out from the perfumed water, she sponged the sweat from his body and dried it with another towel, and from the splashing of water on the other side of the tent he knew that Baba was undergoing the same treatment. When Chatsuba had dried him, she poured a sweet-smelling oil from a flask and motioned for him to lie on the divan, whereupon she rubbed the oil into his skin, kneading all his flesh with her fingers, relaxing all his muscles until there was neither tautness nor tension in his nerves. He felt disembodied, as though all his body had floated away leaving only the throbbing tumescence which now seemed to be his whole being. Here she took special pains, anointing it with a different oil which was so precious that she poured only a few drops of it onto her fingers. It left him with a hot and stinging sensation which caused him a moment's sharp discomfort and then eased while he felt himself further engorged and even more startlingly in evidence.

Reaching with one hand for a small silver ewer on the tabouret beside the divan, she poured a drink into a small porcelain cup and handed it to him.

"Here, my master, take and drink of this," she smiled up at him, her eyes reflecting pinpoints of light under her long lashes. "It is the nectar they drink in Paradise," her voice sank to a whisper. "With one sip of this a man can
146

satisfy each of his forty houris in one night and still have the strength and desire to satisfy them all over again."

Rory took the cup and drank. It smacked of musty rose leaves and left a bittersweet taste in his mouth. When he had handed back the cup, she filled a long slender pipe with kif and handed it to him, picking a coal from the brazier with a pair of tongs to light it. He noticed that Baba had downed the portion offered him by his girl and was already smoking.

He called across to Rory. "Tonight, my brother, you will have the endurance of a stallion and you will need it. The drink, which is supposed to be an essence of sea slugs from China, will kindle a raging holocaust in your blood, but the kif will keep the fires from consuming you and cause them to smolder all night. You will be able to enjoy more and enjoy it longer."

"I needed no essence of sea slugs to prepare me," Rory laughed.

"I doubt it not and indeed my eyes show me the evidence of your ability, but a man with a quiver full of arrows is better prepared than a man who has only one and expends all his ammunition in one shot. Tonight you will find your quiver full," Baba's laugh echoed back. "And now, the lights, Metuq." Baba shoved his girl gently with his foot and she extinguished the lamps. Now there was only the pale light of the moon, shining through the open tent flap, leaving Baba and Metuq in darkness but causing Rory's body to shine with a pearl-white luminescence.

"You are the first man I have ever been with, my lord, and the first white man I have ever seen. True, I feared you when I first saw you in all your glory but now I no longer fear. I have been prepared for you. I was able to accommodate old Miriam's largest wooden peg. We girls called it The Qat and we all dreaded it because of the pain we knew it would cause us when we were impaled upon it. Now the memory of that pain gives me joy because I shall be able to give you greater pleasure."

"A pleasure which I am eager for, little one."

"You will not be disappointed, my lord, and I shall try not to cry out."

147

It was a night of consumate artistry such as Rory had never experienced. It was as far removed from his clumsy fumblings with the Scottish Marys under the hedgerows as day is removed from night. Never before had he attained such heights and never before had he remained so long in an ecstasy so exquisite that it became almost unbearable and he shrieked in suppliance, begging to be released. Chatsubah played on him as she would a musical instrument, uncovering chords of sensation that racked his body while they soothed it. The artistry of both these girls was a result of long and arduous training and yet there was a spontaneity about them coupled with their screams at first penetrations that convinced Rory that this was indeed their first experience with a man. Each time Chatsubah— or it might have been Metuq, for there was a constant interchange between them—raised him to a breathless plateau where he gasped for breath and felt he would explode into infinitesimal fragments, their arts soothed him into a brief hiatus that allowed him to gulp for air and prepare to ascend the heights again. There was not a pinpoint of his body which did not respond to Chatsubah's caresses. Her flicking tongue explored secret areas that caused him to thresh his limbs and moan. She was all woman and she made him all man. Her words glorified him into a god. He remembered a picture he had seen in one of old Jamie's books of the Colossus of Rhodes, and he knew that for the moment he was towering above all men, reaching such a height that ships could sail beneath him without touching him.

She marveled at his endowments, flattering him with a pretty fluttering; cooing and exclaiming in simulated pain that no woman alive could ever accommodate him and that the feared Qat in old Miriam's school was nothing but a pigmy compared to him. He was tearing her apart, she sobbed and she cried out, despite the fact that she did not relinquish him for a second. Her beggings for mercy prevailed upon him and he took pity on her and tempered his violence but she pressed him on, urging him to even more vigorous attacks yet all the time protesting to give pretty credence to the fact that he was her master. When she allowed him a brief breathing spell, he would miss her

148

momentarily only to find her back beside him and again it might have been Metuq for all he knew. Then, once again the fires would be rekindled—those fires which had never entirely died out.

Sometime during the night there was a brief hiatus when a solitary lamp was lighted and by its flame the girls poured another drink while Rory and Baba smoked the second pipe of kif. From the shadows of the other divan, Baba hailed Rory across the tent.

"Confess it now, Rory. You wondered in your own mind if you would really like a black girl."

" 'Tis true, Baba. I did wonder, yet a black girl was not entirely strange to me. I had one once before—Sparks's slut on board ship—and the hatred I had for her afterward probably prejudiced me."

"And now . . . ?"

"And now I live for this one night only. Even were I to die at sunrise, I would still be happy for I have lived as no other man ever lived before in this one night."

"The night is not over my brother. Live some more. Metuq, blow out the light."

The extra potion and the kif lasted throughout the night and at dawn the girls were gone, leaving only the odor of sandalwood on the wet sheets. Rory dozed off into a sleep of utter exhaustion only to be awakened by the sounds of the camp breaking up. He turned wearily onto his side to face the interior of the tent and saw that Baba was up, reaching for his clothes to dress himself. Rory envied the big black fellow who moved as easily as though he had spent the night in restful slumber while Rory himself felt such a sense of desuetude and absolute weakness that he doubted if he could ever lift his tired knees over the side of the divan. But lift them he did at Baba's urging and stumbled off, following Baba to the edge of the river where he hesitated on the bank, trying to collect his thoughts and his courage to enter the water. But Baba, who seemed invigorated instead of drained by the night's excesses, caught him by the ankle and pulled him in. The water was cold and succeeded in waking Rory. Then, after a meager breakfast of dates and coffee, during which the big tents sagged to the ground and were loaded on the

149

horses, they started on the longer part of their journey to Sa'aqs.

The black Arabian stallion with the high-pommeled, silver-mounted saddle was a far cry from the rugged ponies of the Scottish moors. The Scottish moors! Rory was a Sax of the moors of Scotland and Baba was a Sa'aqs of the Moors of Africa. The coincidence struck him as strange and he rode up alongside Baba to explain this other coincidence of nomenclature, thinking it as a pun to pass the time. To his surprise, Baba was impressed and nodded his head wisely, convinced that here again was another substantiation of the words of prophecy.

Tim, who had now discarded his sailor togs and hidden his red hair under the hood of a burnoose, had managed to mount a horse, though not, indeed, such a mettlesome steed nor one as gorgeously caparisoned as Rory's. During the morning, Rory rode back to check on Tim's progress and found his face drawn in pain. The leg was worse, he informed Rory, and every step of the horse caused him intense suffering. But no, he would go on. In truth, both realized that there was no other place for him to go. During the midday halt, Rory took a look at Tim's leg and found it swollen and once again suppurating. He called Baba to look at it and he too seemed disturbed, although it was apparent that he was more disturbed over Rory's concern than over Tim's pain.

"You are very fond of this Tim, your servant?" he asked Rory.

Rory agreed.

"If he can survive three days, we can cure him, otherwise the best thing to do would be to give him a drink of the red water and let him find an easement of his pain in death."

"Three days? But why three days? Why can't we cure him now?"

Baba shook his head. "In three days we come to the land of the Basampos. It is a strange land and the Basampos are a strange people. They are perhaps the oldest and wisest people in all Africa. They have many strange customs and they are savages in that they believe in strange gods. But their knowledge of witchcraft and magic is the greatest in the world. That is why they are so feared and none of them are ever captured as slaves because the slavers fear the deadliness of their magic spells. The King of the Basampos is a vassal of my father's and, although he is young and has seen only fifteen rainy seasons, he is a friend of mine because the Basampos have always been allies of the House of Sa'aqs. I do not believe in their gods or their witchcraft because I am a True Believer of the Prophet and yet," Baba hesitated, "I would not want the King of the Basampos for an enemy." He spat on the ground and rubbed the spittle into the dust with his foot as though to ward off an evil spell.

"Then you believe that the King of the Basampos can cure Tim?"

"His witch doctors can if he so bids them. Of that I am sure, for I have seen them do many marvelous things. I have seen one of the Basampo witch doctors point his stick at a tree and within minutes have seen every leaf on it wither and die. And I have seen even stranger things, as you yourself may. So I say, if this man lives until we reach Basampo, they will cure him. I shall have a palanquin made for him and it will be easier than riding a horse. We shall try to keep him alive because it is important to you."

Tim's eyes pleaded with Rory and Rory nodded his encouragement as he thanked Baba. A hammock was made from the side of one of the tents. Then, by slinging it from two tentpoles and swinging it between two horses, a carrier of sorts was made for Tim and willing hands lifted him into it.

"Am I going to die, Rory?" he asked.

"No, Tim," Rory tried to comfort him. "Baba is sure that when we arrive at Basampo, their doctors will cure you."

"And you'll drink this now," Baba proffered a cup of liquid which Tim downed.

After they had ridden to the head of the caravan, Rory asked, "Was that the red water that you gave Tim?"

"No, my brother. I've promised that we shall do all we can to save your servant and therefore I would not poison him. I gave him opium to make him sleep. You remember

151

the drink that the black girl, Chatubah, gave you last night?"

"The one you said was made of sea slugs from China?"

"The same, but I doubt in my own mind if it ever saw a sea slug. It was opium I am sure—the juice of a white poppy from Persia. When used in quantity it is a beneficial medicine that relieves pain. But a little opium keeps a man so strong and so hard that he can deflower thirty virgins in one night without losing his erection. The kif helps too. Did you notice that you neither tired nor became flaccid?"

Rory laughed. "I merely thought I was becoming a man of greater power."

"Indeed you were, thanks to the opium and the kif. You see, Rory, our women have studied these things. They had to, out of necessity. Even if a man has only the four wives that the Prophet permits and has neither concubines nor slave girls, he can spend only one night with a wife, which leaves the other three alone. Now, if a man has a hundred concubines besides his four wives, you can see how often he must neglect them all. We Moors, Rory, are passionate men. We no sooner mount a woman than we are spent. Therefore the woman who has been waiting days, even weeks for her man does not want her pleasure over in a moment. That is how our women discovered the benefits of opium and kif. It slows a man down. It prolongs his pleasure while it does not destroy it. You can testify to that."

"I can and I wait for tonight."

Baba shook his head vigorously. "No, my brother, not again tonight. A steady indulgence in opium makes it a habit. A man gets so he wants more and more of it and when it is taken in large quantities, such as I gave your man Tim, it causes a deep sleep. The dosage I gave Tim was strong, whereas the one we took was weak. Tim will not feel the pain nor the motion of the horses. We shall keep him sleeping and comfortable until we arrive at Basampo. And as for you, my brother, for several nights you will go back to the gentler ministrations of Almera and I shall seek rest in the arms of Zayah."

152

"To gain strength for another bout with Chatsubah and Metuq."

"Right, but Rory . . ."

"Yes, Baba."

"The women will not be able to enter the city of Basampo. We shall have to leave them outside as it is forbidden for anything female to enter the city. Even the hens are kept outside, and their women are allowed to enter only on special occasions. They have strange customs, the Basampos, and they do not particularly appeal to me, yet I feel it wise while I am there to do as they do. You must promise to do the same as I do not wish you to bring down the curse of their witch doctors on your head. So, my brother, do whatever they require of you."

"I'll try, Baba."

"It will be safer if you do. If you want them to save your man and," he added ominously, "even more important if you wish to save yourself. Not that they would harm you while under my protection. Oh no! But if you were to do something to displease them now, six months from now, a year from now something might happen to you and it would be the result of their witchcraft. Yet, I worry overmuch. The young king will be pleased to see you. He has never seen a man as white as you nor one with hair the color of gold. He has always wanted to, so you can be sure of a warm reception."

"I shall take off my turban."

"Good," Baba edged his horse up close enough to Rory's so he could slap him on the shoulder. "And another thing. Flatter them. Make them think they are the strongest, the handsomest, and the wisest of all the men in Africa. It will not be difficult for perhaps they are. Yes, perhaps they are. Even handsomer and wiser than the men from the Sudan."

"I doubt that, Baba, for remember that you are half Sudanese and certainly nobody could be handsomer or wiser than you."

"Save your flattery, Rory, for the Basampos."

Despite his words, Rory could see that Baba was pleased. "I'm saving my flattery for the Basampos, Baba. The words I speak to you are the truth."

CHAPTER XV

THE THREE WEARY DAYS OF JOURNEYING AND their attendant nights passed. To Rory these were days of blinding hot sun, the discomfort of the high saddle, and the unfamiliarity of the weird African landscape that looked like the unreal topography of another planet. The vast savannahs of high brown grass were dotted with unearthly looking trees—huge baobabs which appeared to have been plucked out of the ground and replanted upside down, making their roots into branches. Strange-looking animals that bore no relation to any that Rory had ever seen stared at their caravan momentarily before taking off in a burst of speed that enveloped them in a cloud of dust. Tawny lions sniffed their scent and then slunk off into the bush; immense stacks of excrement indicated that elephants had passed their way; piglike hippopotami raised bulbous snouts from the sluggish rivers; and at night the hyenas howled around their tents with fiendish human laughter. Nights, however, held the consolation of the cool tent and the warm embraces of Almera which were welcome to Rory after that one fiery touch of Chatsubah. Had it not been for his concern over Tim, he would have thrilled at all the strangeness and the exciting sense of high adventure, but his worry over Tim caused him to ride back frequently to the rude litter where Tim, sleeping in a narcotic stupor, rolled from one side of the improvised hammock to the other.

Tim's leg, when Rory examined it at night, bore no resemblance to anything he had ever seen before. It had swollen to twice its diameter and the skin was taut, dark, angry red, and shiny. The toes, puffed out like misshapen potatoes on the distended foot, were black and appeared to

154

have already died. During the few moments that Tim reached some state of lucidity before Baba again dosed him, he screamed with pain, clinging to Rory's hand as though he felt some measure of strength flowing to him from his friend's nearness.

Every evening Baba also took the time to examine Tim and his only words of comfort were, "He's still alive—the Basampos will cure him."

"But how?" Rory could not see how any power on earth could change that swollen immensity in its stretched sausage skin back into a normal leg again.

"That's not for us to know." Baba shook his head, his eyes imploring Rory to have faith in him. "Although I do not believe in their witchcraft, or at least I am not supposed to, I do know that they can save him. Ask me no more, my brother, for I cannot answer you. I know little of the ways of magic, but I do know that Basampo is known throughout Africa as the kingdom of sorcerers and that their power is very old and very great. *El mektub mektub;* what is to be will be."

The next day several hours of rough traveling, during which the caravan descended from the clear, bright air of the broad savannahs into a steamy alluvial plain, delayed the caravan's progress so that they did not arrive at Basampo until the sun was near the horizon. Once again they had plunged into the jungle, but whereas the jungle which had bordered the river had been merely uncomfortable with its swarms of insects, this one was frightening. The trees with their ropelike lianas made an almost impenetrable wall on each side of the trail. Although the sun had not yet set, it was as dark as night in the forest and only occasionally did they come to a place where an opening in the treetops allowed some light to enter. Rory felt a strange foreboding sense of mystery and danger which recalled old Jamie's tales of haunted woods peopled with ghosties. He half expected wraithlike hands to materialize from out the twisted undergrowth and seize him, open graves to disgorge frightful specters to stalk him. The chattering of small apes in the upper branches as they passed raised goose pimples on Rory's skin, and an occasional glance of one of the strange spider monkeys as it swung from a liana made him think of some shriveled old man with curiously attentuated limbs.

They approached the banks of a sluggish river whose current was not sufficient to move the thick green scum which covered its surface, and as they came nearer Rory could see a company of warriors drawn up alongside the trail. Baba halted his horse to allow Rory to come up alongside him, for they had been traveling in single file. These were, Baba informed him, a guard of honor sent out to escort them into the village. In some way, the Basampos had been apprised of their coming.

Rory was astounded at the men he saw. After the weird forest, he had dreaded his meeting with the Basampos, for surely, in view of the approach to their city, they could be hardly less than human and these men were, Rory believed, the most impressive looking group of super-athletes he had ever seen. Not one them appeared to be over twenty, yet their tall bodies were superbly muscled and oiled so they gleamed like polished ebony in the clear light of the sun that was nearing the horizon. Dancing highlights caught broad, muscle-padded chests with white painted nipples, bulging thighs and tight, round buttocks. Each man wore a high crest of snowy monkey hair which increased his statue and made him look eight feet tall. This was all he wore, except that the calves of his legs were also encircled with the long white hair. Each man carried a tall, bronze-tipped spear and one, from whose spear dangled long strings of what looked like withered and wrinkled black grapes, advanced to meet Baba. His face, although extremely handsome and well modeled, had a blank look—a vacant, faraway stare in his eyes—and Rory noticed as the caravan halted before the line of warriors that all the others had this disembodied appearance—as though their faces were merely empty facades atop their superb bodies.

It was apparent at once that they were not Moslems, for their nakedness showed that they were not circumcized. Quite the opposite. Apparently they made a fetish of not being so, for inserted in each long pendulous foreskin was an intricate and heavy gold ornament about the size of an egg, suspended by a gold chain. It was the weight of these

156

ornaments which had elongated the oversized genitalia until the golden baubles banged against the men's knees. The headman—he with the decorated spear—made a low, but in no way servile, obeisance to Baba and addressed him in some unknown tongue, the words lisping and high-pitched in a falsetto voice that seemed out of place in comparison with so much displayed and startlingly evident masculinity. It was not Hausa because Rory had not forgotten the little of that language that old Jamie had taught him and to which he had now added many more words by his conversations with Baba.

Baba answered the man in the same language, in which he seemed to be fluent, and in speaking it his own voice took on an identical singsong twittering. At a command from the headman, the others came forward, each taking a horse's bridle in his hand. The young Hercules who came to take the bridle of Rory's horse in his hand, stared up at him blankly until Rory threw back the hood of his burnoose. His hair cascaded down to his shoulders and the sight of it caused the man's face to come to life. He pointed to Rory's head, chattered and gesticulated to his companions until they all stared at Rory. Immediately they lost their air of boredom while they giggled among themselves and pointed to him. The fellow who attended Rory bent low, kissed the toe of Rory's babouche and lifted the skirt of his burnous to display the white skin of his calf which sent them all to twittering and giggling again. At the seeming insistence of the others, Rory's guide wet his finger in his mouth and drew it across Rory's leg.

"They think your white skin is painted on with white clay." Baba laughed along with the others. "They have never seen a man like you before. The only white men they have ever seen are Moors and their skin is not as white as yours."

The warriors, now guides, led the horses through a ford of the river which apparently was known only to them, for it meandered up- and downstream but at no time were their horses more than ankle-deep in the green slime. They continued to lead the horses for about another mile after crossing the river. The trail plunged deeper into the

157

jungle until they came to a clearing with a distant view of the village—no, more than a village, a city—which was made up of concentric circles of beehive huts. Mingled with the decaying stench of the jungle, Rory now detected the various effluvia of humanity: the rotting of food and meat, human excrement, and the acrid odor of sweat—although, much to his surprise, he had detected only a pleasantly herbal odor from the man who was walking beside him. Then, as they passed further along the trail, Rory detected the source of this fetor. It was an enormous pit, made further inescapable by a palisade of sharply pointed sticks around the rim, and he could distinguish, from his elevated position on horseback, that it was filled with men. As he eyed the hapless occupants more closely, he could see, much to his surprise, that the prisoners were all strong, young, able-bodied men. It was, he supposed, the slave compound. Later on he was to find out what it actually was. True, the men were slaves, but Rory had no idea of what use was to be made of them and it was fortunate, for the time being, that he remained in ignorance.

After they had passed the pit the trail curved sharply to the left, and as they progressed the foul stink disappeared. Here was another palisaded village of whitewashed bee hive huts, and through the opened gates which were guarded by warriors similar to those who were guiding the caravan, Rory could see women sweeping the paths with bunches of withes. They were bent over so that their pendulous breasts were hanging, and as they moved they waddled like ducks. The reason for their strange spraddle-legged gait, Rory could see, was a band of metal that was locked around their waists, to which was affixed, front and rear, another cumbersome metal band that passed between their legs. On the approach of the caravan, the women all lowered their heads. One, however, who had the temerity to look up, received a swiping blow from the broadside of one of the guards' lances that sent her sprawling in the dust.

After passing the compound of women, they came to a cleanly swept roadway bordered on one side by neat, whitewashed mud huts and on the other by a curving stream of clear limpid water. Their path followed this stream which, as its banks attested, was an artificial canal. Young men were bathing in the canal, splashing water on themselves and others and scrubbing their bodies with the clean sand from the banks. They looked up and stared at the caravan, particularly at Rory, but he was impressed by the fact that there seemed to be an all-pervading air of gloom that prevented the bathers from smiling until they caught sight of his white skin and yellow hair. Then there occurred the same high twittering that had occurred among the guides. Rory came to the conclusion that the water from the river had been dammed up and released into the canals which he could see were in concentric circles, growing ever smaller as they progressed. He was struck by the absolute cleanliness of the huts, the absence of rubbish, the growing flowers, and the occasional bronze standard which supported a basket from which a sweet-smelling smoke of incense issued. Word of their approach traveled among the bathers in the canal and now he was greeted by flashing, white-toothed grins. Several of the fellows waved at him and beckoned to him to join them, while others climbed out of the water and stood on the bank the better to see him.

The guides continued to lead their horses in an ever-narrowing concentric system of circles until they arrived at a clearing of hard-packed earth in the exact center of the city and there, directly in the center of the compound, Rory espied a far grander edifice than any of the houses they had passed. It was circular, with thick walls of mud, painted in bright colors with erotic couplings of men and men, and men and women against a dazzling white background, and supporting a conical thatched roof. A circle of enormous carved and painted wooden pillars whose phallic significance was unmistakable surrounded the hut. Their columnar sides were painted dark brown and the flaring mushroom tops were a dark, purple-red. All except one! This one, larger than the rest, was painted white and its flaring top a brilliant vermilion red. Evidently this particular one had some unusual significance. Bunches of wilted flowers were spread around it and the top glistened from libations of oil.

Baba's horse was halted just before the door of the building and, when Rory's horse was led up, he was helped down with the same courteous assistance Baba had received. Two athletes, even more impressive than those of the guiding party, appeared from inside the structure and arched their spears over the doorway for them to enter. They passed through the lofty portal which was so high that even the tall white headdresses of the warriors did not brush the lintel.

The inside of the building—because of its size it could not be called a hut—was lighted by four gilded bronze candelabra, each one some six feet in height and supporting a thicket of candles. Their elaborate workmanship betrayed their Spanish or Italian origin and Rory wondered what Renaissance palace they might originally have graced before coming to this strange outpost in Africa. A florid gilded throne, obviously from the same source as the candelabra, sat on a dais of leopard skins, and on the throne lolled a Negro youth, dressed in stiff, gold metallic robes. His arms and legs were painted with intricate gold and white arabesques and a glass-bejeweled gilt crown perched precariously on his head. He was extremely handsome in a petulant, spoiled way, and his body under the stiff gold robes seemed slighter and far less muscular than those of his warriors. His mannerisms and his whole bearing seemed extremely effeminate. In addition to the crown, he wore an enormous black phallus made of polished leather and strapped to his waist. This cumbersome appendage was decorated with intricate and multicolored beadwork. When he arose it was even more apparent. Standing beside the throne, seated, lying, and posturing around it, were at least a dozen magnificent athletes, each one chosen for his unusual good looks. These also were as naked as the warrior-guides but their arms and legs were loaded with barbaric gold bracelets and chains and pendants of gold hung around their necks. All wore golden balls suspended from their genitals as did the warriors, except that these were larger and adorned with jewels. They paid no attention to the entry of the strangers, staring only at their standing monarch and murmuring soft phrases which Rory felt were flattering blandishments

160

addressed to the young king. Rory did, however, catch one or two of them appraising him through lash-veiled eyes.

Baba bowed low. Then, taking a step forward, he grasped the huge, artificial phallus in both hands and kissed it. It was the first time Rory had ever seen him make the slightest obeisance to another person. But Baba's gesture of respect was slight in comparison to that of the young king who stepped down from the dais and knelt at Baba's feet, clasping him around the knees and burying his face in Baba's burnoose. When he rose, assisted by two of his men, he spoke to Baba in perfect, although strangely accented, Arabic.

"By the sacred weapon of Basampos, we are happy, great and beautiful Shango, that you visit us once again. We have known for several days the exact hour of your arrival through the predictions of our learned men. Tonight we have ordained the moon and all its stars to shine, but their brilliance will not compare with yours for you are the golden sun and we are but the silver moon, so does your splendor and your beauty overshadow ours. Welcome, great Shango, and who is this beautiful man with white skin and hair of gold who accompanies you? We believe him to be the answer to the great white pillar before our palace which we have today anointed with palm oil and decorated with flowers in honor of his coming."

"We could never hope to contend with your magnificent splendor, oh King Galiah." Baba was flattering the king as he had asked Rory to do. "Your blinding beauty is greater than that of any man I have ever seen in all my travels; the perfection of your face causes me to stare at it in wonder and amazement; your gorgeousness overwhelms me. And now to answer your question, great and glorious king. He of the golden hair is my brother, another lord of Sax, from over the distant seas, who has come to pay his respects to Your Majesty."

"We are pleased that you visit us." Galiah turned and presented the leather phallus to Rory to kiss. "We have been expecting one with hair the color of burnished copper whereas yours is gold."

161

Rory knelt before the king and kissed the phallus as he had observed Baba do.

"I am honored to see such a handsome youth as yourself." Rory felt he could add little to Baba's flowery flatteries.

"And I, my lord Sax, am happy that I have found favor in your eyes. How strangely blue your eyes are. They are the color of the turquoises which we receive in caravans from far-off Persia. See," he stepped toward one of the young men standing near his throne and unhooked the dangling gold ball from him. It was, as Rory could see, set with blue stones, and the king lifted it, comparing their color with Rory's eyes, before he handed it back to its wearer, and resumed his place on the throne.

"Alas, Your Majesty," Baba waited for the king to sit down and for one of the men to place pillows behind his back, "my brother is now in great distress. His servant who accompanies him is sick unto death. We have brought the sick man here for your wise doctors to cure. We knew that if he lived long enough to reach your royal presence, he would not die."

"A servant, my lord Shango? A mere servant? Why then does the golden-haired one bother about a servant? How old is he?"

"About twenty-five, Your Majesty," Rory answered.

"Then it is time that he died. No man, except he be a king or a magician, should live to be more than thirty. We do not believe in old age and death. So let this one die and I will give you ten servants each one better than the man who is dying. Any of my men would be happy to serve a master with hair of gold and eyes of turquoise."

Baba took a step forward, nodding his head wisely. He had remembered something the king had said. "Ah, but, Your Majesty, in this case it is different. Were this man an ordinary servant, we would let him die but he is not just an ordinary servant. You spoke of a man with hair of burnished copper. That is exactly what this man has."

"And does he have a white skin? A skin as white as milk, even whiter than my lord of the golden hair?"

"That he has, Your Majesty."

"Then we shall help him, great Shango, and we trust

162

both he and the white lord of Sax will be grateful. We trust they will show us their gratitude." He turned to Rory. "Will you, my Lord? Will you repay me in that which I ask if I save your servant's life?"

"That I will, Your Majesty. My servant is important to me."

"And to me," the king added. "You say this man here is your brother, my lord Shango? How can that be when your skin is dark and his is light?"

"There is a brotherhood higher than that of blood, Your Majesty. It is that greater brotherhood which exists between my lord of Sax and myself."

The king smiled cunningly as he glanced from Baba to Rory. "Ah, yes"—he closed one eye slowly—"I understand. We here in Basampo understand quite well. Quite well, my lord Shango. Quite well."

Rory had a desire to correct the king's obvious impression, but he decided not to speak. He was anxious that something be done about Tim and he did not want the conversation sidetracked into further ramifications about his friendship to Baba and Baba's to him. Evidently Baba had the same thought.

"Allow me to mention again, Your Majesty, that the man of the copper hair is dying. You know, King Galiah, my sentiments toward you as well as I know yours toward me so, may we dispense with further formalities and have your learned doctors look at the sick man?"

The king made a pretty little moué and slid down from the throne to the dais, pulling one of the young men down beside him and moving the cumbersome phallus so the man could rest his head in his lap. Then openly and without any inhibition he started to fondle the fellow after first removing the golden ball.

"Sick people are so uninteresting, great Shango, but in the case of this man with the copper hair, we must needs do something at once. I had hoped that you and your brother might care to remove your stifling robes and amuse yourselves here while my men bathed you. But, as you say, it is important that we save the man with hair of copper. Is he handsome, my lord Shango?"

Baba nodded in affirmation.

163

"And will he repay me for saving his life?"

This time Rory nodded.

The king continued his manipulations of the man who was lying beside him, quite oblivious to the stares of Rory and Baba. The man arched his body and the king's hands moved faster. As the fellow gasped, the king removed his hand, reached for the napkin that another man handed him, wiped his hands, and pushed his victim away. He summoned another man to him then apparently changed his mind. Instead he spoke to him in a low voice whereupon the man went to the door of the building and let out a loud, ululating screech which Rory felt could be heard back in Scotland. Then the man returned to lie down beside the king.

Once again the king started his dalliance with the new man, ignoring both Baba and Rory, but this time he was not able to complete his manipulations. A fearsome apparition appeared in the doorway and the king removed his hand, pushing the fellow away, and sat up, staring straight ahead. Rory turned, the better to see. One of the figures in the doorway would have been horrible enough, but the sight of some ten of them was frightening. Rory stepped closer to Baba, feeling some protection from this unearthly sight in the big fellow's nearness and unconcern. Except that the figures moved, they bore no resemblance to anything human. They wore tall triangular masks of wood, with horrible grinning features painted on them, through which two eyes regarded Rory and Baba. From neck to toes they were enveloped in long garments of bleached grass, and around their necks they wore gruesome necklaces of monkey skulls, human jawbones, and hundreds of the same dried black objects Rory had noticed hanging from the head guide's spear.

Although Rory had been impressed with the immaculate cleanliness of the village and the interior of the king's house, nay even of his person and those of his courtiers, he was almost overcome by the rank stench of these beings. They smelled of rotted carrion, excrement, and vile sweat, and Rory noticed that the king held a bag of sachet before his nose. But his attitude of reverence to the congregation of rustling, clanking, stinking beings was

164

apparent. It was not only reverence but fear. He spoke to them at length in the unknown tongue, and one by one they replied until the king turned to Baba and in Arabic asked him to have the sick man unloaded from his litter and carried to the open compound. Night had fallen, but the space was brightly illuminated by blazing torches.

When they had laid Tim on the ground, the effects of the opium had been entirely dissipated and poor Tim, dazed and in pain, entirely surrounded by these weird fantastics, reached up for Rory's hand.

"Be they a-going to murder me, Rory lad?"

"They say they are going to cure you."

The king, with the enormous phallus swinging in front of him, came to stand over Tim. He knelt down, the better to see Tim's face.

"He is indeed handsome and he does have hair the color of copper and skin as white as milk. We will save him."

"What are they going to do with me, Rory?" Tim pleaded.

Rory shrugged his shoulders, unable to answer Tim, but when he spoke, his words had a certain assurance.

"I'll be frank with you, Timmy. The way things are, I doubt if you can last through another day. It's up to you, but if I were you, I'd let them do what they can. Baba says they have some sort of black magic, some miraculous power, and they may indeed cure you, Timmy. Just between you and me, this is the damndest place I ever got myself into, and I'll not mind telling you I'm scared half out of my senses, but let's go through with it, huh, Timmy?"

"If you say so, Rory."

But now neither Tim nor Rory had anything to say about it. Outside the circle of firelight, a clatter and a boom of drums reverberated throughout the stillness of the night, echoing from the surrounding huts until the clamor was without beginning or end. In knots of two or three, the inhabitants of the village drifted toward the compound. Even the women, closely guarded by the warriors, were hurrying along with their strange spraddle-legged gait, and were herded together on the opposite side of the canal which encircled the palace compound. None spoke and it was evident to Rory that even these people, who were familiar with rituals such as he was now witnessing, were frightened.

The clamor of the drums continued, increasing in force and tempo until Rory could feel their impact against his eardrums like a pounding hammer. There was some sort of conference among the raffia-skirted doctors around the fire and one of them thrust a spear into the flames. After more excited chattering and wild gesticulating, a semblance of a dance started with one of the doctors leading the others in a clumsy, hopscotching, jigging movement that advanced three or four steps, retreated one or two, and then advanced again. The leader carried a length of grass rope, tufted with parrot feathers, and allowed it to drag on the ground behind him.

Now the ranks of warriors were standing straight and frightened, glancing with downcast eyes at the rope in the leader's hands. The muscles of their arms and legs twitched in nervous tics, and strings of saliva drooled from their mouths. Not until the leader of the procession had passed each trembling warrior did the man relax. However, after having passed all the men, nothing happened. The jigging procession wound its way alongside the canal until it reached the group of women. These, in contrast to the men, did not try to hide their fear but begged and pleaded with the magicians, keeping, as had the men, their eyes on the rope at all times. But still nothing happened, and when the magicians had reached the end of the line of women, they returned to the fire, before which they held another conference.

The king, now seated on a carved stool, surrounded by his courtiers, stood up and came over to where Rory and Baba were standing.

"We are all very happy, beautiful Shango, that none of the men or women of our nation are causing the evil in the man with copper hair. Aye, my lord Shango, he is indeed beautiful with his skin the color of milk and his eyes the color of jade. Now Bora-Boro is sending to the pit to get one of the men there because we cannot lay the blame on any of our warriors. We are glad that none of

166

our people is to blame for the white man's sickness. Now we do not have to sacrifice one of our own men."

"No, Your Majesty," Rory answered the king. "It is I who am to blame for his sickness. I inflicted the wound."

Without answering Rory, the king, unmindful of his dignity, ran to where the magicians were standing and spoke to them. At a signal from one of them, the drums commenced again and the magicians advanced toward Rory with the same jigging trot. When the first man arrived in front of him, Rory heard the drums strike one thunderous high note and then stop. In the awful silence which followed, he saw the limp grass rope suddenly rise from the ground until it stood in the air before him, as rigid as a spear shaft. There was a sudden consternation among the witch doctors and the king, who had come back to stand near Rory, and Baba explained.

"They know now that you are to blame for the evil and they are convinced that you did not inflict the wound with bad intentions. Ordinarily the sacrifice of the man who is to blame for the other man's sickness will cure him, but be not afraid, great lord of Sax, not only are you the brother of the Shango, but you are innocent of all evil. Therefore Bora-Boro will take the man from the pit and put the blame on him. All responsibility for the wound will be taken from you and put in the heart of the man we shall substitute."

While they were waiting, the chief witch doctor removed his mask and Rory was surprised to see a human face emerging from the animated haystack of dried grass. It was the face of an old man, evil and corrupt, but the eyes were those of a man with vast intelligence. It occurred to Rory that this was the only old man he had seen in the village. The fellow came up to Rory, nauseating him with his stench, and gabbled something which Rory could not understand.

"He says," the king interpreted, "that he will demand a payment for curing your servant. He has never seen hair the color of yours and he can make powerful magic with it. He requires only one lock."

It seemed a cheap enough price to pay and Rory nodded his head, whereupon the old man came close to

167

him and, whipping out a knife from under his grassy robes, he cut off a lock of Rory's hair. Slowly he drew it through his fingers, and evidently its silky smoothness pleased him, for he smiled at Rory. He then plucked a piece of grass from his costume and carefully tied the tress, fastening it around the claptrap of his necklace. Looking at Rory and nodding his head knowingly, he began a frantic search among the miscellany of his necklace, finally choosing one of the small round black objects which he cut off and handed to Rory, talking and gesticulating as he did so.

"Bora-Boro does you great honor, my lord," the king whispered to Rory. "He has just presented you with one of the testicles of Amdoola, chief of the Karamangis, who was a very brave man."

Rory bowed his thanks, feeling the leathery thing in his fingers with disgust, then reached inside his djellabah and placed it in the leather bag he wore inside. Now he knew what the things were that dangled from the men's spears and that they wore around their necks. He knelt down beside Tim, reaching for his hand.

"Is it bad, Timmy?"

"Can't stand it much longer. Oh, Rory, give me some more of that stuff to drink. It makes me sleep and I forget the pain."

Rory did not have time to answer. There was a commotion on the other side of the compound and four of the warriors dragged a man into the circle of firelight. Although he might have been a few years older than those superb specimens in the village, he was a strong, well-formed man; but now, in a delirium of fear, he was merely an abject animal, slavering with terror. Nobody paid any attention to his screams and pleas and once again the drums started. The four warriors dragged him over to where Tim was lying and caused the man to kneel by rapping his shins with their spears. He struggled against them but they persisted until he was forced to go down on his knees. Rory himself was kneeling to hold Tim's hand and his face was only inches away from the frightened brute who gazed at him with fear-crazed eyes, babbling his incoherent words.

The drums started on a louder, more frenzied rhythm and now the entire tribe, both men and women, broke into a high-pitched singing which seemed to be merely noise without words. One of the witch doctors seized the spear which had been placed in the fire and withdrew it, red hot, from the embers. Holding it behind his back, he advanced to where Tim rested on the ground and with a motion so quick that neither Tim nor Rory anticipated what he was going to do, he placed the iron in the open wound on Tim's thigh. Tim screamed and struggled to rise but two of the men sat on his shoulders while the spear-blade cauterized both sides of the wound. Then, removing the spear from the wound, the witchdoctor plunged the still-smoking steel into the kneeling man's body, drawing it down from chest to groin. Two more of the witch doctors grabbed at the wretch's body and with their hands, pulled open the trunk, stuffing back his intestines while the victim, still alive, managed to utter faint screams. With the cavity of the torso held open, they managed to force the body down onto Tim's leg, covering the wound. With withes of grass, they bound it tightly over Tim's leg and quickly and neatly disjointed arms and legs, severing them and the head with a dexterity which denoted long practice in butchering. A man appeared with a length of white cloth which the doctors tore into narrow widths and then bandaged the headless, armless, legless torso to Tim's leg until it was entirely hidden from view and appeared only as a gigantic tumefaction.

With their hands forming a litter, the young men bore Tim away and Rory, along with Baba and the king, trailed the jigging, shouting line of magicians. They arrived at a small hut, separated from the palace compound by several canals. The inside was illuminated by the smoking torch and showed a comfortable couch covered with animal skins. Carefully, even tenderly they laid Tim down. Then ensued another chattering conference between the magicians and the king. This time Baba joined in.

"They say the man must stay here for several weeks," Baba turned to address Rory, "until the body of the man they killed rots and putrefies. That is necessary to draw the poison from Tim. We shall have to leave him, but I have arranged with the king that he shall be treated with all the deference that would be accorded to me. Perhaps you had better tell Tim about it because they are going to give him something to make him sleep. These two fellows," Baba pointed to two warriors, "have been assigned to nurse him. They will look after him as though he were the king himself."

Rory knelt on the floor beside Tim.

"Tim lad, can you hear me?"

Tim opened his eyes.

"Aye, Rory, what have they done to me? That poor devil they kilt and tied to me. Oh, Rory, take me away from here. Cut that thing off'n my leg."

"I can't, Tim. They say it will cure you and if I take you away, you'll die as surely as day follows night. I'll have to leave you here but don't fret, Timmy. Baba has arranged for them to take care of you and they'll treat you fine, Timmy. For some reason they want to save you because you have red hair. I don't know what it is but they've got some superstition connected with the color of you hair. I'm not even going to worry about you, for these two lads are going to take good care of you and nurse you back to health. We'll be coming back this way before long and in a few months I'll pick you up. You'll be all hale and hearty, lad. I don't know just what they're doing, but if they're willing to waste a man who'd be worth ten pounds at the coast, they must have something big in mind."

"Then I'll stay here, Rory. It's a long ways from Liverpool to this hellhole, but I'll stay and, by God, I'm going to live too. Don't come in and say farewell to me when you go, though. I might weaken." He essayed a wan smile.

One of the black fellows lifted Tim's head, gently wiping away the sweat with a clean rag. He smoothed Tim's red hair back and Rory could see that the black fingers were touching Tim's face with reverence. The other fellow brought a cup, and the first one, with Tim's head pillowed on his knee, placed the cup to Tim's lips. He drank it and sank back on the bed.

170

"Don't worry about me, Rory, I'll be fine. I'm feeling a hell of a lot better already. I'll be seeing you soon, Rory." Tim's eyes closed and Rory tiptoed out of the hut.

CHAPTER XVI

WITH TIM RESTING COMFORTABLY DESPITE the bandaged horror on his leg—which nauseated Rory every time he thought of it—he and Baba were escorted by their guard of honor to a spacious dwelling, the village guest house. It was situated across from the canal that surrounded the inner circle of the royal palace, a clean and attractive beehive-shaped hut, bright with whitewash. Their escort, stimulated by the recent sacrifice and with the reverberation of the drums still echoing in their ears, jigged as they walked along, their muscles reacting with nervous tics that showed in tiny spasms under their polished skins. Yet for all their exhilaration, Rory detected an ever-present hint of depression in the eyes of the young fellows who accompanied them. The Basampos, he decided, for all their striking beauty of face and powerful physiques, their clean orderly way of living, and their consummate knowledge of black magic, were not a happy people. It was always apparent in their faces. Yet as they danced along this night under the torches of wood saturated with palm oil, even Rory experienced a strange thrill of anticipatory excitement, coupled with an indescribable awe and pity.

When they entered the house, they found it illuminated by standing candelabra which, although not as elaborate as those in the king's house, betrayed their European origin. Two high, carved and gilded beds with mattresses of native silk cotton, nearly filled the interior, leaving only a small aisle barely wide enough for one person to pass in between them. Baba wearily indicated one for Rory and took the other himself. They both sank onto the beds, completely exhausted from the long day's ride and the unbelievable display of witchcraft. But, Baba informed Rory, that was not all he would see. Soon there would be a ceremonial feast and after that the dancing and after that ... well, Baba thought he should explain something about the Basampos to Rory.

They were, as he had previously mentioned, the oldest of the African tribes—true aristocrats of the African Negroes—and so powerful that none of them had ever been captured or sold into slavery, at least until recently. Although they maintained a warrior caste, they never engaged in warfare; nor were they hunters, because they did not eat the flesh of wild animals. Their reputation for black magic was so widely known and so greatly feared that no other tribe had ever dared prey upon them. Baba himself had seen examples of their witchcraft, but of course, as a True Believer, he hastened to assure Rory, he did not believe in it. Nevertheless he could not doubt the testimony of his own eyes. He had seen this same Bora-Boro transfix a man with a baleful stare and watched the man die in seconds. He had heard, although of course he did not put any credence in the story, that at night the Basampo magicians could change themselves into animals—lions, leopards, or other beasts—and that they had the same power to change others into hyenas. That was why hyenas hung around human habitations and why they sounded so much like human beings. They were crying to be transmuted back into men again.

But the strangest thing about the Basampos was that they had no form of marriage rites, and not even a word for marriage in their language. No Basampo man was ever allowed to have sexual relations with a woman. Perhaps Rory had noticed that each woman he had seen in the city—and these women were only servants—wore a strange metal device which was an impregnable chastity belt. Also he must have noticed, because it was one of the most evident things about a Basampo warrior, that all the males were infibulated, although, Baba admitted, the infibulations had now become more of a fashionable doo-dad than anything else. They could be removed in a minute

172

and their main reason was to stretch and increase the size of the men's genitals. However, the iron belts of the women could never be removed, and were worn from early puberty until death. Of course the women Rory had seen in the camp were not the women the Basampos used for breeding; they were only servants. The breeders were kept in another closely guarded city a mile or so away, and these women did not wear the metal guards. They were brought over only on special occasions ordained by either the king or by the magicians. In fact, if the banquet tonight were like others which Baba had been honored with, Rory might see some of them tonight.

Rory was puzzled. If the Basampo men were denied all relationships with women, if the women servants in the city were guarded by metal belts which could not be removed, and if the women who could breed were closely guarded in a city some distance away, how then could the tribe procreate itself? Simple, said Baba. At one time, the king and king alone had sired all the children of the tribe, but that was long ago. Now, Basampo agents were sent to all the slave centers of Africa to choose the finest and most beautiful of all male and female children, for whom premium prices were paid. The usual age of purchase was between six and seven years. Brought back to the women's city, they were carefully tended until they were old enough to breed.

When the time came for mating, no male slave was ever mated with more than three women. Consequently the tribe avoided inbreeding. After having sired three children, the slave was sold to Baba; that is why Basampo was such a valuable trading place for him. The males that resulted from these unions became Basampo warriors at the age of sixteen. The females became servants. Only fresh blood was ever used for breeding. And now, since King Galiah had come to the throne, and that was two years ago when he had reached the age of sixteen, not only were the stud slaves sold to Baba but some of the Basampo warriors as well, as he would explain later.

Then the pit that they had passed was where they kept the stud slaves, Rory said. Baba shook his head. No, those were Basampo warriors who were kept there. When a

173

male member of the tribe reached the age of thirty, he was banished to the pit. This accounted for the look of sadness on the men's faces. Every day brought them nearer to the pit and extinction. Only the king and the witchdoctors were allowed to grow old, for old age was considered loathsome and ugly to the Basampos. When a man's summers totaled thirty, he was consigned to the pit and remained there until the time came for slaughtering him for meat or sacrificing him for medicine. Yes, the Basampos were cannibals and ate human flesh: either male or female, although male was preferred by the men and female by the women. Thus the specially virile parts of a man, such as testicles, penis, heart, and liver were the choice portions, as these parts enriched the parts of the men who ate them. Rory considered that this might be true, for he had never seen such enormously developed men as the Basampo warriors. He had always been proud of his own endowment, but he certainly could not compare with a Basampo.

And the women? Yes, they, too, were consigned to a pit in the women's village—the servants when they reached a certain age and the breeders after they had borne three children.

Rory had still another question. If the Basampos toiled not and merely existed for their few years in this idyllic atmosphere, how then did the tribe support itself? Surely it needed money and a lot of it to support them all in idleness. That it did, Baba answered. They made a levy of gold, ivory, and other valuables on all the surrounding tribes, who were never negligent in paying. They feared the black magic of the Basampos.

But what about the children?

Those were kept in the women's village until it was time for the youths to come to the main village and the girls to come over as servants. Although the Basampos did not practice circumcision—the long foreskins were necessary for infibulation—they did hold an annual ceremony for the youths who had arrived at age that year. After extensive trials, which included fire walking, self-castigation, prolonged manipulation of the genitals to produce a minimum of five consecutive ejaculations, and other practices

174

which Baba said were too disgusting to mention, two youths were chosen and dedicated to the priesthood where they underwent a training that lasted over ten years, after which they graduated as witch doctors. Thus a continuation of the black-magic arts was assured by new blood, the strength of the warriors was maintained in the same way, and the Basampos were always young, handsome, and strong. Surely Rory must have noticed the magnificent physiques of the warriors. By their elimination of age and disease, they at all times presented a tribe of strong young men and healthy females into which neither age nor decrepitude was allowed to enter except for the king and his magicians. In them age was admirable, as it was a sign of wisdom.

Then there were other unusual practices which Baba wanted to warn Rory about, but as he started on these new topics, two youths appeared at the door with an enormous copper pan of steaming water. They were followed by two more with cold water and another carrying some pulpy looking leaves and towels. With profound obsequies they undressed Baba and Rory, bathed them, using the leaves to produce a soapy lather, dried them with towels and then rubbed their bodies with aromatic green leaves. After they had finished, Rory felt an intense stinging and burning in his groin. It was so pronounced and uncomfortable that he mentioned it to Baba, only to be greeted by a guffaw of laughter from his friend.

"They did it to you." He nodded toward the two attendants. "They had some of the leaves of the euphorbium and they rubbed your *mboro* with it. They did it to me too. It's an old African aphrodisiac. It will burn and sting for a while but it won't hurt you although you'll find your djellabah sticking out in front of you as though you had concealed a ramrod under it." Baba pointed to first Rory and then himself. "See! But don't worry, it won't hurt you. It makes a man twice as potent. Come, let's get dressed."

Once again Baba chose imposing robes from the baggage chest, taking as many pains with Rory's as he did with his own. Baba himself sported the green turban of a Hadji because he had been to Mecca, but he insisted that

175

Rory leave the blondness of his hair uncovered for all to see.

Their escorts conducted them around the inner moat and then over a small footbridge into the big center compound where the palace stood. The same fires were burning but the drums were quiet and, as far as Rory could ascertain, there were only men present. He saw none of the women who had attended the witchcraft ceremony, nor did he see any of the magicians. The young warriors were seated in a circle on the ground and the young king was seated on another elaborate throne, this one as long as a divan and piled high with cushions. He stood up as Baba and Rory approached, indicating a place on his right for Baba and on his left for Rory so that all three shared the same divan. They were seated with a flourish of the drums and a din of noise from an orchestra composed of native oboes, wooden rattles, brass European trumpets, pieces of metal banging together, and stringed gourds. There was no attempt at harmony of any kind and yet there was a decided rhythm, like the heartbeat of a huge animal, and it seemed to stir Rory's consciousness with an unusual, inexplicable, brand-new desire. In it he began to sense a little of the great mystery of Africa and he felt his skin crawling with the fear that he alone, as a representative of another race, another age, another culture was about to witness something no white man had ever seen before. He felt his own civilization become puny in comparison with this great and mysterious force, older and far wiser than anything his people had ever known. He was, he could see, not alone in this feeling, for Baba was staring straight ahead with eyes glazed and even the boy king beside him had a strange look of expectancy with nodding head and partly opened lips from which a thread of saliva was pendent. His eyes were curiously glazed and his slender fingers fondled the intricate beadwork on the artificial phallus.

Rory took advantage of the king's vacant stare to study the lad. Strangely enough, although the color of his skin was ebon black, he did not appear particularly Negroid. His hair was not the close-cropped mossy skullcap that was Baba's; it was short and curly but not wiry wool. His nose was finely chiseled without flaring nostrils and his lips, although wide and sensual, were not swollen or blubbery. As Rory regarded him he came to the conclusion that the boy was actually handsome despite the effeminacy of his features and his almost too-graceful mannerisms. He was the only one who was dressed and his robes were even more splendid than those he had worn when they arrived.

After he and Rory and Baba were seated, his courtiers came to stand behind the long divan, one so close to Rory's back that he could feel the heat from the fellow's body. The firelight glinted on black bodies glistening with palm oil, and it gilded dark skins. Yet they were all male bodies—strong young athletes with firm, hard muscles. Rory could admire them for their strength, but he could desire them not a whit.

King Galiah seemed to come back to himself. The faraway look left his eyes and he turned toward Rory, placing one hand on his. It was delicately cared for, with its long, slender, talon-like nails overlaid with gold leaf.

"You are very welcome, my lord of Sax. I have never seen such a beautiful man before. You interest me, my lord of Sax. Tell me, for I am curious, is your body white all over?"

Rory lifted one arm and let the loose sleeve of his djellabah slip down, exposing the even whiter skin of his arm, overlaid with a golden haze of hair which was in contrast to the sunburned bronze of his hand.

"As you can see, Your Majesty."

The dark hand slid provocatively up Rory's arm.

"Your skin is soft, my lord of Sax, but only when I rub it one way. When I stroke it the wrong way, the hair makes it feel less soft than dark skin which is hairless. But I find a coolness to your skin which dark skin does not possess. Perhaps a fire could be lighted under it which might warm it. With us the fire burns all the time so our skin is always warm."

"Have no fear, it can get hot enough," Rory smiled thinking of the intense heat between his legs.

"A little token of my admiration for you." The king slipped a heavy bracelet of curiously wrought gold from his arm and slid it over Rory's hand. "And now, my two

177

lords of Sa'aqs"—he turned to include Baba in his conver--sation—"we dine and I trust the food will fortify you for our evening's entertainment. My men have been waiting for this night, storing up their energy, but tonight we shall break the dam and you will see it spill out in a veritable flood."

From behind the circle of light, a procession of women appeared, all of them in long white robes and each bearing a calabash of food. One glance told Rory that these were not the spraddle-legged women he had previously seen. These women walked straight and tall with regal bearing. Calabashes were presented to the king, Baba, and Rory. They held the dishes in their laps and Rory wondered how the cumbersome appendage which the king wore would allow him to hold the dish, but he saw him untie and remove it. After serving them, the women passed around the circle until there was a calabash of food in each man's lap. When they had served them all they disappeared, to return in a few moments with clay pots on their shoulders. Rory, the king, and Baba were served a potent palm wine in gilded silver goblets, but the other men drank from gourds.

"There is that in the wine which will warm your skin," Galiah again laid his hand on Rory's. "Let us hope it will kindle a blazing fire within."

"To what purpose, Your Majesty?" Rory wished that Galiah would remove his damp, hot hand, but it remained there a long minute. Baba was shaking his head in some warning signal to Rory and Rory understood that he was warning him not to offend the king by taking his hand away.

"The evening is young yet, my lord of Sax," the king gave Rory's hand an affectionate squeeze.

Rory raised his hand slightly, freeing it from Galiah's and adjusting the bracelet. "Your gift is most beautiful." He turned the bracelet to admire it. "And I am most grateful for your hospitality and for your attentions to my servant."

"He of the copper hair is beautiful and he must be saved. And you too are beautiful. But what about me? Do

178

you not think me beautiful too?" The king regarded Rory from under his long lashes.

"I do, Your Majesty. I have just been admiring your beauty."

"Ah, we are indeed a beautiful people, we Basampos," the king's hand made a sweeping gesture to include his warriors. "We are the most beautiful people in the world and the oldest and wisest. We know how to do many things that other peoples do not. We were the first people to inhabit the earth; we came from the moon, and it is from there we brought our knowledge. We never grow old and yet we are older than the world itself. If you were to return here after twenty rainy seasons, you would see that the warriors seated here would not have changed. Only the king grows old because he must bear the burdens of all the others. But I am young now and there are many things I would like to show you."

"I hope to see them all," Rory answered politely, but rather fearful that the king's affection toward him might take another and most distasteful turn.

"Oh, you shall, you most certainly shall. I promise you that. But come, let us eat. Your food grows cold."

Rory dipped his fingers into the bowl. It was a greasy mass of meat, manioc, and vegetables. The first mouthful he carried to his lips had an unusual flavor. It was not unappetizing, although it was highly spiced with pepper and cloves and had a little too much salt—a mark of wealth in Africa where salt is scarce. The meat, cut in small chunks, was stringy but tasteful, and had evidently been roasted before being mixed into the stew. Rory discovered that he was famished and ate quickly and greedily, cleaning his bowl and running his thumb around it to capture the last drops of the rich, greasy gravy. When he had finished, Galiah transferred two bits of meat to Rory from his own bowl.

"A choice part I have been saving for you."

Rory ate them, wondering where the choiceness was for the small pieces of meat were tasteless and rubbery. He glanced across the king's empty bowl to see that Baba had picked out only the pieces of vegetables. Baba's abstinence from the meat made Rory think it might be pork, which

179

Moslems never ate. Well, he had no objection to it; he could even have eaten a second helping, but he did not know if court etiquette would permit him to ask for more.

Now, with the meal finished, the women again appeared bearing calabashes of water and towels.

Galiah excused himself for a moment and left with two of his courtiers, saying that he would be back in a moment and that he was leaving merely to answer a call of nature.

"You ate it!" Baba leaned over across the empty space vacated by the king.

"And why not? I was hungry and it tasted good."

"And you know what it was?"

"Pork, I suppose. I notice you didn't eat it."

Baba shook his head. "Not pork. Man! The meat you ate was a man who was down in the pit, one of those you saw and heard. I suppose you had the choicest cuts. They say that the fingers and the palms of the hands are the tenderest, although the most virile parts are reserved for the king. I warned you that the Basampos were cannibals."

"So you did, but I supposed that was only for special occasions."

"Like this. This *is* a special feast. Galiah even shared some with you and I suppose you know what that was. But don't let it bother you. What's done is done. It's quite common here in Africa. If I were starving I'd do the same thing. Human flesh is a lot cleaner than pig any day. What did it taste like?"

Rory could not answer him. The revulsion to what he had eaten was too much to allow him to dwell on taste or flavor. All he could think was that a few hours ago a man had existed and now parts of him were inside his stomach. And what parts! He swallowed the vomit in his throat and glanced in the direction of Baba's pointing finger.

The music had started again, but it was so entirely unrelated to the booming stridence that had accompanied the witch doctors' trial by rope-end that he had not realized that it had commenced. Now the various instruments which previously had produced only a cacophony of sound were blended in a weird harmony, an emanation

180

from the jungle itself. Rory felt the disgust that had over-whelmed him slipping from his mind and he lounged back on the pillows of the ornate divan, allowing relaxation to ease him. Galiah returned to seat himself between Rory and Baba, pulling them close to himself, so close that Rory could feel the warmth from the king's body through the gold robes. With a seductive smile and a lowering of his lashes, Galiah placed one hand on Rory's knee. Turn-ing to smile at Baba, he placed his other hand on Baba's knee, then commanded one of the warriors to sit on the ground between his own outspread legs.

The warmth of the king's hand on his knee increased the burning sensation in Rory's groin, which had never been absent since his bath. Strange, he thought, that al-though he had not been physically excited in either thought or happening, the burning had of its own accord and most involuntarily on his part, produced an erection which was becoming more assertive as the moments passed. He had never felt this way before without the stimulation of a woman or his erotic thoughts about one, and now he wondered at his involuntary prurience. Had he been alone, he would have been forced to relieve himself. A sidelong glance at Baba disclosed that the big fellow's hands were both in the slits of his robe and judging by the elevation of Baba's robe and the slow movements inside it, Baba was undergoing the same ex-perience as himself. His hands followed the example of Baba's but he found he was unable to rid himself of this persistent engorgement. His fingers had also ascertained another unusual phenomenon—an increased distension which he had never encountered before. But now other things were happening which tended, to some extent, to take his mind off himself.

From the shadows outside the fire, a slow procession entered, pacing in time to the weird music. For the first time since he had arrived in Basampo, he saw naked women—women who were not the duck-waddling females that acted as servants in the kraal. The first thing Rory noticed about them was their long sable tresses, which hung down over their naked bodies, alternately concealing and revealing. Fantastic crude gold jewelry hung from their ears, their necks, their arms and ankles, and the tinkle of the jingling gold, timed to the music, added a further sensual note. Yes, these were women to be desired, from their firm, outstanding, rounded breasts with prominent painted nipples to their protruding buttocks and sleek flanks.

They danced slowly at first, with scarcely any movement of their feet but with a provocative arching of their bellies. The music increased in tempo and volume until one of the black Apollos adjacent to the king's divan stood up to face one of the girls. As though it might have been a prearranged signal, other men from the circle arose until there was a male partner for each of the dancing girls. Rory noticed that the enfibulating appendage had been removed from each man.

Now, with the inspiration of a man before them, erect and pulsating with virility, the dancers redoubled their efforts. Man never touched woman, in fact never came closer than two feet to her, but their movements were as closely intimate as if they had been joined together in an embrace that united their bodies. The couple nearest to Rory claimed his particular attention. The girl was certainly one of the loveliest of all with the smooth rounded skin of adolescence; not quite full grown for she reached only to her partner's shoulders. With her long hair swirling about her hips, she looked down, her eyes fastened on the erect masculinity of her partner. Her mouth was opened wide and her scarlet tongue kept encircling her lips while her hands fondled her breasts. He regarded her through glazed eyes and timed his movements to coincide with hers, thrusting at her while she ground her hips, pantomiming in feverish movements the act of copulation. The dance became wilder, the movements of each more frenzied until suddenly with a high, ululating scream, he spent himself on her, falling to his knees from the violence of the spasm that drained his vigor and quieted his desires. For a moment he swayed, kneeling before her, and then slumped to the ground, prostrate on the hard earth. But the girl, with the smile of a conqueror, backed away only a few paces to make room for another buck to enter the ring and take the place of the vanquished warrior.

Looking beyond the grinding buttocks of this couple, Rory could see that other males were also succumbing and that as soon as they fell to the ground fresh reinforcements were taking their places. The girls seemed tireless for, despite their partners dropping to the ground, they continued as ardently as before, welcoming each newcomer when he entered the contest.

Rory was now beside himself. There was a throbbing in his groin which consumed him like fire and yet he was beyond satisfaction. He felt the warmth of the king's hand slowly making its way up his thigh in warm circles of progress. The royal fingers reached the slit in Rory's djellabah and entered hot against his flesh, seeking then discovering and caressing. He glanced over to discover that the king's other hand was lost in the folds of Baba's robe and saw that Baba's legs were now stretched out straight before him. The man seated at the feet of the king was also slavering over Baba and, although Rory was mindful that the hand that was fondling him was a male hand, he did not dare thrust it away because it belonged to the king. Furthermore, he did not particularly want to, but he was hoping that he would not have to undergo the slavering attentions of the warrior, which Baba seemed so willing to accept. Rory felt his own body straighten out, but whereas Baba's eyes were closed, Rory continued to regard the spectacle before him.

Some of the standing and waiting warriors were not able to contain themselves and yielded to involuntary spasms, sinking to the ground, satiated and exhausted like the others. Just how long it took for the entire assemblage to spend themselves, Rory did not know. Despite Galiah's ministrations, he had been unable to relieve himself and it seemed as though he could no longer contain himself without the release he so much desired. The black fellow on the ground had now turned from Baba to devote himself to Rory and although his attentions were distasteful to Rory, he did not dare to object. He had kept his eyes on the dancing, which had surely started aeons ago and continued throughout his lifetime. When the music came to a sudden stop on a high note in which the drums crashed like thunder, he felt the cessation of the music as

183

an electric shock. In the silence that ensued, the men pulled themselves to their feet, some assisting the weaker to rise. Silently they disappeared into the shadows, and the women followed them. There were none left but Rory, Baba, and the king, together with the warrior seated before them. They were not alone for long before two of the men staggered back from the shadows.

Galiah reluctantly removed his hands and stood up, smiling down at them. At his orders two of the men assisted Rory and Baba to rise, and with Galiah leading the procession, the five of them followed. Rory noticed that the men's steps were uncertain, but whether they were drunk on palm wine or emotionally exhausted, Rory could not tell. He knew only that his own head was whirling and that he had difficulty in walking. He almost felt as though he had an appendage that rivaled the one Galiah had strapped before him.

When they arrived at the visitor's hut, there was a single candle burning inside. While the king stood watching them, the three men stripped Rory and Baba of their robes and sponged their bodies with sandalwood-scented water. Two of the warriors left to stand guard outside the door, and Galiah sat down on Rory's bed while the remaining young warrior sat on Baba's. While Galiah and the warrior engaged in a heated conversation, Baba whispered, "Say or do nothing, my brother. Take what comes along and ask no questions. Oppose nothing. Ordinarily you would be entirely safe here with me, but tonight everyone in the village is drunk on more than wine and I cannot answer for your safety or even my own. Nobody knows what might happen if we were to cross them tonight. Be careful! I can say no more."

Galiah had finished talking to his man, who reached up and extinguished the candle. The interior of the hut was in darkness, and through the doorway they could see the red glow of the dying fire before the palace and the two tall figures of the men standing guard outside. Rory felt a hand reaching for his in the darkness. It pulled him toward the bed and then gently pushed him down on the mattress. He shuddered for a moment, knowing that it was Galiah's and dreading what he knew was going to happen.

184

Ordinarily he would have repulsed any man who wanted to bed him, but tonight he was constrained by two inexorable factors: the fellow beside him was a king and omnipotent, and—possibly a more extenuating reason—Rory's own desire was so painfully unrelieved.

The hand with the long nails reached over to explore Rory's chest. He remained immovable, thinking that passivity might well be his safest procedure, but the hand that was tweaking his paps removed itself, followed down the flesh of Rory's belly until it discovered his hand, lifted it, and moved it to the young king's chest. There was a protruding softness there Rory had not anticipated. His hand moved and he felt, under his fingers, the round outline of a woman's breast and the rigid point of a nipple. He turned on his side toward the king, his hand exploring further. The king, as though to aid him, slipped off his robes and tossed them to the floor, leaning on his elbow over Rory, his round breasts touching Rory's face.

"You are surprised, my lord?"

"You are not a boy, Galiah, you are a girl! Of course I am surprised."

"And you are happy that I am a girl?"

"More happy than you can realize."

"Then you would not care for that particular pleasure with which our good Baba is indulging himself right now?"

"I would not. But tell me—how can a girl be a king?"

"Because a queen would be unheard of in Basampo, yet I alone could inherit the throne. So I must masquerade as a man. And I must make a pretense of being a man even when I give birth to a child. It will be powerful magic to have a king birth a child, but there is one restriction. The child must be born with hair the color of copper. That is why, my lord, I cannot let you father my child tonight. I will satisfy you, my lord, more than you have ever been satisfied before, but it remains for the copper-haired one to put his sperm in me. That is why we must save him. He, and only he, can sire my child. The doctors spoke a long time ago, foretelling his coming, but I would they had foretold that one with hair of gold might father my child." She let her hand slide down over his belly, fasten-

185

ing tightly around him. "I looked at the man tonight while the doctors treated him and I know that he does not support such a palm tree as milord's."

Rory's hand crept down over her glabrous skin, only to be halted by the smooth bandages of silk which encircled her loins.

"It is there for your safety and mine," she whispered. "One or the other of us might yield to a temptation which we could not control. You must not let me remove it in the heat of my desire and I must not let you remove it. No, my lord, we shall resist that temptation but I do not think that you will need to enter me there. There are other ways in which I can satisfy you. Believe me, I have had practice in the arts of satisfying a man. There is nothing for you to do. Lie back, my lord, and let me do what I wish with you. You will enjoy it many times before the sun. Rest, my lord, and let me show you."

Her lips touched his and her exploring tongue entered his mouth while her hands moved over his body. Those slender hands, despite their long nails, were warm and tender and their explorations made him gasp. The hands grasped and clutched, ever moving but seeming to sense just when to stop and allow him time to catch his breath before he exploded. The lips finally removed themselves from his own and started a slow journey over his body, searing it with flame wherever they touched it. No matter how he begged to be released, Galiah denied him. He felt her hot wet mouth envelop him and now he knew he could no longer resist. Sensing his urgency, she tried to pull her head away from him, but he held it, his hands strong in his extreme need. His hips rising, he held her head against him, pushing it down until he heard her choke and gasp for air. He released her momentarily, then allowed her to continue. Now was the moment. Now! His body arched and then sank back onto the bed. Still she did not release him, and his hand which had held her head in a vise now relaxed, content with her kisses until she raised herself, to snuggle into the crook of his arm. In the quiet that followed, he could hear Baba thrashing on the bed and the strangulated breathing of the fellow with him. Then they, too, were quiet and there was no sound in the hut but the breaths that gradually quieted.

A low call from Galiah brought the two guards inside the hut and Rory's fingers touched the hard flesh of a man. What happened after that was a wild phantasmagoria which he was never clearly able to remember. He recalled responding, against his will, to the warmth of lips and the movement of hands and the softness of woman flesh and the hardness of male flesh. He had spent himself once and once again and still he was not satisfied. Again and again he was tortured by indescribable ecstasies; by the moist warmth of places into which he had never ventured before. He became the aggressor and tumbled whatever body was momentarily beneath him into bestial positions he had never dreamed about.

Then, when the first gray streaks of dawn entered the door of the hut, Galiah and the men left, and Rory reached across the narrow space between the beds to touch Baba's hand and make certain that he was still there. After that he slept, but his dreams brought further fantasies. He was no longer Rory Mahound of Sax Castle in Scotland, but some African potentate with a Corybantic hareem. He shed the inhibitions of his own civilization and entered into weird liaisons which, even a few hours before, he would have condemned in others. He explored all the outer fringes of eroticism which he had never known existed previously, until he slept a dreamless slumber which bound up the wounds of desire and quieted him with utter exhaustion.

When he awoke, sunlight was streaming into the hut and Baba was up and dressed. There was nobody else present, and in the sane light of day Rory wondered if the night before had ever really happened. He lifted himself up and then sank back on the pillows. His mouth was so dry he could hardly form the words.

"Tell me, Baba, did I . . .?"

"Day has come, my brother, and it has washed away all memory of the night," Baba grinned.

"I'd never live through another night like that again," Rory propped himself up. "But you seem to think nothing about it."

187

"We in Africa are different, my brother. You said you'd never live through another night with Chatsubah, yet you will. We do not limit our pleasures here in Africa. We realize that there are many things to give us pleasure and we avail ourselves of all of them. Would a man restrict himself to a diet of mealies every day when our land abounds in antelope and buffalo? Similarly, why should a man seek his pleasure in only one way? You have much to learn, my brother."

"But this was different, Baba. I did things I never thought I would or could do. This morning I feel ashamed, dirty, and unspeakably vile."

"We in Islam do not condemn a man for such things. But you had one pleasant surprise. Your little king turned out to be something other than a king after all."

"Yet I sired no royal prince."

"And if you didn't? You found satisfaction, did you not?"

"I did. Never before, not even with Chatsubah, was I so potent."

"You forget the leaves of euphorbium which the men rubbed you with."

"I'll never forget that. It burned like the fires of hell."

"And made you strong as Shaitan. That and the wine, which had the juice of poppies in it."

Rory struggled to get his feet over the edge of the bed. He looked up at Baba and chuckled.

"This plant—this euphorbium—does it grow in Sa'aqs?"

"In quantity, my brother."

"Then we shall not need to take seeds with us and wait for it to grow."

"You're well on your way to being a true African."

"With you to help me, I shall be. Sooner than you think."

CHAPTER XVII

TIM HAD ASKED RORY NOT TO COME TO SEE him before he departed, but Tim was his only link with life as he had always lived it and he had to satisfy himself about him before going ahead into the unknown. When he arrived at Tim's hut, he was happy to see that Tim had come out of his narcotic stupor and seemed much better. His forehead was cool and moist. The fever had left him and he informed Rory that most of the pain had gone from his leg. It still felt sore, but what pain remained was bearable. Poor Tim shuddered when his thoughts dwelt on what was inside the mammoth bandage on his leg. However, even that had been minimized by a brightly hued piece of native cloth that covered it. He essayed a smile at Rory's appearance and waited for one of his two attendants to bring a stool and place it beside his bed.

"Aye, Rory, it's glad I am to see you. My boys are good to me." He gestured to the two fellows who attended him. "Ain't nothing I want but what they do it for me, even to holding a gourd for me to piss in, but nary a word can they say to me. It's good that they're 'round, though; I'd have nobody for company 'cept what's left of this poor devil here," he pointed down to his leg. "That bastard died for me, Rory."

Rory nodded with understanding sympathy. "They all die, Timmy. Even your two pals here will be dead in a few years and they'll have a fate even worse than the lad that's wrapped around your leg." Rory gagged at the remembrance of his supper, and then took a long breath. "I ate one of the buggering cods last night. Goddamn cannibal that I am! Yes, Timmy, I even chewed up his balls, though I didn't know at the time what I was eating.

189

We're in Africa, Timmy, and strange things happen here."
He went on to describe the feast and the dancing of the
night before.

"But that isn't all, Timmy. I slept with the king last
night."

"You, Rory!" Tim sat up, forgetting the pain in his leg.
"You? Now if it had been me, having spent most of my
life at sea, no one would have thought nought 'bout it. But
you who've been a muff-chaser all your life! I can't imagine it." Tim shook his head. "No, me bucko, you bedding
with a boy is too much for me to believe."

"It's not so strange as you might think. The little king
turned out to be a queen."

"Aye yes, Rory, that's what they call 'em, queens."

Rory shook his head. "I didn't mean it that way. This
king is a real queen—a girl—with the nicest pair of tits
you've ever seen and, believe me, you're going to see
them, Timmy. She let me play with them, but the part I
wanted was all bound around and tied up safe and sure so
I couldn't get in. She's saving it for you, my buggerin'
bucko. Yes, you! It seems the next King of Basampo's got
to have red hair. That's what the friggin' witch doctors say
and that's why she's been saving it up, waiting for you to
drop out of the sky. Pretend you don't know, but do your
best, Timmy, when the time comes. I envy you the job.
She's hotter than a poker in a mug of mulled ale. Even if I
didn't screw her, I got it into a lot of places I'd never had
it in before. And, to tell you the truth, Timmy, I did some
other plain and fancy screwing last night such as I've
never done in my life, including two or three of the king's
guards I guess, although I can't seem to remember. Baba
says that everything goes here in Africa. You just put it
into any hot hole you can find. At any rate, I was initiated
into something different, and now that it's over I'm not
shedding any tears. Hell, this is Africa and I may be
humping baboons next. Who knows?"

"At least your first time was better'n mine. A goddamned brownskin Lascar bosun's mate bent me over an
apple barrel. But all cats are gray in the dark and the
main thing is to get yours."

"I'm beginning to think that way." Rory reached down

and gripped Tim's hand. "I'm not going to dilly-dally 'round with any heart-bleedin' tearful farewells, Timmy lad. It's off we go and God only knows where, but we'll be coming back; I don't know when, but Baba won't pass up this place. He gets his best slaves here and saves some of the poor bastards from getting boiled for Sunday's dinner. So get well and get set to stud the little king-queen, and here's hoping you get more in your hand than a pair of bubbies."

Tim clung to Rory's hand, loath to let it go. His eyes were moist but his words were brave. "I'll be after seeing you soon, Rory lad. There's worse things than being the queen's stud, you know. I'm waited on here like Old George himself and, by God, if what you say is true I'm about as much of a king as he is. But don't forget to stop for me, Rory. I'll be glad to get back to being a common seaman after being the queen's fancy boy. Now run along, Rory." Tim released Rory's hand. "Get along with you and don't look back."

The caravan was ready to start by the time Rory had reached the widened circles of the compound. He stopped to chat briefly with the heavily veiled bundles of cloth that were Almera and Chatsubah and then went to mount his horse beside Baba. Soon after leaving Basampo, they quitted the steaming jungles and emerged once more onto broad savannahs of sunburned grass where game was plentiful. The flesh of roasted antelope was welcome after the royal feast, the flavor of which still lingered in Rory's mouth. For several days they enjoyed good hunting and pleasant riding, going higher and higher until the heat became drier and less enervating. They had also left behind the swarms of midges and mosquitoes and the evenings were pleasantly cool so that the warm embraces of Almera and occasionally Chatsubah were welcome.

One night, their camp pitched under a spreading silk-cotton tree with a little brook purling beside it, Baba informed Rory that their days of idyllic traveling were over. Tomorrow, he said, would be the beginning of a grueling journey and, thanks be to Allah the great and the merciful, it would be only two days. Some caravans had to travel through it for weeks. The desert! Yes, tomorrow

191

around noon they would descend the high escarpment down to the desert. Here they would reverse their timetable and camp during the daytime, traveling at night to avoid the worst of the desert heat. Then, after two days of living hell, they would again ascend into and cross over the mountains, where they would shiver in the cold and possibly encounter snow. After that, Baba assured him, they would be in his own country and only three days from Sa'aqs. Tomorrow, at the foot of the escarpment, they would transfer to camels and lead the horses while crossing the desert which, fortunately for them, was only a narrow part of the vast African wasteland. Guides and camels would be waiting for them.

Just as Baba had predicted, early the next morning found them on steep trails leading down through a vast jumble of barren rocks. Below them they could see, shimmering like an ocean, the desert itself—vast, empty, treeless, and forbidding—a dead land that held no signs of life. By noon they had accomplished the descent and come to rest beside a tented settlement whose headman rushed out to greet Baba with respect and affection. But Baba had eyes only for an old man who emerged from a tent and approached them. His pointed gray beard and long straggly moustaches did little to hide a narrow leathery face with a high-bridged aquiline nose and dark eyes that glowed with a fanatical fire.

"This is Sliman," said Baba, "and something unusual must have happened in Sa'aqs to bring him across the desert to meet me."

"It has, my lord Sultan." Sliman ignored Rory. "Something has happened and I am the bearer of sad news for you. Not only is my news sorrowful but filled with danger for you, my lord Sultan."

"You address me as Sultan. . . ."

"Because in your absence Allah sent his Angel of Death to take your father to Paradise, where he is today enjoying the company of the houris."

It was a long time before Baba replied. Try as he could he was not able to hold back the tears, and he clutched at Rory's arm, the fingers tightening convulsively.

"It is the will of Allah," Baba finally spoke. "It was

192

written in my father's book of life. Inshallah! We cannot question the wisdom of the Almighty."

"But it is also written in your book of life, my lord Sultan, that you are to succeed him." Old Sliman was emphatic. "You were his favorite son; the young eagle whom he idolized. Of all his sons, he made you the Shango. It was you he depended on, honored, loved. And now your half brother Hussein has proclaimed himself sultan and swears that you will never reach Sa'aqs alive. He has a following, that villain. Not a big one yet, but give him enough power and he will have. He says that because—"

"Because my mother was a Sudanese, and not that thin-nosed Moorish bitch that spawned him; because he has lived in Cairo and studied at Al Azhar University, while I took slave caravans to the coast; because he thinks he is higher born than I am, I am unworthy of being the sultan.

"He has always been jealous of you." Sliman bowed his head.

"And so Hussein would be sultan. You know Hussein as well as I do, Sliman. Would he make a good ruler?"

Sliman spat on the dirt. "Him? Why do you ask me stupid questions, Baba?" Old Sliman dropped the titles and addressed Baba as a father would a son. "Didn't I teach you both to ride? Didn't I put the first hawks on your wrists? Didn't I teach you to shoot; to seduce the pretty girls of the villages; to conduct yourselves like men in your own hareems; how to judge a slave, and pick the good ones from the bad ones? You were of the same age, you and Hussein, he with his hawk nose and his fair skin and you with your dark. But you were always a man, Baba, even when you were only a colt, and Hussein was always a weakling. The truth does not abide in him. He is treacherous and a liar. His brains are all in his prick, and whoring is all he thinks about."

"We both know Hussein," Baba nodded.

"And so . . . it is Hussein or you. Outside the little circle of friends Hussein has in the palace—those toadying sycophants who fawn over him—all of Sa'aqs wants you, Baba. Just now Hussein has the power because he seized

193

it. He has made himself sultan, awaiting of course the decision of the Ulema in Fez and the word of the Maroc Sultan. Both of these he can buy if he can get you out of the way. He thinks he can control your father's emirs and sheiks and all his men, but we know what they are like, don't we?"

"A hundred men with a hundred different minds. Some of them are faithful to me. Aboukir, for instance."

"Yes, Aboukir and Ibrahin and Saleem."

"How do you know, Sliman?"

"Because they are on the other side of the desert with about three hundred men, awaiting you. We have made plans, Baba, awaiting your decision."

"Then let us start, Sliman. Instead of waiting until sundown, we will start now. We've had a long morning's ride behind us but now I am impatient." He turned to Rory. "Can you do it, my brother? You have never ridden a camel before, and crossing the desert will be hard riding."

"I can do it if you can, Baba, and remember this— when it comes to a showdown I'm a pretty good shot too."

"I may need you." Baba relaxed his grip on Rory's arm. Now he was all business, a real leader. Quickly he and Sliman started to organize the caravan—the transfer of men and stores from horses to camels; the women; the slaves; the long line of horses to be tethered together; the tents and all the other impedimenta that had to be shifted. The sun was just slipping below the horizon when they started out and the heat still lingered on the sands, hitting them in the face with the force of a cudgel. Rory, perched on his pitching camel, could not seem to adjust himself to the awkward stride of the beast. He clung to the high wooden saddle with both hands, sweating under the three heavy layers of wool burnooses Baba had insisted that he wear. His head was swathed in a curiously wound turban, whose loose folds encircled his face, and his hands were discommoded by heavy woolen mittens. The costume would have been far more appropriate on a frosty morning in Sax than in the stifling heat of the desert, but Rory found, as the night passed on, that the desert could be

194

even colder than Scotland, and what had only a few hours before been a fiery furnace quickly cooled to a still cold that seeped through the thick layers of wool.

Tonight, for the first time, Rory rode alone. Baba and old Sliman were ahead, their camels plodding along in measured steps and their conversation seemingly unending. Rory realized the seriousness of the situation not only for Baba but for himself. As the Shango of Sa'aqs, Baba had all the power of his father, the sultan, behind him. If he could overthrow his brother Hussein and seize the reins of government, he would again be powerful. But what if he lost? If Baba lost what would happen to Rory? He did not dare to think about it. Nor did he wish to think about Baba's death. Outside of Old Jamie who had been a father to him, and Tim who treasured his friendship, Baba was the only friend Rory had ever had. Now he was not only Rory's friend but his sole protector.

The stars came out—brilliant diamond-headed pins stuck in a vast pincushion of black velvet. Then the moon appeared, a scrubbed tin plate of pale light that illuminated the waste stretches of desert with an unearthly radiance, etching the shadows of the rocks in black against the pale silver of the arid land. The shadow of the camel on which Rory rode was a traveling inkspot that momentarily dyed the desert and then moved on. He felt strangely alone in this world of gray and black which, discounting the caravan, was empty, lifeless, and above all soulless.

After several hours, Rory finally adjusted himself to the heaving motion of the camel. By coordinating his body to that of his ungainly steed, he found a certain degree of comfort in riding, although it was far removed from the easy seat of his horse.

Several times since the moon had risen, Rory saw the bodies of men stretched in the flinty gravel along the route. Some were merely bleached white skeletons with grinning skulls; some were in a bad state of putrefaction, picked almost bare by vultures; and some, although bloated and misshapen, were still recognizable as humans. Later, when they passed a slow-moving caravan of slaves going in the opposite direction, Rory surmised that the men beside the road were dead slaves from a previous caravan, for in the passing procession he saw a hundred poor devils, roped neck to neck, plodding along in the last stages of exhaustion, whipped into brief moments of activity by the mounted Arabs who rode along beside them.

It was not long after they had passed the last of the straggling line of slaves that Rory saw the form of a black man showing plainly against the moon-etched phosphorescence of the flinty gravel. When Baba and Sliman passed, the man raised himself on his elbows, struggled to his feet, and advanced a step, holding out his hands in supplication, then sank down again, first to his knees and again supine on the sand. When it came Rory's turn to pass him, the man made a final effort and again struggled to his feet. This time he was able to reach the side of the camel; he hooked his hand into one of the ropes and then succumbed again, his body dragging alongside.

Rory halted his camel, clinging to the saddle as the ungainly animal knelt and squatted on the ground. The slave seemed unconscious but as Rory loosened his hand from the rope his eyes opened. He could not summon up strength to speak, but his eyes, white in the moonlight, pleaded with Rory not to abandon him. Rory heaved the heavy body—for he was a big fellow—up into the saddle, climbed on behind, and prodded the beast into rising. The camel, resentful of the double load, bellowed and turned his long neck to bare long yellow tushes, but Rory, using the little goad that Baba had given him, prodded the camel and once again they started.

It took all Rory's strength to encircle the man and get his hands on the high pommel. He felt a stirring of life in the inert body and the man sat up. Rory placed the fellow's hands on the pommel and when he felt the man could support himself momentarily, he reached for the skin of water that Baba had hung on the saddle. With difficulty he managed to withdraw the stopper and, timing his action to the camel's steps, he held it before the Negro's lips, dribbling it into his mouth. The water somewhat revived the man and he spoke for the first time, muttering guttural sounds that Rory supposed were words. However when he had finished the water, his

196

strength returned and he sat up straighter, no longer a dead weight in Rory's arms. He was naked, without even a loin cloth, and his whole body was shaking with the intense cold. Rory stripped himself of his outer burnoose. It was no easy matter while he was trying to hang onto the man in front of him, but he finally succeeded and slipped the heavy garment over the slave's head. Now, warmed by the burnoose and revived by the water, he sat upright in the saddle, pulling Rory's arms around his waist. Occasionally he babbled in an unknown tongue and turned around to reassure Rory with a glittering smile that he had recovered.

The caravan halted for a brief spell at a waterhole—merely a deep black well in the desert with three ragged palms near it. Here they ate a frugal meal of crushed barley in oil and dried dates, washed down with brackish water from the well. When Baba walked over to see how Rory was standing the trip, he was amazed to see his black companion. Rory explained that he could not abandon the man to die, and Baba, calling Sliman, produced another camel.

"You have an affinity for the sick and the ailing, my brother," Baba laughed. "No sooner do you rid yourself of Tim than you adopt another. We'll look at him when we halt at morning light. If he's no good, we'll put a quick end to his suffering," he tapped the hilt of his sword. "In the meantime one camel cannot carry two. Inshallah! Perhaps the All Merciful does not wish this man to die tonight."

Again they started, but now the going was easier. The fellow rode beside Rory throughout the rest of the night until the stars faded and the rose of dawn appeared in the east. Then, when the fiery ball of the sun reached above the horizon, the caravan halted. The tents were put up and they crawled under them for shelter. A fireplace of stones was built outside the tent and soon there was the delicious odor of coffee brewing. The black had never left Rory's side, and now, with the light of day, Rory could see that he was a young man, not more than twenty-five, tall, strong and intelligent-looking. He was pure black—the prune black of undiluted African blood—but in spite of his flattened nose and broad nostrils, his thick lips, tight-curled hair, and low forehead, he was good-looking, even of noble aspect. His dark brown, doelike eyes never left Rory's face. Baba, leaving off his interminable conversation with Sliman, came to where Rory squatted sipping his coffee.

"T think you've picked up something pretty good, my brother." Baba motioned for the man to stand up. "A Kasai. I would judge, and they are rare around here. I've not seen many of them, but they have the reputation of being among the greatest fighters in Africa." He spoke to the man in a dialect Rory could not understand and in answer to his words, the fellow pulled his burnoose up over his head. He was thin. Each of his ribs showed on his emaciated form, but even with his extreme thinness, one could see that there was great power in his well-muscled body. Baba ran a practiced hand over him, judging by his fingers the musculature of the man's body, the soundness of his teeth, and the fellow's response to his impersonal manipulation of his genitals. All the time he kept up a running conversation with him and when he came to the swollen ankle, Baba nodded his head understandingly. He pointed to Rory, turning to Rory.

"He is a Kasai, just as I surmised. He's a fine specimen and in pretty good condition, considering that he's half starved. All that's wrong with him is that he's got a badly sprained ankle and can't walk far. Nothing that can't be cured, and a few good meals of hot couscous will put meat on his bones. You've picked well, Rory. The fellow likes you and wants to serve you." Baba went into the tent and came back with a length of white turban muslin. This he tore into narrow strips and bound them tightly around the man's ankle. He pointed through the opened flap of the tent to a rug beside Rory's couch and the fellow stretched himself out on it.

"That makes three slaves you own, my brother. Soon you will be acquiring a caravan of your own."

"Three, Baba?"

"Yes, you've got Mleeka here—that's what he says his name is—and there's Almera and Chatsubah. We won't disturb either of them this morning. Today we shall need

198

all the sleep we can get because tomorrow night we should arrive at Aboukir's camp before light, and then we shall have no sleep because Sliman tells me that Hussein has started from the city of Sa'aqs and is advancing to meet us. He has a thousand men and we shall have a little over three hundred, but we will beat him."

"And if we don't, Baba?"

"That also is written. *El mektub mektub.* It will be as it will be. He will kill me. If he captures me he will kill me slowly, hoping that I shall be weak and cry out so that all will know that I am a coward and not worthy to rule Sa'aqs. But he will kill me in the end, have no doubt about that, because he would not dare to let me live." Baba shook his head with ominous portent. "As for you, my brother, he will sell you into slavery. With your white skin and yellow hair, you will bring a good price from some emir or pasha who wants a Mameluke slave. You are too old for a bed boy but you would make a good soldier. But do not fear, Rory. Hussein is a jackal, a hyena, a coward. All the men that he leads know what he is. We will defeat him and you will be safe. So sleep! This Mleeka will sleep beside you and guard you. He has already pledged his life to you and he will be faithful. As for me, I shall sleep if I can take the time. I have many more things to discuss with old Sliman."

Rory sought his mattress and sank down upon it, glad of the opportunity to stretch out and soothe his aching muscles. His hand dangled over the edge of the mattress and came to rest on the wiry skullcap of the man on the ground. A black hand clutched his own and held it tight in a warm grip. The words that Mleeka spoke, Rory could not understand; but he knew the significance of the gesture as the man moved Rory's fingers from his eyes to his ears to his mouth and then clasped them around his throat. Mleeka was trying to tell him that he belonged to Rory, body and soul.

Rory's eyes closed and he slept.

CHAPTER XVIII

ALL THROUGH THE BLINDING HEAT OF THE day they rested, and although the black mohair of the tent shadowed them from the incandescence of the sun, it gathered the heat into itself so that the interior of the tent became as stifling as an oven. Following the bitter cold of the previous night, the intense heat of the day seemed even more difficult to bear. Erratic gusts of wind, instead of cooling, were like blasts from a furnace, parching the skin. Rory sweated in his nakedness on the too-soft mattress and then abandoned it for a linen sheet spread on a rug. Mleeka, exhausted, slept despite the rivulets of sweat that channeled over his black skin and soaked the blanket beneath him.

Baba entered the tent long after Rory, shucked off his clothes in a damp heap on the floor, and threw himself on his couch. He did not sleep but stared with open eyes at the black ceiling of the tent and Rory, realizing his friend's grief, did not attempt to break in on his sorrow. Rory somehow sensed that his silence and his proximity were more eloquent to Baba than any words could have been. When eventually Rory found some rest in a disturbed half-doze and then became fully awake, Baba had quitted the tent. Rory realized he was sitting beneath the shadow of the upraised flap, conversing with old Sliman. Their heads were conspiratorily close together, and although they were speaking low Rory could not avoid hearing their conversation.

"It is hard for me to believe it of Mansour," Baba sighed. "He is my own brother, the son of my mother and father. Of Hussein, yes, for he is a worthless cockatrice, more like his Moorish mother than our father." He shook

200

his head in disbelief and his eyes rolled back, showing the ivory-tinted whites. "But of Mansour, whose blood is my own, I cannot understand such treachery." He continued to shake his head with incredulity.

"Yet, whether you believe it or not, my son, it is true." Sliman's solemn, grim-lipped nod confirmed his words. "The young Mansour is Hussein's most trusted lieutenant —fawning on him, calling him 'my lord Sultan,' denouncing you, and swearing that no black skin, nay, not even his own, should have the right to rule Sa'aqs."

"And my mother?" Baba asked fearfully.

"Alas, she, too, is hand in glove with Hussein. It was she who pushed Mansour into Hussein's arms. She has denounced you bitterly while at the same time lavishing praise and flattery on Hussein."

"I lost a father and I gained one in you, Sliman. I lose Mansour and I gain a brother in the fair-haired N'zrani. But I can never have another mother. Now that she has turned against me, I do not want to go back to Sa'aqs. Why should I want to be sultan? It would be better for me to return to Rinktum Castle and go with my white brother to his lands overseas. Believe me, I have no desire to embroil myself in a thousand palace intrigues or to defend myself against the sons of my father who are more numerous than the sands of the desert. He spawned sons like a lion and the palace is full of them, each one like Hussein, wanting to strangle me with a silk cord while I sleep. No, Sliman, without the love of my mother and Mansour, Sa'aqs means nothing to me. I shall not return. Instead I shall go back to Rinktum Castle and take a ship. My white brother is a great lord in his own country and his land of Sax will be mine also."

To Rory, listening to their words, the awfulness of his deception came home to him. Outside of the empty title to Sax and the ruined, roofless castle, what had he to offer Baba in case Baba should come to him? Nothing! Now he regretted his lies and the role that Sparks had forced upon him. Better that he go to Baba and confess the truth—but no, Baba had enough troubles now. There would be time for that. He turned over, not wanting to listen further to the conversation; but it was unavoidable.

"You cannot abandon Sa'aqs to Hussein." Sliman was speaking.

"No, that I really cannot do. I owe that much to my father." Baba sighed. "I shall heed your words, even though I do not desire to. They are wise words, my father. I would be a jackal to abandon Sa'aqs to Hussein. It is either he or myself. I will kill him first and then strangle Mansour. My mother too! She must die. Perchance it is written, however, that they will kill me. *Kismet! El mektub mektub!* If it is written, we cannot change it. When shall we begin, Sliman?"

"As soon as the sun sinks below the horizon. We should arrive at the edge of the desert before the sun rises again and then we will have news from Aboukir who awaits us there." Sliman bowed his head and stood up. Baba sought refuge again under the tent and Rory, ashamed of his eavesdropping, feigned sleep.

All that night Rory, with Mleeka riding beside him, guided his pitching camel over the cold moonlit vastness of the sands. About two or three hours after their midnight halt the sand began to disappear and the camels walked on stretches of sparse grass until these gave way to stronger turf, then to thorn shrubs, and finally, as the sun streaked the sky, Rory saw the feathery fronds of date palms etched against the light and the whitewashed domes of a village.

Suddenly he heard shouting and clamoring interspersed with volleys of gunfire, and from the walled village a horde of men mounted on horses charged toward them. They were certainly not enemies. Rory could see that they were firing their guns into the air and as they came nearer he could distinguish Baba's name in their shouts. Leading the sortie was a young man whose white robes floated behind him and whose long musket spat flame into the air. When he drew nearer, Rory could see that he was black and the resemblance to Baba was unmistakable. Baba, still mounted on the camel, called for his horse, but before it could be brought, the young fellow was before him. Baba's only weapon was the curved dagger that he wore; yet he leaped down from his camel, sprang at the fellow's horse, grabbed it by the bit, and with a strong grip

202

on the young fellow's burnoose pulled him to the ground, holding him there with one foot on his chest.

"I said I would kill Hussein first and then you, Mansour, but Allah decrees otherwise. You die first! But before I kill you I want to tell you how much pleasure I shall have in cutting your throat. Nay, that is too good for you. I shall strangle you with my own hands."

The man on the ground laughed up at Baba, showing two rows of strong white teeth. "Put away your dagger, brother." He arched his back and tried to dislodge Baba's foot. "And take your damned big foot off my chest. Is this the way you receive the son of your mother and the son of your father? I am your brother, Big Baba—your own brother, you great gorilla."

"You are no brother of mine, traitor."

Again Mansour laughed. "How could I be a traitor to you?"

"Do you want me to believe that old Sliman would lie to me?"

"Of course not. Sliman would never lie, but he doesn't know everything."

"He says you are a traitor, working with Hussein."

"How true! I *have* been working with that jackal, that despoiler of infants. But I am not a traitor. Hearken! When our father died—may his soul enjoy the delights of Paradise—Hussein, that violator of little boys, proclaimed his own putrid self sultan. His first thought was to murder my mother and me. Ah, but remember one thing, big Baba! Our mother is wise with the wisdom of her race. She called me to her and told me to go to Hussein, that devourer of camel-dung, and prostrate myself at his feet and kiss the toe of his stinking babouche. She bade me swear fealty to that buggerer of hyenas and to denounce you, as she was prepared to do herself. And so I did and so she did, and that stupid goat-lover was so pleased that he made me captain over his forces. That shows how stupid he is. So then our mother and I made our own plans. She left the hareem at night and together we approached the men of Sa'aqs and convinced them that you, not Hussein, should be sultan. Believe me, it took precious little convincing. We waited until we heard news of your

203

approach and then I entered Hussein's hareem one night, dressed in the robes of my mother. Ay, big Baba, but I made a bewitching houri. Hussein gave up trying to woo his yellow-haired N'zrani slave and started to dally with me but he did not figure on the pistol I carried under my robes. I took him prisoner. I marched him at gunpoint from his hareem and secured him in the lowest dungeon of the palace where he is well guarded day and night by those who wish you to be their sultan. I came on ahead to tell you the news and what a reception I get! Now will you remove your foot, which is as big as that of an elephant, from my chest and let me stand up and take a breath so you can embrace me and tell me what a smart fellow I really am!"

Baba reached down and pulled Mansour up, clasping him in his arms. Pandemonium broke loose. Rory found himself in the midst of a yelling maelstrom of men, all desirous of touching Baba, kneeling before him, cheering him, and offering him their swords. The young Mansour, who had no idea who Rory might be, stood beside him, staring at him with suspicion, until Baba, between accepting the homage of his men and trying to secure a breathing space for himself in the press, had a moment to tell Mansour about Rory and then Mansour, so like his brother, embraced Rory. With this evidence of approval, Rory found himself accepting the homage of those men who could not get close enough to Baba. Through it all the black face of Mleeka grinned at them, and the slave, suddenly transformed from a dying wretch in the desert to a man of prominence in the turbulent crowd, seemed transported to another world.

Gradually the tumult died down and some semblance of peace was restored, sufficient to enable them to mount and ride into the village where their entry precipitated another riotous reception. Then they were granted a brief respite while they washed away the dust of the desert in the local *hammam* and dressed in clean robes. Afterwards they ate a breakfast of dates and bread, washed down with black Arabian coffee, then mounted their horses again. The high-pommeled saddle was a great relief to Rory after the pitching of the camel. It took most of the day for their shouting, triumphal march to reach the city of Sa'aqs.

It was a larger city than Rory had anticipated, sprawling over the dusty ground in a maze of narrow streets that wandered between windowless walls. The huge gateway through which they entered was faced with multi-colored tiles and fretted with plaster arabesques, but the wall itself was merely pounded dirt, streaked in places with wide crevices where the rains had channeled deep furrows. Like the walls, the city itself was of pounded dirt—thick-walled, square houses, some of them limed to a brilliant whiteness, some of them the dun color of the earth. The streets were narrow and winding, ankle-deep in offal and emitting an ancient stench that was overwhelming. At times the extreme narrowness of the streets made necessary their riding in single file. Baba and Mansour were now far ahead of Rory with a column of shouting men between them, but Mleeka kept close to Rory and Rory felt a certain amount of protection from the man who rode behind him. That Rory was a N'zrani and a foreigner was apparent, and some of the wild-eyed followers of Baba, who had now worked themselves into a hysterical frenzy, mistook him for a Christian slave that Baba had purchased and was bringing back to Sa'aqs. They spat on him and reviled him as a Christian dog and some, their eyes blazing with fanaticism, made threatening gestures. Nobody, however, actually touched him and at one of the turnings in the maze of alleys, he found Mansour waiting for him. From that time on, with Baba's brother beside him, he received no further insults and the stares were no longer virulent but friendly or curious. He could not help wonder what life would be like had he actually been a slave in Baba's retinue. His skin crawled and he shuddered. Then he dismissed the thought. He was Baba's friend; nay, more, he was the friend of the sultan.

The palace of the Sultan of Sa'aqs, at least from the outside, was larger but even less impressive than that of the Baron of Sax in Scotland. It presented merely a high, crenelated wall of whitewashed mud with an azure-tiled, tulip-shaped gateway leading to an inner court. The court, once they had entered the narrow gateway, proved to be

205

nothing but a large expanse of hard-packed ground, bounded by another high wall whose only opening was a large double doorway of worn cedar planking, embossed with enormous spiked rosettes of iron upon which a man could be impaled. (Later Rory was to discover that this was indeed their purpose.) They halted at the doors, which swung open with a creaking of unoiled hinges. Exhausted from the confusion and shouting of the day's ride, Rory welcomed his descent from his horse and the comparative quiet of the dim corridor which led to an inner courtyard. Here the heat, sweat, racket, and confusion had never penetrated. There was the tinkling music of a fountain that sprayed a jet of water into a tiled basin; the singing of birds in cages; the perfume of orange blossoms, and the dappled coolness of shadows. The stark severity of the outside of the palace was offset by the calm of the courtyard and the fusty lavishness of the interior.

Baba extricated himself from the adulation of the palace hangers-on and made his way through the press to Rory. "Rest, my brother," he laid a protective hand on Rory's shoulder. "Tonight there will be more festivities and you will need your strength. I shall install you in Hussein's apartments. Everything in them is yours. As you never knew him, you will not object to wearing his clothes or his jewels, so help yourself to anything you desire. He lavished much money on his appearance and he was much of your size. Choose the best of them for tonight because, while Mansour sits on my right hand, you will be on my left. Pick out something suitable for your Kasai, who will stand behind you. There will be feasting and drinking. On a night like this even Moslems have a fondness for palm wine. Later we shall judge Hussein. Rest, Rory, until I send for you; and then I shall make it known to all Sa'aqs that my guest, the Lord of Sax, is my brother."

A young black slave in robes of spotless white conducted Rory, with Mleeka following, through a maze of open courtyards, dim hallways and roofed galleries until they arrived at a wing of the palace which seemed of later construction than the rest. Here the floors were of glazed tiles and the windows had slatted jalousies that tempered the glare of the sun. Rory saw evidences of European

206

furnishings that looked as incongruous in this palace as
they had in the reed huts of Basampo. He noted an
ormolu-and-crystal clock, a lifesize marble of a nude Gre-
cian nymph, and tawdry, gilded French chairs that accomplished a certain purpose in relieving the monotony of the
divan-lined walls of the rest of the palace. They passed
through several rooms, all more or less elaborately furnished, until the slave stopped before a polished wooden
door, opened it, and bowed low for Rory, followed by
Mleeka, to enter. This room, too, contained a strange
hodgepodge of Moorish and European furniture. It
boasted a huge bed that would have done justice to a
Venetian *palazzo,* and Rory was intrigued by the blatantly
pornographic paintings of Greek gods and goddesses on
the towering headboard. Thick eastern rugs covered the
floor; low tables of dark wood glowed with the dull
iridescence of inlaid nacre; hangings of shot silver gauze
shrouded the windows and—this brought a smile to
Rory's lips—sitting importantly alone on a silver inlaid
table, a lidded chamber pot proclaimed its Staffordshire
origin with its liver-colored decorations.

With a languid wave of his black hand, the slave
opened another door and Rory entered a smaller room
with a sunken bath, its walls lined with cedar chests.
When opened, they disclosed sumptuous stuffs which he
took to be the unfortunate Hussein's wardrobe. Unable to
communicate with Mleeka, Rory detained the youth who
had brought him.

"My slave does not speak Arabic and I cannot make
him understand," Rory nodded in the direction of
Mleeka. "Will you attend me?"

"But of course, if my lord commands. I am Oma. Your
slave is stupid, my lord. What business does one who so
recently picked cow dung from between his toes have in
attending so eminent a personage as yourself? He is nothing but a bush nigger and has never been in a house
before. He has no refinement and will probably piss out of
the window and shit on the floor, for he has no knowledge
of how civilized people live. Besides, he stinks like a
baboon. He is also lame, for he walks with a limp. Why
do you not sell him? He is worthless. The great Sultan of

207

Sa'aqs has given me to you and I am a civilized person who knows all the ways of palace life. So, let me take this ape down to the slave market and sell him. He should bring at least ten pieces of silver, worthless though he is."

"And of those ten pieces of silver, how many would you keep?" Rory regarded the fellow, really looking at him for the first time. He had an engaging grin that showed a row of white teeth; his eyes were kohl-darkened and his fingers henna-stained. He was as slender as a willow wand and had a lighter skin than Mleeka's. Although Negroid, he had a finely arched nose and he emitted an almost overpowering odor of jasmine.

Oma considered for a moment before answering. His smile was sly but engaging. "For myself, my lord, I would not keep more than two. I am very honest."

"But we shall not sell Mleeka, no, not even for twenty pieces of silver, for I believe him to be more honest than you. It will be your job to teach him how to serve me. I shall teach him my own language so that he can talk with me and with nobody else. See! I shall teach him one word now." He turned to Mleeka and beckoned. "Come, Mleeka!"

The big black hesitated a moment.

"Come here, Mleeka," Rory beckoned with a crooked index finger and pointed to a spot on the floor in front of him.

"Come," Mleeka answered and walked over to where Rory was standing.

"You see, he is not stupid, Oma. So you shall teach him everything you know. Now, prepare a bath for me and show Mleeka how to do it. When I have finished you will show him where to bathe so that he will no longer stink. He will sleep here in this small room beside my own, but you must tell him where to go for his food and where to obtain mine if I wish to eat here alone."

"I will teach him, my lord, but . . ."

"But what?"

"With ten pieces of silver—"

"Only eight if you keep two."

"With eight pieces of silver you could buy a slave girl. Not a very good one perhaps, but a young one of ten or

208

eleven years. They are the best because their slits have not been opened and they have a certain wonderful tightness —"

"That you would like to try I suppose. No." Rory was firm. "Mleeka is not for sale and if I buy a slave girl I prefer one that is not a child."

"My lord will learn that Oma is right." He grinned, showing all his teeth, then made an obscene gesture of grabbing the finger of one hand tightly with those of the other and slowly moving his finger back and forth. "Aye, my lord is young now; as he grows older he will want younger girls until the time comes when only very little girls will appeal to him. But now, of course, my lord is young and full of fire, straight as a ramrod, big as my arm, and as hard as a steel spear. So, he does not need the narrow slits that old men crave."

"The bath," Rory reminded him.

"Ah yes, the bath! I shall teach this black baboon how to prepare it. While you wait, my lord, let me divest you of those sweaty rags. Do you hunger? See, here are black figs, honey-beaded with sweetness like the lips of a Nubian wench. Here are oranges as round and small as the breasts of Persian girls. Here are melons as big as the tits of a Mandingo female. And, my lord, here are pomegranates that split open to show a red inside like that pretty cleft that all men desire. Aye, and there are bananas which stand upright like the yard of a young lad from the Mahgreb, and here are hazelnuts which are like those in the precious pouch he carries. There is much here for you to enjoy while you wait for your bath, and after you finish, I shall work on your body with my hands and rub it with nard and perfume it with oil of sandalwood and bergamot so that you will excite the senses of your partner from the hareem."

"But I have no hareem," Rory answered.

Oma winked at him. "The hareem of the traitor Hussein is panting for a man and the palace gossip is that the sultan intends to give it to you. This was Hussein's apartment—and see!" Oma separated the gauze curtains and lifted the jalousie.

Rory stepped out on a balcony and looked down on a large courtyard where unveiled women walked.

"Were they not for you, the sultan would not have given you these apartments." Oma slipped off Rory's travel-stained burnoose and motioned to Mleeka to take off the inner djellabah and kaftan. When these were removed, Oma knelt before Rory, untied the string that gathered the voluminous trousers around his waist and let them fall to the floor. Calling Mleeka to him, he showed him how to remove Rory's slippers and how to rub his feet with a coarse towel.

Rory laid his hand on Mleeka's head, touching it lightly. Then, much to Oma's surprise, Rory knelt before Mleeka and touched the bandaged ankle.

"Better?"

Mleeka did not comprehend for a moment and Rory repeated the word, nodding his head in assurance. A light spread over Mleeka's face. Now he understood the strange word. He walked a single step to show Rory that he was not limping as badly as before.

"Better," he answered seriously, then smiled to show Rory that he not only understood the English word but that he would never forget it. "Better," he repeated.

"What does the N'zrani word mean, my lord?" Oma was not to be slighted.

"Ah." Rory look at Mleeka, then turned to Oma and shook his head. "That is something that only Mleeka and I understand."

CHAPTER XIX

THE FEAST THAT NIGHT, HELD IN THE VAST outer courtyard of the palace, was a phantasmagoria of flaming torches, huge platters of couscous, whole roast sheep and sticky honey cakes. All of this was served more or less haphazardly in between dashing sorties of white-robed horsemen who raised clouds of dust as they charged directly at the diners, stopped short, fired their guns into the air with deafening reports, and wheeled their horses to gallop off. It was a scene of utter bedlam—the flickering lights, the incessant movement, and the yelling mob that greeted each sortie of horsemen with howls and high-pitched screaming.

Rory, decked out, he felt, like a Glasgow tart, sported a white djellabah over a sulfur-yellow taffeta kaftan so heavy with gold embroidery it scratched his skin even through his undershirt and the voluminous drawers that he wore. Oma had wound yards and yards of thin white muslin around his head, stuck in a spray of white heron plumes, and pinned them with Baba's ruby, which glowed like a coal of fire. Rory was seated at Baba's left, Mansour on his right. It was evident from the homage paid to him that Rory ranked third in importance that night with Baba playing the leading role and his younger brother a close second. Eating was quite out of the question, for the apparent goal of the horsemen seemed to be to see who could bring their mounts nearest to the platters of cous-cous without stepping into them. Each time it appeared to Rory that the rider would plow through the middle of the platter nearest him, and even though after several frights he discovered that they would not, he was still unable to convey any food to his mouth and he spilled more on the silk kaftan than he succeeded in eating.

Baba stood up and clapped his hands. Suddenly the whole character of the feast changed. The sorties ceased, the shouting was silenced and even the smoking torches seemed to flicker less as four gargantuan Negroes dragged in the pitiful figure of a man and flung him on the ground before Baba. He was so weighted with chains that he could scarcely stand, but the Negroes hoisted him up, supporting him in their arms. Rory could see that he was a young man, tall and slender with a narrow face that attained a degree of good looks despite the hawklike nose and thin lips. He was naked except for a twist of soiled loincloth, and Rory noticed the welts of dried blood across

211

the pale ivory of his body. When he opened his mouth to plead with Baba, there was nothing but a gaping black hole. His teeth had been knocked out, leaving only broken stumps behind his lips.

"Welcome to our feast, Hussein, my brother." Baba tore a chunk of meat from the carcass of the sheep and flung it at him. "You are late for my celebration and you are not dressed in a style that does any particular honor to me. But I forgive you, even though I must admit that iron chains do not become you as do silken kaftans. You have come to pay homage to the new Sultan of Sa'aqs. Ah ha! The title is not unknown to you. You have enjoyed it briefly, so it is no novelty to you. But alas, Allah in all his wisdom and mercy has seen fit to hand the title over to me and now I am sultan instead of you. Rightly so, Hussein. Our father meant for me to be sultan or he would not have made me Shango. But I digress. I am lacking in good manners, for I have not introduced you to my grand vizier, my esteemed brother Mansour, who is as black as I am. Nor to my other brother, the great Lord of Sax, who is far whiter than you. I am a fortunate man to have two such brothers, and my greatest regret is that I do not have another by the name of Hussein who might well be sitting here beside me had he not tried to kill me and take away my birthright."

Hussein lifted his hands as high as the heavy chains permitted.

"As Allah is merciful, Baba, do you be merciful with me. Truly I did not intend to harm you: to take the sultanate of Sa'aqs, yes, but not your life. And, Baba! Listen well to me. It was your brother Mansour who inveigled me into this. Ask him! Ask him who plotted against you!" Hussein tried to lift an arm to point to Mansour, but the weight of his chains dragged it down.

"Ask him yourself, spawn of evil, dog of Shaitan, eater of shit, fucker of camels, splitter of infants, and son of a Maghreb whore." The voice was feminine but deep-throated as it accused Hussein from the latticed casement in the wall above them.

"My gentle mother speaks to you, Hussein." Baba lifted

a finger to denote the origin of the voice. "Do you intend to tell me that she too plotted against me?"

"She——"

"Tell me the truth, Hussein."

"Yes, tell him the truth, you Maghreb bastard. Tell him with the same tongue that despoils little girls," the voice continued.

"Your mother is innocent, oh Baba. So is Mansour! I was only trying to save myself. As Allah is merciful, Baba, be you merciful unto me. I shall be the most faithful of all your followers. Grant me my life that I may serve you, and let me prove that I can serve you better alive than dead. Let me crawl to you on my belly and kiss the toe of your babouche. Let me drag my chains in the dust to touch you. Banish me to the desert, but do not kill me, Baba. I am young and I love life as you do. Our father's blood flows in my veins as it does in yours. We are brothers, Baba. Remember how as boys we slept together, played together, rode together. Remember how we had our first woman together. Save me, Baba, save me."

"Talk on, Hussein." Baba reached into the platter of couscous and rolled a sticky ball together between his thumb and forefinger and then transferred it to his mouth. He chewed it deliberately, eyeing Hussein all the time. "Talk on, my brother, for I delight in your conversation. Yes, I remember your abuse of me when we slept together. I remember how you always took the best horse. I remember how you always insisted that you win every game that we played. And, Hussein, I remember that we did take our first woman together. I remember you said you had to be first. You would not follow me because I was black. Oh yes, Hussein, I remember all those things. You always hated me. Even at this moment you hate me."

"Not *hated* you, Baba—*envied* you! Women desired you more than me. I had only one thing you did not have. My color! Now grant me this tiny favor, Baba. Let me live."

Baba nodded his head slowly, a cruel smile giving his face an expression that Rory had never seen before. "Are

213

there any more favors you want to ask me, Hussein? Because I fear I cannot grant you that one. Yet so long as you are to die, perhaps you would like to choose the way of your death. Would you prefer that my men drag you by the heels from their horses? Perhaps you would like to be spread-eagled on the ground that they might ride their sorties over you. Then we could impale you on the steel spikes at the gate and let the buzzards pick your bones clean. Or, if you prefer a really unusual way to die, we could fit you snugly over a young bamboo sprout after inserting it in your rear. Then it is merely a matter of staking you to the ground. The young bamboo grows quickly and it is as sharp as a dagger. Its sword point would penetrate your vitals in a day, or a little longer."

"Baba. . . ."

Baba languidly waved a hand. "Aye, all these are unpleasant deaths. I prefer a pleasant one for you. You, Hussein, shall have a death such as men dream about. The women of my father's hareem would enjoy a young stalwart like yourself. My father was an old man and not able to serve them often enough or strongly enough and they have sickened of the sterile embraces of their eunuchs. But you, Hussein! Ah, they would glory in you and your stiff yard. We shall feed you a little opium so that you will be able to serve them longer and better. You have always been a man of the hareem, and now you shall have your fill of it. There are even blonde N'zrani slaves in my father's hareem, and those are the kind you enjoy. But I leave the details to my lady mother, who has arranged it all."

Hussein sobbed, his body convulsed with shudders.

"Not that! Not that, Baba! Spare me that! I saw it happen once. If you must kill me, let it be quick with your dagger or let Bistaqa sever my head with one sweep of his scimitar. But do not give me to the women. Mercy, Baba."

A look passed between Baba and Mansour; Baba nodded his head. "Ah, you have made your choice, Hussein. You fear the women most. Therefore it will be the women. Remove his chains! Feed him the opium and let him wash it down with a stiff draught of powdered blister beetles.* Take him to Bistaqa who guards the door of my father's hareem. Let the darboukas play! Let the men dance! Let the feast continue!" Baba rose, his hand on Rory's shoulders. "Come! This is something you have never seen before and may never see again. It is not a pretty sight, but it will teach you how we dispatch traitors here in Sa'aqs. You too, Mansour. This will be a lesson for you. We three shall stand on the balcony and watch." He turned and lifted his face to the latticed window above him. "My mother, are all the women in their rooms and have you instructed them in what they shall do?"

"Yes, my son, and I have promised freedom to those women who acquit themselves well."

"Are the torches lighted in the hareem courtyard?"

"There is a blaze in every cresset."

"Then we go. It is not fitting that anyone but myself, my brother Mansour, and my brother the lord of Sax should see the faces of my father's hareem."

Baba turned his back on the prisoner and entered the door of the palace. Rory and Mansour followed him. This time they walked in an opposite direction from Rory's apartments, yet the corridors were as long and the courtyards as frequent. When they arrived at a silver-bossed door (Rory's had only brass bossings) Baba opened it himself. The room was in darkness and had the musty smell of a place that had not been used recently.

"My father's apartments," Baba explained as he rattled up the jalousies and led them out onto a balcony which was screened with a fine fretwork of wood, enabling the person standing there to observe the courtyard without being seen. But Baba had no desire to remain in hiding tonight and pushed open all the casements to give them an uninterrupted view of the courtyard below. It was like the one below Rory's room, only larger. The entire courtyard was surrounded by a colonnaded portico that shadowed a uniform row of doors. A fountained circular pool occupied the center. Not a person was to be seen. The ruddy glow of the burning torches illuminated the entire space, turning the spray of the fountain into liquid fire. Except

---

*Cantharides, or Spanish fly.

215

for the splash of the fountain there was neither sound nor movement. In the stillness, Rory heard the creak of another casement. A lattice opened at the opposite end of the courtyard and he saw therein the veiled forms of two women. The hands of one were black and those of the other white. They advanced through the opened window to stand on a balcony.

Mansour pointed to the opposite window. "Who accompanies our mother?" he asked of Baba.

"The Maghreb bitch who spawned Hussein." Baba pointed to the pale hands. "It is she who instigated the whole plot." Baba spat over the railing. "She has not long to live but it is fitting that she see Hussein's death because it is through her machinations that it takes place." He turned to Rory.

"I do not glory in the death of my brother Hussein, Rory. Next to Mansour I loved him best of all because he was the companion of my youth. He excelled in everything, but lately we have grown apart. He became a man of the hareem, dominated by his mother and cosseted by his women. The opium that he took daily to enable him to pleasure his women has dulled his brains. Ah, Rory, it is a misfortune to be born the son of the sultan. It takes a strong man not to succumb to all the vices so freely offered him. One becomes surfeited with pleasures of the body until one thinks only of food and drink; of the thighs of willing girls or the buttocks of young boys. Pray Allah for me that I shall be able to resist some of the evils that make a man soft when he indulges in them to excess." He stopped speaking abruptly and motioned toward the single figure that had entered the courtyard.

Rory recognized Hussein. Naked now and without his encumbering chains, he looked arrow slim, the torchlight casting ruddy highlights on his ivory skin. His body was firmly muscled, even powerful in its slenderness. The opiate he had taken had glazed his eyes, but the powerful aphrodisiac of the powdered beetles had already taken effect, and as he walked, his rod-like erection swayed from side to side. His steps were slow and uncertain and when he reached the center of the courtyard, he paused, seemingly hypnotized by the rhythm of the fountain. Slowly he

216

turned his body, his eyes scanning the dark shadows under the overhanging roof of the gallery and then lifting to the second story. The first thing he saw was the two women on the balcony, and his hands instinctively reached down to shield his all-too-apparent maleness. Although the women were veiled, he recognized them.

"Mother!" He stumbled across the tiles to stand directly below the balcony. "Save me, mother!"

The woman with the white hands leaned forward.

"Oh my son! I'd give my life for you if it would save you." She slumped, but the strong arms of the dark woman supported her and forced her back to the railing.

"Then you, Lallah Lalina, save me." He held out his hands to Baba's mother.

She did not answer him until she had pointed across to where Baba stood with Rory and Mansour flanking him.

"I have no authority in Sa'aqs," she said. "Only the sultan himself can save you."

"And as *I* will not save you," Baba answered, "pray to Allah to save you, but if it is written in your fate that you die tonight your prayers will avail you nothing. If you are to die tonight, it was written so forty days ago on your forehead." He leaned far out over the balcony. "May Allah be merciful to you, Hussein. I would that it might have been otherwise." His voice rose higher. "Bistaqa, sound the gong."

A deep reverberation awakened the doves who roosted under the roof of the gallery and sent them wheeling about the courtyard as the boom of the gong echoed from one side of the hollow square to the other. Its echoes were still pounding when all the doors surrounding the courtyard were flung open simultaneously and a crowd of women spewed forth. There were a hundred, perhaps more. In their running urgency, Rory could see that there included old women with gray hair, young matrons, smooth-skinned adolescents, and even young girls who were no more than children. He saw all shades from deep black to white, even one with hair as flaxen blonde as his own. All of them had eyes only for Hussein. With shrill, ululating cries, they converged on him from all four sides. Like a hunted animal he started to run, first in one direction and then in another, but there was no sanctuary. The screaming women closed in on him and he backed up to the rim of the fountain, leaning against it, his body arched backwards so that his still-erect maleness stood out before him like a shaft. In a moment they were upon him—wild-eyed maenads with burning eyes and slavering lips. Hussein was enveloped in a tumbling chaos of arms and legs until the black eunuch, Bistaqa, entered the fray with a stout pole and knocked them away.

"One at a time, my beauties," he roared, letting the pole crack on heads and arms. "One at a time! You'll all have a chance at him, although those who get him first will have the most fun."

Now, for the moment, abandoning Hussein, the women fought among themselves, biting, clawing, scratching and pulling one another's hair. Their flimsy veils were torn off in the wild melee that followed. They reminded Rory of a pack of cats, feral and feline in their viciousness. Four statuesque Negresses, who had evidently banded together in some preconceived and well-formulated plan of their own, stood on the outer perimeter of the snarling mass, awaiting their chance to wade through the combatants to Hussein. With hamlike fists, they started to fell those women in their way, kicking others out of their path, yanking some back by the hair, until they maneuvered their way up to Hussein. Surrounding him, one grabbed his arms, pinning them behind him, while another lifted his flailing heels and tumbled him to the ground. He struggled and managed to knock one of the women down but their combined strength subdued him and he lay on the ground panting. One of the Amazons squatted on his chest, her shiny black thighs immobilizing his head while she rubbed her body in lustful tribadism over his face. Another held his wrists while a third squatted on his feet. The fourth woman, although beset by those rivals who would despoil her of her victory, managed to fend them off. Kicking at those opponents who would drag her away and aided by the flailing arms and legs of her confederates, she squatted on her knees beside Hussein, bending to slaver over his body. Her hands manipulated him ruthlessly and cruelly with so much vigor that despite himself his body arched in

218

an uncontrollable spasm and the woman, shrieking in triumph as he ejaculated, abandoned him, shifting quickly to take the place of the woman who straddled his head. But the one whose place she took was not so fortunate, for another Negress, grossly fat and with breasts like ripe melons, knocked her flat and threw herself upon Hussein, continuing where the other had left off. Her hands flailed even more vigorously as though she would wrench his organ from his body, and when she accomplished her purpose she abandoned him, wiping her hands on the dress of the woman who held his feet. This one cursed and spat like a wildcat, but seeing her chance, she slid up Hussein's legs and worked to revive him, her hand flailing like a piston.

Now the women were quieter and were no longer fighting so much among themselves, for once the first two or three had accomplished their ends, nothing subsequent could compare with what they had achieved.

One by one they worked over him, his body arching no longer in ecstasy but in agony. His screams became hoarser and died away and there was no longer any necessity to pinion his helpless body. It had stopped its ecstatic arching and now twitched on the tiles. At length even their most frantic efforts could no longer arouse him and they fell upon him in a fury. Hands and nails and teeth tore at his flesh. His eyes were gouged out, his ears were torn off, and his mouth was ripped across his cheeks. The slender woman with long golden hair and a skin as white as milk whom Rory had noticed, her eyes glazed with an insane lust, clawed at his genitals with talon-like fingers, emasculated him, and held the bloody trophy of her victory aloft, cackling like a maniac as she rushed across the courtyard to stand below the balcony where the men were and display the torn flesh in her hands. Rory looked down at her. She was the most beautiful woman he had ever seen.

Again they had renewed their fighting among themselves—clawing at him, stripping the skin from his body, tearing at his muscles until Rory prayed that Hussein might be dead. Of this he was sure when he saw one cackling Fury wind his intestines around her neck and dance around the outside of the crowd. But even Hussein's death did not stop them. They were crazed now, and the flesh that came off in their hands seemed to enkindle their bestiality. The same blonde who had emasculated him dropped her trophy and dashed back into the crowd, to return beneath their balcony and toss something up to Baba. He made no move to catch the object and when it landed on the floor beside Rory, he could see that it was a finger.

The tiles of the courtyard were slippery with blood, but the harpies did not abandon their ghoulish saturnalia until Bistaqa, at a signal from Baba, whacked them away with his pole until they retreated to huddle together in a corner.

Rory looked down and his throat engorged with vomit at the shapeless mass of red meat on the tiles and the bloodstained hands of the panting women. While he stared, he heard the thud of Hussein's mother's body as it tumbled from the balcony to the tiles below. It was headless. The women of the hareem looked up to the balcony where Baba's mother stood alone. She threw a bloody scimitar down into the courtyard, raised both arms above her head, and cried out, "Homage! Pay homage to the Sultan of Sa'aqs and learn how the young lion devours the jackals that snap at his heels."

One by one the women of the hareem prostrated themselves on the encarmined tiles, their heads all pointing toward Baba. Slowly one of them—the white-skinned blond—raised her head, looking straight at the Shango.

"Spare us, lord," she pleaded in strangly accented Arabic. "We have served you well tonight. May you live in peace and may you have mercy on us, your servants."

Baba turned his back on her and walked slowly into the room. Someone had lighted a candle in the room and by its feeble light, Rory could see the brightness of a tear as it coursed down Baba's smooth cheek.

"Khallas!" he said. "It is finished."

220

CHAPTER XX

AFTER THE HARROWING EXPERIENCE AT BAsampo, followed by the murder of Hussein that first night in Sa'aqs, Rory was nauseated by brutality, bloodshed, and cruelty. Human life, it seemed, was Africa's cheapest commodity. A man could be sacrificed to propitiate the anger of some potbellied, phallic African god; he could be beheaded at the whim of some local potentate for having stepped on the chief's shadow; or he could be tortured with subtle refinements of cruelty just to relieve a moment of some petty desert sheik's boredom. Africa was indeed a cruel country. Its rivers teemed with crocodiles, its jungles with poisonous snakes, its broad plains with savage beasts, its air with voracious insects; and its people had absorbed all the evil that they were forced to struggle against on the land, in the water, and in the air.

No, that was not entirely true! Rory had discovered kindness, friendship, and hospitality in Africa that transcended anything he might have imagined. Baba had offered Rory something so fine and good in his friendship that it could not be expressed in words. Baba had been generous, too: Rory, who had started out from Liverpool without a shilling, was now as affluent as old George of England. Even the ruby which Baba had so casually given him was worth more than that of the Black Prince which burned in the Hanoverian's crown. The robes that he wore, once Hussein's, were more splendid than anything he had ever worn before, and they were not the only legacy from Hussein. From the window of Rory's apartment, he looked down into the hareem courtyard that housed Hussein's concubines and slaves. Hussein's four wives and their numerous children had all felt the stran-

221

gling caress of a eunuch's silken cord, but the slaves and concubines had been spared. Rory had already investigated them, for he had been told by Baba that they were all his. His property! His slaves! His chattels!

Like a hungry lad in a candy shop, Rory was unable to choose; everywhere he looked he was tempted, and he did not know which appealing sweetmeat he wanted to savor first. Hussein had indeed been a connoisseur of human flesh, and now his carefully selected purchases from the slave markets of Cairo, Khartoum, Tunis, Fez, and Marrakech were spread out in a tempting array for Rory to enjoy. He had only to walk to the balcony of his room, observe the beauties who paraded below him and, when he had finally made a choice, communicate his wish to his own hareem eunuch, Karem. In a few moments, the charmer he had selected would be beside him on his divan, ready to do his bidding.

But even with his amplitude of riches, Rory turned often to Almera, she who had come to him that first night in Baba's tent. He felt freer with her and she had become so accustomed to him that she anticipated his wants even before he expressed them. She was a quiet, gentle girl, soft-spoken and meek in her devotion to Rory; but the quietness and self-effacement which she displayed in the daytime could change into passionate onslaughts at night if he so desired. These, however, he preferred to receive from the other harem denizens.

Chatsubah, that black leopard, was too much for him, and Rory passed her by except for rare occasions when he desired the violence of her lust; it was far too ardent and all-consuming for a steady diet. As a result of her being chosen so seldom, Chatsubah became sulky and unruly. Once Rory had to have her whipped for a clawing attack on another girl. After that she seemed to bear him malice and he was not a little afraid that she might poison him. He decided to give her to Mleeka, who had been womanless far longer than Rory realized. Mleeka received her in the little room that led off Rory's sleeping quarters, and after the first night Chatsubah seemed not only reconciled but chastened. Mleeka, who was adding to his store of words every day, came to Rory and knelt before him and placed Rory's hand on his wiry poll. "Woman good," Mleeka said. "She need . . ." He opened his big hand and brought the pink palm down on his rump with a resounding whack. "You good, Rory Mongo. Me good. Soon baby for Rory Mongo."

Now that Mleeka no longer hobbled from his sprained ankle, he took over Rory and all his possessions as his own. Never had Rory been waited on with such faithfulness and devotion. Mleeka was always behind him and if Rory so much as buttoned a button or tied a string, Mleeka chided him for it. If Mleeka could have chewed Rory's food for him he would willingly have done so. He was a servant to be proud of; his strength and his enormous physique reminded Rory of Baba. Through those who spoke his language, Rory learned something of his history.

He was, as Baba had conjectured, a Kasai, but he had been born in slavery in the household of a Mameluke prince in Cairo. He had been a groom to one of the young princelings and when, through no fault of Mleeka's, a horse threw the young rider, Mleeka was blamed and sold. The trader who bought him sold him again to a caravan that was leaving for the west coast, where his ultimate destination would have been one of the slave factories, from which he would have been put on board ship for a life of servitude in some West Indian island.

During the crossing of the desert, he had slipped on a stone and twisted his ankle. Knowing that he would be abandoned if he could not keep up with the rest, he had painfully hobbled all day until the tortured ankle, so painful that he could no longer step on it, had finally won over his perseverance. He fell and could not rise again. In a few moments he had been cut out of the coffle and abandoned beside the trail, to have perished had not Rory come along. Consequently he worshipped Rory with all the affection a dog might feel for his master, and Rory in turn cherished the big black. He decked him in robes more fitting for a caid than a slave, kept him always by his side, and as they began to communicate with each other in English, came to depend more and more on Mleeka. Even Baba complimented him on his black slave.

223

"You've got something there, Rory my brother, which no amount of gold could buy in the slave market. Outside of you and Mansour and old Sliman there is nobody I can trust, but you can always trust Mleeka." Baba turned and spoke to the big fellow who grinned back and spewed forth his strange jargon. "He says," Baba translated, "that you are his soul. In his belief, every man has a soul as well as a body. Most men never see their soul, but Mleeka says that he is fortunate in that he can see his soul every day because you are it."

With the faithful Mleeka to wait on him, the choice of his hareem women at night, Almera for quiet passion, and the warmth of Baba's friendship, Rory's days at Sa'aqs passed quickly and in a golden haze. Rory usually awoke at the first call of the muezzin from the squat mud minaret which was the highest structure in Sa'aqs. The ululating chant of the *iman* penetrated his slumbers and caused him to open his eyes and stare at whatever woman lay next to him. Somehow, in the cold, gray light of morning, her skin oily with sweat, her mouth agape, and her hair plastered against her cheeks, she never seemed the epitome of eroticism that she had the night before. The kohl that darkened her eyes would be smudged, and her henna-stained hands would look cruel and predatory with their long nails which had, more often than not, raked his back the night before. The alkaline odor of the semen-spotted sheets offended him, and he was prone to shove the woman roughly from his bed, sickened by the memories of what strange and unnatural things they had done with each other in the darkness. Then and there he would make a firm resolution that this day's night would see no such repetition. And ofttimes he kept his promise to himself; instead of one of the trained performers of his hareem, he would call for Almera, whose quietness soothed him and whose soft embraces and gentle words provided a relaxing comfort when he had been satiated with too much female flesh and cloyed with strange indulgences. With Almera he could stretch out and go to sleep without having to prove his virility not only to his companion but to himself. He knew that Almera desired more from him and occasionally he gave it to her, for which he

224

sensed her gratitude; but even desiring him as she did, she was never overtly jealous of those whom he favored. It was she who always attended him before he retired, brought the hareem woman in, set fruit and drink beside his bed, and then whispered instructions to the woman before leaving silently and unobtrusively. Then, timing her actions to the departure of the woman in the morning, she was beside Rory's bed, brushing the flies off him with a whisk, heating his coffee in a small brazier, sponging the sweat and dried semen from his body, and even choosing the clothes he would wear so that Mleeka could dress him.

His body clean, his energy renewed by the pungent coffee, he would walk through the still night-cool corridors of the palace, followed by Mleeka, and out the iron-bossed door to where, in the courtyard, his horse would be waiting for him alongside Baba's and occasionally Mansour's. They would ride out for an hour or two to the open country or to the street of the gem merchants or perhaps that of the armorers, or to the slave market; then they would return to bathe, relax, and talk.

Within the labyrinthine maze of the rambling old palace of Sa'aqs there were several hammams or baths, but they usually headed for the one that had been used exclusively by Baba's father and was adjacent to his hareem. They strode together through the long corridors and shaded colonnades. Familiar as he now was with the palace, the way did not seem as long or as tortuous to Rory as it had the first night he had traversed it. Now he could even find his way around the palace by himself, though he seldom went anywhere alone. Either Mleeka or Oma accompanied him and there was always a heated argument between them as to which would have the honor. Both were jealously devoted to him, but he had more faith in Mleeka than in Oma.

On a certain afternoon, Rory and Baba, with Mleeka at their heels, entered the doors of the hammam. Mleeka helped Rory off with his robes, while the eunuch, Al-Jarir, assisted Baba. It was pleasant to shed their sweaty robes and the heavy wool djellabahs and enter the perfumed steam. It was even pleasanter to relax under the fingers and strong hands of Al-Jarir, whose task it was to scrape

225

the sweat and dirt from their bodies with a bone knife. The knife was, so he informed Rory, carved from the horn of a rhinoceros and possessed magical properties that would make their bodies strong and muscular.

Their bodies scraped clean, they passed into another room where they plunged into a pool of tepid water, which had the sting of cold after the heat of the steam. From there they went to a darkened room where they stretched prone on the cold tiled floor and let Al-Jarir massage them with his hamlike hands. When he had finished, he bade them remain on their bellies while he stood on their backs and walked slowly up and down their spinal columns, massaging their backs with his big, cushioned toes. His weight and the pressure were almost more than they could bear, but the revitalized flow of blood charging through their arteries was proof of the consummate knowledge of the man.

"Al-Jarir is a treasure," grunted Baba. "He can do everything a real man can do except impregnate a woman. In fact, the women of the hareem prefer him to a complete man, as he can swive twenty of them in one night and never lose his vigor."

"You allow that?" Rory in his ignorance had always supposed that no man but the master of the hareem was ever allowed to touch the women.

"Of course. Ask your own Karem and he will tell you that he serves a dual purpose. He not only guards your hareem but he serves it as well. Think you that we go to all the trouble to castrate men merely to guard our hareems? Oh, no! A couple of Senegalese giantesses could do that just as well. Our eunuchs have another reason for being. Think: there are some three hundred women in my father's hareem. He was a man along in years. Even if he took one a night, it would require almost a year for him to lie with them all, and that would mean that each woman would have a man only once a year—and, in the case of my father, an aging man at that. So what would they do while they were waiting for that once-a-year momentous night to come along?"

Rory nodded. Yes, he could see that there might be

many unsatisfied females in a hareem with only one man to serve them.

Baba pointed a finger at him in mock derision. " 'Tis plain to see that the cold-blooded N'zranis are not accustomed to hareems. Not that you, my brother, are cold-blooded or even a N'zrani anymore," he hastened to add, "but we who keep our women in hareems must prepare for everything. I asked you—what would these idle women do? How could they stand going weeks, months, without a man? Why, they would become tribades—lovers of each other. Some of them would remain women, soft and tender. Others would take on the characteristics of a man, dominating and brutal. That is bad. It's common knowledge that once a woman has been loved by another woman she nevermore desires a man. So we have eunuchs and, as they are not real men but are entirely capable of satisfying a woman, we give them to the women to keep them happy."

"My lord," Al-Jarir bowed low to Rory, his teeth showing white in the semidarkness, "it is indeed a fact. Ah, those women! When we enter the hareem courtyard after the evening meal, the women fight over us, clawing at each other to get to us. Of the three hundred in the big hareem I have served all save the cursed English wench."

"An English wench? Did he say English, Baba?"

"That he did. Ah, but she is a viper if ever there was one. A veritable cobra—a mamba—a puff adder! My father was unlucky enough to get her as a present from the Sultan of the Maghreb who had received her from the Governor of Tangier. A toothsome dish she is to look at, Rory, but a she-devil. She swears that no man will ever take her and when my father—may he be at peace—tried, she scratched his face. He should have strangled her then and there, but he was saving her to give to one of his enemies."

"I'd like to see her." Rory leaned forward. "An English girl here! It's almost unbelievable."

"You have seen her, my brother. Remember the night I gave Hussein to the women? Remember the most vicious bitch of all—she who stripped Hussein of his genitals, and

227

later threw his finger up onto the balcony? That is the she-jackal I spoke of."

"A blonde with white skin? Yes, I remember her. How did she get here?"

"The pirates of the Barbary Coast are not particular as to color or nationality. Sometimes they prefer to keep a girl whom they have captured rather than ransom her. Evidently this one was not ransomed. But more about her later. The bitch is yours if you want her, but I advise you to keep away from her. If the Governor of Tangier, the Sultan of Morocco and the Sultan of Sa'aqs could not subdue her, you'll stand little chance; and 'tis said she has a trick with her knee that can make strong men roll on the floor. Also 'tis said that she has a way of seeming to comply and then, just before a man enters her, she reaches down and grabs his precious jewels, squeezing them in her fingers until he screams in agony." Baba turned to the eunuch and the slave. "Leave us now, Al Jarir and Mleeka, we'll rest awhile. But stand guard at the door and see that nobody enters." Baba and Rory walked into an adjoining room where there were divans to stretch out on.

Baba was obviously brimming over with ideas that he wanted to discuss with Rory. There were, he began, a thousand or more women in the palace and that, he admitted, was worse than having a thousand red djinn under one roof. A thousand women—his father's hareem; his brother Hussein's, now Rory's; his brother Mansour's, which was not yet very large; and his own. In addition to these concubines, there were all the women who waited on them and served them, and all the female slaves. A thousand women with nothing to do but try to amuse themselves, cook up diabolical plots, lust after eunuchs and each other, and occasionally serve Rory, Mansour, or himself. May the curse of Shaitan be upon all of them!

According to custom, if not exactly to law, he was supposed to put the women of his father's hareem to death. For any man to touch them would be to defile his father's memory. Yet he remembered that his father had always told him it was a waste of good slave flesh to strangle them all and that when his own father had died, he had sold off the old man's hareem secretly.

Then, of course, Rory's women would be idle after he left and they would be another problem on his hands, besides the numerous women in his own hareem whom he had tired of, and doubtless some that Mansour had ceased using. Allah alone knew how many other female hangers-on there were, hidden away in all the nooks and crannies of the palace. What to do with them? Did Rory have any suggestions?

Rory could only say that it was most inconsiderate of the divine architect of their bodies to design them so that a man could please only one woman at a time. What a pity! However, he could take *one* off Baba's hands—the English wench.

Damn the English wench! Consign her to the deepest of the twenty-one hells! Baba glared at him. The Problem!

For the first time in his life, Rory could see the disadvantage of a glut of women. As he had mentioned, a man could sleep with only one at a time. . . . Well, could Baba sell them?

Slowly, lips pursed, Baba nodded his head. That was exactly what he had wanted to talk to Rory about. Weed out the whole palace, every superfluous female. But—he was emphatic—he couldn't sell the whole lot in Sa'aqs. In addition to the disrespect it would cause to his father's memory, such a number of women would glut the market in Sa'aqs and the choicest female slaves would bring scarcely a tenth of their value.

Why not take them all to Rinktum Castle? Rory suggested.

Alas! Female slaves, no matter how beautiful, were in no great demand on the other side of the water. Hareem slaves and concubines, who had been trained to perform in bed, were useless as field workers. What the slavers were anxious to purchase were strong, healthy young bucks. No, Rinktum Castle and the other coastal slave factories were out. Not only were women not in demand in the new world, but the slavers were none too anxious to ship them over. In another twenty years, there'd be an end to slave trade in Africa if the bucks in America had plenty of women. The plantation owners would be raising their own slaves. But, Baba did have a plan and it was a complicated one. Would Rory be willing to help him? Rory would make a fortune if he cast his lot with Baba and forgot about returning to Rinktum Castle.

Rinktum Castle! Liverpool! Uncle Jabez, whom he had never seen! That old bastard who had not deemed him sufficiently worthy to invite to his home, but had shipped him off to Africa on a slave ship! What allegiance did he owe that unknown man? What, indeed, compared with all he owed Baba, who had made him his brother, shared his palace with him, given unstintingly of his love and his material possessions. He had never been able to repay Baba, and now for the first time Baba had asked him for something. Not even selfishly, because he had said it would make Rory's fortune too. To hell with Rinktum Castle! To hell with Liverpool, Uncle Jabez, Sax, Sparks, the lot! Rory's path lay with Baba and he had no hesitation in proclaiming it.

Baba was happy over his decision. Now that he was Sultan of Sa'aqs he could no longer make the trips to the coast anyway, but had to remain where he could keep his finger on everything that was happening. Of course, he could send Mansour; but he was a stripling, scarcely more than eighteen, and he had no experience taking caravans overland or dealing with those wily robbers, the slave merchants. Yet Baba could depend on Rory. This then was Baba's idea.

The ancient city of Timbuktu was one of the great slave centers of Africa. Here, since time immemorial, the Arab merchants had sold men and women. From Timbuktu, long caravan trails led to all the Maghreb, to Tunis, to Libya, to Egypt, and then on to Ethiopia and Arabia. There, in the slave marts of Timbuktu, a thousand women could be absorbed and the number would not affect their market value. Getting there with a caravan of women would not be too much trouble either—much easier than aiming for the northern cities. To go there they would have to cross miles of desert and the women would have to be carried on camels. But the distance between Sa'aqs and the River Niger was not too great and once at the Niger, they could transport the women by boats right to Timbuktu. There the women disposed of, Rory could join a caravan for Marrakech, which was on the other side of the desert and an important city in the Maghreb. It would be a hard three-week journey for him, Baba said, but from Marrakech to Tangier would be easier, as there were well-traveled paths and he could go by horseback.

Then once in Tangier? Rory prompted.

Ah, Rory would then purchase a ship. There were plenty of ships in Tangier—English, Dutch, American ships, because the Moorish pirates of Tangier were the scourge of the coast and great ship-takers. Of course it would all be made easy for Rory. Baba would send messengers who would arrive in Tangier before Rory and do all the bargaining. The name of the Sultan of Sa'aqs commanded respect, even in Tangier. Once having purchased a good ship, Rory would find a crew: there were plenty of captured sailors among the N'zrani slaves in Tangier.

So now they had a ship and a crew. That was all very fine, Rory agreed. And presumably he would have several bags of gold from the sale of the slaves in Timbuktu. But what in the name of Old Harry would he do with his ship and his bags of gold?

Why, that was as plain as a black mole on a N'zrani girl's ass. Rory would take the gold and buy male slaves in Tangier. To supplement those Rory would buy, Baba would send those he had been gathering together for Rinktum Castle. Strong, healthy men could make the journey across the desert without much difficulty. Rory would then have a full cargo of prime males. He would take them across the ocean and he and Baba would have all the money for themselves. He would never again have to sell his slaves for a pittance on the coast. They would bring full value in whatever place Rory decided to go. Then Rory would send the ship back to some west-coast factory which Baba would set up and Baba would have another shipment waiting for him. They would buy a second ship, then another and another. Rory would stay across the sea, and with Baba supplying him here and Rory selling there, they would have a business which would make anything that the English possessed resemble a eunuch's balls.

It was certainly the will of Allah. Not for nothing had Sax and Sa'aqs come together. He'd send back to Basampo and get Tim; provided, of course, that Tim was alive. Tim would go along with Rory and be his right-hand man. Mansour would to to Tangier with old Sliman and later they'd set up a factory on the coast. Baba snapped his fingers. Well, what did Rory think?

There were so many things to think about, so many seemingly insurmountable obstacles to overcome, that Rory didn't know what to think. It was altogether too fantastic, too improbable, and yet. . . . If men could come from England, set up slave factories and buy slaves in Africa, then transport them to the West Indies and sell them, why couldn't he and Baba do it? There'd be plenty of money behind them. A thousand female slaves at even twenty pounds a head would be twenty thousand pounds, and besides that there were the immense resources of Sa'aqs itself. There were Baba and Mansour and Sliman and yes, by God, there was Tim if he was still alive, and of course there was Mleeka. And, Rory considered the matter, there was he himself. Goddamn it! He was no longer a supercargo on his uncle's slaver. He *was* somebody now.

"Indeed, why not, Baba?" Rory crossed over to sit beside him. "Let's shake hands on it. Where I come from we call this a gentleman's agreement. Sa'aqs and Sax, a real partnership. There are many details we must work out, Baba. When do we start?"

His hand lingered for a long moment in the grasp of the huge dark hand and it seemed to him that something flowed between him and Baba that was more binding than any contract could ever be.

"Tomorrow after the first call of the muezzin. But enough of business, my brother. We need entertainment."

"Yes," said Rory, rising, "I now remember the English girl."

Baba looked up at him.

"If just thinking about her has such an effect on you," he pointed, "she's yours if you want her." He slid off the divan to stand beside Rory. "But remember what I said about the little trick she has with her knee. I wouldn't want you to become as worthless as Al-Jarir."

"Forewarned is forearmed," grinned Rory.

CHAPTER XXI

IT HAD BEEN MORE SPORT GLOZING ONE OF his Scottish Marys until he could tip her on her back under a hedgerow than it was to have these damned perfumed houris deposited beside him in bed with no effort on his part. It was no longer any fun, thought Rory, being the only cock in a barnyard of tame hens. He longed once more to ogle, strut, and conquer; to feel that what he possessed he had won by his own ability. He needed to reestablish his faith in his manhood; to be the victor, not the vanquished. The English girl——that one sounded promising.

Baba, walking through the corridors of the palace, regarded Rory out of the corner of his eye. "All this time you've been conjuring up that N'zrani girl in your thoughts; weaving strange phantasies about her. Right?"

"Huh? The N'zrani girl?" Rory grinned sheepishly. "You're right, Baba, that's just what I've been thinking about."

"Well, you've finally heard something I've said! Get to your apartment and I'll have her sent to you. You're mooning like a mare over a lost foal. To be sure, she's as beautiful as a houri, but she's got the temper of a red djinni. Remember what I told you: she's still a virgin and intends to remain one. Take care how you open the petals of that pale rose; it has thorns."

"Then you don't mind if I leave you?"

"Mind? You're no company as you are. Mayhap when you've broken her in you'll be willing to talk business with me again, but you'll be no good till you get the bitch out of your thoughts. Now go! And if I see you at the evening meal with your face scratched to ribbons and clutching at your crotch while you walk spraddle-legged, I'll know that you fared no better than my father and the others with the N'zrani." Baba faced him in the direction of his own apartments and gave him a little push. "Be off with you!"

"That I shall!" Rory waved over his shoulder as he sped down the hall, Mleeka following. Suddenly he felt stripped of his lassitude, anxious for adventure. In his rooms, he clapped his hands for Almera and Oma. Although he had just bathed, he stripped off his djellabah and had Almera rub his body with attar of musk. He set Mleeka to choosing his most elaborate kaftan and had Oma wind his head with yards of diaphanous white muslin which completely hid his blonde hair. A quick glance in the greenish German mirror assured him that with his tanned face and arms, and his hair hidden, he could well pass for a Moor or at least one of the blue-eyed Berbers. He was adjusting the folds of his embroidered kaftan when the big knocker banged against the outer door of his apartments.

Mleeka rushed to open the heavy brass studded door to disclose Al-Jarir, his big black hand clasped tightly around the wrist of a girl who, veiled and with bowed head, stood behind him. With a forceful jerk of his arm, he pulled her around until she stood in the doorway; then, releasing her, he shoved her inside the room, but before he could close the door she had lashed out and kicked him in the shins. Although she wore only soft leather slippers, he winced and his upraised hand would have slapped her had not Rory intervened.

"Go, I'll handle her."

"You'll handle whom?" the girl snapped her words at him spitefully. "You'll handle no one, least of all me."

She spoke in Arabic, vilely accented, yes, but understandable. He waited until the eunuch had closed the door and signaled for Mleeka to drop the wooden bar and wedge it with the piece of iron which locked it from the inside. Without moving from his position on the other side of the room, he inventoried the veiled figure. She was tall, with a proudly regal carriage that set her apart from the

234

Moorish and Negro girls. He could see from the swift rise and fall of her small breasts—too small for such a tall body, he thought—and the clenching of her hands that she was either frightened or angry. Probably both. Escaping from the turquoise tissue of her veil were two long braids plaited with pearls, and the braids were the color of his own hair. Keeping his eyes on hers, which glittered through the thin silk, he advanced slowly across the floor until he stood before her, then with one hand, quickly lifted the veil and threw it back over her head.

He'd seen her kind before—those fine-featured, alabaster-white English beauties. They came to Scotland for a week of hunting in the autumn when some of the big castles (certainly not Sax) were opened for them. Yes, he'd seen them riding in their long velvet habits and plumed hats, splashing mud on his worn tartan and not even deigning to look at him standing in the hedgerows as they passed by. This was one of them. Her ice-blue eyes now regarded him with all the disdain with which they would have ignored him had he been back in Scotland.

"What do they call you?" he asked in Arabic.

"They call me by the stupid name of Yasmin but that is not my name, Moor."

"You'll address me as 'milord,' and if Yasmin is not your name, what then is it?"

"I am Lady Mary FitzAlbany, not that you would even be able to pronounce it—" she hesitated, then added with a mocking sneer "—milord, if that makes you feel any more important."

"Yes, I can say 'Mary.' " He drew her to him, her body rigid in his arms. With one hand he lifted her face, searching her eyes, but they stared back at him, icy blue and almost unafraid. His lips sought hers and for a fleeting second they touched and then he howled, pushing her away from him. She had bitten his lip until the warm blood ran down his chin. The force of his push had caused her to stumble and she glared up from the floor.

"Damn you, Moor," she spat at him. "So now! Call your slaves! Have them flog me. I've been flogged before. But you may strip the skin from my body. No filthy Moor is going to have me."

235

"Bah!" he sucked the blood from his lip. "Having you would not be too difficult. I've had unwilling virgins before and after having taken them once, they come crawling on their hands and knees, pleading to be taken again. No woman's virginity is important to me. One healthy lunge and it disappears. It is a cheap commodity which I can purchase any hour of the day." He searched in his kaftan to find a kerchief to staunch the flow of blood. Almera gave him a square of lawn and he applied it to his lip. "No, robbing you of your precious virginity would be no problem," he waggled a derisive finger at her, "provided I wanted it. You're a bit too bony for me. I like my wenches better padded and"—he advanced a step to cup one of her breasts under the thin veiling of her robe—"I like them a little more heavily titted. Still, you'll do, I suppose."

"It makes me happy that I do not please you, milord Moor. You barbarians think only of a woman's body. You never think of anything else."

"Such as?" he asked.

"Her intelligence, her love, and her affection."

"My slave Almera," he said, pointing to her, "is intelligent. She has a good mind and she certainly shows me love and affection."

"Then why not cleave to her? Why do you want other women if you have found all you want in one?"

He laughed. "Because I am a man. I like variety. Your pale skin and gold hair intrigue me even if you are scrawny and your bones show through your skin. One way or another I intend to have you even if it serves merely to satisfy my curiosity. Sometimes frigid women, such as you appear to be, have unknown fires smoldering under the ice. I like to kindle them if it is possible."

The English girl appraised him carefully.

"I'll not be raped, milord Moor, but I must say you're a damned sight better looking than those other greasy niggers who have tried to do the same. As a matter of fact, you don't even look like a nigger at all."

He turned on his heel, his back toward her. With a signal, he indicated his desire for Mleeka, Oma, and Almera to remain. When he finally turned to look at the

236

English Mary, she was still staring up at him from the floor. Her bravado had fled and there was a flicker of fear in her eyes. She raised herself on one arm, keeping her eyes on him like a cornered animal.

"What are you going to do to me?"

He held out his hand to her, bowing with a courtly grace he must have inherited from his noble ancestors.

"I might use fancy words, milady, but fancy words do not become me. My answer is, in plain English, I'm going to screw you. It's a simple thing and should not take more than an hour of your time. However, if you are not willing, then I am going to rape you. You have your choice." He had spoken in English.

Without thinking, she stretched out her hand to him and he hoisted her to her feet. Almost immediately she backed away from him, shaking her head in disbelief.

"What did you say?" Her eyes widened in wonder. She had automatically switched to English too.

"I said I was about to rape you, although I hoped it would not be necessary."

"But you speak English!"

"And why not?" he shrugged his shoulders. "I am a Scot, and most Scots can at least attempt the English tongue. Rory Mahound, Baron of Sax, at your service, milady, even though the service which I am about to do you may not be entirely to your liking."

"It can't be true. It can't." She stared at him, her eyes seeking some assurance. "You're the brother of that filthy nigger sultan, or so they told me when they dragged me here."

"That I am indeed, but I am also Rory Mahound, Laird of Kilburnie and fifth Baron of Sax. I am neither a Moor nor filthy. True, my adopted brother is a Moor, but I assure you that he is not filthy either."

"Then save me! For the love of Christ in whom we both believe, save me! Get me back to England." Suddenly she was suspicious. "Is this a trap? Are you trying to cozen me? For all I know you may be a damned Moor who has somehow learned to be glib in English."

He reached up one hand and disengaged the end of his turban and unwound it slowly until it came away and his

237

hair fell to his shoulders. It gleamed as fair and golden as hers. Unbuttoning his kaftan, he slipped one arm out of the sleeve. The whiteness of his skin glowed in the half light.

"To be glib in English would not account for my Scottish burr, nor my hair which is the color of yours, nor my skin which is as white as your own."

"I believe you. Will you help me?"

"I might, Lady Mary, I might. But if I did that for you, what would you do for me in return?"

"My father would reward you."

He laughed, fingering the necklace of gold and pearls around his neck. "With golden guineas, I presume. Alas, Lady Mary, I do not stand in need of money."

"Then what?"

"Aye, it is that little thing we were talking about. You've witheld it from others and it's something that would assuage my vanity. It would be more pleasant to have it given to me than to take it by force."

"You mean. . . ?"

"Exactly."

"Bah! Every man has the same vile thing on his mind, but why is it so important to you? I imagine as the brother of the sultan you can have your pick of a hundred girls."

"Three hundred, to be exact." He waved his hand toward the balcony that overlooked his hareem.

"Any one of whom would be more adept at pleasing you than I."

He nodded in agreement as he reached tentatively for her hand. She did not withdraw it.

"Then why?" she insisted.

"Call it vanity, Lady Mary. My brother, the sultan, said that no man could win you. I would like to brag to him that I've been successful where beys and sultans have failed."

"And if I refuse?"

" 'Twill do you little good. I intend to have you anyway. But if you are unwilling I have only to call Mleeka and Oma to hold you." He waved casually at his servants. "I might inform you that we are making up a caravan of female slaves for the market in Timbuktu. You should

238

passersby. A white-burnoosed Arab, his green turban proclaiming him a Hadji, prodded a young Negro in chains ahead of him, cursing the slave because of his laggard steps. A dog mounted a bitch in the dust, the creature's eyes glazed as he thrust vigorously, until a pack of howling urchins attacked the paired beasts with sticks and staves. A litter passed, borne by two sweating Nubians, one of whom limped painfully as he trotted along. In a shadowy corner between two walls a randy adolescent hoisted his ragged djellabah up over his shoulders with one hand while with the other he shoved a small girl to her knees before him, forcing her to submit to him.

Rory turned from the window and walked back over the polished tiles to where Almera and Lady Mary were standing. He fought against the thoughts that traveled down from his brain to his groin but he could not dispossess himself of them.

Had he become so much a Moor that he thought like one? Was he, too, being possessed by the cruelty of Africa? This woman was no casual slave; she was his own countrywoman, and although he wanted to humble her for her arrogance, he realized that it would be impossible. Mere accidents of birth had given them too much in common. Grudgingly he had to admit that he admired her for fighting for her own birthright against overwhelming odds, while he had been all too willing to forfeit his own. She spoke his language; she had known the snows of an English winter and the springtime flowering of apple trees; she had hung holly branches in the hall at Christmastide and ridden her horses through brown October woods. They shared a common heritage here in this hot, cruel country. He owed her something, but just what he did not know. The sudden sympathy he felt for her made him generous. But no! He was a man. He did desire her. The thought of her white skin after so many brown and black skins inflamed him with irrepressible urges. This was his chance to prove his manhood—not to her but to himself. She was no willing victim, anxious to please him. She was something to be conquered. Yes, he would see to it that she returned to England. He owed her that much. He'd even marry her after a fashion. But first . . .

He pointed to the divan. "You'll carry out your part of the bargain, milady. I'll carry out mine. I'll marry you and send you off to England when the time comes. But your payment of me now will be an evidence of your good faith. If you are unwilling I shall have Mleeka and Oma hold you while I take my pleasure of you that way. I'd prefer that you came to me with some willingness but—"

"You can dismiss the men," she withered him with a glance.

He did so.

"Almera, undress her, then leave."

"Yes, miiord." She started to undo the pins that held Mary FitzAlbany's robe.

Rory walked over and looked out the window again. The passing pageant of the street had changed. There remained, however, the little girl in the corner of the wall. She was sobbing. From the leather bag that hung under Rory's armpit, he drew out a piece of silver and flung it toward the child. She heard it hit the stones and stopped her sniveling long enough to pick it up. Looking to see whence it came, she smiled up at Rory. Her tears stopped. He waved a casual hand to her before turning to walk back to the white form that lay on the divan. Almera had left. They were alone.

He slipped out of his robes and advanced to the bed. The English girl was sobbing. Well, the Arab girl in the street had sobbed too, but a silver coin had quieted her.

"You'll be happy to get back to England, Mary." It was another silver coin which he was offering her. It had its effect. She stopped crying and he reached down, spreading her legs apart. She did not resist him.

"I'll be happy to get back to England, Rory Mahound, but it will not stop me from hating you. Oh, how stupid you are! You might have had what you want along with love too. But you are stupid, like all men. Your thoughts are not in your head, only in *that*." She gazed down at him, and shuddered at what she saw.

He lowered himself onto her and clumsily she accommodated her body to him.

242

"You almost convince me," he said before she screamed.

But after it was all over, she kissed him, and he was surprised at the warmth of her kiss.

CHAPTER XXII

RORY HAD ACCOMPLISHED HIS PURPOSE WITH the English Mary. Now that it was over and his masculine vanity had been satisfied, he recalled it as a particularly uninspired performance. Neither of them had delighted in it, although he had found Mary's final writhings and pantings rather surprising. He sensed that once the fires of her passion had melted the ice of her fear, she would be quite as responsive as the trained women of his harem. He had therefore purposely delayed his own climax until she reached hers. True, at the time, he had developed some slight interest in arousing her, but after it was over, he decided that it was far more pleasant for a woman to arouse him than to go to the sweaty task of arousing her. He was forced to admit the fact that he desired someone far more primitive and uninhibited than the English girl despite her final kiss.

He did not forget his promise to her. He would return her to England and he was sure he might count on Baba to help him. Nor did she forget her promise to him. She continued to hate him for his violation of her—regardless of the fact that she had enjoyed it. He had her transferred to his own harem, even allowing her the luxury of private quarters—those which would have been reserved for his principal wife. Each evening, he summoned her to his room, more because he wanted to speak English than anything else, and although at first meeting they would each conduct themselves with a guarded and armed neutrality, before her visit was up they would be hurling vituperations at one another. There was no evil that she would not accuse him of, and he often thought that she acted more like a jealous wife than a mortal enemy because she seemed to resent his temporary liaisons with the other women of his hareem. She accused him in no uncertain terms of being a libertine, a rake, and a master of all perversions. They would quarrel and wrangle until he would lose his temper and slap her, whereupon she would spit at him. Then he would threaten to include her in the caravan to Timbuktu and she would dare him to do it, both of them knowing that in the end he would relent and send her packing to her rooms. They realized that there was a common bond between them which no insults or threats could break.

One evening, after a particularly violent quarrel when each had exhausted the other with name-calling and even physical violence, Rory called in Mleeka with instructions to take Mary to the little barred cell in the hareem where an occasional recalcitrant inmate was imprisoned. From there she would be destined for Timbuktu. It was Mleeka, with his growing knowledge of English, who had intervened, daring for the first time to oppose his master's temper and his orders. He had acted as mediator and explained to both of them how much easier and pleasanter life would be for them if they agreed upon some sort of workable neutrality that would give them the benefit and pleasure of each other's company and contribute to peace and tranquility. Mary was the first to agree and added her arguments to Mleeka's to convince Rory, who in the end gave his word. From that time on they began—at first slowly—to enjoy some little companionship together.

Despite Mary's jealousy of Almera, she started to teach her English and it became customary for the four of them—Rory, Mary, Mleeka, and Almera—to spend a few hours each evening together in Rory's rooms, discussing the happenings of the day over glasses of hot minted tea.

There was much to discuss. The entire palace was in a turmoil of change. Rory was surprised to see another side of Baba's character. Under the insouciant charm of his friend, there existed the steel-trap mind of a man of business. A plethora of things demanded Rory's and Baba's attention from the morning call of the muezzin until— as the Arabs said—it became too dark to distinguish a white thread from a black. Mansour and old Sliman were taken into their confidence and wheels turned both in and out of the palace. Baba was impatient with inefficiency, and the whole palace adopted a toe-the-mark attitude that found expression in servants running instead of dawdling through the corridors; in guards snapping to attention when the sultan entered or left the palace instead of lounging lackadaisically in doorways; and in palace officials being forced to account for every Maria Theresa dollar that passed through their hands.

A complete inventory was made of all the palace slaves and hareem concubines. Rory was astounded at the total. Every child born in the palace had somehow managed to remain and grow up there with the result that there was not enough work for half of them to do. Those who did have duties were so jealous of them, however slight they might be, that no one else might attend to their tasks. One might sweep half a room, but woe be unto him if he swept the second half, which was the province of another slave. Under the old sultan, things had slowly deteriorated, but now, under Baba's all-seeing rule, the whole palace was spruced up. The outside was freshly limed so that it gleamed like an iceberg instead of a deteriorating mudpie. Inside, dirt that had accumulated in corners for years was removed; worn covers on divans were replaced and pillows re-covered; hangings were washed; and valuable rugs which over the years had lost all pattern and design under the layers of grime, now sparkled in their original jewel-like colors.

It was a slow process to inventory, appraise, and examine all the women, but when the whole lot was toted up there were found to be over eight hundred, each one of whom had been examined by Baba, Rory, and the young Mansour, sitting as a committee of three to decide which were to be sold and which remain. The older women, mainly from the hareem of Baba's father, whose value was neglible, were allowed to live out their lives as servants in the palace. The younger ones were weeded out along with those of Baba's and Mansour's hareems. Into this lot went those of whom the brothers had tired and those of whom they had never been overly fond. It had been a long and tiresome process, for each woman had to be carefully examined as to her age, beauty, health, and disposition, along with any particular specialty she might possess in entertaining her lord and master. With the examinations had come weepings and supplications and even subdued threats, but Baba was ruthless. He callously informed them that they had the choice of being either sold or strangled, and not a single one of them preferred the latter.

There then was the question of the women of Hussein's hareem, now, temporarily at least, under the jurisdiction of Rory.

"They are yours, my brother, to do with as you please. I gave them to you with no strings attached and if you want to keep them here in Sa'aqs until such a time as you return, we shall retain them for your pleasure. If you prefer to have them strangled, we'll lay in a goodly supply of silken cords. Or you can sell them. The money you receive from them will be all yours; I want nothing that belonged to my brother. But whatever you do with them, I suggest that you pick out a few to accompany you on your long journey. A man should not be without women for too long. Just as the women of our hareems need the services of our eunuchs, so does a man need women with him or he will turn in desperation to the beardless boys who follow every caravan. Speak, Rory, and tell me what disposition you wish me to make of your hareem."

Rory considered the mass of women, all ready to do his bidding. He found he could picture only one face of the entire lot. They were all a jumble of writhing limbs, wet mouths, and searching hands. There was only one whom he remembered and wanted.

"I will keep only Almera. I am used to her, fond of her. Sometimes I wonder if I do not really love her. She has been with me since the first night I met you and she is somehow a part of me, demanding nothing yet giving much. All the others can be included in the lot for Timbuktu."

Baba nodded. "Do you include the English girl with the others? Not having seen your face in ribbons or noticed you walking spraddle-legged, I presume you have already succeeded where all others have failed."

"I succeeded. It was not much of a victory. I think she hates me more because I succeeded than she did all the others that failed."

"You are a man among men." Baba eyed him critically, laughing his congratulations. "Where beys, emirs and sultans failed, you have won; yet I must not give you too much credit, Rory. Any girl would prefer you to some doddering, spindle-shanked bey with a limp rope-end hanging between his legs."

"Give me even less credit, Baba. I made a deal with the girl. She spread her legs for me, albeit unwillingly, for my promise to return her to England. After I had accomplished what I wanted, I found that she no longer appealed to me. I am more Arab than English now, Baba. Yet, still being a little English, I recognize the fact that she is my countrywoman, and feel indebted to her. As for bedding her, I feel the same way as I would about a sister. It seems—incestuous."

Yes, she did seem like a sister, one whom he did not love but who was bound to him by ties of blood and a certain indefinable nearness. He had taken it upon himself to transfer her from the hareem of Baba's father to his own, and had given her the private apartment. Sometimes, when he entered his rooms, he called for her before he called for Almera. It was good to talk in English even if their talk was mostly bitter and quarrelsome. Strangely enough it was sometimes more interesting to clash swords in English than to be surfeited with honey in Arabic. But gradually their conversations became less spiteful and they were able to discuss such things as the weather and the palace gossip without rancor. One night he was surprised to find a meal of English food in lieu of the usual couscous. It was not very well cooked but it was a welcome change. Mary admitted preparing it, but she averred that she had preempted a place in the palace kitchen because she was tired of the eternal couscous. She had cooked her own meal and saved the leftovers for him.

247

More and more they took on the relationship of brother and sister. Rory had no desire to bed her, yet he often wondered if she did not feel differently toward him. Although her eyes continued to sparkle with the same dislike of him, occasionally he would catch her off guard looking at him with something that seemed near to desire. At least it was not hate.

Baba had assured him that her freedom would be an easy matter to accomplish. However, he warned, once she was free her position would be a doubtful one. As a slave she merited a certain amount of protection and was inviolate, but as a free woman she would be in constant danger.

"I could marry her," Rory suggested. He recalled the half-promise he had made to her.

But Baba shook his head. "Not unless she professed Islam, which I doubt that she would do. Even I could not force an imam to marry an unbeliever." He pondered the matter for a moment. "But wait! I have the solution. You say she is like your sister. Very well then, we shall make her our sister."

Thinking was acting with Baba. When a slave came at his handclap, he shouted, "Fetch the yellow-haired N'zrani slave! Tell her that the sultan commands her to appear before him and the emir!"

"What emir are you talking about?" asked Rory.

"You!" Baba pointed a finger at him.

"Since when am I an emir?"

"You've been one for all of two minutes. I just decided on it. Mansour is one. He's my brother. You're my brother and so you must be an emir too. And since I've got two emirs, I'll have to busy myself and produce a shango. I've got eight male brats running around the women's quarters, but not one of my wives has produced anything but females so far. As soon as I get you started for Timbuktu, I'm going to divorce them all. One of my bastards is eight years old; perhaps I'll marry his mother and make the boy Shango. He's a likely lad and his mother has good blood." He stopped talking, interrupted by a knock on the door; when he shouted "Open," Lady Mary stood there.

This time she was not pushed into the room, but entered with her head held high. She was veiled, and Rory was pleased to see that as she advanced toward Baba, she had the sense and courtesy to make the customary deep salaam. Baba waved to the slave to close the door, but motioned for both Mansour and old Sliman to remain. He stood up, lifted the veil from Mary's face, and stared at her deeply and searchingly.

"You are called Yasmin?" he asked.

She shot a quick glance at Rory. An almost imperceptible nod reassured her.

"I am, my lord Sultan."

"It seems, Lady Yasmin, that our relationship has suddenly become rather complicated. At one time you were a member of my father's hareem and might well have produced a half-brother to me, which would have made you a step-mother of sorts." He smiled. "But that did not happen and you were transferred to the hareem of my brother, the Emir of Sa'aqs," he spread his hands in a gesture of recognition toward Rory. "So that changed our relationship; now you might almost be considered a sister-in-law. However, my lord Emir tells me that he has no further desire to bed you—and I can see why because you are scrawny—but that he does consider you in the light of a sister. Probably because you have the same yellow hair as his own. That, perforce, makes you my sister, too. So, Lady Yasmin, I hereby proclaim you my sister and grant you all the protection that that relationship carries."

"It is indeed an honor, my lord Sultan."

"Indeed it is, Princess Yasmin."

"You said 'princess,' Baba?" Rory looked at the big fellow, who was grinning from ear to ear.

"In truth, I did say 'princess.' Think you that the sister of the all-too-glorious Sultan of Sa'aqs could be anything else but a princess? Could she be a commoner like some flat-nosed, thick-lipped Bantu wench? So you, my brother, are an emir; our sister is a princess and poor old Sliman sits there with no title at all. Come now, Sliman, I'm in a generous mood today. I'll make you something. I'll make you a sheik. There! In a few moments I've ennobled you all!"

"You are gracious, milord." Sliman bowed his thanks to

249

Baba while Mary straightened herself and lifted her head as though to adjust it to a coronet.

"And may I ask, my lord Sultan—"she took a long breath and her expression became almost coquettish "—if I am a princess of Sa'aqs or Sax?"

"Of Sa'aqs, my sister," Baba replied, making a wide, sweeping gesture to indicate the space around him, "and as such you will be moved from my brother's hareem into your own apartments near my mother's until it comes time for you to leave. You will have your own slaves to wait upon you and I'll instruct my mother to pick them out and also tell her that you will need a wardrobe and jewels befitting your rank. Now that you are my sister I could marry you off to advantage—but I understand you want to return to England."

"I do, my lord Sultan. I have a family in England that has probably mourned me as dead these past three years. They have received no word from me since I took ship from Naples to return home. You can understand my desire to see my father and mother."

"You shall see them, thanks to the intercession of my brother. Had it not been for him you would be bundled off to Timbuktu to be sold to the highest bidder. I hope you are grateful to him."

"And to you, my lord Sultan."

"There is no need to thank me; I have done nothing."

"Except to elevate me to royalty and arrange for my return to England. I shall always feel that I owe you more than I do your white brother." Baba shrugged his shoulders, but Mary persisted. "Mark me down for a vain, selfish creature if you wish. But I take pride in being a Princess of Sa'aqs. Now when I return home, instead of being a spoiled and bedraggled wench at whom everyone would point a finger of scorn and whisper that she had spent three years in a Moorish hareem, I can flaunt my title in their faces. Princess Yasmin of Sa'aqs! They will all be green with envy, and I swear I shall make them curtsy before me. But alas! They will think I am just being fanciful and that I have made it up out of whole cloth. How can I prove it?"

"Documents will be drawn up to prove it," Baba assured her, "and I'll see to it that the parchments are long and impressive with elaborate calligraphy and heavy gold seals so that even the King of England will have to accord full honors to a Princess of Sa'aqs. However, I would have deemed it a greater honor had you been satisfied with being a sister to a sultan and two emirs, rather than deriving your satisfaction from flaunting your title before a lot of ignorant English girls. Be that as it may, my sister, veil yourself. We must grant an audience to a visiting potentate, one of the highest rank, provided that he has rested from his long journey. He will be connected with our enterprise, so it is well that we should all make his acquaintance." Baba clapped his hands, but this time he did not shout to the slave. Instead, he beckoned the man to him and whispered words so low that Rory could not hear, then sent him on his way.

While they waited Baba took his place in the center of a long divan. He designated a place for Rory on one side of himself and for Mansour on the other. Mary he disposed of on a cushion at his feet, with old Sliman on a similar cushion.

The doors swung open and the slave announced, "His Royal Highness, the Half-King of Basampo."

Half-King? Rory expected that the shadowy form emerging from the dimness of the corridor would be the young queen-king, but the first thing he saw was Tim's flaming hair as he strode across the floor, fairly weighted down with heavy gold-encrusted robes and massive gold chains and bracelets. Rory rejoiced that Tim walked on his own two feet, straight and upright without a limp.

"Tim!" Rory was up from the divan and halfway across the room, but Tim, evidently better coached in court etiquette by now than Rory, ignored him to make a deep obeisance to Baba. Only then did he turn to Rory.

"Still Tim to you, indeed, Rory me lad. God, but we've come up in the world, we two, since we met at Liverpool dockside! Here you are hobnobbing with the sultan himself and here am I, poor, ignorant Tim O'Toole, the Half-King of Basampo. Och, man dear, who'd ever think that Tim O'Toole who never had a pot to piss in or a window to throw it out of, would end up as a bloody

251

royal half-king? That's what the Basampo gal has made me. And here you are, as big as billy-be-damned, an emir or something or other so the servants told me, and who could this be," he peered at Mansour, "and her ladyship here," he bowed to Mary, "and the old gent with the goatee?"

And so Rory had to introduce them all and translate for Tim and the others. While they were plying one another with questions, a slave brought in glasses of mint tea. Then, when all the excitement was over and all the questions answered and Tim had explained how the horrible maggoty poultice had drawn the poison from his leg and he was now whole again; and how he had most efficiently gotten the young king-queen pregnant so that her belly was now round and swollen; then it was time for Baba to dismiss Mary and for him and Rory to go over the plans they had been making and explain them to Tim.

Tim admitted that he had had half a mind to stay in Basampo, particularly after he had fathered the heir-presumptive to the Basampo throne. He had, so he confessed, a desire to see if the little one was a boy or a girl. Not that it mattered much—male or female the child would ascend the throne—the important thing, Tim explained, was that it should have red hair.

While the shadows crept across the floor, they put their heads together and planned, perfecting all the details of Rory's coming trip. Tim had brought over a hundred prime male slaves with him, and these would be his contribution to the business. These would not accompany Rory to Timbuktu, but there were altogether some five hundred female slaves to which Baba was adding about a hundred palace youths who, he was sure, would bring higher prices in Timbuktu than either in Sa'aqs or on the coast. Adolescents, no matter how handsome, brought low prices at the slave factories on the coast, whereas there was a great demand for them in the Arab world.

The organization of the caravan would be up to Sliman. He would have charge of the mechanics of transportation, victualing, and the laying-out of routes. He figured that by procuring some two hundred camels, two women could take turns walking and riding each camel. The boys could go on foot if they were properly watered and fed. Sliman informed them that he had already sent messengers ahead to arrange for canoes on the Niger. Tents and baggage camels had been purchased, and supplies were being assembled. After a long discussion, it was agreed that Sliman would accompany Rory to Timbuktu and that Mansour would go with Tim to Tangier, where Tim's knowledge of ships would be helpful in choosing a good vessel. Mansour could arrange for lodgings for the slaves they were taking with them, including those that Tim had brought from Basampo. These would be a clear profit as they were a gift from the grateful queen.

"And the Princess Yasmin?" Baba looked to Rory for his opinion.

It would probably be better for her to go with Tim direct to Tangier, said Rory. Baba agreed. The Sultanate of Sa'aqs owned a small palace there; she could be safely housed, and the Governor of Tangier would never know that the Princess of Sa'aqs was the same vixen who had scratched his pock-marked face.

"It's going to be lonely here without you, Rory," Baba smiled and sighed.

"It's going to be far lonelier for me; but I promise you that each night when it is time for the muezzin to ascend the minaret and call the faithful to prayer, I shall think of you; and I promise you I shall be coming back to Sa'aqs some day. Then I shall see all the improvements you have made."

Baba sighed again. "We will be older then, Rory, and with all the cares that we shall have on our shoulders, we'll not be able to laugh as we do now."

"Oh, yes, we shall," Rory assured him; "you and I will never grow old, Baba. Why, fifty years from now, when I come back to Sa'aqs for the last time, we'll still be riding our horses and—"

"Our hareem fillies." Baba slapped him on the shoulder.

"And how many hareems will you have sold off by that time?" Mansour asked.

"Enough to make us richer than the Ottoman Sultan himself." Baba winked at Rory. "And now, let's seek the hammam and rid ourselves of the day's sweat and worries. The ministrations of Al-Jarir will make even Tim forget his royal spouse."

"You know, I really got to love the wench," Tim admitted, "although she told me that she would never forget Baba, who was an elephant, and Rory, who was a lion."

"And how did the little creature designate you?"

"Me?" Tim parted his robes to expose a leather contraption similar to that worn by the queen, albeit much smaller. "She told me I was a rhinoceros."

"Then you take precedence over us." Baba roared and winked at Rory. " 'Tis said that the rhinoceros' horn is the most powerful weapon in the world!"

CHAPTER XXIII

RORY CLUCKED AT THE WEARY HORSE, TRY-ing to coax a canter into its lagging footsteps. Useless: the poor animal was so completely exhausted it refused to increase its pace. Now with the white minarets of Tangier already ahead of him, Rory was anxious to reach the city and put an end to this, the most fatiguing journey he—or any other man, he was sure—had ever made. He was finally in sight of the end, but he felt he could never accomplish these last few miles. He was pegged out—overtired, overexhausted, overspent, and way-weary. He summoned up enough energy to turn and look back at his two companions, Sliman and Mleeka. He could see that they were as spent as himself. Mleeka's head was bobbing as wearily as his horse's, and Sliman's goatee sagged like an old man's pizzle.

Each day since Rory had left Sa'aqs had seemed a year. He had missed Sa'aqs with a depressing homesickness such as he had never experienced before. It was the only real home he had ever had and he longed for it and the comforts of his hareem, and particularly the ministrations of Almera, who had gone to Tangier along with Mary. Yes, he even missed Mary. He would positively have welcomed a quarrel with her; but this, along with Almera, would be waiting for him in Tangier. Most of all he missed Baba. With Baba beside him, the trip would not have been half so wearisome. A hundred times a day, he found words on the tip of his tongue, ready to communicate with Baba, only to realize that each minute was taking him farther and farther away from the big man who had been his friend. Friend? Bah! Nothing as banal and threadbare as friendship. Wallahi! Baba was his brother!

When he had left Baba at Sa'aqs the long caravan had seemed endless. Now they were reduced to only three—himself, Mleeka, and Sliman. From a business point of view, the trip had been a huge success. He had received far higher prices for the women and youths than he and Baba had ever dreamed of. After the weary days of the caravan from Sa'aqs to the river; after the long, hot days spent in the canoes; and after their arrival in that flea-bitten, sunbaked city of Timbuktu, Rory had been glad to quit himself of his human merchandise. He had lost only two of the women and none of the youths through illness on the journey and the caravan had arrived in Timbuktu at a most opportune time. The city was full of prospective purchasers, all confronted by a dearth of slaves because so many were now being delivered to the factories on the coast. True, the wily merchants had haggled over prices, but Rory knew that he had the upper hand just by the look of worried cupidity on their faces. Never before had such prime merchandise been available to them. Cunningly he played off one against the other, raising his prices bit by bit until he was ashamed to ask for more. Each merchant had offered him bribes and secret inducements, all of which he had accepted and then sold to the one who offered him the most money. Strange to say, their bidding had been highest for the youths of Sa'aqs—those willow-slim palace adolescents with soft hands and smooth skin. Their bee-stung lips and kohl-rimmed eyes had attracted higher prices than the women—and *they* had brought plenty. An astonishing plenty!

The wrangling had taken weeks and Rory had no idea of the total proceeds of the sale. Sufficient to say that their saddlebags were weighty with silver Maria Theresa dollars, Portuguese escudos, Spanish pesetas, English guineas, gold ingots, bags of gold dust, and a miscellaneous assortment of unset emeralds, diamonds, and pearls. He had been too tired to make an accounting but he knew that it was more than Baba had planned on—far more.

During their stay in Timbuktu, he and Sliman had shared a filthy mud house with Mleeka as their only servant. If ever there was a habitation devoid of all comfort, this one certainly had been it. The heat had been so oppressive that Rory had moved his bed to the roof and even there it had been impossible to sleep because of the hordes of insects. For the first few weeks he had had the consolation of one or another of the women from the Sa'aqs hareems until, with the heat and the dirt and the fleas, even women had become distasteful to him and he had been content to roll himself in a djellabah and sleep alone on the roof with Sliman to guard their steadily mounting bags of gold and Mleeka sleeping at the old man's feet.

Then, after an eternity, the whole aggravating business had been finished and he joined the first caravan that was going over the desert and the High Atlas to Marrakech. If the journey to Timbuktu had tried him, it was as nothing compared with the long crossing of the desert. Mostly they traveled by night and slept by day, but the oppressive desolation seemed endless. It wasn't the desert of white sand dunes that he had pictured in his mind—it was dirt and stones and flint and shale; it was sudden windstorms that whipped the gritty soil into clouds that obscured the sun; it was weird, jagged mountains of obscene purple basalt that glowed like molten metal. This desert was a far-spaced well that yielded milky, brackish water with only occasionally a palm-studded oasis and a caravanserai that was hardly fit for camels, let alone men. He had kept on, day after weary day, speaking little and not wishing to be spoken to.

Although Mleeka was as exhausted as Rory, during

their daytime halts the slave did all he could to make Rory comfortable. He erected shelters to shield Rory from the sun. He dug contoured depressions in the dirt to accommodate Rory's body. He hung the porous waterpot in whatever breeze there might be so that the brackish water might have some degree of coolness. But there was little more he could do, and he suffered along with his master.

Once over the High Atlas and down into the verdant oasis that was Marrakech, they had time to catch their breath. Here they parted from the caravan and sought the refuge of a bedbug-ridden caravanserai. Sliman informed Rory that he would be welcome at the emir's palace but in his dirty rags Rory did not want to present himself nor did he have either strength or ambition to buy new clothes. He threw himself on the filthy floor of the caravanserai, as oblivious to the dirty straw and camel dung as he was to the slut with sweaty armpits who tried to rouse him. He remembered kicking her away from him, and then he slept throughout the night and all the next day and the next night, until he finally awoke with a foul taste in his mouth, a week's beard on his face, and his body scarlet-splashed with vermin.

Night came and he stumbled to the souks and there grabbed the first two clean djellabahs he saw, one for himself and one for Mleeka, and together they sought and found a hammam. For an hour he soaked and steamed himself then gave his body over to Mleeka to be massaged and pummeled back into some semblance of sentience. They left the hammam and Rory began to feel almost human. A barber, squatting on his haunches in the Djmna el Fna, shaved him by the light of a flickering wick in a saucer of oil, marveling at the blondness of his beard. Rory did not dare unwind his turban, fearful that his hair would cause more comment than his beard because now it had grown below his shoulders.

Then, clean-shaven, bathed, and dressed in decent clothes, he and Mleeka ate their first decent meal since leaving Sa'aqs—plates of couscous and hot minted tea. They found a cleaner caravanserai by the side of the big square, where they spent their few remaining days in

Marrakech during which they purchased horses, outfitted old Sliman in clean clothes, and prepared for the trip to Tangier. Rory found Marrakech a fascinating city and he spent hours in the Djmna el Fna. It was a continuous fair—a never-ending circus. The perfumed Chleuh boys, their sloe eyes circled with kohl, their hands hennaed, danced for him, their supple limbs writhing in voluptuous rhythms, and while he enjoyed watching them, he. repulsed their advances. He watched the snake charmers pipe their swaying vipers, saw the acrobats perform unbelievable feats of balance, and listened to the storytellers enthrall a charmed circle of listeners with their interminable tales of lust, adventure, and cunning. The whole enormous dusty square was a continuing carnival that never stopped, and he gazed at it as wide-eyed as any Berber down from the mountains.

He found himself desiring a woman, but one look at the dirty whores with running sores on their faces sickened him so that he lost all desire. He had been without a woman for so long, he could go a little longer. Almera would be waiting for him in Tangier and he longed for the touch of her cool hands.

Now, nearing Tangier, along with the ache in his body, he discovered a mounting ache in his loins. Almera! He had not had a woman for so long that he had built up a painful tension within himself. Contact with the warmth and softness of woman's flesh would rest him more than hours of sleep, and then, once his body had been drained, he could sleep, he felt, forever.

The plodding horses had at length reached the gates of the city. The supercilious Moorish guards challenged their entrance, but a word from Sliman and they were allowed to pass. The mood of the guards then changed from arrogance to subservience and their entrance was marked by low salaams from the soldiers. A young lad, conspicuous by his dark skin and the snowy white of his djellabah, who had been squatting in a corner of the gateway, ran over to them, waving his arms and shouting. When he came to Rory he bowed respectfully and asked if Rory were indeed the Emir of Sa'aqs. At his tired acknowledgment, the lad's face lit up with a wide expanse of white teeth and he grabbed Rory's bridle.

"It is two weeks now, my lord, that I have sat at the gate from dawn to sunset waiting for you. 'Twas milord Mansour's orders. He will be happy that you have come, as he has been worried about you. Look! I lead you to your house."

The streets were narrow and ankle-deep in stinking offal which had stained the limed walls and spattered them waist high with brindle dapplings, but Rory was too grateful to be there to complain. Looking behind him to ascertain that Sliman and Mleeka were following, he slouched forward in his saddle, letting the boy guide him through the twisting alleys until they arrived at a blank white-stuccoed wall, indistinguishable from all the rest except that the wooden doors were newly painted and the brass bossings polished to gleam like gold.

At the boy's hammering on the heavy knocker, the doors opened and Rory caught a glimpse of a tinkling fountain splashing into a basin of Persian blue tiles. He smelled the cloying sweetness of orange blossoms and anticipated the coolness of the slatted shadows, then slid from his saddle like a bag of millet into the arms of Mansour and Tim. With an arm over the shoulders of each, he stepped through the doors, across the tiles of the courtyard, and up dark stairs. Then there was a room—cool and dim, with a silk-covered divan and the soft touch of Almera's hands as she stripped off his sweaty garments.

Her searching fingers caressed his skin along with the perfumed water, and although his body responded vigorously to her touch and he was conscious of the throbbing tumescence, his fatigue cheated him of his desire and sleep overpowered him. Dimly he heard her soft footsteps leave the room; he heard the door open and Mansour enter. His consciousness gathered in Mansour's words of praise over the contents of his saddlebags and he distinguished Tim's words, the English phrases sounding strange after so much Arabic. The words drifted off into space and he was too sleepy to understand them. He slept and when he awoke the room was in darkness except for one thin taper burning on a polished brass tray beside his bed.

Sleep would have claimed him again were it not for the forlorn feeling in his stomach. He was thirsty, he was hungry, and, praise be to Allah, he was sufficiently recuperated to be aware of the demands of his body. Summoning his strength, he clapped his hands, listening for the door to open, but when it did, the footsteps were those of a man and it was Mleeka who leaned over him.

"Milord awake?"

"Your lord is goddamned hungry."

"Milord shall eat and if milord wish there is wine of Jerez in the palace but," he cocked his head sideways and winked at Rory, "is forbidden to True Believer such as milord."

"Except in cases where it has a medicinal value, and as Allah is my judge, I am in need of medicine."

"Then it be bringed to you." Mleeka turned to leave, but Rory had one more demand.

"Tell Almera to bring it to me."

"Ah yes, milord." Mleeka grinned and pointed to Rory's body. "It plain milord has more need for Almera than Mleeka. When date palm stand tall and straight, it needs soft finger to pick the fruit."

Rory looked around for something to throw at the grinning black. Instead he reached down and pulled the thin silk up over his body. Mleeka retreated a few steps then stopped.

"Milord has nothing to be ashamed from. He must be proud to display—"

"Get out, you black djinni of Shaitan, and don't come back until tomorrow morning. Seek out some kitchen wench whose skin is as black as your own, because you need her as much as I need Almera."

Mleeka's grin widened. "I did it, milord. While you sleep Mleeka take two women. Mleeka strong man. Women howl. Mleeka like make women howl like hyena. Ay! Ay! Ay! Second she howl more than first and now I seek third who will howl like she-baboon."

This time Rory found energy enough to lean over the side of the divan and pick up one of the bright new babouches aligned on the floor. He hurled it at Mleeka who caught it, juggled it for a moment from one hand to the other and trotted back to replace it on the floor beside the other. With a whirl of the white skirts of his djellabah he was gone; Rory had only a few moments to wait until the door opened again and Almera entered with a tall crystal cruet and a thin-stemmed wine glass.

Never before had wine tasted so good as this amber wine of Spain. Rory downed two glasses. It nestled in his stomach with a spreading glow of warmth and he drew Almera down beside him, kissing her eyes, her cheeks, and her mouth, then nuzzling the soft flesh that was hidden under the gossamer of her gown.

"Your dinner will be here in a moment, milord."

"I can eat later. Sit beside me, Little-love-whose-delight-it-is-to-pick-the-dates. I have hungered for you more than food."

"It is good to hear that, milord. It makes Almera happy."

"Many a night, beloved, I have possessed you in my dreams. You have come to my couch all tender, soft, and sweet-smelling. But always at the most crucial point in our lovemaking I would wake up."

"And then, milord?"

"There was only one way left for me to finish that which you had started in my dreams." He held up his hand and she looked at it and smiled.

"A poor substitute." She leaned over and kissed him.

"A damned poor substitute. But tell me. Have you thought of me?"

"Constantly. I have missed milord but I have found some recompense in waiting on milady Yasmin."

"My lady Yasmin? And how is her Royal Highness, that white-skinned, thin-nosed bitch?"

"She is well. Sometimes she is very kind to me and then she is cruel. She seems to be happiest when she is talking about you. She talks a lot about you."

"Most of it bad, I presume."

"You presume right, milord, yet she is most curious about you. She wants me to talk about you. She wants me to tell her over and over again how you make love to me and what particular things I do to give you the greatest pleasure. Then, when I tell her, she rails against you and vows she would never do such things to a man. She says they are vulgar and bestial, but I tell her that when a woman loves a man's body enough, there is nothing she is not willing to do to give him pleasure. But milady Yasmin says that her lips are too pure, her fingers too delicate, and that she is made too small to accommodate a man such as you. Yet even while she is talking she is asking me more questions and I think she gets some special pleasure out of what I tell her. We can talk about milady Yasmin at some other time, milord. Just now you hunger."

Almera slipped from his arms and went out, to reappear with a heavy salver covered with a white napkin. She fed him, dipping her fingers into the hot semolina, choosing the choicest bits of lamb and the most appetizing vegetables. Rolling the food into a ball, she popped it into his mouth. When he could eat no more, he sank back and threw down the sheet.

"Now," he whispered. "See how straight and tall the date palm stands. Its fruit is ready for plucking."

She blew out the candle, but he heard her retreating footsteps in the darkness. "Where are you going?"

"Only to fetch a jar of unguent. It has been so long, milord, since I have known your caresses, the unguent will make it easier for you and less painful for me."

"Then hurry! I shall count to one hundred, woman, and if you are not back, I swear I shall marry my own right hand and have no use for you. Think you I can wait forever?"

"After all this time, a few seconds will not harm you." Her voice was strained and he heard a suppressed sob. The door closed but it seemed it had no sooner closed than opened again and he heard her footsteps coming toward him across the tiles.

"Now!" his voice was hoarse and he opened his arms to receive her. He was surprised that she struggled a little against his impatience but he forced her down on the bed, pressing his lips against hers. A little moan of protest was smothered by the ruthlessness of his kiss. The jar of perfumed balm which she had pressed into his hand, he flung to the floor, unheedful of her wishes.

He could no longer control himself. The pent-up urgency of months of continence made him inexorable. The powerful thrusts of his hips were cruel and purely bestial without tenderness or pity. It was soon over and he fell exhausted athwart her quivering body, sucking long, deep breaths into his lungs, deaf to her sobs. As some degree of lucidity returned to him, he sensed the paradox of her sobbing. He remembered her insistence on the salve. Why? Certainly she had become accustomed to the enormity of his body. She had never required ointments before. Now, as he listened between breaths, her sobbing seemed one of pain. Perhaps he had hurt her. If so, he was sorry. He had not intended to, but his need of her had been too urgent. To comfort her, he accommodated the curve of her body to his, lifted her head and placed it on his arm. Her long hair smothered him and he pushed it away. Relaxed, he pulled her to him, his lips seeking hers; but he felt her body stiffen in his arms and she turned her face away from him. This was not the Almera he had always known; she had always had only one desire—to please him.

He felt affronted, cheated of his own masculinity; and the desire in his loins, which had so recently been satiated, again asserted itself. He felt himself growing strong and rigid against her and his hands sought her breasts to cup them in his fingers and to bring her to the same point of desire as himself. Her hand pushed them away and she moved from him and sat up.

"But why, Almera? Have I offended you?" His voice pled with her even though all the while, he knew he had only to bend her to his will.

"I am not Almera. Thank God for that." The words were in English. "I do not have to cater to your lusts, Rory Mahound."

He jackknifed up in bed. "My God! Mary? What are you doing here?" He leaned over and fumbled on the table for the tinder box, lit it, and applied the feeble flame to the candle. He turned and saw the gold of her hair.

"I ask myself the same question." Anger pitched her voice high and querulous. "What *am* I doing here? It would be hard to explain. I find it difficult to reconcile my actions even to myself. I am a stupid fool—an idiot, with

263

no more brains than a simpering schoolgirl who has developed an infantile crush on the butcher's boy. What am I doing here? I've always hated you. You're a beast, Rory Mahound."

"Yet I cannot forget that you came here of your own free will. Certainly it was not at my wishing. Damn! I didn't want you. After a man has been without a woman as long as I have, he wants no fair-skinned, ice-cold bitch."

"I suppose you wanted Almera."

"I did."

"I forced her to change places with me. I threatened to have her flogged for stealing a turquoise necklace if she didn't do it. I felt—and only I can realize how utterly stupid I was—that I loved you. Laugh, Rory Mahound, laugh! You! Imagine that? I had forgotten how you ravished me once without mercy and yet I remembered it too. I had hoped that this time things would be different. I had hoped that there might be some semblance of love between us for, in truth, regardless of how odious your body was to me before, I have not been able to get it out of my mind and I found myself desiring it even though I was repulsed by it. But I did not want only your body. I wanted something else. I did not find it. Now I know it is not in you. You are incapable of it."

"Of what? Surely I have but just given you something that most women would be glad to have. Can you complain of my performance? Can you complain of my ability to satisfy a woman?" He pointed down to himself.

"Yes, that is all of you, Rory Mahound. That is your beginning and your end. Besides that you have nothing except a modicum of flashy good looks that might attract some women. You will never know the meaning of the word love." She rose from the bed and sought the tumbled pile of silk that was her robe on the floor. Silently he watched her while she draped it over her shoulders.

He was beginning to hate himself for what he had done. Not that he regretted it. Not at all. But as he looked at her he found her repulsive. Why he did not know. He could not deny her beauty, but it held nothing for him. He did not desire her and even while there throbbed a renewal of his desire, he knew that if he never had another woman he would not take this one again. Never! He sensed when he looked into her eyes that she felt the same way about him. She had sought him, and under cover of the darkness he had found a momentary satisfaction in her. But only that. He rolled sideways on the bed, threw his legs over the edge, and stood up.

"It would seem that we know each other now. You know me for the man I am. I do not woo a woman with frilled nosegays, swoonings, pretty poesies, and moonlight serenades. Bah! Those are for weak men—all this meaningless patter of love which ends up by a tumble among the sheets. I've no time for vaporings. Call me a beast if you will. My heart is not entirely devoid of tenderness. Yet that tenderness—call it love if you will—must go in the way of my own choosing. I know not why you sought me out tonight. I would never have chosen you. The thought of bedding with you seems incestuous and vile. Had I known it was you and not Almera I would have kicked you out. Well, you have satisfied yourself—and yet I do not believe myself to be one half the rogue you picture me. I'm not without feelings. I think I love Almera, and I love her because she has been good to me and loves me in return. That is why I desired her tonight, and not you who have never done anything for me, begrudging me even a kind word. Now go, and after Almera, who is probably waiting outside the door, conducts you to your apartments, she will return to me."

At the door she turned and faced him. "It is strange, Rory Mahound; I hate you and yet, had you but said the right words to me tonight and done the right things, I think I would have loved you. I would have been foolish enough to marry you by priest or imam or even by no vows at all. I shall probably never forget you, but I shall have my revenge. Someday, believe me, I shall have the upper hand. Then watch out! I shall be as cruel, as ruthless, and as evil as you are."

He acknowledged her words, looking past her to Almera who stood on the threshold of the opened door.

"When you have conducted milady to her room, return

here, Almera. I have not decided whether or not I shall have you whipped for trying to deceive me."

She bowed her head but Mary straightened up, her eyes flashing. "And if you do, it is something I want to witness."

"Your jealousy ill becomes you, Mary," Rory laughed. With a swoop of his hand he picked up the jar of ointment and walked over to her, to set it in her hand. "Perhaps had I used this, Lady Mary, you would not have had so much to complain about. Keep it handy. You will need it for that nosegay-toting English husband you've set your cap for." He smiled at her although it was a smile that had neither warmth nor affection. "On second thought," he continued, with that puny Englishman whom you will probably pick out, I doubt if you will ever need it, nor—" he hesitated for a moment "—do I imagine that now that you have tasted a real man you will ever be satisfied by anything England can produce." He turned on his heel, but before he heard the door close, he shouted, "Return quickly, Almera, I have urgent need for you."

CHAPTER XXIV

THE WHIRL OF ACTIVITIES THAT FOLLOWED Rory's arrival in Tangier was every bit as hectic and at times even more frustrating than those in Sa'aqs before he left. Although Mansour and Tim had laid much of the groundwork, there remained an endless number of things for Rory to do. His, after all, was the final word—his the judgment, his the decision. First there was the accounting of money, accomplished through a money-lender and a jeweler. When the gold was weighed and the jewels appraised and sold, when the various coins were counted up and all exchanged into Spanish gold pieces, Rory mentally translated them back into pounds. He was astonished at the figure—some forty thousand pounds sterling! This divided between himself and Baba would mean a considerable fortune if they never did anything else in their lives. Yet it was merely the nest egg that would be turned into more "black ivory," which in turn would be transformed into more golden pounds.

Mansour had brought with him a coffle of about a hundred and fifty male slaves from Sa'aqs. These he had lodged in an old warehouse near the waterfront. All were prime specimens—Fans, Mandingos, Hausas, Wolofs, Fulanis, Lobis, and Adjukrus—the most-wanted tribes— whom Baba had purchased from itinerant Arab slave dealers to augment the fifty or more fine Basampos that Tim had brought with him. Fortunately there had been no casualties in the long march from Sa'aqs to Tangier. Mansour had been well briefed by Baba as to the value of his merchandise and had seen to it that the men received humane treatment while in the caravan. Mansour, astute in his own right, had the good sense to use psychology on the slaves. He imbued them with the adventure of going overseas to what, as he described it to them, would be a land of perpetual pleasure—a nightly procession of beautiful women, bounteous meals, continuous hunting, and a paucity of labor. No wonder the prospects appealed to them in contrast to the shackled slavery they had undergone. In fact, unlike the miserable members of most slave caravans, they were not shackled, and they marched on, drunk with their first taste of freedom and looking forward to the future without fear or dread. Not one of them had absconded. Since their arrival they had rested for several weeks, had eaten good food, had been allowed to bathe and exercise, and had had their bodies rubbed daily with palm oil. Rory visited them in their temporary barracoons and found them in good spirits, anxious to make the trip across the ocean to enjoy all the delights that had been so wondrously depicted to them.

Rory knew he would need more slaves, although the exact number depended on the capacity of whatever ship he could find to transport them to the Caribbean. After a talk with Mansour, this turned out to be not quite the problem Rory had anticipated. The entire matter, Mansour explained, would be settled after a visit to Sidi Mohammed el Khatib, the Governor of Tangier and the representative in Tangier of the great and supreme Sultan of Morocco. The audience would take place *bokra*—tomorrow.

Sidi Mohammed el Khatib was a man of about fifty years, with an enormous bushy black beard and a bronze complexion. He was, Rory thought, the fattest man he had ever seen and a momentary picture of that gross belly attempting to make love to Lady Mary crossed his mind. No wonder she had scratched his face to ribbons. Yet, as man to man, Rory could not help but take to him immediately. Like all fat men, he exuded jollity and good humor; his little black eyes, sunk in rolls of fat like raisins in some spicy cinnamon dough, twinkled merrily, and a smile, outlined by moist red lips, appeared in the enormous black beard.

"Two Emirs of Sa'aqs together!" He spread his pudgy hands in an open gesture of welcome. " 'Tis too much of an honor! The new Sultan of Sa'aqs—may Allah give him a long and prosperous reign, for he is indeed a vassal of which His Sublimity the Sultan of the Maghreb is exceedingly proud—shows me great esteem in sending both his brothers here. Pray be seated."

He waited for Rory and Mansour to sink onto the two cushions which slaves brought. There was none for Tim, who was forced to stand. It was apparent that, as Half-King of Basampo, he did not rank with either of the Emirs of Sa'aqs.

"We are, you see"—Sidi Mohammed was overextending himself in graciousness—"most anxious to be of service to your brother, the sultan. His Sublimity, the Sultan of the Maghreb—may Allah bless every hair in his beard—is particularly fond of Sa'aqs. It is one of the provinces in his realm to which he has never had to send his tax collectors. Sa'aqs has been not only most prompt always, but most generous. I am therefore instructed to place all the resources of my city at your disposal—which at present means a fine ship—" he paused for a moment to show his red lips in another smile "—as well as a captain and crew."

"You are most kind," Rory bowed in acknowledgment.

The finger of the governor hovered over his lips in a little gesture of caution against Rory's consideration of his offer as a gift. "But at a price, of course. Oh my, yes indeed, at a price." He lowered his voice and whispered, "His Sublimity is always pleased to receive presents but he does not like to give them."

"And that price?" Rory asked.

Sidi Mohammed waved the matter aside as of little importance. "Who are we, my illustrious Emir, to discuss such trivial matters as money? That is for dusty-fingered accountants and ledger-blind clerks. The bill will be rendered in due time and because of His Sublimity's regard for Sa'aqs, it will not be exorbitant, either for the ship itself or for the crew of N'zrani slaves which I propose to sell you. Experienced men they are, all seaman, from a grim-faced captain right down to a pretty cabin boy. You'll find them familiar with the ship, too. They should be. They were captured on it. I've been giving them all a more-severe-than-usual taste of Moorish hospitality, so that when you appear to deliver them they will think you the Archangel Michael come to rescue them from the fiery depths of hell." He closed one eye slowly and knowingly. "Their treatment has been such that they'll be glad to rid themselves of our hospitality. I've been softening them up for you, although I must admit that the captain is a hard one to soften."

"He must be a man of spirit. So much the better," Rory answered. "But I trust the others have not been so softened they will not be able to work."

"Not at all. They still have all their hands and feet, plus a few stripes on their backs. But we would not want them to become so enamoured of our fair city that they prefer to serve us rather than you. Besides," the governor sipped at his mint tea, "there's a glut of N'zrani slaves today. Our corsairs have been fortunate lately, thanks to Allah, and have brought in many ships. That's why I can let you have the ship and the entire crew cheap—dirt cheap."

"I find words inadequate to express my gratitude."

"They are unnecessary. All Islam glories in your conversion from a N'zrani to a True Believer. We are not the savages we are supposed to be, my lord Emir. And now may I present Signore Tancredo Vogliano, late of Turin in the land of Italy. Signore Vogliano is a man of business who stands high in our favor because he, like yourself, has proclaimed Mohammed the only True Prophet of the one God. He has our instructions and he will arrange many things for you and, should you feel inclined to reward him for his services, he will, I am sure, be most willing to accept some small pecuniary reward." He motioned for a man in European clothing to come forward. "May I present Signore Vogliano, my lords of Sa'aqs, who acts as our representative in our dealings with the N'zrani nations."

There was a certain air of oily unctuousness about the man which Rory did not like. He was too fawning and subservient and the streaks of gray in his black hair testified to the fact that he had had the experience of many years of surviving and adapting himself to any situation. Rory would have preferred to do business with Sidi Mohammed himself but the Sidi's rising from the divan was a sign that the audience was over. He departed with a languid wave of his hand. The Italian came over to Rory and Mansour. His bow was too low, his smile too much of a smirk, and his eyes a bit too crafty. Tim heaved a sigh of relief that the interview was over and poor Mleeka hoisted himself to his knees and stood up, along with Sliman. With more expressions of gratitude, blessings from Allah, deep salaams and wishes for long life and peace, the Sa'aqs delegation saluted the remaining members of the Sidi's council and departed, escorted by Signore Vogliano who continued to bubble with affability.

Once out of the audience chamber, Vogliano led them through devious corridors of the palace to a small room which he described as his office. It was the first room Rory had seen in Morocco that boasted chairs and a desk. When he seated himself, at Vogliano's invitation, he discovered the hard seat of the chair uncomfortable after the soft divans to which he had become accustomed.

Vogliano's manner changed as he seated himself behind

his desk. His air of obsequiousness vanished and he became a hardheaded businessman. A servant brought a carafe of wine at which Rory looked askance, but which Vogliano poured, speaking in English as he handed a glass to Rory.

"Your health, Sir Roderick."

Surprise showed in Rory's eyes.

"Oh yes, Sir Roderick, I speak English. Also French, Spanish, and Portuguese if you prefer, and although I find German difficult, I can at least make myself understood. However for the benefit of the Emir Mansour perhaps we had better carry on our conversation in Arabic."

"But you know my name?" It had come as a shock to Rory to be so addressed.

"Of course. It is our business to know everything. We know of your friendship with the Sultan of Sa'aqs and we approve. At first I must confess we were somewhat suspicious that your relationship with him partook of something more than friendship. Alas, such things are common here in the Maghreb. But our informants in Sa'aqs who are most trustworthy have told us that it is indeed a friendship that exists between you two and nothing else. The business venture that you are starting sounds good to us. You got good prices for the female slaves and the youths you sold in Timbuktu and you are well capitalized for your new venture.

"The Maghreb needs foreign trade and your business will have an important future. The new world is avid for slaves and we have a glut of them in Africa. The only difficulty has been in getting them across the ocean. To do this we have had to accept low prices for them and allow the immense profit they bring to fall into the hands of Englishmen and Portuguese. We are willing to cooperate with you provided. . . ." He held up an index finger which glittered with the multi-faceted encrustations of rubies, sapphires and diamonds.

"Provided?" Rory already saw a goodly share of the money he had brought from Timbuktu vanishing.

"Provided His Excellency the governor and I have a share in the proceeds. Oh, it need be a very small one. Say two per centum for the governor and the same for myself.

271

That means we shall not be too hard on you in charging you for the ship and the crew. Ten thousand Maria Theresa dollars for the ship and one hundred dollars for each of the thirty crew members. Where else could you get a sturdy three-master and a crew for such a paltry sum?"

It sounded like an exceeding lot of money to Rory, but Tim's almost imperceptible nod of his head signified his approval, so Rory felt it might be a good bargain.

Vogliano's voice droned on. The ship had been captured about two months ago some fifty miles off Gibraltar. It was an American ship, bearing a cargo of rum, whale oil, and timber from a place called Salem in Massachusetts to Livorno. The Moorish pirates had captured it and brought it to Tangier. Alerted by Mansour's need of a ship, they had kept the crew intact. Instead of stripping the ship and burning it for its copper and iron, they had merely altered it so it could not be easily recognized.

Instead of a three-master, it was now a barque with square-rigged foremast and mainmast and a mizzenmast fore-and-aft rigged. Its black paint had been covered with a coat of dazzling white and it had been armed with four brass cannon. They had had, so Vogliano informed them, some trouble with the figurehead. The ship had been called the *Juno* and the figurehead it sported was a voluptuous goddess with huge crimson-nippled breasts and flowing robes. As the delineation of any human figure was forbidden to the followers of Islam, they had had to search among the N'zrani slaves to find a man skilled in woodcarving. He had, Vogliano beamed, done a commendable job.

The swelling breasts of the goddess had been recarved into the massive pectorals of a man; the simpering features made masculine and ferocious; the flowing hair turned into two small horns and a gilded trident placed in the figure's hand. A coat of scarlet paint had metamorphosed the goddess into the devil himself, and the name of the ship had been changed from *Juno* to *Shaitan* which, Vogliano smirked at Rory, seemed a most appropriate name for an owner by the name of Mahound. Let the devil serve the devil—and besides, the fiery figure on the prow of the white ship was most picturesque.

Then there was the matter of ship's papers. These had been cleverly forged—the Moors were adept at calligraphy—and now instead of the ship *Juno* out of Salem bound for Livorno, it was the barque *Shaitan* from her home port of Goree in Senegal, flying the flag of the Ottoman Empire and bound for . . .?

Vogliano shrugged his shoulders. What exactly was Rory's destination to be?

It was Rory's turn to shrug his own shoulders. Frankly, he did not know. He and Baba had not discussed it and lately things had been happening too fast for him to keep up with them. Suddenly he found himself the prospective owner of a ship and a full crew. He had a half, or a third, of a cargo of slaves, but he was damned if he knew where he was going to take them.

His indecision did not faze the redoubtable Vogliano. He merely twirled a globe that stood beside his desk, waiting for it to stop, and then put a blunt finger on a tiny spot which appeared to be an excrescence on the shoulder of South America.

"Trinidad," he said.

Rory regarded the map closely. It was, he could see, an island off the coast of South America, the southernmost in the chain of islands that made up the West Indies.

"But why a Spanish island?" he queried.

Vogliano shook his head. "A Spanish name, true, but now an English island. It has been a colony of Spain for many years but recently Spain ceded it to England. Now England is busy changing it from a sleepy Spanish outpost to a vast sugar-producing plantation. English capital is being invested there and slaves are desperately needed to work on the plantations. The English in Trinidad are paying the highest prices of all the American markets."

So that determined his destination. Trinidad! But where was he leaving from? What was to be his home port, Tangier?

Vogliano shook his head. No, that city enjoyed a rather disreputable odor throughout the world of shipping because of its pirates. No, something a little more respectable and convenient. It seemed that the Sherifian government had once been a part owner in a slave factory on the island of Goree, offshore from the city of Dakar in Senegal. It had made money for a few years until the English took over the slave trade and established slave factories of their own, preferring to do business among themselves rather than with the Moors. The factory had been abandoned, but now it was being refurbished and garrisoned. Couldn't the Emir Mansour take up his residence there and be prepared when the *Shaitan* returned for another black cargo? With a self-effacing smirk, Vogliano admitted that he had attended to all the details, even to designing a houseflag that would be flown over the factory at Goree. It was red with two gold *S*'s entwined—one for Sa'aqs and one for Sax.

Then, of course, there were a few other details. The *Shaitan* had accommodations for some four hundred slaves. It would be necessary to purchase additional bodies to fill out the complement, and Vogliano promised the finest possible merchandise. These would be more expensive than the N'zrani sailors, but he was willing to sell them for a hundred and fifty dollars a head which, of course did not include the infinitesimal one per centum which Vogliano was entitled to as his commission. Then, in addition, there would be the ten Moorish soldiers that would accompany them on the voyage.

"Ten soldiers?" Rory didn't understand.

Of course. A ship manned by a slave crew could well be a hotbed of mutiny. Rory would need protection. Agreed?

Vogliano thought of everything, Rory was forced to agree.

Then there would be the matter of clothing for the crew, who could hardly man a ship in the filthy rags they were now wearing. The captain would need decent clothes, as would Rory and Tim who could not arrive in Trinidad dressed in Moorish robes. And there was the victualing and watering of the ship for the voyage. Both clothes and provisions Vogliano could supply from his own stores. Rory was not to worry; everything would be taken care of. At a price, of course, at a price!

When he arrived back at his own house, Rory sat down with Mansour, Tim, and Sliman to figure out how deeply indebted they might be to the wily Italian, but in the midst of their figuring Tim excused himself. He was gone for some few minutes and when he returned he was followed by two slaves carrying a small wooden chest.

"If I'm to be part of this company, it's time I invested something in it besides me own pretty face and a few black buckos." Tim opened the chest. "Never say that Timmy's talents didn't come in handy. The little king thought so anyway. See!" He pointed to the chest which was filled with bracelets, chains and ear pendants, all of heavy barbaric gold.

Mansour arose from the divan and threw his arms around Tim's shoulders. "We'll never underrate your talents, Tim, Your Half-Majesty. Any man can impregnate a woman, but it takes a real man to get a king with child."

Tim fumbled in the chest and took out one of the gold chains and hung it around Mansour's neck. " 'Twas a pleasant job, bucko, and I must say a profitable one. Me, who's always had to pay some stinking whore for my screwing, getting paid for it. Aye, it's the cushiest money I ever earned and I come by it so easy-like, I'll never miss it. Should make me a full-fledged member of the corporation, I'd say?"

"It does, Timmy, it does," Rory assured him.

CHAPTER XXV

RORY AND ALMERA WERE STILL DAWDLING over breakfast. It was a period of the day that Rory particularly enjoyed. The passions of the night had been fully spent and he felt relaxed in mind and body. The jalousies were open and a cool breeze entered to caress his skin along with the soft fingers of Almera.

Rory was surprised that Almera spoke so often of Mary. A strange bond had grown between the two women—a bond which Rory felt had its roots in himself. Almera's was born of a desire to serve him. She delighted in nothing more than humbling herself before him. Mary, on the other hand, seemed to take special pleasure in hating him, and in the rare intervals when they saw each other, trying to humiliate him.

This morning, Almera startled him with the news that Mary—the Princess Yasmin as she called her—wanted Almera to go to England with her. It would not be fitting, Mary had told Almera, that she return without a waiting maid, and she'd be damned if she'd take along any thick-lipped nigger wench.

Rory looked long at her, admiring, as always, her beauty. Although he often took Almera for granted, he was never entirely forgetful that she was one of the most beautiful women he had ever seen. The dusky olive of her skin, the blackness of her hair, the luminosity of her dark eyes appealed to him far more than Mary's bleached English pallidity. "But do you want to go, my Little-picker-of-dates-from-the-tall-palm?"

She shook her head. "I would rather go with my lord, wherever that might be."

"This time I cannot take you with me, little dove."

Her hand, slippery with the oil of musk, traced an arabesque of meandering circles on his belly.

"Then let me go with the Princess Yasmin."

"To England?"

"Yes, to England, wherever that is. But not forever, milord. Not forever! I would return when my lord returns, to be with him again. I would speak his language and I would be more of a companion for him. As it is I am only a poor, ignorant girl. I cannot even talk with my lord in his tongue."

He smiled. "You do not need to speak it, Almera. I love you as you are."

It was her turn to smile. "That is the first time you have ever said that you love me, milord. I am grateful. I know I please you in bed, but I would do more than that. I would be someone you could talk to and discuss your plans with. That I could do, could I but go to England and become more like the Princess Yasmin."

276

"God forbid!"

Yet as he spoke Rory wondered if this would not be a solution. It had disturbed him as to what Almera would do after he had gone. He could not leave her alone in the palace in Tangier. He could not send her to Goree with Mansour as she was not a woman of Mansour's hareem, and for the same reason he could not return her to Baba. Without him, she would have no place, neither in Morocco nor in Sa'aqs, for she would be a woman without a man, a slave without a master. Why not allow Mary to take her to England? There she would learn the English language and English ways, and when Rory returned from the Indies he could send for her. With an English background she would, as she professed, be more of a companion. Allah! He might even marry her. He gave his consent, wondering as he did so exactly why Mary wanted her, wondering if she would be good to her. Almera smiled her appreciation.

"Mleeka calls," the words came through the cedar panels of the door.

Rory bade him enter for, although Mleeka was far from being a eunuch, he shared the secrets of Rory's hareem now that it consisted only of Almera. The big black closed the door behind him while Almera covered herself with a veil of silk and modestly drew the sheet up over Rory.

"Signore Vogliano waiting you below, my lord." Mleeka averted his eyes from Almera. "The Emir Mansour pace his apartment asking if you ready. The Sheik Sliman gone to look over a caravan of slaves from Meknes, and I, my lord, have sitting outside door for an hour, waiting for you to call."

"And listening too, I suppose," Rory grinned.

"The door thin, milord, and I hear, though it difficult when milord speak in whispers to his woman and she does not reply in word but in gesture. Hard for Mleeka to hear gesture."

"You've made her blush, you black rascal. But go now! Ask Mansour to come here while I dress. Advise that Italian Judas, who has probably thought up more ways to separate us from our money, that Mansour and I will see him in a few moments; then wake Tim and tell him he is

277

no longer the pampered stud of Basampo but has important work to do."

Mleeka departed and Rory threw down the sheet. Almera had almost finished dressing him when Mansour entered. The boy was growing up and getting handsomer every day, Rory thought. Lately there had been a new closeness between them, almost approximating that intimacy that existed between Baba and himself. Rory trusted the boy and he knew that Mansour had a deep regard for him.

"I've toted up all the bills," Mansour said, "and we'll have enough money to pay for the ship, crew, and slaves. But we are going to be hard pressed for the provisioning of the ship."

"Are you forgetting Tim's contribution?"

"I am not. Tim's a real friend. But first I must take it to the goldsmith's and have the pieces weighed and changed into money. With his contribution we'll have enough, unless that flea-skinning Italian has not already thought of other ways to spend our money."

"He most certainly has. You can count on that. Otherwise he would not be waiting for us below." Rory adjusted the folds of his djellabah, slipped his feet into yellow babouches, and gave Almera a lingering pat on her curved little rump. He signaled to Mleeka to accompany him and Mansour. "Come, little brother, we'll see what the wily Italian wants now."

It took a second glance for them to ascertain that the swarthy Moor sitting cross-legged in the courtyard was the same man who had appeared in European clothes the day before. But it was: Vogliano's smile was as bland and as ingratiating as ever. He rose to his knees and bent over, touching his head to the pavement.

"My lords Emirs." He was most servile. Glancing up and noting Tim's arrival, he salaamed again. "And Your Half-Majesty."

The three acknowledged him with curt nods.

"This morning, if it please my lords, I shall take you to see the captain of your new ship, and later your crew. I have been preparing them for this visit of yours. I have taken the liberty of asking your grooms to have your horses saddled, even that of your black slave whom you take everywhere with you."

"And how much is all this going to cost us?" Mansour asked.

Vogliano spread his hands, palms up to minimize his answer, and shrugged his shoulders.

"Only a little *baksheesh* to the guards of the captain and a little more to the guards of the sailors. They have gone out of their way to help you and it is only right that they should be rewarded. Yes?" He climbed upon his white mule and motioned for them to follow.

Once again they ascended the hill that was crowned by the kasbah, but prior to arriving at the small square before the governor's palace, they turned off and traversed a narrow alleyway which led to a heavily barred door. A slouching soldier in a dirt-encrusted djellabah grudgingly rose from squatting on the cobblestones, but when he saw the Italian's face under its hood, he hastened to unlock the door and let them enter. He even deigned to watch their horses while they were inside. Following Vogliano, they descended several steps into a large hall lighted by windows high up in the walls. A group of soldiers sat on the floor, their tall guns stacked beside them; one of them, an evil-looking old man with a sparse beard, arose and advanced toward them across the littered floor.

Vogliano effected a brief introduction, stressing Rory's title as well as those of Mansour and Tim. The old man turned out to be the chief warden of the governor's prison, by name Yousof ben Maktoub.

"*Aselamu, Aleikum!* He awaits you." The old genie walked across the room and raised a filthy piece of sacking that hung over an alcove. The narrow space inside was lighted by a deep-set barred window.

Rory gasped.

He was a tall man, the man hanging there, and once he had been a strong man, but now his body was so emaciated that each of his ribs could be counted. He was hanging by one finger from a rope in the ceiling with the tips of his toes barely touching the floor. A wide strap around his narrow waist supported a chain from which hung a heavy iron cannon ball. The finger from which he

279

was hanging was turgid and purple; his head lolled at an awkward angle and his eyes were closed, blinding him to the plate of couscous, the dish of fruit, and the druse of water that were on the floor, well out of his reach.

Old Yousof pointed a talon of a finger with a cracked and blackened nail at him.

"The Captain Porter," he cackled. "An American. He does not like the meals we serve him so he threw his bowl at a guard. Therefore we have found it necessary to punish him."

"Nothing but goddamned garbage. . . ." The swollen lips uttered the words in English, but the eyes did not open.

"To be sure." Yousof, who evidently understood English too, poked at the man's ribs with his finger. "But such excellent garbage—straight from the governor's table."

"And decorated with some son-of-a-bitching guard's snot, too."

The palms of Yousof's hands were upturned and he made a deprecatory gesture as though to absolve himself from all blame. "Aye, what a stubborn man! Why doesn't he accept Islam and be free?"

"That will not be necessary," Rory said in English, "not if he is willing to listen to me."

The head lifted, the eyes opened slowly and focused on Rory with difficulty.

"You're the first bastard I've heard speak a civilized word. Who in hell are you?"

"That question will be answered in time." Rory spoke to the prisoner but gestured to Yousof. "Cut him down. I can't talk to a man who's strung up like that. You can string him up again if he is not willing to listen to my proposal, but for the time being, cut him down."

"He has twenty more lashes coming to him at noon." Yousof seemed to regret being denied the pleasure. "Should I give them to him now, before I cut him down?"

"If he listens to me, he won't need them. If you string him back up again, give him fifty."

"*Allahu Akbari,*" said Yousof admiringly.

The process involved dragging in a stool and sawing the rope with a dull scimitar, but eventually the rope was severed and the wretch dropped to the floor. At Rory's

280

bidding they also unloosed the belt and freed him from the iron weight. Underneath the matted hair and the vermin-crawling beard, Rory could see a man of perhaps thirty.

"You were a ship's captain?" he asked.

"Was and *am*." Porter made an effort and rose to his feet, while he tried to shield his nakedness with his uninjured hand. "Captain of the ship *Juno* out of Salem, Massachusetts, of the United States of America and wishing to hell I was back there instead of in this heathen hole."

"Then if your common sense is equal to your desire to leave here, perhaps we can talk business, you and I. I am in need of a ship's captain. You are a captain. I offer you freedom along with a bath, a barber, and a decent meal to start off with."

"Damn it to hell! You tempt me, but what's the catch? Nobody in this godforsook land ever offers anyone anything for nothing."

"Neither do I." Rory answered the other's curtness with a quiet suavity. "I expect you to take my ship safely across the ocean and dock it in Trinidad. Can you do it?"

"I can if I want to, and I can't if I don't want to."

"String him up again," Rory spoke to Yousof and pointed to the dangling rope. "Why wait until noon for the lashes? I'll stay here and watch."

"Just a minute!" Porter became a little more humble. "Suppose I do take your ship across the Atlantic and dock it in Trinidad. What then? Will I still be a slave?"

"No, you will have a choice. Either you can return to your United States, or continue on with me if we get along together. We'll be carrying a cargo of slaves and you'll have the usual captain's percentage of the profits. You don't know me and I don't know you. We may well hate each other's guts. On the other hand, we may turn out to be friends. In the position you're in now I think you'd be better off taking your chances with me than being hoisted up again. I have heard"—Rory decided to lay it on as thick as possible—"that white eunuchs are in great demand in the Sublime Porte and that's what they've got in

281

mind for you. Not many survive the operation; with your balls sliced off you'll probably bleed to death."

"Or wish I had." Porter supported himself with one hand on the wall and took a step toward Rory, so close that Rory could smell the fetor of his filthy body.

"You ain't one of these stinking Moors?"

Rory laughed in the man's face. "I've never smelt a Moor that stinks as badly as yourself."

"But are you?"

"No, only by adoption. By adoption I am the Emir of Sa'aqs, brother of the Sultan of Sa'aqs and also of His Highness here"—he indicated Mansour—"likewise an Emir of Sa'aqs. But I am also Roderick Mahound of Scotland, Baron of Sax, although that would mean nothing to you."

"Then you ain't a real Moor?"

Rory denied it with a shake of his head.

Porter appraised Rory carefully. "I might as well cast in my lot with you. At least I'll save my balls, though they've been no good to me here. I may be jumping from the frying pan into the fire, but at least I'll still be a man when I sizzle. Whatever it is you offer me, it can't be worse than this place."

"Then come with me."

"Buck-naked like this?"

Rory ripped down the piece of sacking and handed it to Porter. While he was tying it around his waist, Vogliano spoke. "We can return for this man. It is necessary for us to go outside the walls to see the other prisoners—the sailors."

"I've seen enough of prisons today," Rory shook his head, sickened already by the misery, the stench, and the degradation he had seen. "Mansour, you and Tim go. Tell those men if they prefer freedom with us to slavery here, it is their choice. Let those who wish to come with us be housed and fed and rested in the barracoons with the slaves, but see that they are treated well. Make your arrangements with Signore Vogliano. I'm taking the captain back to the palace. I want to talk with him."

Mleeka relinquished his horse and the near-naked white man rode while Mleeka trotted alongside. When they reached the palace of Sa'aqs and the heavy doors opened, they stepped inside, but before the street doors closed, Rory had Porter take off the rag and fling it out into the street. With Rory leading, Porter following, and Mleeka bringing up the rear, they ascended the steps to Rory's apartments and Rory gestured toward the bathroom.

"Clean him up, Mleeka, and I shall await him here."

"I can goddamn well clean myself," Porter smiled for the first time. "Always have before and can't say I want another man scrubbing me."

"You'd better get used to it. That's what we have slaves for. While you're here you will avail yourself of their services. In this country you are either waited on by a slave or you are a slave yourself. You've been a slave; now see what it is like to be a man." Rory watched them enter the bath and saw the curtain that draped the door fall. He sat down on the divan, nibbling a tamarind that had been left on the breakfast tray.

There was something about the man that Rory admired. Despite his position, he had not been servile. He had not begged to be released or promised anything. Rory respected him—nay, even felt the germ of liking for him. He needed him and he was determined to have him. Rory had become confident of his own power over people. He realized that his looks and his body attracted women. He also knew that there was something about his personality that drew men to him. Almera, even Mary, had capitulated to his body and many more had desired it and slavered over it. Baba, Tim, other men had surrendered to his charm. True, he had not consciously used this power to bring about these results; he had, as a matter of fact, been quite unaware of it, and he could truthfully say that he returned all the affection that people had given to him. But now, conscious of this power, he was determined to use it to suborn Porter. The whole success of their adventure depended on it. Some sixth sense told Rory that the man was a good captain.

Now, while waiting for him to regain some semblance of humanity, Rory began to understand Vogliano's shrewd use of psychology. He had had the captain tortured that he might hate more. He had degraded him, starved him,

283

humbled his pride, flogged and tormented him that he might be willing to trade his miserable lot for anything that would seem better. Now it behooved Rory to offer him exactly the opposite treatment from what the poor wretch had received and thus bind him closer to him. Where the Moorish gaolers had starved him, Rory would feed him; where they had degraded him in filth and animality, Rory would surround him with ease and comfort. It was a cheap price to pay for a man's loyalty.

The splashing ceased in the bathroom. There followed the sound of the rhythmic slaps of Mleeka's hands on the other man's bare flesh. His nostrils caught the heavy odor of musk; so Mleeka was using Rory's own attar to make more supple this poor fellow's skin. Then followed the slap-slap of the razor being stropped and the sluff of Mleeka's feet on the tiles as he shaved the man. Finally Mleeka held up the curtains and Porter entered, clad in a thin white silk kaftan, his feet in yellow babouches.

Although the lines of suffering still showed in his lean face and the thinness of the silk did not hide his emaciated body, it was a new man who looked at Rory. Gone was the matted beard and the tangled hair. He was clean-shaven and Mleeka had clubbed his black hair in back, drawing it smoothly over his head. Rory's first estimate of his age was correct. He was a man of about thirty and rather good-looking in a hawklike fashion. Strangely enough, he resembled a Moor rather than an Englishman, with his dark, copperish coloring, his black hair, his high cheekbones, and thin-nostriled, aquiline nose.

He stopped halfway across the floor and cocked his head to one side, listening to Mleeka's whispered command to abase himself.

Rory intervened. "The salaam is not necessary between us two when there is nobody here. In public, as long as we are in Africa, it will be necessary, for here I am an emir and you are still a slave—my slave, in fact. Now, however, that we are alone together let us talk without the formalities of my rank and without my being a master and you a slave." He indicated a cushion on the floor before his divan. A finger, pointed to his mouth, and a nod to Mleeka sent the big black scurrying off for food.

"First let me thank you." Porter sat down facing Rory. "If nothing more ever happens to me than that bath and that shave I'll always be grateful to you, sir."

"Then you did not find it too difficult to be bathed rather than to bathe?"

"Your black's got magic in his fingers. I feel like a man again."

"And you must be hungry too. I have ordered food. Your name is Porter—Captain Porter—but I do not know your first name."

"Jehu."

"Then I shall call you Jehu. While we are here today you will call me Rory, for that is what my friends call me and I hope to have you for a friend. You are an American. I have never met an American. Do you want to tell me about yourself?"

"First I want to say thanks, Rory. Thanks for cutting me down and restoring my self-respect, so I don't think of myself as a damn hog, crawling through the mud of a sty to feed on slops." After a pause he went on. "There isn't much I can tell you about myself. I was born thirty-one years ago in a seaport town in New Hampshire; that's in the United States. My father was English, my mother a Merrimac Indian. They weren't married. A white man doesn't marry an Indian squaw. She's only a convenient warm hole where he can let his seed go without thinking that it may result in a man—a half-breed. So I'm that half-breed, a bastard. The name of Porter was the name of the man who sired me, and my mother gave me that name.

"I was bound out—actually, sold into slavery—to a white family. At fourteen I ran away to sea as a cabin boy. I made able seaman and then third mate. On three different voyages, death befriended me. A second mate was murdered and me promoted; a first mate was swept overboard and I moved up again. Then a captain was stabbed in a waterfront whorehouse in Cartagena, and I took command of a ship. I'm a damn good captain if I say it myself. My men obey me and respect me. They know I've taken all the hardships a seaman can."

Rory nodded for him to continue.

"Then, on our last voyage, our ship was taken. It wasn't nothing I could help. We were outnumbered and with only a five-pounder mounted aft and six muskets. My second mate and two seamen were killed. I surrendered on the promise that we'd get good treatment. Good treatment! From what I hear, my crew's had far worse treatment than I did, and God knows that was bad enough. These fucking Arabs have a way of degrading a man so that he ain't a man any more—so he crawls on his belly like a worm." Jehu looked up at Rory, his eyes narrowed to slits as he scanned his face. "But you, sir, who are you and what are you doing in this bloody hellhole?"

"Hellhole for some but not for others." Rory remembered all the bounty he had received in Africa. "As to what and who I am, I'll tell you when the time comes, if it ever does. I have a ship and a cargo of prime black flesh, but I need a captain and a crew to sail it. Your own crew is being delivered to my brother, the Emir Mansour, and being transported to clean quarters where they will receive decent food, humane treatment, clothing, and a chance to rest up. Later you can talk with them and ascertain their willingness to sail with you. Each man will be paid the same amount you paid him, and as for yourself, you'll have the usual captain's percentage.

"I shall be obliged to hold you under house arrest for two reasons. One is that technically you are still a slave of the Sherifian Empire; the second is that as a foreigner and a N'zrani unbeliever, you would not be safe on the streets alone. The freedom of this house is yours, provided you do not enter the apartments of my women. You'll have your own room on the other side of the courtyard where you will be comfortable. I'll assign a slave to wait on you. You have only to clap your hands and he'll furnish you with whatever you require. Here you are my slave, but at the same time you are a master instead of a slave. Do I have your word for it that you won't try to escape?"

"Escape? Good God, man, what'd I escape to? You have my word and my hand on it"—Porter stretched out the hand with the bandaged finger—"if you don't squeeze it too hard. 'Twill not be a difficult pledge to keep. Besides, just now I got a dang few wants—a meal, a score of ripe oranges to suck, and a clean bed where I can stretch myself out and sleep."

"The bed awaits you, the food and fruit will be sent to you, and my man Mleeka will conduct you to your room. You have the entrée to me whenever I am in the house. In public you will have to address me by my full title and prostrate yourself to the floor. Alone, we'll remain on a first-name basis. And now I bid you good day and I trust you will not regret the step you have taken."

Captain Jehu Porter started for the door where Mleeka was waiting. Rory's question halted him halfway. "Are you married, Jehu?"

"Me? Married? No decent American girl would marry an Indian half-breed, and I've no liking for the harbor scum that's available to me, leastwise not for marrying up with any of them."

"So you have no ties to draw you back to this Salem place that you mention?"

"None! Neither wife, sweetheart, nor mistress."

"But a man needs a woman, Jehu."

"You're goddamned right, Rory. I sometimes think it's the Indian blood in me that makes me so hot-cocked."

"Taking into consideration your long voyage and your imprisonment here, it must have been some time since you had one."

"Not since the night before we sailed from Salem, when I paid two shillings to a waterfront doxy for half an hour of her time behind some cotton bales on the wharf. I'd been looking forward to a visit to a bawdyhouse in Leghorn when we docked."

"Then," Rory smiled because he knew that what he was about to say would bind the man even closer to him, "along with the food and the fruit and the wine, I'll send a slave girl to serve you. She'll be black but comely, and if you think your red Indian blood has fire in it, wait 'til you taste black African blood. It's twice as hot, I assure you."

"After that offer, Rory, a man'd go through hell for you."

"Perhaps that's where we're headed, Jehu. I'm the Ma-

287

hound; our ship's the *Shaitan*; and what better place could there be for all of us than hell itself, Jehu man?"

"At least we'll have company along the road, eh, Rory?"

"Then take your first step with the black wench I'm sending you. If she's like all the rest of them, she'll burn you hotter than the fires of hell."

CHAPTER XXVI

RORY DISCOVERED THAT VOGLIANO WAS A true jack-of-all-trades. There was nothing that the wily Italian could not do and no item that he could not supply —at a price, of course. Within two days he had produced complete European wardrobes for Rory and Tim. The clothes appeared to be new and of finest materials cut in the latest fashions. Rory could not but wonder from what English nobleman's or Spanish grandee's trunk they might have come. In addition, Jehu Porter was supplied with naval uniforms and the motley collection comprising his crew were all accoutered as sailors with a full share of a good slop chest for each man.

Rory had taken Jehu to see them and found them, to a man, willing to quit the slave gangs of Morocco for a ship—any ship. Rory and Jehu had inspected the ship also, smart now in its white paint with the scarlet Satan for a figurehead. Despite its transformation from a ship to a bark, Jehu recognized it as his former command. He intimated as much to Rory although he did not press the matter. Rory recognized Jehu's allegiance to him when the captain informed him that the ill-fated ship *Juno* had been insured, which was as much as to say that the American owners would not be out of pocket and that the *Juno* had disappeared forever. As for the insurance brokers in their Boston coffeehouses, who cared about them anyway?

The slaves needed to complete their cargo had been purchased. They were not, in Rory's opinion, as high quality as those Tim had brought from Basampo and the others Mansour had brought from Sa'aqs, but the miscellaneous lot of Fans, Hausas, Dahomeys, and a few thin-lipped Ethiopians was the pick of the Tangier market—all healthy young bucks and all eminently salable. Vogliano had seen to provisioning and watering the ship. Rory's cabin had been furnished with a certain degree of elegance, as were Tim's and the captain's. Between decks the ship had been fitted out with tiers of wooden shelves for the slaves, with fetters and leg irons provided. All was in readiness for departure.

And now came the farewells between Rory and Mary and Rory and Almera—because Mary had been firm in her decision to take Almera along. Rory had not demurred. He suspected that Mary knew of his attachment for Almera and was loath to leave her behind, fearful that Rory might take her along with him. He had indeed been tempted. A slaver was no place for a lone woman— Captain Sparks's example notwithstanding. She would be better off with Mary. His farewell to Mary was cool and strangely enough friendly. She had actually embraced him, offering her lips for a chaste kiss. But . . . if her lips were cool the pressure of her body against his was not. He knew that she was conscious of his response by the way she ground her hips against him. For a moment she hung limp in his arms, then pushed him away for a formal good-bye. Later, when he was beside Almera on his divan for their last night together, he realized that his feeling for the Moorish girl was far deeper than he had imagined. She assented to his demands, but strangely enough without her usual ardor.

"My lord has noticed nothing?" she inquired.

"Nothing except that you are more beautiful and desirable than you have ever been before."

"Not even this?" She guided his hand over her belly. He discovered that it was a swollen mound.

"You mean . . .?"

289

"That the sweet moisture from milord's body which entered me found its place. I am about to have a son for milord; I am sure that with milord's strength and vigor it will be a son. It is well that I have him with me, because now I shall not miss milord so much."

His desire was swallowed up in his love for her.

"I've probably left a hundred swollen bellies behind me, scattered from Scotland to the Maghreb and from Sa'aqs to Timbuktu. Those children I shall never see, but this one seems more truly mine than any of the rest ever could be. This child shall be born free and to make sure of this, I shall free you. You are no longer a slave, Almera." He rose from the bed and walked to a chest, from which he took a heavy bag of gold. "This is for the boy. He will be born in England, and someday I shall see him. He will be a handsome boy because he has a beautiful mother."

"Milord is too good to me."

"I've not been half good enough. Know, Almera, that you have my love. Perhaps someday we shall see Sa'aqs together again."

"Allah is merciful." She took his hand and covered it with kisses; as he relaxed under her, her lips sought the hardness of his body, and when he had released the torrent within him, he slept with her in his arms.

The next morning Mary departed with Almera. A swift felucca—the private yacht of the governor himself—slipped out of the harbor of Tangier to head for Gibraltar. Rory had conducted the veiled ladies on board and once more he bade them farewell. Mary took her leave of him with all due formality: she addressed him as "Your Highness" and he responded by calling her "Princess Yasmin." Yet Rory sensed that underneath it all some desire still smoldered within her. The formality was for the Moors who were looking on, and he wondered if she would have pressed against him ardently once more had they been alone.

When he kissed Almera, and he did it before Mary and the gaping Moors, he gloated at the red flush of jealousy that mounted Mary's cheeks. But what she could not know was that his kiss for Almera was different this time.

Its tenderness surprised even himself. It was more than tender—it was reverent. Yes, goddamn it, it was reverent and he despised himself for a brief moment in giving it to her. He, Rory Mahound, mooning over a woman. It nearly made him curse her in the midst of loving her, and then, the curse dying on his lips, he kissed her again with such an overwhelming emotion that he wondered, somewhere deep within himself, if it might truly be love.

Love? What had he to do with love? For the few nights that remained to him before sailing on the *Shaitan* he would sate himself with love. Love, love, love! Yes, he knew what love was. It was embedding himself in another; nothing more nor less than that. He and Mansour would send out for dancing girls. He'd invite Tim and the sober-faced Jehu to share them and they'd all get roaring drunk. That would make him forget Almera and the life he had implanted within her. By all means, dancing girls! A dozen of them! Why, he was almost anxious to see the felucca leave. He would steep himself so thoroughly in adder-slim sweaty bodies that he would not think about leaving Africa. He would be so drunk and so drained that he would not remember parting from Mansour and severing his last tangible link with Baba.

The next few days were all but an oblivion for him. There was wine, an ocean of wine which Vogliano supplied from his warehouses. There were dancing girls with apricot-colored limbs that smelled of patchouli and amber. There were lithe Chleuh boys who were able to contort their bodies into weird feats of acrobatic copulation which Rory had never envisioned before. There were hot wet mouths; hands that stroked gently and flogged roughly; bodies with entrances which he had never sought before; and strange lusts that even he had never encountered. Through the fumes of wine and sweat and animal heat, he saw Mansour and Tim and Jehu, their clothes stripped from them, their bodies beslavered by red lips and questing fingers and violated, as was his own, by sweet pains that made them gasp in unknown ecstasies. Finally he sank into the deep, warm caverns of flesh and became so exhausted that he slept, nor could all the artifices of the motley crew that surrounded him revive him for one more bout or to shoot one more bolt. He was limp, spent, and oblivious of everything.

Until . . . he awoke one morning, conscious of the movement of his narrow bed and the dappled reflections that chased each other across the white ceiling. He was at sea both mentally and physically.

He lay there, gathering together the tangled threads of his consciousness, until with a superhuman effort he lifted his legs over the side of the bunk and placed his feet on the deck. Planning each move carefully, he stumbled to the small washstand where a crockery pitcher chattered in a bowl, and, leaning forward, he clutched the handle of the pitcher and poured the water over his head. It revived him sufficiently to make his way across the tiny cabin and open the door that led to the companionway. It opened only an inch, but enough for him to see Mleeka's form stretched out on a pallet on the floor. Mleeka jackknifed up and came inside.

"Milord!"

"How long ago did we sail?"

"At noon of yesterday, milord."

"Then get me shaved and dressed, man. I should be out on deck. What about Tim?"

"With the captain, milord."

Rory remembered Sparks's strategy of always appearing before his crew in his finest regalia so, while he was drinking the coffee Mleeka brought, he had him rummage through the chests to discover just what Vogliano had supplied him with. There were several suits in the new French style which eschewed the elaborate satins and brocades and featured the skin-hugging pantaloons of fine white wool tricot with a long-tailed waistcoat that was cut short across the front. Rory donned one of these with a white shirt that had a high collar and a wide black stock. His hat was an enormous half-moon affair that made him look at least eight feet tall. The short white silk socks and the thin leather pumps were also new to him, but when he dressed he realized that he must cut a rather dashing figure. With Mleeka leading the way, he left his cabin and went up onto the quarterdeck. Jehu and Tim were talking with a third man. All three were leaning over the rail,

292

staring down at the main deck where a long line of naked bucks shuffled around and around, keeping time to the beat of a drum which increased and decreased its tempo so that they changed from a slow pacing to a rapid trot and back again.

So rapt were the three with the movement of the blacks that Rory reached the rail unnoticed. He stood beside Tim and rested his hand on Tim's shoulder. Tim wheeled in surprise and when he recognized Rory, he was jubilant.

"Was beginning to feel, me hearty," he held Rory at arms' length to admire his sartorial finery, "that them lads and lassies might have proved too much for you. But you managed to come out on top. At least the last time I laid eyes on you you were."

"Seems to me, Tim, that when I saw you, you were on the bottom with a Chleuh boy in the saddle."

"Away with you, me bucko! 'Tis trying anything more than once, I am, but here's Jehu to tell you that it's all in your own mind that you're castigating poor Tim when there's not a word of truth in what you say."

"No, Tim?" Jehu winked at Rory. "I do remember seeing you that-a-way, but I thought you and the lad were dancing a new kind of Irish jig."

" 'Tis plain to see I've shipped off with me mortal enemies." He nearly pumped Rory's arm off. " 'N this here is Mr. Jenkins, our first mate."

Rory bowed and offered his hand to a glum-faced personage of about fifty. His black beard, streaked with gray, and bushy eyebrows almost hid his face. His greeting was short and barely civil. Here, it was evident, was one man who did not immediately respond to Rory's charm.

Rory bowed to the man nevertheless. "Mr. Jenkins, will you have all blacks confined below decks and will you, Captain Porter, order all hands to stand muster on deck. I'd have a word with them." Rory found that giving orders came naturally now.

"What about them dozen Ay-rab soldiers we've got on board, sir?" Jenkins asked, his lower lip a moist red line in his beard. " 'Twon't do me a bit of good to talk to them. Cain't speak a word of their heathen lingo."

"More's the pity." Rory felt a sudden antagonism

toward the man. "If you had mastered Arabic as the captain did, you might have learned something of value during your stay in Morocco. But never mind the soldiers, I want only to speak to the crew."

It took some time to clear the deck of the slaves, and Rory was pleased to see that they all appeared to be in good condition. Their skins glistened with oil; they looked well fed; most of them were grinning. He was glad when Tim informed him that he had taken over charge of the slaves. Tim, Rory knew, would see to it that all were well treated and not abused by the sailors.

At length the blacks were below and Rory noted the well-scrubbed decks, the glistening paint, and the shiny brasswork. Jehu certainly knew how to keep a trim ship. The bosun's whistle trilled and one by one the crew came out onto the main deck, dropping down from the rigging, coming out from the fo'c'sle, from the galley, and from the carpenter's shop. They assembled, all looking up to him.

"Gentlemen!" Rory smiled down, remembering Captain Sparks. "I address you as gentlemen for the first and last time on this voyage. My purpose in calling you to muster here is to introduce myself. I am Sir Roderick Mahound, owner of this vessel. Captain Jehu Porter is in command, and Captain Porter acts under my orders or those of Mr. O'Toole, my associate. We sail under the Star and Crescent of the Ottoman Empire, through the authority of the Grand Sultan of the Sublime Porte and of my brother, the Sultan of Sa'aqs. Neither British law nor American law prevails on this ship. I am the law and what I say becomes the law.

"I have rescued all of you from slavery in Morocco—a slavery which is a sure road to death. You've had a taste of it and I don't think you'll ever want to return to it. Therefore you owe me a certain amount of gratitude, and I shall expect you to show it by good will and good work. Once we have landed our cargo safely in port, you will be free to sign on again with me for a return voyage, or to return to your own country. You are being paid regular wages and I will see to it that you have a share in the profits of this voyage. Does that seem fair and just to you?"

294

"Aye, aye, sir!" The assent sounded enthusiastic and genuine. Some of the men threw their caps in the air while they cheered Rory.

"Our cargo is slaves," Rory continued. "Be they men or cattle, I'll not dispute with you; but even if they be cattle, they are valuable cattle. Each one we land in port means more for all of us. They deserve humane treatment."

Another cheer followed.

"And now, although I shall not remember all your names this first time, I want each of you to advance"— Rory pointed to a spot directly beneath him—"and tell me your name and rating. Before the voyage is over, I'll get to know you all." He pointed to a tall man with a shaven poll. "You start."

"Johanssen, sir, ship's carpenter."

One by one the members of the crew came up to call out their names and ratings. Rory remembered almost none of their names, but he noticed that most of them looked up and met his eye. There were a few that didn't. These, Rory realized, might be potential trouble-makers, along with the first mate, Jenkins, whom he already mistrusted. But of course there was never a ship's crew without some malcontents. The sight of the small group of Moorish soldiers in the background reassured him. These men were armed with long muskets and had heavy bandoliers of ammunition around their shoulders.

It took some time for the introductions to be over and when they were finished, the crowd dispersed. Rory saw that they were making preparations for the midday meal for the slaves who were once again being herded up on deck. He noted with approval that large baskets of limes appeared and were placed beside the big kettles. Each man, as he presented his wooden bowl to be filled, received one of the limes. When they had finished, buckets of water were passed around and each man had a dipperful to drink. After that buckets of sea water were drawn up and thrown over the men who scrubbed themselves and trotted around the deck until they were dry. Then they were sent below and another lot emerged. Rory learned, through Tim, that the slaves were divided into three companies. Each company had its time on deck and was then taken below. As each company came up, the decks and bulkheads of their section were swabbed down and policed by those remaining below.

Later, Rory, sitting with Jehu and Tim in the trig captain's cabin, complimented Jehu on the appearance of the ship and the order and discipline he maintained with his crew.

"I told you I was a good captain, Rory. Now I'll prove it to you."

"Your first mate, Jehu, what's his name again?"

"Jenkins."

"Yes, what about him?"

"A good man, Rory. Oh, at first he was a little pissed off to have to serve under me, saying as how he'd never taken orders from a goddamned half-breed. But he's come 'round. Never's been very talkative or friendly, but dependable; yes sir, dependable."

"I don't doubt it, but I feel that for some reason he doesn't like me."

"Oh that's just Jenkins's way. He's a surly cuss; hates to give anyone the time of day and"——he stared at Rory, shaking his head to add portent to his words——"his brother-in-law was one of the owners of the *Juno*."

"Which was covered by insurance. Then there were three other seamen with whom I was not overly impressed. One's name I remember. It was Carver. There were two more. One had an eagle tattooed on his chest and the other—a young and rather pretty fellow—had long black hair that fell to his shoulders. What about them?"

"Carver's a good man, able seaman. He's taken his capture and imprisonment hard 'cause he's got an invalid wife back home. The one with the tattoo is Barnes and it's my first trip with him. He's a fo'c'sle lawyer if ever there was one. The long-haired lad is a Portugee from Cape Cod, named Barbosa. Why do you ask about those three?"

"They were the only three that did not look me in the eye when they stepped forward to tell me their names."

"Barbosa's all right," Tim laughed. "He was looking at me instead of you, that's all. Him and me've got something going. I've been a sailor most of my life, Rory, and I always believe in making a ..." he hesitated a moment and winked at Rory, "a 'connection' shall we say. It's going to be a long voyage, you know."

"It's not well to mix with the crew, Tim. Times have changed. You're a part-owner of the ship now. Quarterdeck and fo'c'sle don't mix."

"Sorry, Rory." Tim was chastened. "It's my first voyage on the quarterdeck, you know. I feel more at home in the fo'c'sle and Manoel—that's the Portugee—and I seem to hit it off."

"All right, I'll keep my eyes closed, Tim."

"You've nothing to worry about, Rory." Jehu sensed Tim's embarrassment and hastened to change the subject. "The men are all right. I've never had no trouble with one of them. Carver's been with me on three voyages. I know him. Barbosa's got long hair and his lips are a little too red, but he's a good fellow despite his looks. This is my first trip with Barnes and he's kind of an unknown quantity, but I never had trouble with him. We're all glad to be quit of Morocco and feel a ship under us again."

"I'll vouch for Manoel." Tim was quick to recommend the Portugee.

"Let's hope so." Rory pulled up his chair to the long table. "Seems to me if those blacks have been fed, it's about time I was too. Outside of the cup of coffee Mleeka gave me, I don't believe I've eaten for two days. I'm starved."

"Then eat up, Rory." Jehu crossed the cabin to pull the bell cord. "It's the last fresh meat we'll have till we get to Funchal."

CHAPTER XXVII

NOTHING BUT NOSTALGIA MARRED THE GLO-
rious days of blue skies, blue seas, and brilliant sunshine
while the *Shaitan* sped along under a steady and constant
breeze, swallowing the miles between Africa and Madeira.
Day followed day with the white plume of spray curling
under the golden trident of the figurehead, and Rory relaxed in the purely masculine atmosphere of the ship.

Good God, though, but he missed his hareem! The
nights of purple shadows and a soft, warm, receptive body
beside him; the touch of Almera's hands and lips—these
things his body missed, but beyond this physical yearning
there was an even greater feeling. He missed Almera
herself. She was ever present in his mind, blotting out all
the nameless bodies he had clutched momentarily in his
arms. Added to his longing for her was another nostalgia:
his longing to be back in the vast mud palace of Sa'aqs; he
was homesick. Yes, he missed them all.

Activity helped. He was up mornings at six bells, eating
a hearty breakfast with Jehu, Tim, and the sober-faced
Mr. Jenkins (Rory had never learned the man's first
name). After breakfast, with Tim and Mleeka following,
he descended through the big hatch amidships to the slave
quarters. The open portholes on both port and starboard
filled the dim place with a fresh salt breeze and the men
confined there were not unhappy. Their minds were filled
with the promise of Elysian fields to come. Soon they
would be there and they envisioned a nightly procession
of voluptuous women, each waiting to be mastered.

Rory had grown to recognize a few of the Negroes and
as he passed them he would lay an avuncular hand on the
satin smoothness of a shoulder, pat a kinky head, or squat

down on his knees to speak a few words of Hausa or Arabic. They responded by reaching out for his hand, nuzzling against him, or grinning to show a row of white teeth in the semidarkness. When they came on deck, he would encourage them to indulge in horseplay, to wrestle, or to dance to the booming of an empty iron kettle pounded with a marlinspike.

So far the voyage had been fortunate. Neither sickness nor death had claimed a single man. Most important of all, the spirits of the blacks were good. They had all been slaves before leaving Africa and the clean ship, the plentiful meals, and the prospects of a better life to come obviated depression, sadness, and the overwhelming desire for death which ofttimes caused homesick Negroes to throw themselves over the rail.

In the long afternoons, Rory succumbed to sleep, dozing away the hot hours under a sailcloth awning on the quarterdeck. His cabin, without the cross ventilation that the slaves enjoyed, was hot and stifling. Tim sometimes napped alongside him and when they awoke they indulged in long talks. For all his varied experiences before the mast, Tim was a naive chap, really a child mentally. With the big heart of a true Irishman, he worshipped Rory because, as had never happened before, he had found a friend.

Rory learned through his talks with Tim that there had never before been anyone in Tim's life who had accepted him as an equal; never anyone whom he could respect, look up to, and consider as a friend who in turn reciprocated that friendship and respect. Never until Rory. His friendships in the fo'c'sles of the ships he had sailed on and in the various ports at which he had called had been but casual affairs, more physical than anything else, for Tim had learned to satisfy himself with whomever he found. Tim had learned much from Rory. He had also learned much in Basampo, where he had been a person of authority, and after his return to Sa'aqs, where he had been treated as an equal in the sultanate court. Gradually he was forgetting his dockside lingo and taking on the airs of a gentleman. Not only that; he was fast becoming one.

Along with the ripening of his friendship for Tim, Rory

found new respect and liking for the grim Jehu. Where Tim was all warmth, demonstrative affection, and proffered friendship, Jehu was quiet and deep: but Rory sensed an innate dependability in the man and felt that in his way Jehu was as dependent upon him as Tim was.

In the evenings they would all three sit on deck talking, or just being silent with a certain tacit understanding among them that required no words. Sometimes they would bring up a few of the more talented slaves who would dance for them and sing their weird barbaric chants, in which Mleeka would join when the words were familiar to him. It was a strange hiatus for Rory—like those few moments after ejaculation when he had neither desires, thoughts, nor words. It was a time of merely existing without cares or worries; a time of eating and sleeping and drinking a little wine. Sufficient it was to feel the warm sun on his back in the daytime and enjoy the star-pricked nights. It was a time to sweat out all the excesses of Africa from his body; to feel so satiated that the mind recoiled from excesses and desired only an infinite boredom which made no demands either mentally or physically. Rory ceased even to think; he let others do it for him. He permitted Jehu to run the ship; he let Mleeka attend to all his wants; and he allowed Tim to take care of their living cargo. He was content to sit alongside of Tim, listening to his voice as it spoke words that he sometimes comprehended and at other times did not even hear. While the *Shaitan* scudded along before continuing favorable winds, Rory drifted into a comfortable lethargy of *dolce far niente*.

One sunny morning exactly like the ones which had preceded it, Rory made out the purple outline of Madeira rising above the blue water. He stirred himself sufficiently to bid Mleeka brush and press his clothes for a day on shore. By the time they had swung inside the breakwater, he was dressed and awaiting the little boat that came white-winging across the water, bringing the harbor master. This man, a sweaty, fat little Portuguese with a meager command of English, had considerable difficulty deciphering the ship's papers and he was quite nonplussed as to how a ship sailing under the Star and Crescent of the

Sublime Porte could be manned by men who spoke English. Tim's summons for Manoel Barbosa settled the matter, for the lad was fluent in Portuguese and soon had the harbor master signing entry papers for the *Shaitan*.

They intended to dock only long enough for provisions and water. Rory had specified that they load as much fruit and fresh meat on board as would keep, besides a few head of cattle. After Funchal there was nothing but the broad Atlantic until they arrived at Port of Spain in Trinidad.

Captain Jehu dispatched Jenkins to arrange for the necessary purchases and declined Rory's invitation to come ashore with him, saying that it was necessary for him to remain aboard. He pointed out a gaily painted house on the waterfront and added, closing one eye slowly, that if a girl named Rosa happened to be still there, she was the best of the lot. Rory nodded in understanding. When he stepped ashore, he saw Tim and Manoel walking some distance ahead of him. He recalled Tim's invitation to walk up the mountain when they had been in Funchal before. Tim had not invited him this time, and despite Rory's warning not to mix with the fo'c'sle, he was glad that Tim had found companionship.

Later he wished he had gone with Tim and Manoel. Rosa turned out to be a muddy-complexioned slattern with an all-too-evident black moustache who would never see thirty again. Her caresses were professional and perfunctory until he slipped out of his clothes, whereupon she flogged up some latent passion and dug her sharp fingernails into his back, moaning and protesting and pretending to suffer as though she were being ravished for the first time. Nevertheless, in her writhings and clawings she did not forget to inform him with every other breath that because he was hurting her so she expected a double payment. Rory's days of continence at sea stood him in good stead and the bout was soon over. He hurried into his clothes, flung a gold piece on the woman's naked belly and sought the sunshine again. What he found most strange was that he had had to picture Lady Mary beneath him in order to reach his climax. It was her body that he had loved instead of the slattern's. But he was relieved that it was over. Now he could saunter along the cobbled streets in a drift of violet jacaranda blossoms, quite satisfied with himself and the world.

He passed Jenkins and the seaman Barnes standing together in a doorway, conversing earnestly. They had not seen him coming, and the usually imperturbable Jenkins was laying down the law to Barnes, punctuating his remarks by striking one fist into the hollow of his hand and then wagging an admonishing finger. They stopped suspiciously short when Jenkins spied Rory and nudged Barnes to keep still. Much to Rory's surprise, Jenkins was almost affable. "Plenty of good food coming aboard, sir," he saluted, and pointed down the street.

Rory saw a strange procession of heavy wooden sleds pulled by plodding oxen. A boy ran before each of them, dropping greased rags under the runners, then after the sled had passed, picking up the rags and dropping them again. The sleds screeched across the smooth cobbles and Rory saw that they were laden with calves and chickens, piled high with panniers of fruits and groaning under hogsheads of water. All the rest of the afternoon the crew loaded the ship, putting the livestock in an enclosure which the carpenter had hastily knocked together, the hens in coops, and the fruits and vegetables in the hold. Tim and Manoel returned, and by the time the sun set, the *Shaitan* was loaded and they were able to slip out on the tide. The glittering lights on the mountain twinkled, faded, and were gone. Even the land smell vanished from the air. The next land they would see, if Allah willed would be Trinidad.

Common sense told Rory that Jenkins and Barnes had been merely attending to business when he had seen them ashore. Jenkins preserved his impassive expression during the evening meal and Rory dismissed his vague suspicions about the man. Perhaps it was merely that he disliked him and was only too willing to think the worst of him. With the lassitude that the Portuguese trollop had engendered in him, he sought his bed early. Almost immediately he fell asleep. Sometime during the night, he awoke to hear Tim enter the cabin next door, then heard him leave and the door close after him. Once again he slept.

A hand on his shoulder awoke him, and a voice whispered in his ear. "Rory, lad, wake up! It's me, Timmy."

"What in hell do you want?" Rory's first thought was that Tim might have designs on him. "Go find your Portugee bugger."

"Sh-h-h! I already have. He's with me and so is Mleeka." Tim struck a spark and blew on the tinder, applying it to the candle by Rory's bunk. "Quick, Rory! Up and dress!"

By the light of the candle, Rory saw Tim and Mleeka and in the background the long-haired Manoel. He swung his legs over the edge of the bunk.

"We got no time to lose." Tim found Rory's pantaloons and handed them to him, edging the narrow legs over Rory's big feet. "You said it wasn't good for quarterdeck and fo'c'sle to mix, but now you can thank God they did. Manoel and I. . . ." Tim hesitated a moment. "Well, goddamn it, you know how it is. We was both in the dory aft, snuggled down under the sailcloth, when we heard voices right under us so we kept quiet and listened. It was Jenkins talking with that bastard Carver and that other tattooed son of a bitch, Barnes. They've got a mutiny started. Waiting till eight bells when Jehu's watch is up and Jenkins takes over. They've already slit the throats of the three Moors on guard and stolen their guns. Now they plan to kill you 'n me 'n Jehu and take over the ship. We ain't got much time."

"You heard all this?" Rory was fumbling with the buttons of his pants.

"And Manoel did too, didn't you?"

"That I did, sir." It was the first time the fellow had spoken. "They're coming here, sir. Going to get you with a knife, sir, after they've done away with your black boy. Then they're going to get Timmy, and after that the captain."

Rory was dressed. "You, Manoel, slip up on deck. If Jehu's at the wheel speak to him and warn him. Here." He reached for a pewter mug on the chest. "Take this with you and if anyone stops you tell them that the captain sent you down to the galley for some coffee. Take the helm and tell him to go down to his cabin, unlock the

303

arsenal, and send you back with side arms for Tim and me." He looked at the watch with which Vogliano had supplied him. "If they're waiting till eight bells, we've got about half an hour. Are you with us, Manoel?"

"With all of you, sir; especially with Timmy."

"Then hurry!" Rory glanced about the cabin. "We can ambush them here better than anywhere else. It's cramped in here and we'll have them at a disadvantage." He yanked at his clothes that were hanging from a hook, threw them on the bed and rolled the blanket around them so that they took on the semblance of a sleeping form. "You, Tim, creep under the bunk. One of them will come in here, thinking I'm sleeping. And you, Mleeka, go outside the door and bed down as usual. Make no resistance and they won't harm you. It's me they're after. I'll be behind the door." He waited for them to take their places and then doused the candle. The cabin was in darkness except for the dim circle of night sky that was the porthole.

"Rory!" It was Jehu's whisper on the other side of the door. "Captain, sir," was Mleeka's identification.

Rory opened the door and Jehu slipped inside. "Manoel told me. So it's mutiny, is it? I trusted Jenkins. Never thought he'd mutiny against me after I gave him his freedom. Here, they're loaded." He held out his hands in the darkness and Rory, fumbling, felt the cold steel of the pistols. He took them, knelt and slipped one to Tim under the bunk, closing his fingers around it. "Go back up on deck, Jehu. They are going to try to get us before they tackle you. Arm the Portugee. He's to be trusted. Send him to rouse the Moors if they aren't all dead."

"Good luck, Rory." Jehu crept out and the door closed. Rory heard Mleeka adjusting his long body to the mat before the door and then his simulated snores. That was the only sound except the faint whistle of the wind in the rigging, the creak of ship's timbers, and the sound of water slapping against the hull. The time that they waited in the darkness, not daring even to whisper, seemed interminable; at last they heard the faintest of footsteps coming down the companionway outside. Rory's ears caught the sound of a dull thud. Then there was silence, which

304

was finally broken by the stealthy movement of somebody trying the latch. Instinctively Rory knew that Mleeka was dead, but his sorrow was wiped out in his rage.

He cocked his pistol and the faint click that followed it from under the bunk informed him that Tim was also prepared. After a long moment of silence, in which Rory hardly dared to draw a breath, he heard the slightest scraping of metal on metal as the latch was lifted and a thin sliver of light from the lantern outside crept into the cabin. Inch by cautious inch, the door opened until Rory, standing just behind it, could see the dark shadows of two heads, grotesquely magnified, on the floor. There followed a cautious step and then an arm was raised and pointed to the stuffed blanket on the bed. A few more steps, stealthy and cautious, brought the two men to the side of the bunk and Rory could see the glint of light on a raised cutlass and a shiny dirk as both dark forms raised their arms.

But they never lowered them. An explosion from Tim's pistol, followed by an almost simultaneous report from Rory's, brought a high-pitched shriek from one man and a gasp from the other as his body fell to the floor. The one still on his feet staggered and continued to screech. Neither Rory nor Tim had a chance to reload, but Rory could see the glimmer of the cutlass blade which one man had dropped on the floor. He crouched to clutch the hilt and then, his foot behind him to give him leverage, he sprang up suddenly and lunged with the weapon, feeling it pierce the body of the enemy.

"They're both done for, Tim."

A spark appeared from under the bed. "Hand me a candle."

Rory located the candle stub, knelt, and placed it in Tim's hand. The tinder flamed and Tim lit the wick, then crawled out from under the bunk and over the two bodies. Rory helped him to his feet.

"It's Barnes and Carver," Tim said, lowering the candle to identify the faces. "By all the saints, I shot Carver's balls off. You must have got Barnes with your first shot and then finished off Carver with the cutlass."

But Rory, with a quick glance to see that both men were dead, was out in the companionway. He slipped and fell in the puddle of blood that was before his door. He had been right to mourn Mleeka. The poor fellow's head was rolling back and forth from one wall to the other with the motion of the ship while his body was still outstretched before the door. He'd never had a chance. They had sneaked up on him and decapitated him while he was feigning sleep. Tim reached a helping hand to Rory and with the other crossed himself. He picked up Mleeka's head and tenderly laid it alongside his body. "Poor fellow."

Rory's grief made him hoarse. "They'll pay for this."

Tim gestured with his thumb toward the cabin. "They already have."

"Bastards! But now we've a score to settle with that double clocker, Jenkins." Rory started for the ladder and when he stepped out on deck, he stumbled, catching himself before he fell. The body of Manoel was stretched out on the deck before the threshold, and he delayed a moment to warn Tim. His hand was on Tim's arm when they heard the shout.

"Rory!" It was Jehu's voice calling from the helm. "I've got him." They stepped over Manoel's body. The captain was standing, pistol drawn, and crouching before him on the deck was another man. It was Jenkins.

CHAPTER XXVIII

"WE WAS IN IT ALONE; JIM CARVER 'N ED Barnes 'n me." Jenkins had entirely lost his bluster and bravado and cringed hopelessly while he stood facing the tribunal of Rory, Tim, and Jehu across the long, baize-covered table in Jehu's cabin. "We figured that once we'd taken over the ship, the others'd go along with us 'cept possible them Arab sons-o'-bitches." He pointed to the nine soldiers lined stiffly at attention behind Rory. "But then we figured as to how we could sell 'em with the niggers. They're black enough; nothing but niggers they are."

Rory and Tim, their anger heightened by the loss of Mleeka and Manoel, sat grim-faced and silent while Jehu questioned the man whose manacled hands and spanceled legs clanked when he shifted his posture.

Jehu's finger stabbed the air. "You've always hated me, haven't you, Jenkins?"

"Oh, no, Cap'n, no! Cain' say I ever hated you."

"You lie, you goddamned, psalm-singing, self-righteous New England son of a bitch. You lie! You hate me because I'm part Indian, younger than you are, and a captain. You hate me because you don't like taking orders from a half-breed. Tell me, you white-livered Congregational bastard, was it your silly hatred of me that impelled you to do this?" Jehu lowered his accusing finger and picked up a pistol from the table, deliberately cocked it, and pointed it at Jenkins. "Answer me or I'll put a bullet through your guts."

"You ain' a-going to shoot me, Cap'n. Don't shoot. Remember we're white men on a ship filled with niggers."

"White men, huh? That's the first time one of you whey-faced Puritans ever called me a white man. I'm not white. I'm half redskin, remember?" Jehu aimed the gun at Jenkin's belly.

"Oh, Cap'n. I've got a wife and daughter back in Portsmouth. Remember? She's B. C. Adams's sister and he's part-owner of the *Juno*. I was jes' takin' back stolen property, that's all. Any court in the States would uphold me for that. You know that this's the *Juno* jes' as well as I do."

"This is the *Shaitan*." Rory's words were short and cut through the air like a whiplash. "We know nothing about the *Juno*. We purchased this ship for hard cash and it's ours. The ship and the cargo belong to us. Had it not been for me, your days as a slave would have been numbered. No Christian dog lasts more than a few years building walls for the Sultan of the Maghreb. I rescued you from that, and you tried to kill me."

"We was jes' wantin' to get the ship back to its rightful

307

owners." Jenkins stirred himself to a sudden bravado. " 'N you know, Cap'n, this is the *Juno*. You know damned well it is."

Rory half rose from his chair, but Jenkins continued, discovering some hidden well of courage. "A coat of white paint and a devil for a figurehead cain' change a ship. Captured by pirates it was 'n you're one o' them, Mr. Mahound. You're an Ay-rab too, Mr. Mahound, even if'n you do mouth English."

Rory's face flushed red with rage. He stood and reached across the table, slapping Jenkins with so much strength that he nearly felled the man.

"You! You were trying to get the ship back to its rightful owners? I'm the rightful owner along with this man here." His gesture included Tim. "And you, you bastard, you were willing to crimp a whole cargo of slaves which would have made you a rich man. Bah, you filthy stinkard! I suppose you had to kill my man Mleeka in cold blood just to get this ship back to its rightful owners."

"And Manoel was my friend and you killed him." Tim's hand was raised.

"Dirty little cocksuckin' buggerer!" Jenkins lower lip curled. "Low-life Portugee! Birds of a feather, I'd say."

Tim was around the table, his hands on Jenkins's throat, but Rory moved as quickly as Tim and pulled him away. "If you're thinking of butchering the pig, Tim, don't do it now. Daylight's better than darkness to punish a man. Let him think things over the rest of the night. Jehu, detail two of the Moors to guard him in his cabin, with two more outside the door. Have all hands piped amidships in the morning and I'll settle the matter then, provided"—he deferred to Jehu—"you will allow me."

Jehu gave tacit assent by taking the keys for Jenkin's manacles and spancels from his pocket and handing them to Rory. "He's your man, Rory. You attend to him and I'll take care of the rest. I'll have Manoel and Mleeka sewn up in sailcloth for burial along with the Arabs and the mutineers. Whatever you do with this rum scutch is all right with me. I only wish his brother-in-law, that pompous ass B. C. Adams, was here to share in it."

Neither Rory nor Tim slept the remainder of that night. Over countless cups of strong black coffee, sometimes laced with brandy, they sat at the table in Jehu's cabin while one by one every member of the crew was brought to them for questioning. They came into the cabin, some of them rubbing their eyes to get the sleep out of them, having slept through the shots and confusion. Jenkins was obviously right: none had been involved in the plot. Those on watch had heard the confusion and wondered what it was about; those who had been sleeping in the fo'c'sle were in absolute ignorance. Evidently Jenkins and his two cronies had planned to take over the ship themselves and had counted on the willingness of the others to go along with them.

By daybreak the sailmaker had sewn the seven bodies into weighted canvas shrouds which were lined up on deck amidships; a wide plank was propped against the rail. Tim wept openly when he viewed them, although there was no way for him to identify poor Manoel's corpse in its sailcloth covering. Rory, gazing down at them and even not knowing which one was Mleeka, restrained his own tears with difficulty. From the night Rory had picked him up on the desert, the Kasai had served him faithfully, and Rory now realized the intense loyalty that Mleeka had always given him. The Moorish soldiers were permitted to mourn their comrades and they prostrated themselves on the deck in the direction of the rising sun, which they took to be the direction of Mecca, and intoned their prayers. The sun broke over the horizon and the ship's bell struck four times. The strokes started the shrill piping of the bosun's whistle and all work stopped on the ship. The entire crew, with the exception of the helmsman, assembled on the main deck. Rory and Tim climbed the ladder to the quarterdeck and stood alongside Jehu. Rory leaned over the rail and spoke a few words in Arabic to one of the Moors, who disappeared to return with Jenkins in irons. Following Rory's gesture, he placed the man directly below Rory.

"Gentlemen"—Rory looked down on the motley throng below him—"I told you before when I addressed you by such a flattering term that that would be the first and last

309

time I would do so on this voyage. I was wrong. I do so again. You see here"—he pointed down at Jenkins—"a man who was formerly our first mate. During the night he, Carver, and Barnes plotted mutiny on this ship. In so doing they killed my servant Mleeka. They also killed a seaman, Manoel Barbosa, along with three of the Moors. Five innocent men died last night, besides Carver and Barnes whom we blasted into hell while they were about to kill me."

There was a muttering in the crowd while Rory waited for his words to penetrate their sodden mentalities. Not that there was anything new in his announcement, because each man had been questioned previously. But now, with the canvas-shrouded bodies laid out on the deck, there was a certain dramatic quality in Rory's words that impressed the crew anew with the heinousness of the crime. Then Rory repeated his words in Arabic for the benefit of the Moors who, when he had finished, set up a loud keening. He held up his hand for silence. Again Rory pointed to Jenkins.

"Have you anything to say for yourself?"

Evidently Jenkins had rehearsed his speech during the night; he recited it glibly. "I demand to be taken in protective custody to the nearest port and turned over to the American consul. I'm an American citizen and I have rights."

"Rights?" Rory tried to keep his voice down. "What rights? To kill five men, not one of whom ever harmed you? Sure, get yourself to an American consul. Go ahead! Jump overboard! The nearest port is Funchal and you'll have a goddamned nice swim back to it. But there's no American consul there, so you'd better head for Liverpool or Le Havre."

"You a-goin' to kill me?" Jenkins looked up, searching for some relenting expression in Rory's face. There was none. "Oh, please, Mr. Mahound. I'm sorry I ever done it. 'Twas Carver 'n Barnes what talked me into it. I didn't want to believe me, I didn't. Swear on a stack of Bibles, I didn't. Think of my wife, Mr. Mahound, 'n my little girl what's waiting for me. For the love of God, don't kill me."

"I'll not lay a hand on your dirty carcass, I can assure you of that." Rory looked beyond Jenkins who, momentarily with the assurance of Rory's words, felt that he had a chance to live. His confidence was bolstered by the keys that Rory flung down to him. He scrambled for them, unlocking his handcuffs and spancels. Free now, he straightened up and a ghost of a smile appeared on his face.

"Thank you, Mr. Mahound, thank you."

Rory ignored him. Speaking in Arabic, he addressed the soldiers, the nine scowling Moors who looked almost ready to leap up onto the quarterdeck and assassinate Rory himself.

"Men of Islam, this N'zrani dog has killed three True Believers. Ali, Edris, and Hussein were your friends and companions. By this man's bloody hands they have entered into the gates of Paradise and even now enjoy all the delights of that place. But," as he pointed to the sailcloth shrouds, "their bodies are still with us and these three men, faithful followers of the Prophet Mohammed, will never see their homeland again. I leave it to you to punish this man. Do with him as you see fit."

The scowls disappeared. They cheered Rory.

"Ali was my brother." A brown hand was raised in vengeance.

"And Edris was a beardless youth whose kisses were sweeter than the dripping honeycomb." Another raised his clenched fist.

"Hussein was my brother, my father, my protector, and my lover." A third arm was raised.

"Their names were written in the Book of Life to die by the hands of unbelievers, but we will avenge them." A bearded Moor started pulling his djellabah over his head.

Although Jenkins did not understand their words, the maniacal expressions on the Moors' faces caused him to sense that he had been premature in his gratitude.

"What's he a-sayin' to them Moors, Jehu? You ain' a-goin' to let them heathens hurt me, be you Jehu?"

Jehu started to speak but Rory silenced him with an uplifted hand, pointing to the Moorish soldiers below. Each of the Moors was undressing. They took off their yellow babouches and stood clad only in their loose cotton trousers. Slowly, their eyes never off Jenkins, they formed a circle around him. Each man spaced himself about six feet from his comrades and all faced Jenkins in the center of the circle. Deliberately they closed in on him and he, gazing from one to the other in terror, decided to make a dash for it, attempting to slip between two of them. The long arm of one of the Moors reached out and caught him on the shoulder, spinning him around and hurling him into the arms of another Moor. He caught Jenkins, grabbed him by the shirt and ripped off one sleeve, then held him, punching him with two sharp blows which sent him reeling into the arms of another Moor. The next one caught him, ripped off another sleeve of his shirt and pushed the now dazed Jenkins into the arms of his nearest comrade. Had they not been grim-lipped and serious it would have seemed like some childish game, with Jenkins being flung from one to the other like a ball. As he proceeded around the circle, each of the Moors ripped off part of his clothing, pummeled him, and passed him on to another until he was naked. They flung him, screaming for mercy, into the center of the circle.

The old Moor in command of the soldiers unsheathed his yataghan, the slim curved short-sword that every Moor carried. He flourished it in the sunlight.

"We avenge our comrades with a *jehad*," he yelled, froth on his lips. "We accomplish a holy purpose." He stepped forward to stand over Jenkins, and the quick stroke of his sword was like a flash of light. The small bronze nipple on Jenkins's chest disappeared, and in its place there was a wider circle of scarlet. For a moment Jenkins stared at it, his eyes unable to believe what had happened to him until the blood started to flow.

"Mercy, Jehu, mercy! They be cuttin' me. Help me!"

"You had no mercy on my man Mleeka," Rory answered.

"He was only a nigger. I'm a white man. . . ."

Another flash of another blade, then another and another and another. The Moors took careful aim. They had no desire to kill the man yet. Red stripes appeared over Jenkins's body as the sharp steel sliced at him. Where there had been an ear, there was nothing but an expanse of bleeding flesh; his nose disappeared with a swipe of a dagger; his lips gave place to bloody teeth. He turned from one side to the other, seeking some refuge, but the yataghans continued to slice at him; a buttock, a calf, a cheek, a thigh, another ear. He discovered an opening between two of the Moors and started to crawl through it, but the relentless blades pursued him, chopping hunks of flesh from him. He was screaming with crazed shrieks, beating the bodies of his tormentors with bloody fists while their blades wreaked more havoc on his suffering body.

With one final gasp of energy, he darted for the shrouds, and the horrified men on the ropes, who had been watching from this vantage point, climbed higher to the yards. For one brief moment, Jenkins was free from his pursuers and with practiced hands he forced his bleeding arms and legs to carry him aloft. But there was no haven for him. The Moors swarmed below him, and although they were unaccustomed to the ropes, they were not far behind him. Still he kept going until he reached the main-royal yardarm and, perhaps thinking that the Moors would not dare to follow, he inched his way out to the very end of the yard. The Moors were undaunted. In their fanatical desire to kill they would have trodden on thin air to get him. They came nearer, clinging to the yardarm, inching their buttocks along it. Through the curtain of blood over his eyes, Jenkins watched them approach, slowly, inexorably. He tried to scream, but the wind carried his voice away.

"Goddamn it, Rory, I can't stand it any longer." Jehu raised his pistol and cocked it. He would have fired not at the Moors but at Jenkins. Rory pulled at his arm.

"Let matters take their course, Jehu. You heard old Abdullah. This is a jehad, a holy avenging. At this moment the Moors are crazed fanatics. Rob them of their prey and they will turn on you."

"Christ, Rory! I can't stand here and see them torture the poor devil any more."

"It's out of our hands. He'd have had no mercy on you last night."

313

"He might have killed me, but he wouldn't have tortured me." He pointed up. "Look at them."

Abdullah, his beard blown out at an angle, his sword in his mouth, was almost near enough to reach Jenkins, who was clinging to the very tip of the yardarm. The old Moor balanced himself, taking the yataghan in one hand. Leaning over carefully so as not to lose his balance, he hacked at Jenkins's fingers. Bloody bits of flesh fell to the deck and Jenkins's hold was broken. His stumps of hands opened and his body poised motionless for a fleeting moment; then, plummeting in an arc, he fell, clearing the deck, into the sea. His head reappeared, laved of blood, his arms raised momentarily above the white foam of the wake, and then he sank.

Rory motioned for the bosun to pipe the men back to muster and they lined up. He waited for the Moors to descend to the deck.

"If there's any man among you feels he wants to lead another mutiny, let him step forward." Rory placed his hands on the rail and looked down at the upturned faces below him.

"We're all with you, sir."

"We'd rather be here with you than back in prison."

"You saved us, sir, and we're grateful, we are."

"We ain' a-thinkin' o' mutiny, sir. We ain' had no hand in it."

"Then a double ration of grog for each man today and you, cook, slaughter one of the calves and feed these men well. Make the best plum duff you can. There'll be easy duty for all men out of respect to those we bury—good and bad alike." He turned to Jehu. "Will you conduct the services, Captain?"

Jehu opened the ship's Bible. Due to the awe and reverence which Mohammedans have for printed books, it had been allowed to remain on board. Rory did not know whether he had opened it at random and started to read, or whether he had planned it; but the words seemed strangely appropriate.

Save me, Oh God: for the waters are come in unto my soul.

314

*I sink in deep mire where there is no standing: I am come
   into deep waters where the floods overflow me.*

*Let not the water flood overflow me, neither let the deep
   swallow me up and let not the pit shut her mouth upon
   me.*

*Draw nigh unto my soul and redeem it; deliver me because
   of mine enemies.*

*I am poor and sorrowful: let thy salvation, Oh God, set
   me up on high.*

*I will praise the name of God with a song and will magnify
   Him with thanksgiving.*

While Jehu was reading, the canvas-shrouded bodies,
one by one, were lifted onto the plank, the plank was
tilted, and each one slid off noiselessly into the water.
There was a splash, a plume of wind-drifted foam, and the
blue water erased everything.

Jehu's "amen" sounded deep-throated and clear.

Tears were streaming down Tim's cheeks. "Manoel was
a Catholic like myself." Tim's fingers made the sign of the
cross. "I'll have masses said for him when we get to port."

"I don't even know what Mleeka was," Rory sighed,
turning his back to the rail and walking toward the companionway, "but whatever Paradise he believed in, I'm
sure he's there now. I'm sorry for one thing; I never gave
him his freedom."

Jehu walked beside Rory. "You know," he shook his
head slowly, "I don't think freedom would have meant
much to Mleeka. If he had a god, Rory, it was you."

Rory nodded his assent slowly. "He was a good man."

"What better epitaph could any man wish?" Jehu laid a
comforting hand on Rory's shoulder.

CHAPTER XXIX

NEITHER RORY NOR TIM HAD SLEPT MUCH THE night before, but despite their exhaustion, they could not seek the seclusion of their cabins for an afternoon nap. Following the grim events of the morning, neither of them wanted to be alone. Napping on deck was also out of the question because the crew, making the most of their day of easy duty, were celebrating. One of the men had bought an accordion in Funchal and this, aided by thumpings on the upturned kettle, provoked a bull dance on deck for which, with Rory's permission, some of the handsomer and more adolescent blacks had been suborned. Buck-naked, their ebony skin agleam with a patina of sweat, and their animal spirits aroused as was so obviously apparent with their complete absence of clothing, the black boys were as gallantly whirled and petted as waterfront doxies in a dance hall. Occasional brawls broke out, engendered by some seaman's grog-flared jealousy over being robbed of his partner, but they were good-natured disputes. The good meal, the festive air, the extra grog, the wine brought aboard in Madeira, and the affectionate reciprocations of the black boys all served to erase the horrors of the morning—at least for the sailors.

Rory, however, was not so fortunate. Neither rum nor stout Madeira, which he mixed together, were able to blot out the bloody stains on the mainsail. He hoped that Mleeka had never known what struck him and that Manoel had died without suffering. When he dared to remember Jenkins, he consoled himself that death by drowning had eased the wretch's tortures. In his present drunken stupor, he did not notice that scudding black clouds had covered the sun or that the warm air had taken

316

on a sudden damp chill while the freshening wind tossed spray up onto the quarterdeck. Tim had not imbibed as much as Rory and realized the situation more acutely. After a particularly high wave had drenched them both, he managed to get Rory to his feet and led him down the companionway and into his cabin. Rory's knees collapsed under him and he fell on the bed dead drunk; but Tim, gathering what few wits he had, straightened him, removed his wet clothes, screwed shut the porthole and doused the candle, leaving Rory alone.

. .Later that night Rory awoke from a concupiscent dream of dalliance with the long-forgotten Mary Davis of Glasgow. He was glad that his dreaming thoughts had been kind enough to him to carry the dream through to completion. Now awake, he was aware of the violent pitching of the vessel which tossed him from one side of his bunk to the other. He had to brace himself to keep from rolling onto the floor. As his mind emerged from the hot lust of his dream into cold reality, he was conscious that there was someone else in the cabin—someone kneeling beside his bunk. He sat up quickly but was reassured when he heard Tim's voice.

"It's only me, Rory lad. Forgot to put the sideboards on your bunk when I tucked you in, and was afeared you'd fall out. We're in for a blow, I reckon. But don't worry. Jehu's on deck and this here's a staunch ship. Always heard that those American rebels were good shipbuilders and good sailors too." He gently pushed Rory back and pulled the rough blanket up over him. "Sure there ain't nothing else you want while I'm up?"

"Sick as a horse, I am." Rory swallowed the winy vomit in his throat. "But there's nothing you can do for me, Tim. Feel about as bad as I did that first morning on the *Ariadne*. Bad weather and I don't mix, lad. Go back to bed. You don't need to watch over me like a mother hen with one chick. Not that I don't appreciate it, though." He felt Tim's hand rest for a second on his forehead, and then came Tim's good-night before he closed the cabin door.

Rory wished he could go back to sleep and have another dream about Mary Davis as pleasant as the one before.

Mary Davis! Here in the creaking timbers and rushing waters, he longed for the snug stability of the little room in Glasgow with the flickering, dying peat fire and Mary's warm body beside him on the pallet. He hadn't thought about her in months. Mary Davis! His dream of her had temporarily blotted out his constant longing for Almera. For the moment he wanted Mary. Then he reconciled himself: he had just had her, albeit in a dream.

Now what was the name of the boy he had sent her? Fayal, that was it. Had Sparks ever delivered him? And if he had—sick as he was, he smiled in the darkness—had Fayal proved a worthy substitute for himself? Had Mary forgotten the Mahound and Old Harry in her dalliance with Fayal, or did Fayal's presence serve to remind her of himself? . . . With these thoughts he drifted off into a fitful sleep.

Finally a pale watery light appeared through the porthole, and waking, he knew that it was nearly morning. Then Jehu entered with Tim behind him.

"Bit of a blow, Rory." Jehu was cheerful. "But the old *Juno* weathered worse nor this, and now that she's Scratch himself, she'll be twice as stout. Who ever heard of a little wind and water stopping the devil?" He cocked his head toward Tim. "Tim, this here owner looks green around the gills."

"Best get yourself up, Rory. Cabin's no place to stay if you're going to heave the gorge. Best be up on deck and let the fresh air blow it out of you."

With Tim's assistance, Rory got dressed and negotiated the companionway and the steep steps to the deck. An arc of black-green clouds had settled heavily on the churning sea, pouring down a torrent of slanting rain that beat against his face. The sails had been furled and there was a weird howling in the lines such as Rory had never heard. The ship staggered as each mountainous wave hit it. The *Shaitan* heeled over so far that the seas washed over the main deck, smashing everything loose against the lee bulwarks.

Rory clung to the rail, welcoming the cold spray in his face while he gagged on the sour vomit in his throat. The hatches had been battened down. Another wave, higher, vaulted the bulwarks and swept over the rails the flimsy timbers that had caged the livestock. A calf bleated, tried to regain its balance on wobbly legs and then disappeared as another wave crashed over the deck. Rory clawed his way over to Tim, and roaring in Tim's ear, managed to make himself heard.

"The blacks, Tim—how are they?"

"Battened down. They'll come through."

"We've got to get to them. The poor devils are chained, Tim, and they'll be injured. Can't sell them with broken arms and legs."

"Can't get down through hatches. Got to go below, go through supercargo's cabin," bawled Tim.

No lights burned below deck, and with all portholes closed it was as black as the inside of a vat; but with Tim in advance and Rory clinging to him, they descended to the lower deck and entered a small cabin. Tim found a candle lantern and lighted it. Books and ledgers mingled with a storm of papers on the floor. They passed through a small door that led amidships. Here in the 'tween decks, the stench was nauseous. The feeble light of Tim's lantern showed naked black bodies writhing on the floor, their legs and arms immobile in the stanchions, their torsos curved and whipped as comber after comber hit the ship. The deck was awash with vomit, urine and excrement and Rory could contain himself no longer. He stumbled and fell over a welter of black legs, coming to rest athwart a strong brown body. The puke filled his throat and gushed from his mouth onto the fellow beneath him. For moments he could not move, then he pushed himself up, placing his hands on the other's shoulders.

"Courage, boy," he was able to gasp, forgetting that his English words would be meaningless to the man. He heaved again, but this time it was only a dry wracking. "We'll try to help you." This was his cargo and it was a valuable one. Unless the men were released they would break arms and legs. Now, seeing Rory in their midst, they braced themselves as well as they could, beseeching him in a multitude of shouted jargons, their eyes rolling white in their fright, their faces livid in the dim light.

The terrified black under Rory clutched at his hand

with one of his manacled ones. Fright caused the Hausa words to spill from him in a torrent, but Rory was unable to understand most of them. He knelt beside the fellow and although the fetid man-stench was enough to make him heave again had he anything left to throw up, he tried to calm the fellow.

"Listen, boy," Rory's Hausa came haltingly. "I don't know who you are, but you must have a good disposition to let me vomit all over you and do nothing about it. I'm making you a headman here. See if you can help me keep the others in order."

"Yes, master, I will be your headman. I am from Sa'aqs. All the others know me and my word will be obeyed. Free us, master, or we will all die."

Rory dispatched Tim back to Jehu's cabin for the master key that unlocked the long leg chains and the manacles. Then he continued to talk with the black. He felt he had made a good choice, albeit accidentally. The man was a big fellow, young and strong; he had a well-favored and intelligent face, handsome in a savage way.

"I want you to pick out ten men here—men who can take authority. You will be headman and they will be headmen under you. You will see to it that they keep all the others in order. Yes?"

"Yes, master, but hurry and unlock the chains."

Rory nodded in assurance and stumbled up and down the narrow lane between the feet of one row and the heads of the others, stooping, reassuring, comforting. He felt sorry for the poor blacks. The groaning of the ship's timbers and the crash of combers against the side were enough to frighten even seasoned sailors. He tried to stifle his own sickness and terror in order to give assurance to these poor devils. They represented Baba's and his entire investment—they were the alpha and omega of all his endeavors. But his interest, he realized, somewhat to his surprise, was now more than merely commercial. He recognized their helplessness and he wanted to help them. His very presence quieted them somewhat, and although he had had a chance to speak with only a few before Tim returned with the keys, those few in turn quieted others.

The locks snapped open and the chains rattled out from

320

between the leg irons and the manacles, coiling over the deck like long black snakes. There was no time to unfasten all the individual leg irons and manacles, but now, freed from the long chains, the men could sit up or stand and were able to keep their balance. Rory did, however, return to the first man he had spoken to and freed his hands and feet.

"What's your name?" he asked.

"I am called K'tu."

"K'tu, come with me. We will pick out the men to help you."

Much of the moaning had stopped when the men were released. Now they huddled together, bracing each other for support, while K'tu led Rory in and out of the various groups. He would point out a man and call his name. When the fellow stood up, Rory unlocked his irons and he accompanied them to the next man and on again until K'tu had selected ten stalwart bucks. That these men might be malcontent ringleaders, Rory never considered. Some slight resemblance in the fellow K'tu to Baba had caused Rory to trust the man even though he realized that he was banking on something so ephemeral that it could be laid to intuition only.

K'tu, speaking rapidly in Hausa and other tongues which Rory did not understand, placed each of his chosen men in different sections of the deck, giving each to understand that those on the floor within the vague circumference of K'tu's gesture were to be that man's particular responsibility. The ship, now struggling out of the trough of the sea, began to run before the storm and was somewhat steadier. Gradually the slave deck took on some semblance of order. The stench had not abated and the floor was still slippery from vomit and excrement but the men themselves were beginning to clean their skins, wiping themselves with their hands and scrubbing off each other's backs.

Feeding them was out of the question. No fires could be lighted in the galley and even if food was prepared there, it could not be brought below. But there were water casks on this deck and Rory knew that some of the stores were forward. He sent Tim with two of the freed slaves; when

321

they came back, the men were carrying sacks and buckets and Tim had a long-handled iron spoon.

"Ever eat loblolly, Rory?"

"I'll never eat anything again as long as I live."

"It ain't much, but it will fill these poor devils' bellies." Tim went forward to the water casks and half-filled one bucket with water. Punching a small hole in one of the sacks, he had the black fellow lift it over the pail, allowing the yellow cornmeal to dribble into the water. Stirring as the meal trickled in, he evolved a water mush, which became thicker and thicker until he could make a ball of it with his fingers. This he dispatched with the black to his group, then called up another and one by one mixed the gruel for each section.

Tim rolled a ball in his fingers and plopped it into his own mouth. He swallowed it, then rolled up another ball for Rory, who refused it. But the boys ate it voraciously, plunging their hands into the buckets and gobbling it mouthful by mouthful. They scraped the buckets clean with their fingers and sat back grinning, their teeth making bright points in the dim light of the 'tween decks.

Rory suggested to Tim that he go to Jehu, thinking that in the absence of his first mate, Jehu might find Tim's experience valuable. As for himself, Rory decided to stay below with the blacks. There was motion, activity, and to a certain extent, companionship here. He had K'tu carry two of the full sacks of meal up to where the mainmast rose like a treetrunk through the deck, and by sitting on the sacks and bracing his back against the mast, he found some stability; the ship too, was now somewhat steadier. He motioned to K'tu to sit on the floor beside him and encouraged him to talk.

Glad of an audience, K'tu talked. He was a soft-spoken boy of about eighteen, with an agreeable grin. From his Fulani mother he had inherited the thin lips and hawklike nose and lighter coloring of the Fulanis. His Hausa father had bequeathed him his height and strength. An Arab slave trader had brought him to Sa'aqs and sold him to Baba. Now, K'tu grinned, he was with the sultan's famous white brother. He grabbed Rory's hand, laid it on his head, and pleaded with Rory to take him as his servant.

Rory reminded himself that he had no servant. Poor Mleeka was dead. Why shouldn't he avail himself of this willing young colt? If he didn't work out, he could relegate him to the hold again and try another.

"You think you'd like to be my boy, K'tu? How do you know that I won't be a bad master and whip you?"

"Because you are a good master and I am a good boy. If I am good to you and serve you well, you will be good to me and not beat me. I know you are a good man. Today when you were as sick as we were you came here to help us. You sprayed your vomit on me but I didn't mind because I knew you could not help it. I have known you a long time, my master, because I have seen you in Sa'aqs and in the big house where we stayed before we got on this canoe. Then I have looked for you each time we came up in the air to eat. Each time my eyes seek you out and they worship you because you are not like any man I have ever seen before. You smile much, and it is a good omen when a man smiles. It shows he has a good soul. I smile much, even if I am a slave, for I too have a good soul. I will serve you well, my master and my lord."

"Then when I leave here, you have permission to come with me."

K'tu took Rory's hand from his wiry pate and rubbed it against his cheek.

"I will go with you, milord, but now because you have put me in charge it is best that I leave you and go to the other ten men, one by one, and talk to them or they will not remember that I am the headman here."

Rory nodded and K'tu left him. During the long day, he half sat and half lay against the mast. His nostrils became accustomed to the stench and his eyes to the darkness. His stomach rebelled against food, although he drank often of the tepid water K'tu brought in a bucket. He had no way of telling time because he could not hear the ship's bells, but he knew that the ship was running out of the storm because the deck beneath him became more and more steady. K'tu returned to sit at his feet and then, dozing off, laid his head on Rory's knees and slept. Rory, too, slept.

The stamping of feet and noises on the hatch above

323

awoke him. One by one the heavy planks were removed and the light burst through. A patch of sunlight gilded the filthy deck and Tim's aureole of red hair appeared over the edge of the hatch.

"You all right down there, Rory lad?"

"Practically recovered," Rory yelled back.

"Storm's all over. Come on up."

Rory prodded K'tu and bade him follow him up the ladder which had been lowered through the hatch. The strong light almost blinded him but it was good to see bright sunlight again. The sea was a wide expanse of whitecaps, sparkling in the light.

"I want all those boys brought up on deck and doused with sea water. Issue a double portion of palm oil to them so they can rub themselves down. Then I want fifty to take swabs and scrub the slave deck clean. Have cook get some sort of meal for them; if there's any fruit left, issue it. Then have them all taken down and bedded."

"Who's the big black foo-foo what's following you like your own shadow?" Tim pointed to K'tu.

"His name's K'tu. I'm taking him to replace Mleeka. About time you had a boy of your own too, Timmy. I don't think we'll have another mutiny, but you'd be safer with a boy sleeping outside your door."

Tim winked slowly. "I'm way ahead of you, Rory. Got one all picked out, I have. Was going to ask you if I could have him. He's one of my own boys. Brought him all the way from Basampo with me."

Rory shook his head sadly. "How short a time sorrow lives, Timmy. Two days ago I mourned Mleeka and you Manoel, and even now we have replaced them."

"It's life, Rory. When you've been at sea as long as I have you know that it's here today, gone tomorrow. I no sooner got bosom-pally with a fellow then we changed ships or something and I had to find another. Got to get used to it and not let it tear your heart out." Tim walked over to where K'tu was standing and appraised him, then shook his head. "Rory, there are times when I think you a bit daft in the head."

"And so do I, but why do you think so now?"

"Because you pick out someone like this K'tu. Look at

324

him. He's another big bruiser like your Mleeka. Now if you'd picked out someone like that melon-assed boy named Darba that I chose, you'd have more than some stupid bastard sleepin' outside your door. You'd have a nice bedmate a-sleepin' alongside you where he'd do you some good. You'd better learn, Rory, that life at sea is different from life on land. I know, I've been doing it most of my life."

"Each to his own," Rory smiled. "At least I can dream." He remembered Mary Davis again.

"Aye, aye, that you can." Tim poked a finger in Rory's ribs. "And I'm thinking you dream pretty goddamn well, bucko. When I went in last night to put up the sideboards on your bed you were fair thrashing around 'n breathing hard and fast." Tim winked. "Don't know who she was, Rory, but you sure was a-going strong. Too bad she missed it, whoever she was."

"She was Mary Davis, a Glasgow doxy, Timmy, and if I know Mary she isn't missing a hell of a lot. She's the one I sent the young stud to. Remember?"

Timmy scratched his head. "The black bucko what looked like an elephant in front and a palm tree behind? I remember him, and a likely lad he was. Faith, Rory me lad, he was almost a worthy substitute for you."

"Let's hope Mary Davis found him so."

CHAPTER XXX

THERE FOLLOWED SEVERAL WEEKS OF CALM, uneventful sailing. Then one morning Rory awoke half-blinded by a brilliant circle of sunshine on the deck of his cabin. Something was wrong; something was missing. Then he realized the strange hush, the calm that came from in-action. The ship was moving only with a gentle, almost imperceptible rolling. Jumping out of bed, he ran to the port-hole, but from it he could see nothing but the same expanse of water he had been looking at for weeks. Grabbing a towel from the nail by his washbowl, he tied it around his middle and yanked at the latch of the door. Outside, K'tu was sitting up on his pallet idly playing with his toes. Rory leaped over him and took the stairs to the companionway two at a time, K'tu following, his frightened Hausa words making no sense. Tim, already dressed, was at the rail, shading his eyes with his hand as he stared at the land.

"Where are we, Timmy lad?" Rory came up beside him, panting. He laid a reassuring hand on K'tu's shoulder to calm the frightened boy.

"According to Jehu that there's Port of Spain." Tim pointed to a stone spire rising above the trees some distance from shore. "He says this is Trinidad and he damned well ought to know."

"Get me a glass, will you, Timmy?" Rory continued to enjoy the green and solid vista and to calm K'tu who was wildly exuberant over the sight of land. Tim returned with the telescope. With it Rory could see buildings among the distant trees and nearer, small boats drawn up on the shore. One jerry-built pier extended into the water, but the *Shaitan* was anchored at least a half mile off shore.

"Waiting to be cleared," Tim explained. "Some red-faced, English, high and mighty son of a bitch who thinks his shit don't stink and who's all prettied up in white breeches and a blue coat with gold braid will be a-coming out pretty soon, soon's he's had breakfast. He'll sweat up the ladder and stand here a-huffin' and a-puffin' like billy-be-damned. Then Jehu'll invite him down to his cabin for a glass of Madeiry and slip the bastard a couple of cases on the side and Johnny Bull Boy'll look over our papers and, if we are lucky and the bastard likes our Madeiry, he'll let us in to His Bloody Majesty's bloody colony of bloody Trinidad."

"He's coming now." Rory's glass had espied the trimly painted boat oared by eight blacks. "And as you say, the bastard's red-faced and dressed in white breeches and a blue coat."

"They always are." Tim took the glass that Rory

326

offered him and peered through it. "Likely as not the old boy's madder'n hell because he had to get himself dressed so early; but Jehu'll soften him up with the Madeiry."

Just as Timmy had prophesied, the man (whose name turned out to be Elphinstone) huffed and puffed his way up the rope ladder and stumbled onto the deck. His manner was brusque and patronizing until he discovered that Rory was a baron, after which he became fawningly subservient and sirred Rory with every sentence. Once in Jehu's cabin, he hemmed and hawed over the fact that theirs was a ship under the Star and Crescent of the Sublime Porte, but he was somewhat mollified by the five cases of Madeira that Jehu pressed on him. Then, when he discovered that they were carrying a cargo of prime black meat, he literally welcomed them with open arms.

"Slaves?" He shook out a freshly ironed handkerchief and mopped his brow. "Demn-it-all, gentlemen, they're worth their weight in gold in Trinidad. Plantations screaming for 'em. Need 'em! Can't get 'em! All the demned slave ships drop their cargoes at Barbados or carry them through to Jamaica. We're a new colony here; just starting! Willing to pay double for them. Need a nice wench myself to help my wife in the house." He winked with newborn intimacy at Rory.

"We've brought no wenches, Your Honor." Rory was at a loss how to address the man. "But we've a cargo of prime bucks."

Elphinstone's jaw dropped, then his lips broke into a jowly smile.

"It's bucks we're really wanting, Lord knows, Sir Roderick; good strong bucks to build up the colony. Bucks like that one there." He pointed to K'tu whose black nakedness was partially hidden behind Rory. "Now there's a fine specimen. Got any more like him?"

"Plenty more below, sir."

"Come over here, boy," Elphinstone beckoned to K'tu who, unable to understand the words, looked to Rory for instruction.

"Go to the man." Rory spoke in Hausa. "He won't hurt you."

"Permission?" Elphinstone's question was perfunctory

327

as he started moving his hands over K'tu's arms and shoulders. "Fine boy, fine!" He continued his inspection, his hands pinching at the muscles of K'tu's chest, a stiff finger poking at the hard abdominal muscles, and then a hand cupping the pendent genitals. "Fine boy, fine!" he repeated, nodding his head in admiration. "This boy for sale?"

Rory could see the nervous tics of fear as they contracted the muscles under K'tu's polished skin.

"Sorry, Mr. Elphinstone, this particular boy's not for sale. He's my personal body servant, although you'd not guess it because I've not gotten around to giving him clothes yet. But I assure you, there are many more below who are his peers and if you're interested, I'll give you first look at them."

"Thank'ee, Sir Roderick, thank'ee." He hastily scratched his name on the papers which he had previously looked at so suspiciously and handed them back to Jehu. "Glad to meet you all, gentlemen, and I'll be seeing you on shore. If you've got more like him, you'll be as welcome in Trinidad as the flowers in May!" He shook hands with them and with an appraising glance at K'tu, he departed, his face a shade redder from the glasses of Madeira he had downed.

After he had gone, Rory, with K'tu's help, dressed himself in all the finery that Vogliano had provided for him. That it was French in cut and material did not detract from its richness, and although the long-tailed blue coat and the white tricot pantaloons were tight, hot, and uncomfortable, they did transform Rory into an imposing spectacle. The ruby that Baba had given him glowed on his shirtfront and his thin pumps shone like black jet. He called K'tu to stand beside him and held up a pair of white canvas pantaloons against the black skin. "These ought to fit you." He handed the pantaloons to K'tu. "Put them on, and this too." He reached for a white shirt. "If you're going to be my servant, we can't have you going around bare-assed naked."

K'tu accepted the garments and slipped them on. "You are going to sell me to that red-faced man?" His voice trembled with fear.

"Not as long as you and I get along together. Don't let it frighten you if a white man examines you. It doesn't mean I'm selling you. I'm going ashore now. I won't take you this time because I don't know what we're running into; but hereafter I'll want you with me wherever I go. Understand?"

"Like your shadow, master?"

"Like my shadow."

K'tu raised Rory's hand and placed it against his cheek. "Your shadow is black, master, and I am that shadow."

Rory cuffed him good-naturedly and, leaving him in the cabin, knocked on Tim's door. Although Tim's accoutrements were somewhat less splendid, he sported Mechlin lace at the throat and wrists of a garnet red jacket and wore white pantaloons.

"Look at me, Rory me lad." Tim turned slowly around for Rory's inspection. "A bleeding toff, a regular la-dee-da bloke, I am. Not even a pigtail to put a bit of tar on and feeling more like the Lord Mayor himself. I've come up in the world, Rory."

"You're the Half-King of Basampo, remember that, Timmy."

"That I am, and I warrant a salute of eleven guns, if the Johnny Bulls only knew it. Should I make them acquainted with my high-and-mightiness?"

"Better stick to being Timothy O'Toole, Esquire, I'm thinking, Timmy. They don't know what a half-king is here, and now that you're dabbling in trade, you'd best forget that you're royalty. Come, man, let's set foot on Trinidad and see what it's like to have honest soil under us instead of oaken planking."

A striped awning had been hastily erected over the gig and the four sailors who manned it were attired in fresh white trousers, blue jackets, and leather hats. Rory, seated in the gig, looked up to wave to Jehu and to K'tu, proud in his new finery. Jehu called to them over the widening expanse of water, "We'll be anchored yonder when you return." He pointed in the direction of the long, rickety wooden pier.

It was good to be on land again, but Rory was sorely disappointed in Trinidad, if the rest of the island was to

329

be judged by the slatternly appearance of the waterfront. There were a few rickety piers besides the long one, but they were so small that they hardly merited the name; three or four small boats, none larger than a coasting vessel, and on the shore a clutch of low huts of palm-leaf thatching. Nothing more, unless one were to consider the mangy curs that sniffed at the piles of offal, the black buzzards that wheeled lazily in the overwhelmingly blue sky, and the general air of decaying somnolence that pervaded the place. Rory already regretted his finery in the intense heat of the sun. He was sweating like a grenadier and had the uncomfortable feeling that his fine clothes were sticking to him in a sodden mass.

"One hell of a glory hole, if you ask me." Tim sniffed at the stink and dust and heat. "But lookee, Rory, there's a lean-to with a green branch over the door, which is an old Irish custom for saying there's drink inside. Warm beer's better than warm air to wet my whistle."

The shade, if not the fetid odor of the waterside tavern, was welcome after the incandescent glare of the sun, and once inside, a black wench whose dirt-encrusted shift made no attempt to imprison her huge swaying breasts provided them with tankards of warm ale.

"Tastes more like donkey piss." Tim made a wry face.

"Don't know, Timmy." Rory pointed an accusing finger at him. "Never tasted it myself, but you may well have. However, I can imagine that it might taste something like this."

Inquiries to the barmaid elicited the appearance of the owner, an obese Spaniard who spoke a little English. He informed them that it was some distance to the town; too far indeed for such extremely handsome and well-dressed young dons to walk. He would find them a conveyance to take them there. Rory agreed, but when it arrived they discovered it to be a cart with high solid wooden wheels drawn by two plodding oxen. The inside of the cart was liberally bespattered with fresh dung which necessitated their standing, and the old black driver accomplished nothing with his goads and shouts. The oxen moved along at their own creeping pace, completely oblivious to his prods. All the spit and polish of the gig with its freshly

330

uniformed sailors and the splendor of Rory's attire had been wasted, for upon their arrival in the town, he found one side of his coat liberally besmeared with a wet brindle stain from his having been thrown against the side of the cart. His linen was dusty and bedraggled, his face lined with sweaty channels of dirt, and his temper none too even. Tim was equally disheveled, but nothing seemed to disturb the evenness of his disposition. Their aged driver abandoned them before a substantial stone weatherbeaten building with wooden awnings and a weatherbeaten sign that read, in fading letters, ELPHINSTONE & COMPANY, FACTORS. They entered the open door, finding it somewhat cooler inside, to discover that Elphinstone—he of the company—was quite a different man from the official who had met them earlier. This Elphinstone was a young fellow of about Rory's age and he needed no introduction to Rory, for it had been his uncle who had come to the ship and had already spread the news of Rory's arrival.

"You'd be the Baron of Sax?" The graciousness of the young man was apparent as he advanced in the semi-darkness of the louvered office to greet them. "My uncle was telling me about you not more than an hour ago. Tells me that you have a shipload of slaves and that they are all prime specimens." He proffered chairs for Rory and Tim, rang a bell which summoned a colored porter, insisted that they remove their coats, sent Rory's coat out to have the manure sponged from it, supplied them with cool drinks from the sweating *olla* which the servant brought in, and in a few moments had them cool, refreshed, and comfortable.

Young Elphinstone—Noel as he introduced himself— seemed likable and honest. He had, so he said, intended to go to the ship himself, but now that Rory had saved him the trip, they could do business together—that is, if Rory wished—in the cool comfort of his counting room. Rory did wish.

Young Elphinstone explained that he had been in business only a couple of years because the colony, so recently taken from Spain, was a new one. There was not, he informed them, any great wealth there. But the few Englishmen who had settled there were doing well, with even

331

better prospects, for their plantations had great potentialities. The old Spanish families who had been intrenched there for generations were extremely well off. The soil was rich, the crops good, and there was every chance of success and riches could they but get slaves to till the land and do the work. That was why this shipment of Rory's was so welcome. Young Noel reiterated what his uncle had said: that most slavers coming from Africa stopped first at Barbados or went on further to the more populous islands of English Jamaica or French Haiti, even to Spanish Cuba. It was seldom that they, in Trinidad, had an opportunity to buy slaves. They needed them badly.

Now young Elphinstone leaned forward confidentially and tapped Rory's knee. He would be willing to help Rory dispose of his cargo. Of course, it would be as Rory desired. He had no wish to push himself forward, but as Rory was a stranger, perhaps he could be of assistance. He did have a large compound, unroofed but enclosed with high stone walls. There was an open shed at one end of it which Rory could use as a barracoon. The shed was large enough so that the slaves could sleep under cover, albeit on the ground, and they would have space to exercise in the open court. However, they would be there such a short time that they would experience no discomfort. What did Rory think?

He would think it over. He appreciated Elphinstone's cooperation, but he would like time to think about it.

But that was not all, Elphinstone continued. He advised Rory to hold an auction because competitive bidding would bring higher prices. He would even be willing to do the auctioneering himself. He'd have hand bills printed up and send them out by messengers to all the plantations, setting the date of the sale. Yes, if Rory desired, he'd be willing to handle all the business once the cargo of slaves were installed in the barracoon. He'd slop them, providing adequate food with plenty of fresh fruit. He'd allow them a few days to rest up and get their land legs, and it might be a good idea to exercise them to pump up their muscles and get them in the pink of condition. He'd be willing to do all this for a mere ten per centum of the sales price.

Rory felt that in the end he would agree. He was, more

332

or less, at the mercy of this engaging young fellow anyway, because he did not know where else to go. A cargo of livestock had to be taken care of, housed, and fed. Animals were not like lumber or cotton cloth or iron kettles. They were alive, and having been so fortunate as to lose none of them during the middle passage, Rory was anxious to get them off his hands. Yes, he would let Elphinstone know—he most certainly would.

Then at least, Elphinstone suggested, let them write up an agreement. He rang a bell and a stooped and elderly clerk appeared, who at Elphinstone's dictation wrote up an articled agreement with a place for Rory to sign when he had—and Elphinstone hoped it would be soon—made up his mind. Refusing Elphinstone's invitation to dinner at his home up in the hills, Rory did, however, accept the offer of a cart and driver to convey him back to the waterfront. Elphinstone apologized for the cart which was an island product, but at least it was clean and the seat cushioned with sailcloth which allowed for somewhat easier riding than the dung cart in which they had arrived.

Although the cart was unsprung, the wheels spoked instead of solid, and the horses trotted instead of plodding like oxen, Rory had a sudden longing for Sa'aqs and the swift Arabian horses that he and Baba had ridden together. He wanted to gallop out to the ruined mosque; to listen to the licentious tales of the old storyteller, and then, most of all, to ride back to the mud palace of Sa'aqs and choose one of his hareem. Not Almera. Almera was for quiet love and his body demanded something more than that after his long continence. He remembered his hareem; there was a certain Persian girl there—he had forgotten her name—whose warm lips had a way of milking him of all desire. It was she whom he would choose. He became aware of an expansive burgeoning in his crotch. Persian girl? Hell! He'd take any one of them. Any one if he could have her at this moment. In fact, he'd take anything. Good God! He'd had nothing since Madeira and that cow Rosa.

He sighed and gritted his teeth, hoping that Tim would not notice the all-too-apparent signs of his excitement, but Tim had. After all, it was impossible to hide it.

"You gotta learn something, Rory me goozlum, if you're going to go a-sailin'. There ain't a man yet but needs to get his stones off every so often and you might as well get used to the fact that there's more ways than one when you're out of sight of land and women."

"But now we're on land and certain as hell there must be women here. If there are I'm sure going to find them."

He spoke to the driver, an intelligent-looking Negro youth who spoke English fairly well, instructing him to drive them about the town. The impression it made on Rory, after the slatternly appearance of the waterfront, was most favorable. Until a few years ago it had been a Spanish colony and Spain had always been a good builder—a permanent one. The houses, stores, and churches were solidly built of masonry because the Spaniards did not believe in wooden construction. The streets, even though narrow, were shaded with palms and blooming tropical shrubs. Swags of brilliant magenta bougainvillea were draped across blinding white plastered walls; weird plants with leaves of orange, red, yellow, and green were as brilliant as flowers, and through wrought iron gates set in solid walls of white, there were glimpses of gardens half-hidden from the road. Although only a few people were abroad at this hour, those whom Rory saw in the better section of the town were well dressed and prosperous looking.

After circling through the residential and business section of the town, the driver, almost as though guessing Rory's thoughts, turned around and addressed him.

"Yo' might be a-wantin' a woman, sah masta man? Got one street in this town what hab women, sah masta. If'n yo' like I take yo' to see."

Rory mentally thanked the fellow for not beating around the bush. Delicate words and subtle innuendoes had no bearing on his feelings now. The driver had stated succinctly exactly what he wanted—a woman. *A* woman. Not *the* woman or any *particular* woman, merely *a* woman. If she were young and pretty, so much the better; but the most important thing was that she be a woman.

He flipped a silver coin to the driver who grabbed it in

midair. "That's what I'm wanting, boy. Jog up those horses."

"Yes sah, masta man." The driver laid his whip on the horses.

"Can't be any worse than old Mother Blood-and-Guts where you took me in Liverpool, Timmy. Seems a long time ago, doesn't it?"

" 'Druther not think about it, Rory. We're good friends now. Then you was just another sailor I was crimping for a fartin' guinea. Things are different now."

They turned a corner and Rory let his gaze wander in the direction of the driver's pointing whip.

"That here it am," the fellow said, slowing the horses.

It was a narrow street, but far from being sordid, the little houses were neatly kept. The older ones were of stone and the new ones of wood. Each had its own small plot of flowers, and on the wide steps that led up to each front door bevies of girls in brightly colored dresses sat waving to them as they passed. They were in all shades of brown, sepia, and white, some of the latter Spanish in appearance with here and there a blonde with fair English skin. The occupants of each house tempted them and Rory was prone to stop at the first, but the driver, with a wide grin, proudly pointed to a larger and more substantial building at the end of the street. Its two stories dominated all the others, and brightly dressed young ladies filled a gallery around the second story. These occupants were thus set apart from those who had merely steps to sit on.

"There at's the bestest." White teeth sparkled in the plum-dark lips as the fellow flourished his whip. "The prettiest gals there sah, masta man." He pulled up to the entrance door and alighted to hold the horses' heads.

A young colored fellow dressed in the most fantastic costume Rory had ever seen came through the door and jogged over to the cart, grinning an invitation and gesturing toward the house. His skin-tight pantaloons of vivid emerald-green silk tricot were apparently designed especially to attract attention to the superabundance of his manhood, which bulged grotesquely and incredibly. He wore a flared coat of glazed white chintz covered with

335

enormous red roses, a waistcoat of orange satin, a stock of fuchsia taffeta, and a high turban of acid purple adorned with white cock's feathers.

A few steps from the cart, he looked up into Rory's face, his grin changing to a bewildered stare. Rory returned the stare. The boy's face seemed strangely familiar, but Rory was entirely unprepared for the torrent of Arabic words that poured from the boy's mouth.

"Bismillah! My lord and master." He bowed so low that his top-heavy turban fell off, disclosing his matte black hair. "My lord and master, the brother of my lord the Shango."

For a moment Rory could not answer, and then he remembered back to the river at Castle Rinktum when he and Baba stood on the bank and he had picked out one Negro lad because of his phenomenal development.

He was out of the carriage in a moment, his hands on the boy's shoulders. In his excitement, he shook the lad.

"You are Fayal!"

"Yes, my lord, I am Fayal."

"And Mary Davis? Good God, boy, is she here?"

The boy took one of Rory's hands and kissed it. "Mrs. Fortescue is here."

"Mrs. Fortescue?"

"She who was Mary Davis, my lord and master."

CHAPTER XXXI

IT SEEMED IMPOSSIBLE BUT IT WAS TRUE. HERE in Port of Spain, halfway around the world from Glasgow and even farther from Rinktum Castle, Rory had come upon Fayal—and even more important than Fayal, he had been reunited with Mary Davis, although she was now Mrs. Fortescue. Who the hell was Fortescue? Well, whoever he was, Rory intended to cuckold him. He'd put a longer pair of horns on the bastard than any stag in the Highlands could boast. With a quick leavetaking of Tim and instructions to the coachman to take him back to the waterfront, Rory followed Fayal through the open door of the house. It was dark and cool under the arched passageway, and even in the flower-filled patio he sensed a feeling of shadowy coolness from the palms and the tiny fountain that dripped into a tiled basin surrounded by dewy ferns.

"Please, you wait here, lord and master." Fayal pointed to a stone bench shaded from the sun by the broad metallic green leaves of a banana plant. "I go to tell Mrs. Fortescue you are here." He slipped off the fantastic turban and wiped the sweat from his forehead with the back of his hand. "Goddamn monkey suit," he said in English. "Goddam tight pants. Mrs. Fortescue say I wear him, I wear him, but he hot as hell. Get business though but I tell Mrs. Fortescue don' I wear any pants I get more business but she say I ain' no goddamn black savage no more."

"Wait a minute." Rory continued to speak in Arabic, glad of this opportunity once more to use the language which took him back to Africa. "Don't tell Mrs. Fortescue who's here. Just say a gentleman wants to see her."

"Will do; mean will not do. Goddamn English hard to speak but mos' forgot other speaking." He turned and ran up the stairs as fast as the sausage-tight casings of his legs would allow. He was back in a moment, breathless. "Mrs. Fortescue say man wait a minute. She come down. Better you stay there behind banana." Fayal grinned. "She not see you so soon; she be goddamn surprised."

Rory discovered that he was trembling with excitement and anticipation. Also desire, for he felt a hot engorgement in his groin. True, he had never been in love with Mary Davis; at least he did not think so. But he had never been able to forget the night they spent together, and even more than that, he was eternally grateful for her goodness to him. Now the prospect of seeing her made him realize that she occupied a more important place in his heart than he ever considered. Mary Davis! A wharfside doxy from

337

Glasgow! Yet he would never forget the snugness of her little room, her inspired lovemaking, and her offer for him to remain in Glasgow. Mary Davis! His recent dream about her had renewed his desire for her.

He heard steps coming down the stairs, then the staccato tapping of high heels on the tiles. Peeking out through the leaves, he could hardly connect this *grande dame* with the slattern he had left in Glasgow. The only thing that had not changed was her face, but her bearing, her clothes, and her demeanor were a far cry from those of a dockside whore. She wore a gown of some filmy white stuff cut in the new, extreme French fashion which exposed her breasts to her rosy nipples and allowed those to show through like ripe berries. It was evident as she walked with the sunlight behind her that she wore nothing under the dress. A girdle of woven gold clasped the diaphanous material under her swelling breasts, and the gown hung straight and loose to her feet. The mop of frowzy curls that had bedecked her head in Scotland was now sleekly coifed, piled high in a chignon which allowed the pendant earrings of brilliants to show to good advantage. A scarf of white and cherry striped tissue fell from her elbows and floated behind her. Little cherry-colored satin shoes peeped out from the hem of her dress.

"My God! She's ravishing," he whispered to himself; yet in spying on this woman of the world, he hoped that the Mary Davis he had known had changed only outwardly.

Halfway across the courtyard she halted for a moment, looking around the patio, and catching sight of his broad back between the leaves, she came around the little fountain to where he sat. No sooner had she parted the leaves than he sprang up and enfolded her in his arms; she responded by squirming and fighting him off.

"You son-of-a-bitching bastard, whoever you are!" She pounded at his chest with futile blows. "I'm no two-shilling doxy. If you want a wench I'll get you one, but the devil take me if I'll let you maul me."

He released her at arms' length, grinning down at her.

"And that's just who's taking you, Mary Davis, the devil himself—the Mahound—Old Harry—Satan—

Lucifer—Shaitan, whatever name you want to call him. The last time I saw you you were clutching a woolen shawl around your shoulders as the Liverpool coach left Glasgow, shivering in the cold dampness, and now here you are, decked out like billy-be-damned and answering to the name of Mrs. Fortescue and not even a kiss for poor Rory Mahound who's been a-sea for nigh onto a lifetime it would seem without anything to kiss except his own right hand."

"Rory Mahound!" She stared at him for a long moment to verify the fact, then fell into his arms, smothering him with kisses. "Rory Mahound, my love, my bairn, my rum damber, my very life itself! And did you bring Old Harry with you, Rory Mahound?" She let her hand slip down between his legs, her fingers clutching. "Aye, that you did, as big as life and growing bigger by the second. Now tell me, what are you doing in Port of Spain and did you ever forget me, Rory Mahound? Aye, lad, it's all due to you that I'm now the elegant and the Honorable Mrs. Fortescue with my own stable of fillies to do all the work for me and I'm here in Port of Spain. And, oh, Rory Mahound, it's glad I am to see you." She covered his face with kisses. "My own Rory Mahound."

"My Mary Davis." He returned her kisses. "But come, sit down and tell me all about yourself now that you're the elegant and Honourable Mrs. Fortescue of Port of Spain." He pulled her down on the bench beside him, enveloping her in his arms, one hand on the soft flesh of an exposed breast.

"But not here, Rory Mahound." She pointed to the stairs. "I'd never trust myself here with you and all my little girls peeking over the rail and Fayal spying on us from behind the palms. Although my hands itch for you, we're not putting on any raree show. It's better that we go upstairs to my rooms where I can close the door and lock it and be as foolish as I want to be with you." She led him to the stairs and they ascended a step at a time, between kisses and fondlings and arm-in-arm squeezings. Then they were safely along the corridor and into her room. He pulled her close and pushed her hand down to his bursting buttons.

339

"Oh, it is Old Harry himself," she laughed, "and glad I am to see him again with his hat doffed and ready for a fracas. He's still champion, you know, although I must admit he has a most serious rival in the young Fayal, who's made my fortune for me."

And then, then, after more kissing and more fondling, squeezing and pressing, followed by more sweet words, they disengaged themselves with Mary's flimsy dress up over her shoulders and Rory's jacket on the floor and his pantaloons around his ankles.

Though there was much to be talked about between the two of them, there was much more to be done, and not until some two hours had passed were either of them in the mood for serious conversation. During that time Rory returned to the hard pallet in the dingy room in Glasgow. He whiffed the odor of peat smoke from the little fire in the grate, felt the warmth and security of Mary's arms around him and, with all the memories, he put Old Harry through such a series of performances as left Mary gasping yet swearing that no other man but the Mahound himself could stage such a spectacular *tour de force*.

At length, with the fires in his blood smoldering but not quenched, Rory swung his long legs over the edge of the tousled bed, picked Mary up in his arms, and deposited her in a chair beside the louvered window. Pulling up a cushion, he sat on the floor at her feet, but she would have none of that and made him sit in the chair as she preempted the cushion for herself, leaning her head, now not so sleekly coifed, between his knees.

"So now, Mrs. Fortescue, or should I say the Honorable Mrs. Fortescue who can still be so charmingly dishonorable." Rory lifted her face, cupping her chin in his hands. "Let's hear what brought *you* to Port of Spain along with your Fayal—and who, by the way, is Fortescue?"

She kissed the tips of his fingers, then, laying her head against his thigh, she teased him with her warm mouth until he gently pushed her away.

"Fortescue?" She smiled up at him. "Why bring up that fluffy-fugger now when Old Harry's doffing his cap to me?"

"Curiosity maybe. Jealousy perhaps."

"You've nothing to be jealous about. Captain The Honorable Jeremy Algernon Philip Fortescue was nothing but a drunken little whippersnapper—a mincer from the Grenadier Guards—who stumbled into my place one night, having heard of Fayal whose fame it seems had reached even to London. Jemmy was the younger son of the Earl of Dugane and a perverted little bastard if ever there was one. Wanted both me below and Fayal above at the same time and was willing to pay through the nose for it. And I did make him pay plenty in the end." She nodded her head knowingly. "Stayed in my place day and night for a week until both Fayal and me were fair worn out. Then he had no money left and wanted to stay another week. So I made him a proposition. If he married me he'd have both Fayal and me for free. He accepted. In his state, what with drink and his circus ideas of having fun, I knew he wouldn't last much longer. So married we were, and he lasted just three months. I woke up one morning and he wasn't breathing, that's all. I notified the old laird and his lady and they came and got what was left of poor Jemmy, turning up their elegant noses at me, but half thanking me that he'd passed on private-like without causing any scandal."

Rory pushed her hand away. "And then what happened?"

"Then comes their grand solicitor who wanted to see my marriage certificate, and after hemming and hawing he had to admit that it was all legal and aboveboard. So, wanting to get me out of the country along with Fayal— that nothing would ever be said about their precious Jemmy and his queer likes—he up and offers me two thousand gold guineas if I'd light out and shake the mist of Scotland from my rags forever. 'But where am I to go?' says I. 'Anyplace you please,' says he, 'as long as it's out of Scotland, Ireland, or England. How about Trinidad?' says he. I'd never even heard of Trinidad before, but it seems the old laird had bought a plantation here, which he didn't much want, so he was willing to throw that in, too, if I'd only go. What did I have to lose? I sold my little house in Glasgow, took Fayal, and went to London where

341

I stayed a month, waiting for a ship that would take me to Trinidad. During that month I took lodgings in Chelsea and made friends with an old lady, a Mrs. Edwards, who lived in the same house. She'd been an actress and in that one short month, she made a lady out of me—a silk purse out'n a sow's ear. Almost!

"We took the ship, me and Fayal, and we landed here. At first I thought I'd live on my plantation and be a decent lady, all la-di-da and proper-like as an Honorable Mrs. Fortescue should be, but, my dear Rory, one week of that and listening to the sugar cane grow and I was fit to be tied. Lonesome I was, and fair bored to death with being a lady. I found there was no proper entertainment for the poor men of Trinidad here and all the poor sailors who come to this port. To be sure, there's a whole street of cheap whores, but none of them really know their business. With them it's on and off and pay me a shilling and that's it. I decided to do something about it. I sold a bit of the land I had got from the old laird. I'd of opened up a place out at the plantation but it's too far for the sailors to ever find it. This was once a warehouse and a good sturdy place, so I bought it and fixed it up. Then I sent back to my friend Hannah MacTavish who's a trollop in Glasgow to send me over six pretty girls what knew their business and who wanted to trade the fogs of Glasgow for the sunshine of Trinidad.

"And here I am in business, and a damned good business if I do say so. What with all my girls white girls and busy every night, and with Fayal performing when asked— at a gold guinea if he's alone or two if he puts on a show with one of my girls—I'm fairly coining money." Her mouth slavered Rory with kisses. "Ain't never found no one to compare with you, Rory. Of course Fayal does as well as he can, and he's big, but he's not much fun."

Rory stiffened in his chair, spreading his legs out straight before him, but Mary, sensing another explosion, desisted.

"So, here I am in business and being such an elegant lady." She made a derisive *moue* at herself. "I don't work myself anymore unless the mood strikes me and some particularly handsome sailor comes along. I keep a respectable house, if you can consider a whorehouse respectable, and I've made friends with all the bigwigs here, even the governor himself, Sir Basil Cleverden. He's a good customer of mine though he's so old and feeble he can only look on. They say his lady-wife won't let him between her legs and I don't know as I can blame her. He's nigh onto seventy and limp as a rope, and she's not a day older than twenty so I've heard. But la! How I do go on like Dame Gossip herself with my everlasting blib-blab. And that's my story, Rory Mahound, and now that you're here and brought Old Harry with you, bless his shiny red head, that's all that matters."

For long moments there was silence in the room while Rory, through half-closed eyes, saw the changing bars of light sift through the louvered windows onto Mary's moving head. She pursued her course to its final denouement, until Rory once more gasped for air and fell back exhausted in his chair. She rose from the floor, poured out a glass of brandy, and gave it to him to drink, then seated herself in a chair across from him, at a proper distance.

"I'll keep my hands off now." She leaned forward and patted his knee. "Enough's enough for the time being and Old Harry needs his rest. See how cute he's sleeping now, all curled up and happy. But you, Rory, me gosling, I've told you my story. It's your turn to tell me yours."

The brandy had revived Rory and it was indeed his turn to tell her about himself—his journey to Africa, his friendship with Baba, his hareem, his love for Almera, and his child by her which must by now have been born. He told her of his rise in the world, his being an Emir of Sa'aqs, his ship in the harbor, and his cargo of slaves. He told her of Tim and his adventures in Africa. He told her of all the things that had happened to him, blushing over none of his exploits, knowing that she had been frank with him.

"And now that you're here, Rory Mahound, will you be staying?" she asked.

"For a while at least," he answered. "I'm to set up an establishment here as a permanent market for our slaves. Tim returns with the *Shaitan* to Goree in Senegal for more slaves which Baba will supply. Soon we hope to get more ships. With Baba in Africa and me here, we'll all make a fortune."

Mary interrupted him with an uplifted hand.

"No need to look longer for a place, me breakneck bucko. There's a nice house out on Melrose Plantation that I own. Nobody lives there because I have to spend my time here. 'Tis yours, Rory, for as long as you want it, and I'd appreciate it if there were someone there to look after it because the place's going to wrack and ruin. It's all furnished and you've got enough blacks to train for servants. You can even make money on the place if you want to work it. Set yourself up as a gentleman planter— milord the Baron of Sax—and do your slave business on the side; slave dealers ain't much thought of here. Take yourself out to Melrose and make it your home."

He walked over and kissed her on the forehead. "You solved all my problems once, Mary dear, and now you've solved them again. You took me in once and gave me a home and the warmth of your body. Now you're giving me a home again. Am I always to be indebted to you, Mary Davis?"

"Ah, Rory, it's a debt you can easily pay."

"That I can. I'll marry you, Mary Davis who is now the Honorable Mrs. Fortescue, and I'll make you Milady of Sax in Scotland and a Princess of Sa'aqs in Africa."

"That you will not," she stood up facing him. "The la-di-da Mrs. Fortescue is nothing but a dockside trollop after all, as you can well tell by the way she's plagued you this day. It's true she's a whore no longer, but she's mistress of a whorehouse and mayhap that's even worse. No, Rory, as much as I'd like to be Lady Sax and look down my nose at all the other women here, even Milady Cleverden, the wife of the governor, it would be they, in the end, who'd be looking down their noses at me. I thank you for the offer, Rory; there's no man I'd rather be married to than you, with Old Harry to keep me company always, but I'll not do it. I'd just be taking advantage of you."

"But I love you, Mary Davis."

"I love to hear you say it to me. No words were ever sweeter; but it's not love you feel for me. It's just meeting an old friend whom you never expected to see; it's having a wonderful tumble in bed you never anticipated; it's having Old Harry stand straight and tall and then curl up and go to sleep. Sure I know. It's a sort of loneliness and want of mothering and some pity and mayhap a wee bit of love, too, and as much as I'd like it, I'll still say nay, but. . . ." She let her hand linger on one of his bronze paps.

"But what?"

"It's only five miles from Port of Spain to Melrose Plantation. Two times a week, maybe three if you'll allow it, I'll drive out in my coach after it gets dark and I'll stay till just before daybreak. That's all the payment I'll need. Just to know that you and Old Harry'll be waiting for me."

"That's little enough, Mary Davis. I'll welcome you with open arms and Old Harry will be standing at attention, straight as a ramrod."

"The cute little big-man's starting to do it now." She kissed him and turned him around, facing him toward the bed. "Just wait till I spread the sheets smooth and clean."

"Then hurry while you do it," Rory allowed himself to be led across the room. "After all these weeks, Old Harry doesn't need much rest. He's fair to boiling over now."

"And mark my words, Rory lad," she pulled him down beside her, "he wouldn't enjoy it half as much if we were married. He just wouldn't, you know."

"I know, Mary Davis. You're always right."

CHAPTER XXXII

THE FIRST GLIMPSE THAT RORY HAD OF MELrose Plantation was disappointing. Its name had conjured up visions of an English country seat or possibly some moated Scottish castle, but the squat, sprawling farmhouse was far more Spanish than English and not unlike an Arab dwelling with its whitewashed stucco walls and red-tiled roof. It sat in a broad expanse of fields which were covered with tall brown grass where they were not a rampant jungle of weeds. Trees—many palms and some towering hardwoods—surrounded the house which was only one story high. The outside walls, merely blank expanses of once-whitened but now stained stucco, were devoid of windows, and the only entrance seemed to be the sagging iron gates at the front. Rory was alone with K'tu, having left Tim back at Port of Spain. After having heard Rory's description of the late and unlamented Mr. Fortescue's predeliction for being sandwiched between Fayal and a woman, Tim was all too anxious to experiment with one of Mary's girls and the redoubtable Fayal.

Nor had Mary been willing to accompany him. "Let them suspect all they want, Rory, 'bout you and me, but if they don't see us together they can't say nothing malicious 'bout us. If you're going to be a respectable dealer in slaves—if such can ever be respectable—it won't do no good to have your name tied up too close with mine." He could see her wisdom, but he missed her company as well as the easy familiarity of Tim's. So Rory had come alone with K'tu on the horses he had purchased for them both in Port of Spain.

He alighted before the gates. A rusty iron chain was suspended from a bell outside the closed gate and when Rory pulled it, the clamor started a flock of pigeons wheeling in the courtyard. He had to pull the chain several times before he detected any signs of life within the house, but finally the sloughing footsteps of bare feet on the tiles brought a young Negro buck—a gangling adolescent—who was lazily buttoning his ragged pantaloons around his slim waist.

"Whaffor yo' a-ringin' de bell, mista? Ain' no one a-livin' here, mista."

"You're living here, aren't you, you worthless hunk of black meat? I'm going to be living here, too. What's your name, boy?"

"I bin called Petah. Yas, I a-livin' here mista, alongside

346

my sister. She call Maria." He pronounced it with a long "eye" instead of the Spanish "ee".

"Then get your ass moving and open these gates. I'm going to live here and I'd like to see what the place looks like."

The boy fumbled with the chain on the gates, opening the rusty padlock, which was not locked, with his fingers. He made no effort to come outside and tether Rory's and K'tu's horses. Instead he leaned sleepily against the unopened gate, watching K'tu while he looped the reins around a tree branch.

"Looks to me, you lazy bastard, like you're going to need a little touching up with a whip." Rory's voice was stern with anger and impatience. "Someone's got to teach you a few manners. After this you'll jump when you see me. And when you address me, you call me 'master.' Now, take me inside and show me the place." Rory tickled the boy's calves with a switch which, in lieu of a riding crop, he had torn from a tree on the way out. "How long have you been here?"

"I always bin here, masta, me 'n Maria. Ol' Masta Kendall he go back to England, but afore he go he sell off all de niggers 'cept me 'n Maria. We runned 'n hid, we did. Then new masta he comed out from England but he not stay. Say this place no goddamn good thout'n niggers. We runs agin, me'n Maria, 'n then we comes back 'n now Missus Fortescue she say we stay here 'n look after things for her." He was fumbling with his buttons and Rory's eyes shifted to the boy's clumsy fingers and to the tattered pantaloons which did little even when buttoned to hide the boy's slowly receding erection.

"What were you doing when I arrived? Why did it take you so long to answer the bell?"

Peter lowered his head and his bare toe made circles in the dust of the tiles.

"Wan't a-doin' nothin' bad, masta. Nothin' bad 'tall. Ain't my fault. Maria she a-makin' me do it. Every day she a-makin' me 'n nights too. But ain' wrong, masta. She a-sayin' it ain' 'n she oldern me."

"You been screwing your sister?"

The boy Peter shook his head. "Ain' screwin' her,

347

master, leastwise not in de day. Jes' a-playin' wid myself so's she kin watch me. She a-likin' to see me a-shootin' my milk. Nights she a-makin' me sleep with her but ain' sleepin'. Ain' nobody what kin sleep wid Maria, she so goddamn cock-hungry." He raised his head with a shame-faced grin.

"Go fetch this Maria. I'll wait here." Rory dusted off one of the patio benches and sat down. He had only a short time to wait until a mulatto girl, several shades lighter than Peter and extremely handsome in a sluttish, unkempt way, sauntered onto the patio, dressed in a tat-tered ball gown which, although dirt-encrusted, showed a richness of material and cut which might have been in style twenty years ago.

"I'se Maria," she announced. "Petah a-claimin' yo' a-wantin' me."

"I do." Rory did not rise from the bench. "Mrs. Fortes-cue has turned this place over to me. I'm going to live here. First I want to look around and then we'll have to get it cleaned up. Suppose you take me around the house and then later your brother will take me around the buildings outside."

She eyed him speculatively, letting her eyes sweep from his head to his bootsoles, lingering overlong on the conspic-uous bulge of his crotch. He felt her eyes penetrating through the cloth of his pantaloons and knew that he was rising to meet her inspection although he cursed himself for it. She lifted her eyes to meet him. Her smile was conspiratorial.

"Glad yo' a-goin' to come here to live, masta. If'n yo' don' min' I goes fust to show you de way. Yo', Petah, yo' stays here 'n how's about him?" She pointed to K'tu. "We ain' wantin' no nigger buck alongside us' n's." Gathering up the voluminous train of her gown, she swept across the patio.

Rory bid K'tu remain with Peter. The girl, sluttish as she was, fascinated him. He caught up with her on the farther side of the courtyard.

Despite its squat, one-story appearance, it was a large house, with all the rooms opening off the enormous cen-tral patio, which was surrounded by a roofed and stone-pillared gallery. The patio itself was a tangle of overgrown weeds, flowers, and ragged banana plants, and the rooms were equally filthy with the dust and disorder of many months. One room, Maria's, contained an enormous double bed with tumbled, stained, and dirty sheets. Its tester was draped with festoons of cobwebs where damask should have hung. Another room contained a single cot, obviously Peter's. The kitchen showed signs of use. The embers of a charcoal fire still glowed and there was a dish of black beans and rice on the table, alongside dirty crockery plates.

The entire house was furnished in heavy, carved Spanish furniture which showed worn and rotting upholstery, with tattered rags of damask and moth-chewed tapestries on the walls.

When they had completed the tour of the various rooms, most of them bedrooms except for a dining room and a large salon, Maria led Rory back to her own room.

"Dis de bes' room for sleepin' in de house," she informed him. "It cool in her 'cause dis de only room what have an outside window." She indicated the heavy iron bars in the masonry. "If'n yo' likes, kin fix this room up for yo' and," she came closer to Rory, slipping an arm under his jacket, "if'n yo' likes, kin sleep in here too. Mighty sick o' that boy Petah I am. All he a'wantin' to do is jack himself all day. Come night he ain' got no strength for screwin'." She sidled closer to him.

The strong musk from her body was sickening to Rory, but there was a certain allure to the heart-shaped face and the long-lashed eyes. He pushed her away but he did it gently.

"We'll see," he temporized. "Now call Peter and my own boy K'tu and we'll look at the outside."

"Shore yo' ain' wantin' to rest up a bit?" She arched her body to him so that the points of her breasts protruded under the frowsy satin of her dress. "Kin lay yo'self down on de bed. Mighty hot out dere in de sun."

Once again she sidled up to him, and this time her fingers brushed against the bulge she had been eyeing. He wanted to protest, but the pressure of her fingers was so tantalizing he did not, for the moment, have the courage.

She fumbled with the buttons in an endeavor to open his fly, and he realized that once she had accomplished her purpose he was lost. He wanted to tell her that he could not accept her invitation without first an application of a bucket of warm suds and a good brush for her body. His fingers disengaged hers and her hand dropped. He walked away. She accepted his dismissal, hoping that it might be only temporary, and sucked in a thread of saliva that had drooled from her lips.

On the patio, he found Peter waiting for him, a broad straw hat on his head and a grin that seemed to be his usual expression. K'tu was behind him—too close behind him, Rory thought. But then he remembered the averted preliminaries between himself and Maria and he felt he could hardly blame K'tu.

"That Maria, she jes' a-dyin' for a man," Peter cackled in a high-pitched falsetto. "She bin a-night-roamin' to other plantations tryin' to snare herself a buck 'n if'n she cain' get one, she a-makin' me screw her, but she say I ain' so much-a-much. I ain' lastin' long 'cause I too young. This way, masta." He doffed his straw hat and gestured.

The plantation buildings were in the same state of disrepair as the house, but Rory discovered one enormous building which Peter told him had been used at one time for tobacco storage. It was of superior construction, large, and well ventilated, and Rory decided to use this building for his barracoon. He could still employ Elphinstone as an auctioneer, but he preferred to house his slaves where he could oversee them personally. Thinking of the plantation and its possibilities he was almost tempted to keep all the slaves for himself and put the plantation back on a working basis. He had, however, no knowledge of planting, and it appeared from the rundown condition of everything that it would take a long time to get things operating again. He would have a quick and substantial profit from the slaves, and after all, that was the business that he and Baba had decided upon. He did decide to go through the lot and pick out a number for house servants, but as to who would train them, he had no idea. Possibly Tim? But no, Tim would be returning to Africa. Well, he'd train

350

them himself. He'd start with Maria and Peter. Washed up and in clean clothes, Maria would be a handsome wench and Peter seemed fairly intelligent. Mayhap Mary Davis could find an experienced black woman who could take charge of the household and act as cook. He'd want two or three men for the house and another half dozen or so to care for the slaves before they were sold. Going to the house with Peter, he informed Maria of his imminent return.

At Port of Spain, he stopped to see Mary Davis and found Tim still there, looking rather the worse for wear after his bout with one of Mary's girls and the redoubtable Fayal. Rory expressed his gratitude to Mary for the loan of Melrose and assured her it would exactly fit his needs both for a residence while he was in Trinidad and for a barracoon for the slaves, not only those on board ship but those he intended to bring on future voyages. He mentioned having met Maria and she waggled a finger at him, saying that the girl was nothing but a dirty slut who was willing to spread her legs for any chance-encountered black. Then, with his plea for someone to get a general clean-up started, Mary, who always seemed to be able to solve Rory's problems, came to the rescue. She pulled a bellcord and when it was answered by Fayal (who, in contrast to poor Tim, seemed as fresh as ever) she sent him back again downstairs with orders to bring up Mama Phoebe.

This was the most colossal Negro woman Rory had ever seen. She was a veritable giantess, standing over six feet tall and probably weighing three hundred pounds. (He was afterwards to find out that she was a Luo from Uganda.) Huge melon-like breasts threatened to burst the thin cotton material of her dress, and her enormous thighs taughtened the cloth of her skirt. Her broad black face held a perpetual crescent smile, displaying a row of strong white teeth, and her small eyes, nearly buried in her rounded cheeks, stared out on the world with vast good humor. There was a clean fresh smell of newly baked bread about the woman, and Rory noticed that her clothes were white and spotless. Mary regarded her with considerably more deference than was usual between slave and mistress.

"I've got just the one to help you, Rory lad." She beckoned Mama Phoebe to her and took the black hand in her own. "This is my very own Mama Phoebe who not only has a heart to match her frame but is positively the best cook in all Trinidad. Not only that but she manages my household with a rod of iron. I don't know how I'm going to get along without her except that her daughter Phoebe-Two has been trained by her mother and equals her in nearly everything. I'm not going to sell her to you. There ain't enough money in all Trinidad to buy her. But I'm going to loan her to you provided"—Mary held up a warning finger—"she is willing to go. How about it, Mama Phoebe? Would you mind going out to Melrose and getting things in order for my lord of Sax?"

The colored woman peered at Rory, scanning him from head to foot and then burst out in a high-pitched cackle which she eventually transformed into words. "With him, Missus Fortescue? Wid dat mos' handsome fellow? I goes anywhere wid him. Likin' me to serve a man onct 'gain. Ain' nothin' here but gals, 'ceptin' that Fayal boy, tho' he worth three ordin'ry men anytime. Yas'm, shore would like to serve this pretty white man, if'n yo' wants me."

"Then it's all settled," Mary smiled. "Mama'll be ready tomorrow morning. And you," she questioned Rory, "you'll be setting out from here yourself tomorrow morning?"

"I can't refuse the invitation that implies." Rory winked at her. "And as for you, Mama Phoebe, I've already fallen madly in love with you and I'm going to choose the five handsomest bucks I've got on the ship to help you out in the house. I can't guarantee that each one will be worth three men like Fayal, but I'll do my best to get some that will be worth at least two men each."

The big woman's cackles and giggles reached an even higher pitch and she turned with an immense swirl of starched white cotton skirts and petticoats, kissing Rory's hand and then Mary's, even sidling up to Tim and making a curtsy before him. Hesitating a moment on the threshold to show her pleasure by an even wider grin, she skipped out the door with a lightness of foot that was surprising for such a behemoth.

"And now, Mary, I'll have to get back to the ship." Rory took her hand and covered it with kisses. "Unless Tim wants another bout with your Fayal. . . ."

"One's enough to last me for a day at least." Tim was almost blushing before Mary despite the fact that he was well aware that she had arranged for his pleasure.

"Then I'll take you with me," Rory continued. "Mary, I've a need to talk with Jehu my captain, get out of these sweaty clothes, and then come ashore for another conference with Elphinstone, after which I'll be back to see you around ten o'clock. All right?"

"Oh, Rory lad, it's wonderful to have you here with me. They say there's nothing but bad comes as a recompense for a life of sin such as I've lived, but I've found otherwise. Nothing but good fortune has come my way and having you back again is the best fortune of all. I'll be waiting. Now go and take poor Timmy with you and see that he gets a bottle of good port wine to build up his strength before he tackles Fayal again."

Tim preceded Rory down the stairs. Halfway down Rory halted, hearing Mary's call. "Don't forget to bring Old Harry back with you!"

"I'll build up his strength with another bottle of port, too."

"That one!" She leaned forward so that Rory could see her breasts over the confines of her bodice. "That one! It's never port Old Harry'll be needing."

CHAPTER XXXIII

RORY, WITH AN UNCOMFORTABLE TIM, RE-turned to the *Shaitan* to find Jehu dining alone under an awning on the quarterdeck. Below him, the slaves, who were now allowed the freedom of the main deck during the daytime because of the intense heat between decks, were sleeping, leaning over the rail or talking in little groups. Jehu beckoned for Rory and Tim, who took chairs at the table, welcoming the shade of the awning after the hot drive to the ship. Rory launched into an account of his day and his intention of taking the cargo off the ship and keeping them at Melrose to condition them fore the sale.

"You two et?" Jehu asked after he had agreed with Rory's plans.

Rory shook his head. He had thought of an intimate supper with Mary, but his day's activities had made him hungry, and Tim, in his present exhausted state, certainly needed nourishment. He agreed to eat then and accepted Jehu's invitation for the evening meal. Without smiling, his long face as serious as usual, Jehu pushed over a small wooden bowl to Rory. It was filled with a viscuous black substance.

"What's this?" Rory looked at the contents of the bowl and scowled. "This some goddam native concoction you expect me to eat, Jehu? If it's a joke, it's a hell of a time to play one on a hungry man."

The ghost of a smile touched Jehu's lips. "We're going to be eating that the rest of our lives, I hope. The gold that that stuff is going to bring us will buy any kind of food we want. Look, Rory! What did you have in mind for a cargo back to Goree?"

Rory shrugged his shoulders. He had not thought that far ahead. Sugar perhaps; rum maybe.

Jehu looked at him as though he did not consider Rory overequipped with brains. "Sugar? Now what in hell would them friggin' Arabs want sugar for 'cept maybe a few spoonfuls to sweeten their goddamn mint tea? And as for rum, they only drink it on the sly, the bastards. No, Rory, we've got something here to make our fortunes, and it ain' a-goin' to cost us one copper cent. You know what this stuff is?"

Rory examined the contents of the bowl which he pushed over to Tim, shaking his in ignorance.

"Well, it's pitch." Jehu jabbed a forefinger into it. "Remember the delay we had in getting the *Shaitan* keeled and caulked in Tangier? You know why? 'Cause they just

354

ain' got no pitch there 'n it's scarcer than hell to come by. Well, that stuff in there's pitch and this is the one place in all the world where they got so much of it they don't know what to do with it. Kin have all you want free just for carting it off."

"How're we going to cart it?" Tim asked.

"Lord God Almighty!" Jehu felt he was dealing with a couple of noddleheads. "Look down there," he pointed to the milling slaves on the main deck. "You bin a-talkin' 'bout getting them bucks into condition. A couple o' weeks work in sacking that pitch, transporting it to the ship by oxcart, and loading it, and you'll have every man jack of 'em conditioned to hell, with his muscles all swole. *Then* you can sell 'em."

"You're sure there's a market for this stuff in Goree?" Rory took a poke at the pitch with his own forefinger.

"It's plain to see you ain' much of a sea-farin' man, Rory. How about it Tim? You ought to know. You been a sailor yourself."

"It's worth its weight in gold, Rory. Every one of them slavers will be wanting to be keeled and caulked there when they know we've got it. And, if it's as Jehu says and it ain' going' to cost us nothing 'cept the hire of a few oxcarts, it'll be all clear profit."

Jehu nodded in assent. "Then after you gits the slaves all sleek and muscled up you sell them; meantimes, we'll have the ship loaded with the most valuable cargo we could take to Africa, three quarters pitch, and the rest something just as valuable."

"What's that?"

"Indigo."

It was Rory's turn to treat Jehu with contempt. "Now what in hell will those frigging Arabs want of indigo?"

"And what in hell would you do without me to find out things for you?" Jehu laughed. "Think back, Rory. Remember when we took some of these buckos aboard in Tangier, that some was blue on top of their black—or didn't you notice?"

"Now that you speak of it, I do remember." Rory nodded his head in recollection of the peculiar blue-black skin hue of several slaves.

"Well, they're blue men," Jehu explained. "There's some Arabs in Africa what reverses the custom of others. Instead of the women being veiled and the men not, it's the big buckos who hide their faces in modesty and let the women have their faces bare-assed naked. Call themselves Tuaregs. They ain't niggers themselves, but they do have nigger slaves and that's where some of our boys came from—the blue ones. Well these Tuaregs wear only blue djellabahs, and the dye comes off and sinks into their skins. Their slaves wear the same blue cloth.

"Now indigo is the best of all blue dyes. So we gives some room in the hold to indigo and barter it to the Tuaregs for more niggers. With a cargo of pitch and indigo, we'll be a hell of a lot better off than them Liverpool and Bristol slavers loaded up with the same old bugle beads and mirrors and copper buckets. We'll have something the Africans really need, not just something to please their silly fancy."

Tim and Rory agreed. Pitch and indigo! An unusual cargo, but Jehu knew what he was talking about, as Rory found out later from Mary. The pitch lake, which she had heard of but never seen, was indeed a local phenomenon, a curiosity for visitors and noted throughout the Indies as a source of ships' caulking. As a matter of fact, many ships put in here for that special purpose.

K'tu appeared along with Tim's boy, Darba, and served them something more appetizing than the dish of pitch Jehu had offered them. They had fresh-water fish delicately fried in butter, baked yams, a salad of hearts of palm, and, as a dessert, a compote of oranges, bananas and mangoes, sprinkled with freshly grated coconut; then steaming coffee and cigars to finish off with.

Rory excused himself and went below to his cabin where he had K'tu bring in a pitcher of hot water. He had decided he would not call on Elphinstone but go directly to Mary's. K'tu had learned to shave him, and after shaving, Rory scrubbed his body to remove the accumulation of dust and perspiration that clung to it. Then with K'tu's help, he dressed himself in another suit of his best clothes. Scattered glimpses of himself in the small mirror assured him, by piecemeal, that he was fit for inspection.

He eased the bulge in his trousers to a more comfortable position, smiling as he thought of Old Harry and the work laid out for him, cocked his half-moon hat at an even jauntier angle, and went up on deck, bidding K'tu follow him.

He had instructed the driver to call back for him, and fortunately the man was waiting before that decrepit hovel, the waterfront bar. When they reached Mary's house, Rory was surprised to see it in darkness: girls on the balcony, no lights in the main salon, and no Fayal to welcome him. Dismissing the cabby, Rory walked up to the front door only to find it locked. His repeated bangings brought no one to open it.

He turned away from the door, cursing himself for sending away the hackman and wondering how he was going to get back to the ship, when an upper window opened, the casement rasping despite apparent caution. A woman's head showed dimly behind the opened casement. "Rory?" came a whisper.

"Yes, Mary. What's the matter?"

"Go around back. I'll let you in. Quick!"

Sensing the need for secrecy, he made his way around the house, tramping through the high weeds and tripping in the masses of convolvulus. When he arrived at the back he saw a door open cautiously and spied Mary, a dim white blur in the darkness.

"In here," she whispered, pulling him inside and closing the door, then fastening it with an iron bar that slipped into two brackets. "Sh-h-h," she cautioned, taking him by the hand and leading him through the darkness of the kitchen and up the back stairs. Even the gallery around the patio was dark and he saw no light nor any person moving until they entered her room, bright-lit with many candles. Before he could speak, she silenced him with her lips.

"What has happened?" he said in a moment. "Are you out of business?"

She shook her head. "There are times in this business when you make more money closed than open."

"Which shows that I don't know your business very well, my dear."

357

"No man could." She smiled up at him condescendingly. "Whoring is a woman's business, Rory darlin'. It's women who do it and women who understand it. The pounds and shillings I might make tonight from my ordinary traffic are dwarfed by the gold sovereigns I'm coining right this minute, and my girls get a well-earned rest. Poor Fayal is the only one who works tonight. Do you understand now why he's been such a godsend?"

He shook his head, unable to comprehend.

"Well, let's say this. There's a certain lady—and indeed she is a lady—whose husband is three times older 'n her. She's young, full blooded, very rich, and likes nothing better than a good healthy poke by a strong healthy young man, especially one equipped like Fayal. So when she can get away from the old dodderer, she sends her maid here. The maid, poor thing, can't speak hardly a word of English, but brings me a note saying that milady will be here at such-and-such a time. She arrives, milady does, all covered from head to toe in black veils, and once she's here, all other business is suspended. If her old dodo of a husband is away, she stays till near daybreak. She pays well and has made me promise that nobody else will come here while she's being serviced. Well, I've broken my rule tonight, but I've as much right to my pleasure as she has to hers."

"And the lady?" Rory was more than a little curious to know who, in a place so remote as this new colony, had developed such erotic tastes. Somewhere in the back of his mind there lay the thought that he might serve her as well as Fayal, and at considerably less expense to her.

"His Excellency the governor, Sir Basil Cleverden—I think I mentioned him to you once before—who stands in lieu of His Britannic Majesty here, is in his sixties. He arrived back from London a month or so ago with a wife of twenty. She's a beauty—a real, stark raving beauty. She soon found out about Fayal. Her maid, who's some sort of a dark-skinned heathen, but pretty's all get-out, met Fayal when she first arrived here, and he speaks her language. The maid told milady, and milady, who was sick and tired of that limp rope-end that Sir Basil sports, made arrangements to come here and get serviced by Fayal. So now when the governor has to go over to Tobago on His Majesty's business, Lady Mary takes advantage of his absence. 'Tis become a common thing for her; she can't live without it! And, I found out, she speaks the same language Fayal speaks, too. It's Ay-rab, I guess."

Rory had been listening with only half an ear. He was not particularly interested in the peccadilloes of some unknown Englishwoman who had more of a predeliction for Fayal's black and puissant python than for the insignificant white worm her husband sported. That was indeed her own business; and if she chose to pay Mary for being studded, that was Mary's business and certainly not his.

But! There were certain coincidences that warranted more than a passing attention to this lady. Not many English ladies were accomplished in Arabic. Then too, this lady had a maid who also spoke Fayal's language and was, to use Mary's words, "a dark-skinned heathen and pretty as all get-out." It couldn't, no it couldn't possibly by any stretch of the imagination be *his* Lady Mary, but on the other hand it just might be, and her maid might be Almera, though common sense denied it. Lady Mary had never had an itch for any man, not even for Rory who'd despoiled her and made her less than a virgin. And yet he remembered his second bout with her, when she had passed herself off as Almera. That time she had sought him. Certainly, his conceit insisted, she should have been satisfied with his performance which he remembered as being more than adequate. His vanity asserted itself. If she had not had a yen to spread her legs for him again, she would scarcely be willing to do so for Fayal. And pay him for it too! Yet. . . ?

"Rory?" Mary was curious now. "Just who is this Englishwoman? If you've a yen for her, forget it. Old Harry's a mighty important little grenadier but he's no match for Fayal's dragoon. Besides, I'd be jealous of her, and I'd be losing money if you have any idea of giving it away free when she's willing to pay me for Fayal. You'd not like her, anyway. She's one of those high-nosed, thin-lipped English bitches with golden hair who look like they never used a chamber pot in their lives, they're so high and

359

mighty; but she's a plain woman underneath, same as the rest of us."

"And her maid? Tell me about her."

"I told you. Pretty as hell in her dusky fashion."

Rory paced the room. Of course it was impossible. Lady Mary and Almera here in this godforsaken part of the world. But . . . he had to know. He had to be sure. Mary sat on the floor, her head against his knee, and stared up at him, her lips in a thin line, her brow wrinkled in vague fear.

"Rory! What's happened? You see a ghost?"

"Not a ghost. But there's something I've got to know; something I've got to be sure of. My common sense tells me I must be wrong and yet I've got to see this English-woman and make sure."

"You've known her before?"

"Mayhap."

"And you're in love with her?"

He shook his head in such vehement denial, his entire body shook. "God, no! I've never disliked a woman more. She's a real bitch."

"Then I have no reason to be jealous of her?"

"None at all. If she is the one, and she just possibly may be, I robbed her of her maidenhead and she's hated me ever since. How can I see her, Mary, without her seeing me?"

"That's not difficult, my goslin'. Remember this's a whorehouse and a whoremistress never loses a chance to turn an honest penny. Some of the buckos who come, like Old Sir Basil, have queer tastes. They need to look on before they can turn proper randy and get it up."

"Like in Fanny Hill?"

"Pish! I've read about that trollop. She was just an amateur compared with me."

"Then?"

"Then I'll be telling you. There's a peephole into the room where she's with Fayal. I rent it out sometimes. And if she's kept the candles burning, which she usually does, you can get a good look at her. But you're sure it's not going to make any difference between us? Sure?"

360

He answered her by leaning over to kiss her. "Show me, Mary."

"That I'll do. If I don't, you'll be so full of conjecturin' you and Old Harry will both disappoint me. Come!"

With her fingers on his lips, cautioning him to be quiet, they tiptoed out onto the dark gallery, past a closed door which showed a thin sliver of light on the threshold, and into an adjoining room. She reached out her hand in the darkness and drew him to the wall. Together they knelt on a bed and she reached up to remove a framed picture from the wall. A ray of light entered the room from an inch-wide hole in the wall.

He squinted through, fitting his eye against the brightness of the aperture. The room he saw was a small one, with a bed on the opposite side, in full view of the peephole. Fayal was stretched out there, a writhing of dark copper flesh against the whiteness of the sheet. His head rolled from side to side in a frenzy of ecstasy. Straddling him was a woman with skin the color of milk and long blond hair which fell over her face like a veil. She was riding Fayal, and her frenzy equaled—perhaps exceeded—his. The boy's writhings and buckings obviously increased her pleasure.

Her hair! Damn it, her hair! It covered her face so that Rory could not see who she was. He continued to stare, feeling a tightening in his groin, which was further enhanced by the warmth of Mary's fingers sliding over the stretched cloth of his pantaloons. By Fayal's clutching hands and arching back, Rory could see that he was about to erupt in a torrential climax. It came. Fayal gulped in a lungful of air and expelled it in a strangled yell that mingled with the sharper falsetto screams of the woman. For a few brief moments she poised above him, immobile except for the nervous tics that chased each other under her skin. Then, with an effort which seemed to sap all her strength, she released him, rolled over and stood up, taking a final appraisal of Fayal's freed body and touching his swiftly drooping totem with her hand. She turned, unconsciously facing Rory, and brushed her wild hair up over her forehead, staring—albeit unseeingly—into Rory's eye.

It was his turn to gasp. By God! It *was* Mary—Lady Mary FitzAlbany, Princess Yasmin—whom he had last seen when he put her aboard the ship in Tangier. And if this was Mary, as it so patently was, then Almera must be with her and with Almera his son—because it must be a son!

He slumped down on the bed beside Mary. She nudged him, bringing him back to reality. "Is it the one you thought?"

"It is."

"Do you want to watch her anymore?"

"I never *want* to see her again—not really. But her being here is important to me. I've *got* to see her."

"You'll no doubt be invited to Government House. It's probably already known there that milord the Baron of Sax is in Trinidad. Of course, you could pay her a call uninvited. . . ."

"The lady and I have much to talk about. But I think I'll wait awhile before visiting. I've a lot to attend to right now."

"Such as what, Rory?"

"Disposing of the slaves."

"Alas, I was thinking of something else you might be wanting to do 'right now.' "

"Such as, Mary?"

"Such as giving Old Harry the exercise he's needing so badly after what he's been watching."

He smiled at her in the darkness. "Old Harry can't be denied after that."

"So I've already discovered." She rose from the bed and extended a hand to him. Before he accepted it, he took a quick glance into the other room. Lady Mary was dressing without so much as a glance toward Fayal. She was hurrying. Well, let her. He was in a hurry, too. He climbed down from the bed and tiptoed out of the room, following Mary down the hall. He had to hasten to keep up with her. But Old Harry was in the greatest hurry of them all. No matter how fast Rory sped, Old Harry was bound to be there before him. He was already ahead.

362

CHAPTER XXXIV

RORY FOUND IT DIFFICULT TO LEAVE MARY Fortescue the next morning. Willingly would he have lingered in bed alongside her, sipping her strong black coffee and responding time and time again to her caresses. Unwilling, he bestirred himself, but then found it even more difficult to return to the ship and leave the town without further knowledge of Almera. A brief conversation with Fayal had corroborated his thinking that it must be Almera. It was; Fayal had assured him. Then, if Rory's reckoning was correct, she must by this time have given birth to his son. Although his first inclination was to rush to Government House, storm its citadel, and take Almera away, some sense of caution overruled his impetuousness and bade him wait. There would always be Lady Mary to deal with. What reception might he expect from her? At least he was cognizant of one thing. She was no longer the icy virgin who had defended that virginity by scratching the faces of emirs and beys. He could not understand, even after having seen with his own eyes what amounted to her frenzied raping of the willing Fayal, how she, the aloof and virginal, could generate such bestial heat. But she had, and now she was there in Government House and so was Almera, and neither of them would go away immediately; so he must pay attention to the living cargo so entirely dependent on himself.

Once aboard the *Shaitan*, Rory tried to push his emotional upheaval into the background. It was so difficult to sort out all his feelings! He realized that the feeling he had for Mary Fortescue was not love, but if not, what was it? He enjoyed being with her, and for a romp in bed she had no equal. Now that he had seen Lady Mary's performance with Fayal though, he realized that he would willingly have traded places with the lad. He would enjoy Lady Mary in her new role of being quite capable of matching his fire with her own. But perhaps more than Mary Fortescue's unbridled lust and Lady Mary's newly ignited fire, he wanted the relaxing satisfaction he had always experienced with Almera. Yet, intruding in all these thoughts was a troublesome remembrance of the mulatto girl he had seen out at Melrose. What was the slut's name? Maria! Under the grime that had covered her there was something worth remembering. But just now, to hell with all of them. Fuck 'em all! He smiled. That he had done with the exception of Maria. Some day he'd douse her in a kettle of water and scrub her up. Enough of these meanderings! He'd better get his mind on his slaves.

Jehu was standing beside the long line of slaves, surrounded by piles of canvas, a sharp knife in his hand. As each black came up to him, Jehu measured off two armlengths of the canvas, ripped it off with his knife, and handed it to the slave, who then descended the gangplank to the pier. At Rory's look of surprised wonderment, Jehu merely shrugged his shoulders.

"Cain' have these buckos paradin' bare-assed naked through the streets of Port of Spain. Beasts they may be, but them tassels 'twixt their legs look goddamn human to me, and it ain' a good sight for no white woman to look on. Won't never be satisfied with their short-peckered husbands ever again. Don't think I'm a-usin' up our good canvas just to protect the modesty of the good wives of Trinidad, tho'. No siree, not by a damned sight! I'm sending along needles, thread, and wax. Each man wears his piece of canvas through town and when he gits to your place, sews up the sides and he's got a stout sturdy bag to bring the pitch back in. How's that for using the old noodle to kill two birds with one stone?"

Rory nodded in agreement, impressed with Jehu's foresight. When the last fellow had been landed, Rory followed to find them crowded together on the jetty under Tim's watchful eye, each with his piece of canvas tied around his waist, and all of them grinning widely at the feel of land under their feet after so many weeks at sea.

With the help of some of the sailors, Rory lined them up four abreast, and with himself leading the procession on horseback, K'tu acting as a sort of marshal, and Tim, also mounted, following in the rear, they made their way through the streets to Mary's house. There Mama Phoebe was waiting for them astride a rawboned gray mule whose back was even more swayed under her enormous weight. She cackled with delight at seeing them, and took particular notice of the column of boys, reminding Rory that he had given her *carte blanche* to choose those she felt best suited for house servants, and also that he would need men for the stables, the grounds, and some for the raising of vegetables, milch goats, hens, and other food supplies.

The slaves soon found it too dull to march along sedately. Their jubilant spirts overflowed and they skipped, jumped in the air, high-stepped, and trotted, the white soles of their feet kicking up the dust, and their flapping canvas aprons more often than not waving in the air like flags which did little to hide their swinging genitals. Everything was new and different to them, and they gesticulated and called out to each other to notice a house, a bird, a tree, an oxcart, or a white man driving along the road in his coach.

On their way to the plantation, they forded a small river and the sight of the fresh water was too much for them. They had come to recognize Rory as their master on the voyage, and K'tu, along with those to whom he had previously delegated authority, danced up to him, gamboling like overgrown puppies, and asked his permission for a halt that they might wash themselves. He granted it willingly, and for an hour they sported in the water, scrubbing themselves with the white sand of the river bottom and bunches of grass. Now clean and clean-smelling for the first time in months, many of them came to where Rory was seated on his horse to fondle his hand and place it on their damp hair, stroking his knee and reveling in the affection of his pats on their satin-smooth, sun-warmed shoulders.

At Melrose, it took Rory and Tim the rest of the day to get the boys stabled, fed, and bedded. At last they were under cover, although their beds were only piles of dried grass and their first meal only boiled plantains; but Mama Phoebe promised Rory there would be more on the morrow and nothing dulled the boys' euphoria at being once again on land. Late in the afternoon, when things had approached some state of order, Rory called Mama Phoebe out to the shed to pick out six of the men to train for house servants. He lined them up. They had long ago discarded their canvas aprons. Mama Phoebe slowly walked down the line to make her choice. She inventoried each one carefully, passing up and down the line several times, then settled on her choices. Rory noticed a certain similarity in those she had picked out, and when he questioned her about it, she replied with her high, good-humored cackle.

"Laws, Masta Rory, I picks 'em young 'n tender. Those mens what comes to Missus Fortescue's house, they al'ays a-lookin' for virgins. They likes to bust 'em 'n break 'em in. Jes' so I likes young mens, so's I kin learn 'em to do things the way I likes. 'N too, young lads they stiffer'n a ramrod 'n they quicker on the trigger 'n the older boys," she giggled brazenly. "That's how I likes 'em. 'N sides, it easier to train young lads to be good servants. Learn 'em young 'n train 'em in the way I wants 'em. Then too, thinkin' I'm a-goin ter bring these boys up ter be good breeders for yo', come the time that yo' gits me some wenches ter bed 'em wid. That's one reason I picks 'em all so big-peckered. We ain' a-wantin' ter raise no runts 'round here. 'N besides," she winked at Rory, "Mama got herself kind-a used to that young stallion Fayal 'n she a-hopin' one o' these boys a-goin' to turn out like'n him, come he gits hisself growed up in a couple o' years."

Although Rory could not imagine anyone, even Fayal, being able to make any connection with Mama Phoebe—'twould be like bedding with an elephant—he winked back at her and set her to cackling again.

"Shore a-goin' ter have a surprise fer yo' tonight, Masta Rory. Big surprise! Yo' jes' wait 'n see. Yore frien, Masta Timmy, he a-goin' back ter town fer me with a message for Missus Fortescue. Sort o' secret it be 'n yo' ain' needin' ter try ter wheedle it out-a me. But yo' a-gain' ter see, come nightfall. Yes siree! Yo' shore as hell a-goin' ter see it'n yo' a-goin' ter feel it too. Um-huh! But jes' now, I'm a-takin' these here colts inter the house 'n put 'em ter work. Place more like'n a pig sty 'n anythin' else."

For the rest of the afternoon, Rory stayed out of the house where the brigade of Negro youths under the able generalship of Mama Phoebe attacked the rooms with buckets, swabs, and brooms. He sat out in the slave compound where he supervised the work of the slaves, picking out about a dozen men, including those to whom he had delegated authority on shipboard. But, whereas Mama Phoebe had been more concerned with youth, good looks and special physical endowments, Rory picked the strongest and most intelligent of the lot. Once having chosen them, he got out the sail needles and thread that Jehu had sent along and showed them how to sew up two sides of the doubled-up canvas to make bags. They caught on quickly and before he left, his lieutenants were teaching the other men how to do it while the pile of finished bags grew high in the corner of the compound.

Late in the afternoon Tim arrived at Melrose, leading a pack mule laden down with panniers. He refused to tell Rory what was in the baskets but drove around to the back door, delivered them to Mama, and then came out to sit with Rory. K'tu, escaping from Mama's relentless generalship, also came to squat on the ground beside Rory. He laid his head against Rory's knee, partly to assure himself of his closeness to Rory and partly to impress the other blacks that he alone shared this intimacy with his master.

Tim and Rory sat quietly, hearing nothing but the hum of the slaves as they plied their needles until the light became so dim that they could no longer see. The quick tropical twilight passed into night and they heard a bell ringing from the big house. Not knowing what it meant, they left the slave quarters and walked along in the gathering dusk to the house. Mama Phoebe was at the front gate, a luminescent mountain of starched white. She ushered them in, her stiff petticoats rattling.

She had turned it into a completely different world from the cobwebbed debris of the morning. It was now all polished floors and candlelight, with the clean smell of soap and beeswax. Through the big drawing room she led

367

them into the dining room, where a polished expanse of mahogany was laid for two. K'tu, in a clean white shirt and pantaloons which had miraculously appeared from nowhere, was standing at attention behind Rory's chair, while a scrubbed and gleaming Peter, also in white drill, stood behind Tim's. An island of light in the middle of the big table reflected the candles in the big silver candelabrum. Chairs were pulled out for them, and Mama, with a whirl of starched petticoats, left.

Then her boys, all in white breeches, brought in a soup tureen, and she returned to stand guard over them, directing their motions as they ladled out a rich soup and placed it before Rory and Tim. There followed a dish of rice and chicken, sharp with curry, and a salad of heart of palm rich with oil. The meal ended with a custard oozing caramel and cups of dark steaming coffee laced with brandy. Rory pushed his chair from the table, grabbed Mama Phoebe around the waist (or at least the place where a waist should have been) and kissed her.

"Is this the surprise you had for me?" His arms tried vainly to encircle her massive girth.

"Laws no, Masta Rory, this am jes' somethin' ter eat. Big surprise a-comin' soon. If'n yo' gen'lemen a-ready ter go ter bed, mayhap's yo' fin's my surprise." Once again she led Rory and Tim out through the drawing room and onto the gallery. She pointed to a lighted doorway where an adolescent girl leaned negligently against the door jamb.

"This yere's my very own granddaughter Pentecost what we calls Penny." She pushed the girl up close to Tim, who put an arm around her, drawing her to him where she snuggled against his shoulder. "A-thinkin' Masta Timmy he ain' a-wantin' ter sleep 'lone way out here in the country. Penny she ain' too well titted out seein' as how she's pretty young, but she bin busted, so Masta Timmy he ain' a-goin' ter have ter strive too much."

With a hurried good night, Tim pushed the willing Penny into the bedroom and closed the door, then opened it for a second to wink knowingly at Rory. He stepped quickly over the threshold, bussed Mama Phoebe soundly

368

on the cheek, then retreated into the room a second time, closing the door with a final bang.

Mama escorted Rory down the gallery to the bedroom he had seen previously. K'tu stood in the doorway, silhouetted against the brightly lighted interior.

"Git out'n my way." Mama pushed the big black aside. "Ain' yo' a-knowin' it bad luck ter stand in a doorway. Yo' so big 'n gigantic-like! Ghostes might jes' want ter pass through, 'n if'n they does, they a-goin' ter have ter bresh past yo' 'cause they ain' no room lef' fer 'em, 'n if'n they touches yo', yo' a-goin' ter git a sudden mizry in your stomick, 'n yore head it a-goin' to swell ten times its size."

Although K'tu did not understand her, he slipped from the doorway out onto the gallery, frightened by the look in Mama's eyes.

"Masta a-goin' ter bed, 'n he not a-needin' any big buck nigger a-helpin' him git his clothes off." She dismissed K'tu with a wave of her hamlike hand.

"Whoa there, Mama Phoebe. That's why I own him."

"Ain' no need fer him this night." She nodded her head with an authority that sent K'tu striding sulkily away down the gallery. "Missus Fortescue she a-plannin' on bein' here some nights, but she ain' here tonight 'n she a-sayin' ter me that it ain' good fer her Mista Ol' Harry ter be sleepin' all night 'n a-gittin out-a practice. So, says I, a bird in the han' worth a dozen a-roostin' out in the trees 'n ain' no reason fer yo' ter have some big black buck a-strippin' off yore clothes." She gave Rory a push through the doorway.

In the mellow candlelight of the bedroom, he saw a girl standing, partly in shadow, her gown of rose satin catching the highlights of the candles. Slowly she turned to face him and he saw that she was beautiful. An oval face the color of old ivory was stained with a blood-red mouth and the brilliant blackness of eyes, all framed by lustrous curls which fell to her shoulders. The low bodice of the rose gown disclosed rounded breasts as satin smooth as the fabric which covered only a part of them. Mama went over to her and nudged her closer to Rory.

"Here it am, Masta Rory, the surprise I done promised

369

yo'," Mama giggled in a rising crescendo. "Don' yo' know who-at she be? She that harum-scarum Maria what bin there a-fore. I jes' got her washed up 'n dressed fer yo', tho' it a-takin a bucketful o' lye ter scrub the crut 'n the stench off 'n her."

It was indeed Maria, but what a change had come over the girl! She was beautiful. The snarled rat's nest of hair was smooth and fell from her head like skeins of thick black silk. Her ivory skin overlaid a rosy underglow which might have been a reflection from her dress, and her eyes, staring at him from under long lashes, smoldered with banked fires. An aroma of jasmine and musk, heady and provocative, clung to her. The hand she extended touched him and her fingers burned like live coals.

"She jes' achin' ter get screwed, that one," Mama stated, turning toward the door. "Not that she ain' bin a-fore, but she mighty tired o' that little runt brother o' hers what cain' do nothin' but jack hisself off so she a-tellin' me. Now I a-thinkin' she goin' ter git herself a real man. Uh-huh!" She closed the door and Rory could hear her high-pitched cackle as she lumbered down the gallery.

He moved closer to Maria, bringing her hand up to his face. There was no false modesty in her approach to him. She neither lowered her head nor avoided his gaze. Her eyes stared back at him while she disengaged her hand from his and sunk to her knees before him.

"If'n I a-goin' to git yo' undressed, better start at the bottom, huh?" She unbuckled and slipped off his shoes, then his light socks. Her hot fingers massaged his bare feet before they moved up his legs to clasp themselves around his waist. She pressed her head against the bulge of his groin. Lifting her head she looked up at him and slowly relaxed the pressure of her arms, sliding her hands around front, her fingers fumbling with the buckle of his belt. They loosened it while he sucked in his belly to make it easier for her. One by one she undid the buttons of his pantaloons, pulling down the skin-clinging tricot to his knees, then down over the calves to his ankles.

Lifting one foot and then the other, he allowed her to free him. Again she leaned her cheek against him but only

370

for a moment before her fingers ripped at the buttons of his smallclothes, releasing them to fall to his feet. He sprang forth to meet her while his own fingers tore the buttons of his shirt, casting it, along with his jacket, to the floor. He stood naked before her. She was still on her knees and the warm wetness of her mouth nuzzled him. His hand rested on her soft hair, and slowly guided her head until, shaking off his restraining hand, she accelerated her motion. He endured it for a few brief moments, then forced her head away.

"You indeed a man, my masta." She fought against his restraint, looking up at him. He lifted her in his arms so that her face was on a level with his own.

"You tread on dangerous ground, Maria. In another moment I would have been less than a man for you. Come! The bed awaits us and I have no desire to have my knees buckle under me which would surely happen were we to remain where we are."

She did not reply, although he was certain she understood what he said. He watched the rose satin gown join the tumble of his pantaloons and shirt while he yanked the counterpane from the bed. She blew out the candles, not bothering to use a snuffer, but in her hurry she missed two or three which guttered for a moment, then resumed the brightness of their flames. He pulled her down on the mattress beside him, but in a moment they were both a tangle of limbs. There was nothing studied or affectionate about her passion. None of the savage beauties of his harem in Sa'aqs had ever devoured him with such a feral appetite. Her caresses were violent and rough. She was a lioness, chained to him, whose fingers, mouth, tongue, and teeth ravaged his body in a frantic turmoil of dementia in which Rory lost all sense of time, place, and reason. He became a concentrated bundle of raw nerves, unable to keep up with her acrobatics, not knowing where or how she was about to impale herself next. Then, when his finely tautened nerves could no longer hold against the pressure of her onslaught, he broke through his delirium to burst like volcanic lava with ejections of liquid fire and then abruptly descended into an abyss of panting release where he struggled for breath until a measure of calmness

371

enabled him to move his sweating body away from the torrid heat of the woman's flesh beside him. Even then, he had to fend off her attacks.

Suddenly and without warning he was aroused from his lethargy by a sharp pain that lacerated his lips. His own blood was hot and salty in his mouth, and he pushed the girl off him, but despite his strength, she clung to him, sucking the blood from his torn lip.

"You fucking bitch!" He tried to free himself, but her lips clung to his lacerated lower lip like a leech while her arms gripped him with the strength of a madwoman. Releasing his grip on her, he raised his hand bringing it down on her cheek with a resounding slap. Momentarily her mouth released him and the moment was enough. He rolled to the edge of the bed and jackknifed up. The burning candles had guttered out and he fumbled on the candlestand beside the bed, found a tinder box, struck the flint, and with the feeble flame lighted the candle. She was sprawled on the bed, her mouth and face encarmined with his blood. From under the rumpled pillows he saw the curling black feathers of a dead cock, its limp body flattened by the pressure of their bodies and its lifeless eyes staring at him.

"What the hell. . . ?" He snatched at the dead rooster and flung it to the floor. "What's going on here?" He grabbed a corner of the sheet and held it to his lip to stanch the stream of blood.

She pulled herself up slowly and with feline grace. One hand rubbed her cheek where he had struck her, but she stared at him unabashed and unafraid, her eyes widened in defiance, her scarlet tongue licking at the blood on her lips. One shoulder lifted and she pointed at him. Her index finger moved from his eyes down his body to the limpness which had now supplanted turgidity.

"Maria never a-goin' to give yo' to 'nother woman, big man. She jes' ain'. Never no mo'. She a-likin' yo' too well. Maria a-savin' yo' all fer herself, now on. Ain' never a-goin' ter let no woman touch yo'. No mo'."

"That's what you think, you black bitch. Now get out." He stepped to the edge of the bed, his hand upraised to strike her, but she slithered across the rumpled sheets to wind her arms around his legs. Despite himself the feeling of her hot flesh pressing against him restrained his uplifted hand. It came down softly to nestle in her thick, black hair. Her bloodied lips caressed him until he found the willpower to pull her head back. She stared up at him.

"Yo' a-knowin' what I is, Mista Big Man? I'se a Diabless, tha's what I am. An obeah girl. Tonight I make strong magic with yo'. Tonight I drink yore blood, Mista Big Man. Yo' ain' never a-goin' ter leave me. Yo' cain'. Not even if'n yo' wish. I'se swallowed yo'. All o' yo'. Yo' inside me 'n yo' part o' me now. Obeah fix it so's yo' cain' never get away from me. Ain' never a-wantin' to. See!"

Her clutching fingers proved how expertly she had revived him. He was powerless; he could not resist her maneuvered caresses. Although somewhere in his mind he despised her, his body responded to her and he dropped to the bed pulling her to him. The eyes of the dead cockerel on the floor looked up at him and he could swear that one of the eyes closed in a lascivious wink.

Her arms drew him down to the bloodstained pillow. He supported his head on his hands, lying back passively to allow her free reign.

She stopped toying with him, looked up at him, and smiled. "Yo' jes' damn lucky I ain' no Soucouyan, Mista Big Man. I jes' a Diabless. Cain' take off my skin 'n go flyin' through the night 'n drinkin' blood. But I kin love yo', Mista Big Man. Kin love yo' so's yo'll come a-beggin' me mornin', noon, 'n night to love yo' up. Man, yo' ain' seen nothin' yet. Wait till I gits started."

He relaxed after plumping up the bloodied pillow so that he could better watch her. She began to prove her words with a consummate artistry which he had not experienced since Chatsubah. Dawn streaked the sky with salmon pink and violet, entering the room to cast barred shadows on the floor from the one window. He turned on his side, freeing himself from her, and slept. After a moment she got up, grabbed the rose satin dress from the floor, and wrapped it around her. Then she reached down for the dead bird on the floor, plucked a long curling tail feather from it, and stuck it between Rory's legs. Laughing to herself, she left the room.

CHAPTER XXXV

RORY AWOKE SLOWLY, FIGHTING AN OVER-
powering lethargy which wooed him back to sleep. The
room was flooded with bright sunlight, so bright it must be
midmorning. He moved his head gingerly from side to
side, conscious of the stinging pain in his lip, then managed a long breath which expanded his chest wide. He
almost retched. His nostrils were offended by a fetid odor
of sweat, musk, and the flat, alkaline odor of dried semen.
The whole room, despite the opened window, reeked of
the vile stenches. He raised his head from the pillow and
stared down at his own body which was covered with
purple blotches where Maria's mouth had engorged his
skin. The black cock feather, erect and curved, stood in
decided contrast to his own limpness which was unusual
because he usually awoke with a pulsing vigor which was
not dispeled until after he had relieved himself. The upstanding cockfeather, blackly curved against the whiteness
of his skin, brought back the episodes of the previous
night.

Good God! He had never felt so completely exhausted,
so entirely drained. Gently, as if fearing that Old Harry
might have entirely disappeared, he examined himself and
was grateful when his fingers assured him that he was still
complete—not the eunuch he almost feared himself to be.
He flung the cock feather away and it circled lazily to the
floor with a seeming life of its own. Goddamn that Maria!
No, she did not deserve curses. What a fabulous price she
would bring in Africa! She was even better than Chatsubah who had so exhausted him long ago in the tents of
Sa'aqs. Chatsubah had been expertly trained. Nobody had
ever trained Maria. Nobody had ever had to. She knew

374

instinctively how to please a man; but the bitch was more animal than human.

And what was all that humbugging tomfoolery she had blathered about. Something connected with *obeah*? Yes, but what was obeah? He remembered: it was some kind of damned fool African high jinx; silly superstition, that's all. He'd not even mention it to Mama Phoebe. But man! If obeah was what it took to make a wench hotter than a majigger-majaggus, then more power to obeah. All women should take it up. He started to smile as he pictured a world full of women who were all like Maria. Hot damnation! After a week there wouldn't be a man left.

Well, up and at 'em! He maneuvered his long legs over the edge of the bed and stumbled across the cool tiles of the floor. Spilling a pitcherful of tepid water into a porcelain bowl, he dashed it over his face, drying with a coarse towel and running a wooden comb through his hair. The skin of his body felt soiled and sweat-scummed, but there wasn't enough water in the bowl to take a bath. He lifted one arm and sniffed of his armpit. What a stench! And the dried and crusty white spots on his belly and the hairs of his groin! His lips contorted and he shook his head. He'd like to be in the river where the boys had bathed the day before and wash some of Maria's and his own spunk off his skin. And why not? He'd go back to Port of Spain this morning. There was nothing in particular for him to do at Melrose; the boys were all stabled and Tim and Mama Phoeba were in charge. He had implicit faith in Mama Phoebe. When that old girl died and went to heaven—or it might be hell where she was headed— she'd take over as soon as she arrived and put everything in good running order.

He pulled his clothes on haphazardly and stumbled out onto the gallery, finding his way along it to the kitchen, where Mama Phoebe welcomed him and ushered him into the dining room. Answering the question in her eyes, he grinned shamefacedly and admitted that it had been one hell of a night while she, knowing that he was telling the truth, only pursed her lips and nodded her head wisely as if to say that she knew what a hot-blooded young rakehell would enjoy and, knowing it, had provided it.

375

His early morning lassitude was partially dissipated by Mama Phoebe's good breakfast and several cups of chicory-spiced strong black coffee, and although Tim had already eaten and been out to inspect the blacks, he wandered into the dining room and joined Rory for another cup. Rory announced his intentions of returning to Port of Spain, but Tim declined, and said he would return later in the day. Mama's granddaughter had proven so entertaining that Tim was planning on an afternoon siesta with her and a possible recruitment of young Peter in the role that Fayal had played. Rory made a note that the Pentecostal achievements could not possibly have rivaled those of Maria or Tim would not have been so eagerminded. Penny should take up obeah too; but perhaps Maria's brother had had some instructions, and if so, he would lend spices to Timmy's threesome.

With K'tu mounted on his own horse, Rory started off for town, not forgetting to take towels and soap both for K'tu and himself. They stopped at the river and Rory scrubbed himself until his flesh glowed pink, regretting that he had not brought other clothes with him. Once his body was clean, he was finally free of Maria's clinging odor. When he arrived at Elphinstone's, he was glad to avail himself of the deep cooling shade of the counting room. Over a Havana cheroot, he outlined Jehu's plan to young Elphinstone, who agreed to furnish the oxcarts for the transportation of the pitch from the distant lake to the ship and agreed with Rory that it was probably the most valuable cargo he could take out of Trinidad. Then, when Rory spoke of including indigo, Elphinstone agreed to procure that for them also. He advised a three-week interval which he felt would be sufficient to load the ship with the pitch and the indigo and suggested that after that, with the boys at the height of their physical fitness, the auction should be held.

"Unless," he looked quizzically at Rory, "you change your mind and decide to settle down at Melrose and become a Trinidad planter. It's damned good land but it's never really been worked. Milord Dugane bought it sight unseen as an investment when all England wanted to get in on the opening up of a new colony. He sent out first one man and then another to oversee. They came over from England and not one of the highfalutin' bastards knew anything about the tropics. They'd never grown anything but potatoes in Ireland or oats in Scotland. Then, when Mrs. Fortescue came out here, she thought she'd have a go at farming, but she soon decided on a more lucrative business." He closed one eye in an obscene wink. "Thank God, she did. She's saved the lives of all the white men on the island."

"Plus my own," Rory nodded back.

"But you, Sir Roderick"—Young Elphinstone did not seem surprised that Rory had already acquainted himself with Mrs. Fortescue's merchandise—"you are in an enviable position. You've got enough blacks to make planting a real business. Why not use them? That would be my advice even though I'm talking myself out of a commission on their sale."

For a brief moment Rory considered it: set himself up at Melrose, dress in white drill and be a respectable colonial planter instead of a slave merchant. Respectablity would be a new guise for him. He'd settle down and marry Mary Fortescue: make her marry him if he had to. No, he'd marry Almera and become a real father to his son. For another fleeting moment, he toyed with the idea of Lady Mary becoming a widow—her husband would probably die soon—and certainly if she were willing to pay out money to enjoy Fayal as much as she apparently did, she'd enjoy riding Rory equally well. But hell no! Let her buy her stud services; he'd not act as stallion to that blue-white, skimmed-milk bitch. In contrast to her there was Maria back at Melrose. She was like spitting on one's finger and touching a red-hot iron. Pssst! Forget the damned women and get back to Melrose. Yes, that's what he was supposed to be thinking about—becoming a plantation owner. He decided it was not for him. Respectability was just another name for boredom and—for an instant recalling Captain Sparks—he had begun to fear boredom more than anything else. He'd never be able to settle down to a life built around a field of sugar cane or stand of coffee bushes. He'd die of *ennui* in a month even if he had

Lady Mary, Mary Fortescue, Almera, and Maria all with him.

He shook his head in answer to Elphinstone's question. No, it was not for him and he advised Elphinstone to go ahead with his plans for the auction, informing him that he would keep out a few of the boys for house servants to make the place more comfortable during the time he intended to remain in Trinidad.

After a glass of rum, not the raw Trinidad product but the real old Jamaica rum, Rory took his leave and traded the cool obscurity of the counting room for the blazing heat of outdoors. He'd go back to the ship. No, he wouldn't. As usual, Mary Davis Fortescue was the solution to his problems. He'd go there first. The effects of the river bath had long worn off and he could feel the sweat chaneling down his back, soaking through the thin cloth of his trousers and starting an unholy itch in his groin. He called K'tu to him and dispatched him to the ship for his razors, a change of clothes, and polished shoes; he was to bring the lot to Mary's house, which K'tu knew. He'd go there, eat a light lunch, take a long hot soak to get the dust and sweat out of his pores. Then, he decided, he would be ready to present himself to Lady Mary at Government House in a manner that would do credit if not to a Prince of Sa'aqs, at least to Sir Roderick Mahound.

All the jalousies were drawn at Mary's house and Fayal was not at the door pimping. Rory wondered if by chance the house was closed because Lady Mary was being studded again, but at his rap on the front door, it was quickly opened and a little maidservant ushered him in. Mary had evidently been awakened by his rapping and she was halfway down the stairs to meet him before he had crossed the flowering patio. He explained to her what he wanted and a loud clapping of her hands brought girls scurrying to follow her instructions. First she ordered them to prepare a bite of cold luncheon for him, then to heat water and bring it to her room, along with scented soap and big towels.

She ushered him up the stairs to her own apartment, petting and fussing over him, propping him up on the

378

chaise longue with pillows behind his back as though he were an invalid. Rushing to the door, she opened it and screamed down into the patio below, ordering in addition a cooling drink made of limes and sugar with just a touch of ginger in the cooled water from a porous *olla*.

When it arrived, he rested, sipping at his drink while Fayal brought a napkin-covered tray and pitchers of water, and the girls brought in soap and towels and pulled out the big tin tub and filled it with water. Mary finally shooed them all out of the room, despite the covetous glances they directed at him. She cut the cold meat on the plate and fed it to him, alternating it with bites of buttered bread.

"So, it's to Government House you're a-going?" Her statement became a question with the final Scottish lilt at the end. "Going to beard the high and mighty Lady Cleverden, huh? But you just be careful, Rory me lad, that she don't beard you first. With the gov'nor away and she so hot after what's in Fayal's britches, no telling what'll happen to *you*."

"She already knows what's in my pants, Mary my love."

"Then all the more reason for her a-wantin' it."

"But she's no use for Old Harry, now nor never. She could have had him time and time again, but she doesn't fancy the little grenadier."

"Then more's the pity and a stupid one she sure must be. But now, methinks, she'll be remembering him and she'll want him more than ever before. White meat will be a change for her after black."

"The color won't make any difference—not after having tasted Fayal."

"Pshaw! The lad may be hung like a stallion but he don't really know how to use it. He ain't got the technique that you have. How's that for a real ten-shilling word? I learned it from the old gal in London."

He grinned and allowed her to feed him the remainder of his lunch. After she had wiped his lips with a napkin, he stood up and she stripped the damp garments from him, scrubbing the wet from his body with a dry towel before he bathed. Her hands, always gentle, fondled him

379

and he, like she, was surprised to find that Old Harry did not respond. It was the first time in his whole life that the warm touch of a woman's hands had not aroused him. Mary looked her question at him, her face plainly showing her disappointment.

"Now what's come over Old Harry?" she asked when even more vigorous efforts on her part had failed to make any response. "You been a. . . ?"

"Might as well confess, Mary." He was apologetically rueful. "I was unfaithful to you last night."

She negated his confession by clasping him even more tightly. "And when did I ever ask you to be faithful to me, Rory? I'd not tie any man down more than I'd want him to tie me down. You asked me to marry you and I said no. If I'd a-said yes, I'd a-raised holy hell if I found out you'd been with some other woman, but I didn't. Sure, lad, I'm always jealous of you and I'd like you all to myself, but that just ain't fair. Now at least, with me making no scene at all and not tearing out my hair and beating my chest, you might tell me who the lucky girl was what put Old Harry on the shelf."

" 'Twas Maria, the colored wench at Melrose. Mama Phoebe scrubbed her and dressed her up and . . . "

"So that's what my rose satin dress was for?"

"Generous of you to loan it." He managed a shame-faced grin.

"Had I known it was for that bitch, I'd have torn it into rags. I thought Mama Phoebe intended it for Penny."

"That was Tim's bit of nippy. I had Maria."

"And you must have had her about ten times to cause Old Harry to curl up and go to sleep."

"Nigh onto that, but that's not all." Rory went on to describe the dead cock under his pillow and Maria's sucking of his blood, pointing to his lacerated lip in proof. He was unprepared for Mary's action. She sprang away from him, her face contorted with fear, her eyes staring blindly, her hands trembling. "You mean she . . . ?"

He nodded.

"Truly then she's a bitch, a spawn of the Evil One and it's evil I mean, I do. A Diabless, you said? Well, that's what she is. A she-devil. Oh, Rory, I've not lived here

380

these many months for nothing. I know what obeah is. I've seen it work its deviltry time and again. You can't say it's just superstition. It's real and it's wicked and powerful too. Ask anyone who's lived here. They'll tell you. But, thank God, she's only a Diabless. If she had been a Soucouyan, you'd be in real trouble."

"She said something about that too." Rory looked at the tub of steaming water, but did not feel like availing himself of it in Mary's present agitated condition. "I don't take any stock in what she said. Nothing but a mare's nest of superstition. Some African mumbo jumbo and God knows I've seen enough of that not to believe in it."

"No, then you'd damned well better start believing in it now, my bucko. You've got proof of it right there. Look!" She pointed to his limpness. "That never happened to you before, did it?" The shake of his head confirmed her question. "I tell you the girl's a menace. She's put a spell on you so's she can have you all to herself and no other woman ever will. She's been studying under some damned she-witch-doctor and learned a few of the secrets. She's just a beginner—they call one o' them a Diabless—but that's bad enough. As I said, it's a good thing she's not a Soucouyan. Do you know what *they* do?"

He shook his head in ignorance, edging toward the tub.

"Well, they're real devils. It's the truth. They can take off their skins and put 'em back on again. They have to wait till after midnight to do it and they always stash their skins under a crock. Then they take off into the night, flying right through the air to find someone that's sleeping. They prefer good strong men because their blood's stronger. They creep up on him and bite him with their teeth which have been filed sharp. Did you notice this bitch's teeth?"

Rory thought for a moment. No, he had not noticed Maria's teeth but, judging by the way she had torn his lip, he would not doubt but what her teeth had been sharpened.

"Then they suck the blood out of the poor man." Mary pursed her lips as though she were draining a man's life blood herself. "It's what they live on. When they've had their fill, off they go home again to put their skin back on.

381

But they don't ever eat food. Did you see this Maria eating?"

"I've not seen enough of her to know whether she eats or not. But wait! The first time I was there I saw some food on the table."

"Then probably she does. She ain't a Soucouyan yet so's she has to eat. And that brat brother of hers does, too. But all that makes no nevermind. She's got you under her spell. That's what's happened to Old Harry. Don't think it was galloping all night that wore him out. He'll not stand up for another woman in the world but her. She's drunk your blood and she's swallowed your man-juice; that's given her a power over you because she's got your vital fluids in her. Then to clinch matters, she put some sort of a spell over you with that dead rooster."

"It'll take more than a few sips of my blood and a dead rooster to keep Old Harry down. Look, I'll prove it to you." But Rory's own efforts were to no avail.

"I'll be out to Melrose tonight," Mary was emphatic. "I'll not let you stay in that vampire's clutches. There's only one way to fight obeah and that's with obeah. Fire with fire. Mama Phoebe'll know."

"Mayhap I should've told her. She seems to know everything." Rory tested the water with his toe and stepped in. He allowed Mary to soap him and once again he was chagrined over his lack of response. Oh well, tomorrow he would be all right. All this obeah talk was pure foolishness—old wives, tales. Nothing like this could ever happen to him and Old Harry. Nonsense!

While he was bathing K'tu arrived from the ship. Rory shaved and dressed. He scarcely dared look Mary in the face when he left. If anyone ever deserved a beating, it was Old Harry, who had deserted him.

"There's always a bright side, Rory darling." Mary tried to make light of a bad situation. "At least I'll not be worrying about what goes on at Government House with His Excellency away. If the obstinate fellow wouldn't stand up for Mary he sure as hell won't come to attention for her High-and-Mightiness."

Rory smiled wanly.

"And another thing," Mary pointed a commanding

finger at him. "You heist yourself back to Melrose as soon as you can. I'll be waiting for you there. There'll be no brouhaha tonight, me goslin'. I'll send that Maria packing. She's mine and I'll sell her tomorrow, get shut of her lock, stock, and barrel, then we'll exorcise you with bell, book, and candle, and every antidote that obeah has—and there's another ten-shilling word you didn't think this dock trollop knew. Did you, Rory?"

"The more I see of the Honorable Mrs. Fortescue, the more I find out she knows. You, Mary, and Mama Phoebe, that girl Maria, and even Lady Mary. You all seem to know a hell of a lot more than I do."

"Laws, Rory, all women know more than men! How do you think we handle 'em if we don't know more than they do?"

"Something tells me you're right." He took her arm and led her down the stairs beside him, across the courtyard, stopping at the entrance gate. "You're going to protect me tonight?" He squeezed her hand.

"Damned right I am." She rose on tiptoe to kiss him. "We've got to put life back into the little grenadier one way or another."

"Then you be his commanding officer, Mary."

"That I will, and when I tell him to stand at attention, he'd better or . . ."

"Or what?"

"I'll court-martial the little bastard. Thirty days solitary confinement."

"That should make him behave; that's longer than he's ever been alone in his whole life."

CHAPTER XXXVI

RORY STOMPED HIS FEET ON THE TILED floor of the bougainvillea-shaded terrace of Government House to remove the thin coating of dust which had settled on his shoes during his short ride over from Mary's house. He adjusted the black satin stock, smoothed down his coat, pulled up the white trousers and removed the big half-moon hat. Feeling quite satisfied with his appearance, he reached up to yank at the brass chain that hung beside the door. Somewhere in the depths of the house he could hear the answering tinkle of a bell. He listened. The sound died away and there came the hurried tread of soft footsteps, the rattle of a chain and the slipping of a bolt. A sentry, pacing back and forth on the terrace and sweating in the woolen fustiness of his English uniform, turned his head and their eyes met momentarily, as though the man wanted to assure him that there was somebody coming to serve him and take over the responsibility of his presence.

The door opened slowly to a semidarkness which gave a promise of coolness inside. A form, ghostly white in the crepuscular light, bowed to him and he stepped inside, trying to adjust his eyes to the darkness as the door swung to. Immediately he felt himself enveloped in a clinging embrace of soft arms that, despite their trembling, enfolded him with an almost overwhelming fervor.

"Milord, milord!" It was such a familiar and well-loved voice. "Fayal told me that you were here but I could not believe it. Oh, milord, it is really you. I thought never to see you again so far away in this barbarous country. Allah is merciful. He has seen fit to return you to me. Wallahi! He ordained that I should suffer no longer." Her fingers reached up to his face, touching his cheeks lightly as

384

though they were afraid that his solid flesh might vanish into nothingness.

There was no mistaking Almera's voice or the soft Arabic words. He clasped her to him, pressing her mouth against his own, conscious of her tears and the spasms that convulsed her slight body pressed so tightly against his own. Her slender body! Yes, it was the willow wand it always had been. Then she had already accomplished the miracle for which he had been hoping, although, his conscience reprimanded him, he had given far too little thought to it.

"Almera." He lifted his mouth from hers, pushing her body away from his only enough to let his hand slide down over her flat belly. "Yes, little one, I am here but tell me—oh, tell me quickly—how is my son?"

"Your son, milord? You knew you had a son?"

"I knew it would have to be a son. I could never have planted a girl child in you."

"Yes, Rory, you have a son and he has yellow hair and a white skin like yours and he is the biggest baby you have ever seen with the loudest voice."

"And his name, Almera?"

"I call him Ismail. But you, milord, must give him an English name, for I know of none, in truth."

"That he shall have, Almera. Two names. One Moorish and one Scotch. We shall call him Ismail as you have chosen but he will also be a Mahound because he is half Moorish and half Scotch. Ismail Mahound of Sa'aqs and Sax. We'll make him a Prince of Sa'aqs and a Baron of Sax. Let's hope he'll be proud of his father some day. Ismail Mahound of Sa'aqs and Sax. What an unholy mouthful! But now, my very dear, about yourself? Where can we talk? We can't stand here, and we have so much to say to each other."

She reached for his hand, leading him down the long gallery, his heels clicking on the tiled floor. "Walk softly, milord," she warned, but it was too late; a door opened, flooding a patch of brightness onto the tiles. A woman stood in the sunlight, her hair blazing like an aureole in the light.

"Who is it, Almera?" There was a cutting edge to her

385

voice and Rory stepped from the shadows into the light that surrounded her.

"You must have been expecting me, Mary. Surely you knew I was here in Trinidad."

"My lord of Sax," she extended a slender hand to him which felt cool and dry in his sweaty palm. "I must say you have been most dilatory in calling on an old friend."

"A friend?" He brushed the hand with his lips. It was like a piece of ivory. "Since when were we ever friends, milady Yasmin?"

She started at the name, but the ghost of a smile showed that it was not entirely beclouded by unpleasant memories.

"Then if not friends, surely we can no longer be enemies, Rory. We've been through too much together." She stepped between him and Almera, linking her arm into his, then turned abruptly. "Go, Almera, before that brat starts squalling again." Almera hesitated and Lady Mary turned, slapping her lightly across the cheek. "Go, I said."

Rory restrained the girl. "She's not your slave, Mary. If she belongs to anyone, it's to me. And the brat you speak about is my own. If we've much to say to each other, I've much to say to Almera. . . ."

"But more to me. She can wait. There's no reason for you to be so puffed up about fathering another half-breed bastard. I dare say there must be a string of them reaching all the way from here to Timbuktu."

"Granted, Mary, and a baker's dozen or more of them in Scotland perhaps." He bowed slightly. "And remember, there could well have been another, whiter and more yellow-haired than either of us, had the seed I planted in you fallen on more fertile ground."

She reddened, the carmine spreading quickly over her face. Her lifted hand was about to descend on his cheek with even more force than it had on Almera's. It halted in midair and descended slowly, even affectionately, to his shoulder.

"Thank God that seed didn't sprout. But let us not quarrel. There's been too much bitterness on my side and too many regrets. I'm cognizant of all you did for me. I owe you much and most of all gratitude. Come, Rory. I'll not deny you the right to see Almera later, but now I am anxious to talk with you. Alone! Go, Almera." She dismissed the girl and turned again to Rory. "You can't make this an official visit anyway. My husband's away. It's the only time we can talk because the old fool's frightfully jealous of me. As for Almera, you can talk with her any time but with me. . . ." She made a little gesture of futility with her fluttering fingers and pushed him over the threshold. The door closed behind them and he heard the faint click of a well-oiled bolt.

It was a small sitting room, tastefully furnished in the style of Mr. Sheraton, with slender-legged chairs and a settee, all upholstered in white damask. The spindly furniture, which had evidently come from England along with Her Ladyship, looked strangely incongruous in the rough Spanish interior. Through an arched door, netting was draped over a disheveled bed, and now that he could see Lady Mary plainly, he noticed that she was in a thin deshabille. It was evident she had been indulging in the tropical custom of taking a siesta in the afternoon and his entrance had awakened her. He sat down gingerly in a chair, wondering if it would bear his weight, while she tripped nervously about the room, picking up a pair of gossamer silk stockings from the floor, adjusting the blinds to temper the light, finally pouring him a glass of wine.

Her hand was trembling. Damn! was he destined to send every woman into a fit of the vapors today? She came to stand beside him after he had accepted the wine; so near that he could have touched her with the slightest motion of his hand, so near that he could see the blue-veined marble of her flesh through the transparent *mousseline de soie* of her robe. He sipped at the wine, waiting for her to sit down, but she remained standing beside him. His eyes raised to meet hers, he lifted the glass with the gesture of a toast and smiled up at her.

"After all, why shouldn't we be friends, Yasmin? We could have been a long time ago and it would have made matters far pleasanter for both of us. I'm sorry now that I forced you. I shouldn't have done it, you being a countrywoman of mine and, to a certain extent, under my protection. But you see, it was necessary. . . ."

387

"Necessary? What a cowardly thing to say! Even more cowardly than the deed itself."

"Necessary I said, and necessary it was. You see, I had to prove something, not only to myself but to Baba. Everyone else had tried knocking at your door and nobody had ever succeeded in entering. It was a challenge. I had to prove that I was more of a man than any Moor, that my virility exceeded that of every Arab. Furthermore," his lips drew down at the corners and his smile was an attempt at humility, "I'd never had a woman refuse me before and mastering you would be a sop to my vanity. So, I had to force my way in and I'm sorry for it now. In truth 'twas an empty victory. You deserved better from me."

"Indeed I did." Her hand rested on his head and her fingers twined a strand of his hair. "I deserved to be raped again. Once was not enough, Rory. You kindled a fire and then let it rage within me without a thought of ever extinguishing it. Having entered once, you should have had a desire to do it again, but no, you treated me with the cool respect which you might have used toward a sister of whom you were not particularly fond."

"But you? You treated me even worse."

"I came to you a second time, literally on my knees, begging for it, and I am not the type of woman who asks for favors, from any man, Rory Mahound. I wanted you to take me, not make me beg you for it."

"A hundred or more in my hareem were doing it. Why not you?"

"You always were a conceited scoundrel, so secure in your power over women. Do you never tire of having them beg you for your favors? Well, I didn't beg you then, but now I have lost whatever pride I had and now I do beg for it. Think you that you could kindle such a holocaust within me and then never do anything more about putting it out? Where, oh where, could I ever find another like you?"

It was on the tip of Rory's tongue to tell her that she had undoubtedly found a fair substitute in young Fayal who seemed adept at putting out such fires as raged in her, but he swallowed his words. Events had taken a turn

388

which he had never expected. Well, so be it. It was little enough to ask of him. Reaching up, he pulled her down to him and she sank into his lap, but he bethought himself of the spindly chair. He lifted her, feeling how strangely light she was in his arms, and settled her in the chair opposite. Sinking down on the floor in front of her, he encircled her waist with his arms, leaning his face against the warmth of her body which penetrated through the thin silk.

"Oh, I've wanted you so, Rory." She bent down to lift his face and kiss him on the lips. "So much, so very much. But my silly pride would never let me ask you after you kicked me out of your bed when I entered there by pretense. All the time I was hoping you would woo me, yea, even force me again and I ached with jealousy over the Moorish wenches that shared your bed and your body. And yet, although I burned with jealousy over Almera who carried a proof of your love in her belly, I wanted her with me. Just talking about you assuaged my grief when we were separated."

"Tell me all that happened." He drew her closer to him, delighting in the lavender scent of her skin.

Her hands pressed on his head and her fingers twisted in his hair as she began on the long tale of the many things that had happened to her since that day she had left him in Tangier. They had gone, she and Almera, across to Gibraltar where they had had some difficulty in landing. The English were not welcoming any ships from their Moorish neighbors on the other continent, but when she had screamed from the deck to the stiff-necked soldiers on the jetty that she was an Englishwoman and returning home and had cursed them for a company of stupid bastards, they relented and allowed her to land along with Almera without impounding the ship.

Then, when they discovered her rank, they took her to the commander of the garrison, whose lady supplied her with civilized clothing. Almost immediately she was able to return to England and sought her father's house in London.

Alas, nobody had believed that she was a Princess of Sa'aqs, not even when she waved the sheets of parchment with their Moorish writing and their heavy seals before them. She had been a prisoner of the Moors—so it was whispered around all London to the clatter of teacups and the clicking of fans. What delightfully terrible things must have happened to her, because of course she must have spent her time in a Moorish harem. Everyone knew what happened to girls in *those* places. And, they whispered, if she had managed to get away from those terrible Turks, who did *anything*—positively *anything*—to a young girl, she must have been more complaisant than all the others in order to win her freedom and the bogus title she flaunted in their faces. Oh, it was all most titillating to talk about, but it put her beyond the pale, most definitely.

She was not invited to a single dinner or party or even tea. She was ignored and snubbed and left alone to think about Rory and to wish that she had stayed in Sa'aqs. By her improbable, implausible story she had become the laughingstock of Mayfair and Belgravia, though she was sure there wasn't one of the stiff-necked, horsey-faced women who did not secretly envy her.

Even her own family did not believe her. There remained only one thing to do, her father insisted, and that was to marry her off, provided of course anyone would want such a piece of damaged goods, even with a considerable dowry. But there was always somebody who would want the dowry if not herself. Sir Basil Cleverden was the man, a cousin of her father's. True he was older than her father and so pockmarked that he resembled a crocodile, but he had wangled an appointment as governor of His Majesty's colony of Trinidad and was to leave immediately. He needed all the money he could get to bolster up his rat-gnawed coffers, and he didn't mind a young wife who had lost her maidenhead. She might help him rekindle what remained of a passion that had long been exhausted by London's most expensive whores. It was only an expensive strumpet who would accommodate him; even a Thamesside doxy would turn up her nose at him. But Lady Mary's father didn't. Old FitzAlbany jumped at the chance to get his much-gossiped-about daughter off his hands and once again safely out of the way across an ocean. So she was married, without her consent and with only memories of Rory to console her for the inept and impotent fumblings of Sir Basil.

What a silly idiot she had been! Yes, she admitted it now. She should have stayed in Sa'aqs and languished in Rory's hareem with the hope that someday he would return and notice her. Even the hareem eunuchs would have been better than Sir Basil and she would have belonged to Rory, who couldn't have ignored her forever. She would even have preferred to be sold in slavery, provided her master was some young and virile Arab. Her marriage was just another form of slavery and, please to believe her, Sir Horatio was no young Arab, although the old lecher was frightfully jealous of her.

But to sum it up, it was all Rory's fault. She pointed an accusing finger at him, and then leaned over and kissed him. It was he who had created the burning desire in her and then abandoned her. Did he think any other man would ever be able to satisfy her? He started to demur, but she silenced him with a finger on his lips. He should have paid no attention to her maidenly foibles; he had taken her by force once and he should have done it again and again even in the face of her silly refusals. He should have been wise enough to see that she needed a master, someone to break her stubborn spirit and realize that she actually didn't know what she wanted. Even a touch of the whip would have been useful to bring her around to her senses.

Suddenly, in the midst of her recriminations, she was on the floor beside him, her lips pressed against his; his arms were around her, his hands pushing aside the thin silk of her robe.

"Oh, Rory, can you ever forgive me?"

His answer was to pick her up, cradling her head against his shoulder, his hands under the robe, feeling the warm pressure of her flesh. The tumbled bed beckoned him, and he carried her in to ease her gently down under the fall of netting. His fingers sought the buttons of his garments and her hands, pushing aside the white tent, stripped them from him. His body fell beside her, adjusting itself to all her contours while their lips met, this time without hesitation, recrimination or apologies. She had

391

finally achieved that of which she had dreamed so long—
that which was not merely a stopgap to her passions,
which was all that Fayal had ever been, but the one
person she had, despite her ignorance of the fact, always
wanted.

There was a warmth and impetuosity to his love play
which she had missed with Fayal who had always seemed
only to have one thing in mind—to impale her as quickly
as possible. Rory's hands roved over her body and his lips
sought out all the hidden places that served to set her on
fire. As his hands explored, so did hers, down through the
thick curling hair of his chest, tweaking at the hardened
paps, then further beyond the conchoidal convolutions of
his navel into the thick fleece, and then to grasp—what?
Not what she had magnified in her memory since that
unforgettable day at Sa'aqs (as if Rory had ever needed
magnifying). Far from it. It was there with its well-
remembered potential, but that was all. No amount of
kissing, fondling, or frenzied manipulation could increase
that potential and bring it to the turgid, adamantine rigidity that would transform it to a *tour de force*. She gave up;
it was impossible. To make matters even worse, he tried
himself but no amount of self-castigation accomplished the
desired result. After half an hour of inept fumbling which
placed them both in an absurd light, he was forced to call
quits. There was no use in further flogging a dead horse.
Humbly and with a shame which he had never experienced before, he apologized, and she, bereft of the one
thing she had longed for every moment of the past
months, took refuge in the icy scorn that had always been
her best weapon. Her words, cold with frustrated desire,
poured over him with such glacial sarcasm that they
burned him like scalding water.

"Out!" She beat upon his chest with her fists. "Get into
your clothes and get out of here. Damn you, damn you,
damn you! Go back to your whoremistress, that Mrs.
Fortescue who has so drained you that you are no longer a
man. Oh, I know all about your visits to her house, I
know you've just come from her. No wonder you are
impotent, useless, a poor imitation of a man. How dare
you come from her bed to mine, your body reeking with

the stench of her cheap perfume, your strength sapped by her jaded practices? Get out!" Her sharp nails raked his chest and she flailed him with her fists.

Rory extricated himself from her fury and slipped from the bed, clutching at his clothes and trying to struggle into them while he fended off her attacks.

"Go back to your whore!" She was screaming now. "Go back to that common trollop in her filthy house. She probably knows some tricks that will arouse you. Would that I knew as much as she does. Perhaps I could have succeeded. I'll have my husband close her down; I'll have her place burned to the ground; I'll have her put in the stocks and branded with a red-hot iron. I'll . . ."

"Softly, Mary." Rory found an opportunity to wedge a word into her tirade. "Softly with your threats against her. Would you cut off your own nose to spite that pretty face of yours? Remember, Fayal is there. You'll be needing him again and soon, I wager."

She became quiet; the color drained from her face. "Fayal? She told you about him? Oh, damn her to hell for a lying bitch."

"She never had to tell me about him. It was I who sent him to her."

"I didn't mean that. . . ."

"If you mean did Mary Fortescue tell me about you and him—no, words were not necessary. I saw with my own eyes how you rode that lusty buck and how you reveled in every minute of it."

"You devil! You spied on me! You saw! Then all the more reason for me to ruin that woman."

He shook his head while he buttoned up his shirt and twisted his stock around his neck.

"You'll ruin nobody. Nobody, do you hear me? You'll not ruin Mary Fortescue and you'll not take vengeance on me for something that is not my fault. As God's my witness, I wanted as much as you to give you what you craved. Something has happened to me; I don't know what, though believe me, it's more of a disappointment to me than to you. But you'll keep your mouth shut, my pretty. You say your husband is a jealous man. So bide your time and be careful what you blab to him or I swear

393

he'll find out about your visits to Fayal. 'Twas no fault of yours that I failed you today. That I could not rise to the occasion was not through any dislike of you. I tell you again, something has happened to me. Just what I do not know . . ."

"Oh, but I do! You're a dissolute rakehell, a libertine, a whoremonger, that's what you are, milord of Sax. You're worn out before your time. You're drained, sapped, unmanned by all the dirty hareem sluts you've crawled over and that have sucked you dry like an orange. You're probably poxed by all the strumpets you've had, or even worse, you've succumbed to the Moorish vice and become so enamoured of pretty boys that no woman can arouse you. Well, go back to your catamites. I never want to see you again. Never, never, never! Now go!"

"Not before I see Almera and my son."

Suddenly it occurred to her that she still had the upper hand over him. She retreated from him and the ugly scowl that had distorted her features gave way to a crafty smile.

"You threatened me, Rory Mahound. Because you managed through connivance with that Fortescue bitch to see me with Fayal you think you can blackmail me. You threatened to go to my husband, and although I loathe the senile old dodderer, I'll not have more scandal gossiped around about me. But now, Rory Mahound, you'll keep your mouth shut if you ever want to see Almera and the precious brat you call your son. I'd as soon strangle her with a cord and smother the little bastard under a pile of pillows. Don't think I won't do it if word of Fayal leaks out."

"I remember Hussein. You're capable of it."

"You can wager on that." She shook a fist at him.

"But you'll not harm them. I, too, can threaten. Harm either one of them and I'll do far more than blacken your reputation. I'll kill you. You know me well enough to know I'll do it. Yes, I'll kill you and, as God is my witness, no woman ever deserved killing more than you do."

"A pact then, milord of Sax." She unclenched her fists and her hands fell to her side. Suddenly remembering that she stood before him naked, she grabbed her robe from among the tumbled sheets of the bed and held it before her. "I'll keep my hands off Almera and the brat. You keep your mouth shut."

"Agreed, milady Cleverden. My silence for their safety. But before I go, I'll see Almera and talk with her."

"And warn her? Oh, no! You'll leave at once or I'll put my head out of the windows and scream that you're raping me. The sentry at the door will come a-running. You'll not see Almera or the child either."

He strode toward the door of the little sitting room. He shot back the bolt—it had proved unnecessary after all—and with his hand on the latch, he turned, took off his hat, and swept the air with it in a low bow.

"Allow me, milady, to congratulate you. You are undoubtedly the most consummate jezebel I've ever had the bad fortune to come across."

She bowed quite as low and quite as formally as he. "Allow me, milord, to return your compliment. Let me say that you are undoubtedly the handsomest man I've ever had the misfortune to meet and I shall spend the rest of my life regretting that you are not really a man. There is nothing more despicable than a creature who walks around on two legs with only a limp rope-end between them. Good day, milord of Sax, I hope our paths never cross again."

"Ah, but they will. They must. And the next time they do, milady, watch out. I'll show you once more what a real man is like."

"Braggart!" She had managed to have the last word as he closed the door.

CHAPTER XXXVII

RORY WALKED HIS HORSE SLOWLY ALONG dusty Charlotte Street, which was now almost completely overcast with the drift of late afternoon shadows. His brief flare-up of anger against Lady Mary had now been turned inward against himself. After all, perhaps she was right. Had he, in his profligate excesses, wasted the seemingly inexhaustible reservoirs of his own body? Had he, as she had accused, spilled his manhood so frequently and so indiscriminately into whatever convenient receptacle came to hand that there was nothing left? Could it be that he, young as he was, had completely burned himself out? God forbid! Could he be a mere husk, a sucked-out orange, as she had so aptly put it, devoid of all its juices, used up and ready to be cast away? No, no! He could not be that—he of all people.

He could comfort himself with one thing, though bare comfort it was. He had never—well, hardly ever—wasted any of his seed on those adder-slim boys with bee-stung lips who were always so much in evidence in Moorish courts. Damn it, no! Of that one accusation he was innocent; well, perhaps not entirely innocent. There had been, for one thing, that orgy in which Tim and Jehu had also indulged. But such occasions were rare in his life, and certainly not habitual or necessary. Anyway, look at Baba and Mansour. They indulged from time to time for the sake of variety—it was a common practice in Morocco—and their manhood seemed none the worse for it. He was glad that he could prove his tormentress wrong in one thing.

Perhaps, he continued to argue with himself, all might not be lost forever. He could embark on a period of continence and see if by some miracle complete abstinence would replenish his empty reservoirs. Alas, although his physical capacity seemed to be paralyzed, he realized that his desires were as strong as ever.

From populous Charlotte Street, he turned his horse into a narrow lane, realizing as he did so that he was heading back toward Mary Fortescue's house. He seemed always to be seeking her protection. Only a short distance from the corner, a form emerged from a shadowed doorway. It was a woman, completely enveloped in dark cloth, carrying a bundle. Just as he approached she drew back the veil that covered her face. He stopped, recognizing the familiar gesture with which Moorish women were wont to uncover their faces.

"Almera."

"Milord. Forgive me. I had to see you. I was listening outside the door. I am frightened." She looked carefully up and down the narrow lane, and seeing nobody, she lifted the cloth-wrapped bundle up to Rory who opened his arms to take it.

"There is nothing to be frightened of, little one."

He opened the folds of cloth and looked down at his son's face. The child looked like all other babies to him, but he could see that the boy was white-skinned, strong, and healthy and that a wisp of blond hair straggled across his scalp. He felt an emotion that surprised him. The weight and warmth of the bundle in his arms gave him a peculiar sense of accomplishment. This indeed was his own flesh and blood which he shared with the girl standing near him. He handed him back to Almera, suddenly aware of the extreme fragility of his burden.

"For myself I am not frightened." She reached up to receive the baby. "Nor for Ismail. I can protect him, but it is for you that I fear. She may harm you."

He found himself able to smile. "I've still got something that she wants; she'll not harm me, at least not until she gets it, and by the way it looks now, that will be a long time."

"It's something I want too, milord. Oh, take me with you!"

The prospect of having Almera with him again was

alluring, but where could he take her? Certainly not to Mary Fortescue's, with her collection of hoydens; not to Melrose, where Maria was to be feared far more than Lady Mary, nor to the *Shaitan* where she would be one lone woman among a crew of rough sailors. Possibly he could take her to Elphinstone's, but that would cause a lot of talk—Lady Mary's servant under the protection of the newly arrived slave trader.

"Just now I cannot, Almera. And in the matter of that which you desire along with Lady Mary, I fear that I'll be useless to you. Something has happened. Don't ask me why, but I'm less of a man than any eunuch in the hareems of Sa'aqs." He slid down from his horse to hold her in his arms. It was a brief embrace, interrupted by a lumbering ox cart which turned the corner.

He waited for the ox cart to pass and kissed her.

"Go back, little one. You'll be all right there for the time being. Let me think about it. I'll settle on some safe place for you and Ismail. If you were to disappear now there'd be a hue and cry after you. Trust me, Almera. I'll work the whole thing out. Guard my son well. Allah is merciful; he'll protect you and so will I. Go now before you are missed, and know this: I love you. I always have and now I love you doubly because you are the mother of Ismail."

He released her, mounted, and with the touch of her fingers still warm on his own, rode away. At the end of the lane he looked back to see the black figure, its shoulders drooping, turn the corner. An overpowering desire to race back and sweep her up beside him came over him, but he resisted it, turning his horse toward Mary Fortescue's house.

He found her sitting in her upstairs drawing room, a look of grim determination on her face.

"Your man K'tu is here. He's been to the ship; Captain Jehu sends word that everything is fine there."

"You could understand him?"

"Fayal interpreted for me. Now, for heaven's sake, sit down and rest. You've been flying around like a blind-folded crow all day, and getting nowhere."

"How true! What's happened to me? Suddenly, overnight, I've become a eunuch. Old Harry's dead. He can no longer come to attention."

"As Milady Cleverden probably found out, judging by the look on your face. I reckon she was no more successful than I was."

"No more." He grinned at her sheepishly. "The little rascal's dead."

"He's far from a *little* rascal, and he's not dead either. I know what's wrong with him and we'll get him on his feet and standing straight and tall in two jerks of a lamb's tail. It's that damned Maria and her double-damned obeah curse on you. I'll wager he'll stand up for her whenever she wants him but for no one else. We'll attend to that, my lad. If she can put a curse on you to keep Old Harry for herself, we'll go a step further and remove the curse. See, Rory", she lifted the skirt of her dark dress, "I'm all ready to go out to Melrose with you although you wouldn't notice. We'll have a bite to eat, and then we'll beard the lioness in her den. Have no fear. Mama Phoebe'll make short shrift of that lass. A Diabless, huh? Well, Mama's brother is a Soucouyan. He's an old rascal who's always coming around to the back door a-begging his dinner. Now it's time for him to pay me back for all the meals he's whined out of me. The old foozle and that young polly-boy flunky who always goes along with him are both stuffing their faces in my kitchen right now. They both stink to high heaven and I'll need a clothespin on my nose to sit in the same coach with them, but the stenchin' old rascal will put that chocolate-colored floozy back where she belongs. He's got a whole bag full of dried leaves and rat skulls and rooster feathers with him so's to be prepared for anything."

He reached out both hands to her. "No matter what happens to me, Mary, I've always got you to help me, whether it's giving me a bit of cold meat and warm love in Glasgow or trying to make Old Harry stand up again and doff his cap. You always have the solution."

"And always will, lad. I told you, any man's helpless without a woman to think for him. So take warning of all women, Rory. What would life be like if you married me? I'd wear the pants all the time and you'd be nothing but a

399

henpecked husband. I've delivered you from a fate worse'n death by refusing to marry you. You'd better thank me for it."

He shook his head, glad to be back with her again and wanting nothing more than to eat and to stretch out his long legs and forget all his problems for a while. He leaned back in one of Mary's comfortable chairs, closed his eyes, and dozed off until the clatter of dishes and the smell of food brought him to his senses.

They dined *à deux* and he realized that he was hungry. Afterward there was the bustle of preparation for leaving and as it was now dark, he instructed K'tu to ride on one side of Mary's coach and he would ride on the other. The shapeless pile of dirty rags on the ground beside the coach metamorphosed into a man. "Tio Carlo," Mary introduced him from her seat inside the coach, and he waggled the carved handle of a cane up toward Rory in place of a hand. "And Ganimedes." Mary designated the slender tobacco-brown youth with a ravaged prettiness of face who stood beside him, holding a bulging sack. The boy helped the bundle of rags to his feet and pushed him into the coach, crawling in beside him. They both smelled of carrion and excrement and Rory noticed that in place of a clothespin, Mary held a pomander before her nose; but whether its spicy smell would dispel the odor, he had serious doubts.

A pale moon, strained through jagged palm leaves, gave sufficient light to silver the waving tassels of sugar cane and light the road. When they arrived at Melrose, Tim met them at the door, with Mama Phoebe beside him and a radiant Maria, once again resplendent in the rose dress, behind them. The arrival of Mary along with Tio Carlo and the languishing Ganimedes brought a cry of surprise from Mama Phoebe and a look of consternation to Maria's sullen features. Mary shooed the old man and his boy off to the kitchen with instructions to Mama Phoebe to have them start on whatever preparations they were to make—anything to keep them and their carrion odor out of the way for a time. She then made a point of having her small valise placed in Rory's room, ordering Maria to carry it there herself so there could be no mistake in the girl's mind but what Mary and none other was to sleep there with him. Maria flounced away, but her scornful leer, not unnoticed by Mary, gave evidence that the girl felt it would do her mistress little good.

"Wipe that grin off your face, girl," Mary's hand descended on Maria's rear, "and mind your manners or I'll have your back a-smarting with twenty lashes. One thing I won't stand for is impudence."

Her face averted from Mary's anger, Maria picked up the valise and left, but the set of her shoulders and her quickening steps betokened her anger. With a flurry of skirts she disappeared down the gallery. Now, with Maria away on her errand and the two obeah men in the kitchen, Mary quickly explained to Mama Phoebe and Tim her version of what she surmised had happened to Rory. Tim shook his head in disbelief. Nothing like that, he was sure, could ever happen to his idol, but Rory affirmed that it had. Mama Phoebe agreed that such a misfortune was possible. If the girl Maria was a Diabless, as she had boasted, she could cast such a spell. They were not uncommon, and often used by jealous women on philandering husbands and lovers. When Mary told her about the dead cock, the biting of Rory's lips—he stuck out his lower lip to show the scar—the old woman nodded her head in portentous affirmation of Mary's wisdom in bringing Tio Carlo out from town.

"He kin do it, Miss Mary. He not worth much, that shiftless brother o' mine, but if'n they's one thing he a-knowin' 'bout it's obeah. He bin a obeah man all his life, he have, 'n that li'l squidgereen what he got wid him, that Ganimedes, he don' look like more'n a missy but he do be knowin' 'bout obeah too. Come night he kin take off his skin 'n go a-flyin' all over de worl'." She waddled over to Rory and placed a cautioning hand on his elbow. "Yo' ready ter go through wid this? Don' know myself what a-goin' ter happen, but obeah kin be skeery at times— mighty skeery, son." With a look of grim determination on her face and her shoulders planted squarely, she led them out of the room with all the aplomb of a drum major. "Come on! Le's all go ter de kitchen. Ain' havin' that

401

no-good Tio Carlo in here a-stinking up ma house. He work better in de kitchen anyway."

K'tu was standing outside the door and Rory signaled to him to follow. "You come with me, boy, and don't leave me. Stay with me whatever happens." Rory felt safer with K'tu along.

They all followed Mama Phoebe down the patio. Halfway to the kitchen, she turned around. "Whereat that sneakin' bitch, Maria?"

"I sent her with my valise to the bedroom."

"That so-'n-so, she a-lookin' fer trouble. Better we lock her up somewheres." Mama Phoebe turned with a speed that belied her corpulence and bounded down the passageway to Rory's room. "She ain' here," she called. "Done left the v'lise 'n skinned out. Ain' no tellin' whereat she be."

That she was not around, however, was, for the moment, more important than where she had gone, so they resumed their interrupted parade to the kitchen. Tio Carlo was there, seated, as usual, on the floor. Ganimedes and Peter, who seemed to have formed an immediate attachment, were sitting together holding hands in the dark shadows of the kitchen where the one tallow candle was unable to send its flickering light.

"Yo' think yo' kin do somethin' fer this po' young gen'l'man, Carlo?" Mama Phoebe positioned herself before him.

"Shore kin, Sista Phoebe. Hear some wench done put a spell on him 'n he ain' able to git it up for no one else. Kin do it if'n he believe in me. If'n he don', cain'. Hard ter work wi' white folkses what ain' believin' in obeah, Sista Phoebe, like'n yo' knows. He believin'?" His wizened head turned to stare up at Rory.

"I believe, Tio Carlo." Rory would have believed in the Mahound himself—the one in hell—if it would cure him.

"It somethin' yo' ain' a-goin' to like much. Maybe hurt some."

"If it brings results, it doesn't matter much whether I like it or not."

"Then clear out of the room." Old Tio Carlo managed to get to his feet. Yo', Sista Phoebe, drag yore fat ass out'a here and yo', beggin' yore pardon, Missus Fortescue,

402

please to leave us 'n take that brown-faced young spadger out with yo'." He pointed to Peter. "Ganimedes' not keepin' his mind on nothin', he havin' a fresh-sapped young squirt like'n that a-hangin' roun'. Now git, all o' yo'."

"But K'tu is to remain," Rory insisted. He wanted something familiar to offset the esoteric strangeness of Tio Carlo.

"He that there big bozal?" Tio Carlo pointed to K'tu. At Rory's nod, Tio Carlo consented, after exchanging a quick look with Ganimedes. "Kin stay if'n yo' wants, but gotta tie him up. Cain' have him a-rampagin' roun'."

Rory explained to K'tu and he agreed.

"You'd better let me stay too, Rory," Tim insisted. "I goddamned *do* believe in nigger magic after what happened to me in Basampo, and remember, you stayed with me then, Rory. The least I can do is stand by you."

"This ain' for no white man to see, less'n he the one we a-workin' on. Don' min' the black, but white gotta go." Tio Carlo was emphatic.

Mama Phoebe protested that she could be of help; that she knew as much about obeah as Tio Carlo and a damned sight more than Ganimedes, but her protests were to no avail. Mary Fortescue also elected to stay, averring that she wanted to be there to see that no evil might befall Rory, but again Tio Carlo was adamant. Only K'tu, and he bound hand and foot. Ganimedes suggested that Peter could help him, but Tio Carlo cuffed him and pushed Peter out the door. Finally the room was cleared of all save Rory, the old man and his minion, and K'tu, who submitted meekly to thongs about his wrists and ankles.

With one broomstick-thin black arm, Tio Carlo cleared the big white-scrubbed kitchen table and signalled for Rory to mount it. "Better take off your clotheses first, man."

Rory stripped himself and climbed on the table, lying there, awaiting whatever might come, ignorant of what was to happen and cursing himself for a fool to put any credence in this old man and his mumbo-jumbo. Yet, despite all his reservations, he somehow felt that Tio Carlo might be the only one who could help him. He'd seen what black magic had done for Timmy back in Africa.

403

Timmy had been as good as dead, and now he was walking around as healthy as any man. It had helped Tim, now let it help Rory. God knows he needed it.

He watched while Tio Carlo lighted four tallow dips and smeared their molten wax on each of the four corners of the table, waiting for it to cool slightly before he anchored the candles in the congealing wax. He laid a venturous hand on Rory's bare arm.

"Ain' a-goin' to hurt you' more'n I have to, son, but it better if'n I tie yo' up. Yo' ain' a-goin' to get mad at ol' Uncle Carlo if'n I do?"

"No. Do what you have to."

Tio Carlo spread-eagled Rory's arms and legs to the four corners of the table. With a thin hempen rope, he secured wrists and ankles to the table legs. Before tightening the bonds so that Rory could not move, he was careful to pad Rory's wrists and ankles with old rags so that the thongs would not cut into his skin. He was most solicitous of Rory's comfort, and except for being unable to move, he was fairly comfortable.

With Rory tightly trussed and his bonds thoroughly tested, Tio Carlo produced another rag, passably clean, with which he intended to blindfold Rory; but Rory objected. "If I'm going through with this, I want to know what's going on. Don't batten down my eyes."

"Some thin's a man ain' supposed to see." Tio Carlo looked toward Ganimedes. "Kin fix that tho'. Come the time we a-needin' to, kin put out the candles." He fumbled in the bag on the floor and took out a bleached human skull which he placed at Rory's head. He then proceeded to stick black, red, and white cock feathers in the gaping eyesockets, making a studied and fanciful pattern of the various colors. The arrangement seemed to be part of some complex ritual for when the old man had finished, Ganimedes rearranged it slightly, bringing a nod of approval from the old man. Next he drew out a crumpled paper packet from the bag, opening it to disclose an iridescent, coarse powder, and to Rory, who strained his neck to see, it looked like the pulverized wings of flies. Calling to his assistant, Tio Carlo asked for a cup of water which was brought to him. Judiciously measuring

404

three pinches of the powder into the water, he had Ganimedes stir it with a spoon and held up Rory's head so he could drink it. The powder had not dissolved in the water but it was tasteless, albeit scratchy in his throat.

This done, Tio Carlo motioned for Ganimedes to bring a small pot from the stove. It exuded a strong odor of pepper—the fiery red capsicum from Cayenne in the Guinean province on the South American mainland. With a swab of rags tied to a stick, Tio Carlo sopped it up from the pot and applied it to Rory's upper thighs, his belly, and yes, even to Old Harry himself. Ganimedes, his hands well greased with fat, massaged it into Rory's skin. Rory yelled out, squirming under the biting broth. It burned like the stabbing pitchforks of ten thousand devils and his only wish was to bound from the table and plunge into the cool water of the horse trough beside the stables. Tio Carlo held him down with a strength amazing for such scrawny arms, nor did he yield to either Rory's curses or the howls of K'tu, who was belching forth murderous threats against anyone who would so harm his beloved master.

While the old man was holding Rory's arching body down on the table, Ganimedes produced a bunch of slender withes, bark-peeled to a whiteness and tied together with a string. He handed them to Tio Carlo who released his hold on Rory and bade him be quiet and then proceeded to belabor him with the switches. At first he did not lay on very hard and there was only a tingling sensation added to the fiery smarting of the broth, but as Tio Carlo increased his tempo, so did he increase the force of his strokes, until each descent of the birches seemed to cut into Rory's flesh, although he could see by raising his head that the strokes were so expertly applied that they did not break the skin.

K'tu was screaming as though each blow cut into his own flesh. Rory rolled from side to side on the table as much as his bonds would allow while the switching continued without mercy along the tender skin inside his thighs and up onto the tautness of his belly. Tio Carlo's flogging tapered off more from exhaustion than any desire on his part to stop, but now the smarting of Rory's skin was augmented by a fierce fire in his belly which the mysterious draught had kindled. Tio Carlo pinched out the four tapers, gasping for breath so violently that he could hardly mutter in his high sing-song voice some unintelligible jargon that Rory could not understand. The words were, he felt, some sort of prayer to an African heirarchy of gods who were malevolent and benevolent at the same time. Evidently they had some meaning for K'tu, for he stopped his keening and droned along with the old man.

For a few moments nothing happened. Then Rory felt cool, expert fingers grasp him with a pleasant rhythm of manipulations, timed to the rapidly mounting tempo of Tio Carlo's chanting. Despite the burning of his skin, the fire in his belly, and the soreness of his welted thighs, the pleasurable rhythm coursed through his body making him arch his back, this time in pure animal gratification rather than pain. Old Harry was standing once again and it seemed to Rory that he had never before achieved such puissant potency, such steel-like rigidity and such an infinite capability of pure sensuality. He gasped, sucking in his breath. The pleasure of those fingers' titillation was reaching a pitch which was well-nigh unbearable. He could contain himself no longer. With a scream of relief, he spilled out in a drenching torrent over his heated body. His relief was only temporary before the same overwhelming desire mounted again. He felt his bonds released, and his own anxious fingers probed in the darkness, prying away the fingers that had pleasured him so much. He identified them by their smoothness as those of Ganimedes. Now it was Rory's own turn to handle, to excite himself, and to assure himself once more that all was well. Thank whatever black gods had intervened for him, he was himself again. His fingers did not lie.

He heard the click of a flint and saw the glow of tinder breaking into a flame. Tio Carlo lit one of the candles and helped him down from the table.

"The spell broken, suh. You never be troubled again. Do never fear that yo'll lose any of dat power. See, it like a coconut palm." He grinned and pointed down to Rory. "Yo' goin' ter have ter work hard tonight ter git him down. He a-goin ter keep on a-spoutin' all night, suh." He leaned forward, his little black eyes sparkling in the candlelight. "Missus Fortescue tol' me she be a-waitin' fer yo' in her room. She a-goin' ter be plenty happy, too, 'bout that coconut palm. Yessuh! Mighty happy she a-goin' ter be. Go, man! Go jes' like'n yo' are. Ganimedes he 'tend to yon rantin' black man." His head nodded in K'tu's direction.

Rory reached out to grasp the birdlike claw of the old man. With the other he clutched the slim, cool fingers of Ganimedes—those same fingers which had so aroused him moments ago.

"I owe you much, both of you." He released Ganimedes' hand. "My jacket." He pointed to the crumpled garment on a chair.

Ganimedes handed it to him. Rory reached in the inside pocket and drew out a purse. The gold pieces he proffered were a liberal reward for both of them and they accepted them along with his praises and his gratitude. Hanging his clothes over one arm, he reached for one of the candles. Its light flickered out as he walked from the room, but he knew the way in the dark. Was not Old Harry there ahead of him, leading the way? He certainly was and Rory had Tio Carlo's promise that he would never fail him again, certainly not this night with Mary waiting for him in his bed.

CHAPTER XXXVIII

THE DOOR TO RORY'S ROOM STOOD AJAR, BUT despite the heat of the night the louvers at the single window in the room were tightly closed and the air was still and heavy. The feeble light that entered from the door did not extend much beyond the threshold, and the interior of the room was black with a darkness that seemed solid. Although Rory's thighs still burned fiercely from the pepper broth and the flogging, and the fire in his belly still smoldered, he was jubilant as he groped his way through the darkness, his hands outstretched before him as he explored the room for the bed. His hands located it and, with the knowledge that he was once again a man——complete, ready and rigid——he dropped his clothes on the floor. Never before that he could remember had he craved a woman more lustily or more immediately, and never had the prospects of a night with Mary been more alluring or stimulating. He eased himself down on the bed, physically exhausted from his ordeal yet not too tired to move his hand across the smooth sheet to where Mary lay.

Much to his surprise there was no answering move to meet him. She must have dropped off to sleep, he rationalized, and yet, knowing Mary as he did, it would be so unlike her to doze. She should be, so his male egotism prompted him, awake and anxious to know the results of the experiment she had instigated. But then, he grinned with self-satisfaction, the results were so startling as to satisfy even her——and how he would satisfy her this night! This one bout would make up for all the frustrations of the day. His other hand, reaching down with prideful assurance, confirmed that he had never been more able, not even when as a horny lad he had tipped over his first Mary in a hedgerow. Releasing himself, albeit not without a powerful throb of self-satisfaction, he heaved closer to Mary's sleeping body, stretching out his hand to cup her breast. Strangely enough she did not wake up nor did she respond by any move toward him; she did not even whisper his name, and her silence made him a bit resentful. After all, it was she who had arranged all this; it was she who should be rejoicing with him instead of lying there, stupefied by sleep. His hand moved from the flaccid nipple which had, much to his surprise, not responded as usual by hardening under his touch, down into the cleft between her breasts. It encountered a sticky substance, cold and gelled. Now his exploring fingers moved faster, frightened by this strange encounter, until they finally touched the cold hardness of steel. Moving upward, his

408

fingers felt the wooden handle and confirmed his worst fears—it was a knife, deeply embedded in Mary's chest.

"Mary!" What left his lungs as a shout of terror froze in his throat, and he was conscious that his scream was nothing but a hoarse whisper. Frantically his fingers sought her face, lingering for a moment over her breathless mouth. He raised himself up on one elbow, shaking her, knowing even as he did that there could be no response. Bounding out of bed with a sudden revulsion for the lifeless body beside him, he searched his jacket for his tinder box, and with shaking hands he managed to strike the flint and steel together and forced enough breath from his lips to blow on the tinder until it burst into flame. It gave sufficient light for him to locate the candle on the stand beside the bed, and he applied the flame, letting it come alive and soar up to rive the darkness.

Its light proved that what he had dreaded was true. Mary was dead. She lay a little on her side, and the edge of the bed away from him was encarmined with her blood. The knife buried in her breast was one of the big wooden-handled carving knives from the kitchen. Now, gulping his lungs full of air, he was finally able to scream, and he ran from the room, stumbling and falling over the supine figure of K'tu, who had followed him and stretched himself across his doorway. He recovered himself and dashed along the passageway, banging on all the doors until the whole patio echoed and re-echoed with his cries.

Lights appeared first in one room and then another. Tim and a trembling Penny emerged; then Mama Phoebe, clutching a sheet about her mountain of flesh and almost hiding the slim black boy who had been picked out for her night's pleasuring. Peter and Ganimedes sheepishly emerged from another room, clutching their pantaloons at the waist; and lastly, old Tio Carlo, still in his rags, crawled out from the kitchen.

They all stood around Rory, waiting for him to stop his screaming gibberish. Awed into momentary silence, they stared at him stark naked before them, questioning him with their frightened eyes and each wondering what had caused him, even now in his frenzy, to appear so mastlike rampant before them. During that moment which stretched into an eternity, he stared back at them without the ability to stop his meaningless howling. It was Tim who recovered first, sufficient to form intelligible words.

"What is it? Before God, what's happened, Rory? Are you sick or mad or both?"

Rory came to what senses he had left. "Mary, Mary, Mary! Don't you understand? It's Mary! She's been murdered!"

"Miss Mary?" Mama Phoebe tightened her sheet about her. "You say Miss Mary, Missus Fortescue?"

Rory could only point dumbly toward his room where the light of the candle gilded the tiles of the passageway. Mama Phoebe she ran toward it. The rest followed her.

"My God in heaven, it true." She knelt beside the bed, her two black hands chafing Mary's lifeless white one. "Someun did her in. Killed my Missus Fortescue. Oh, God in heaven, who all did that dirty thing? Who killed my Miss Mary?"

"And why?" Rory's tears stung his eyes, and he came nearer as Mama Phoebe struggled to her feet and enveloped him with one black arm.

"Let me in dere." It was Tio Carlo's piping voice. He edged his way past Tim and Penny, past Peter and Ganimedes. His hand reached out to take Mary's in his. With birdlike talons he groped for her wrist, seeking some pulse, but there was none. His lips in a grim line, he shook his head dolefully. "She shore daid. Cain' he'p that pore missy nohow. Thinkin' mayhap I could if'n she not all daid, but she a-gone. Pore li'l missy."

A weird wailing came from Penny, which was taken up by Mama Phoebe—a high-pitched ululating keening that stopped as abruptly as it had started.

Mama Phoebe cut her keening on a high note. She released Rory, grabbed the screaming Penny, and shook her. "Ain' no use us'n's standing here a-doin' nothin'. Ain' no time fer mournin' now. Got ter do what we kin fer pore Missus Fortescue and got ter find us who done it. Thinkin' I know."

"I think I know too," Rory's brain had begun to function with a bodily return to normalcy.

410

"It that good-fer-nothin' bitch, Maria, that's who 'tis." Mama Phoebe pronounced sentence on the Diabless.

"It her. She not a-wantin' no other woman ter have him." Tio Carlo confirmed his sister's pronouncement.

"Then whereat she be now?" Mama Phoebe peered around the room as though Maria might be hiding in the shadows.

"She done kited out, that whereat she be," Tio Carlo answered her. "Jes' a-kited out."

"If'n we could fin' her skin under a crock, whereat she a-hidin' it, could keep her from gittin' back into it." It was the first time Ganimedes had spoken.

"She ain' a-flyin' 'round 'thout'n her skin tonight. She lit out somewhere. 'Sides, you know she ain' no Soucouyan 'n cain't do it nohow."

Rory recalled how Maria had said that she and Peter had hidden themselves while all the other slaves had been sold and then had returned to the plantation afterward. He questioned Peter, who said they had never really left the house but had hidden in a dark closet off the kitchen used for storing vegetables. Rory dispatched him, along with Tim, to look there.

"Yo' better git yore clotheses on," Mama Phoebe told Rory. " 'N yo' boy." She pointed to the nameless boy who had accompanied her. "Go 'n git yo'sel' dressed. Ain' no one interested in seein' yore bare ass now, least o' all me. Yo', Penny, climb inta yore shift, h'ist yo'self ter the kitchen, blow up the fire, 'n put on a kittle o' water 'n come back here. We got to wash Missus Fortescue 'n git her laid out 'fore she start ter stiffen up. Now git, all o' yo'. Take yore boy, that Ganimedes there, Carlo, 'n tell him ter git a pot o' coffee started. If'n he kin cook up them brews o' you 'n 'pears like'n he kin make coffee. Gits ourselves somethin' in our stomachs, better we send Mr. Tim off ter town 'n report this ter the 'Lustrious Cabildo. This's murder 'n better we git started a-findin' out 'bout that goddamn Maria. She done it, sure's hell's a-tootin'."

"She did it, Mama; she did it," Rory agreed.

"Co'se the bitch done done it. Ain' no questionin' in mah min', but accusin's one thing 'n findin' her's another. Better yo' go, too, Mista Rory. Doin' what we kin fer pore

411

Missus Fortescue's a woman's job. Ain' much we kin do, but necessary we do what we kin, Penny 'n me."

He struggled into his clothes and left the room, wandering disconsolately up and down the gallery. Now, with Mary gone, he was more convinced than ever that he had really loved her. She was good, Mary was, good through and through. Yes, she had been a whore, a dockside strumpet in Glasgow and a whoremistress in Trinidad, but above and beyond all that, she'd been a fine warm-hearted woman. The finest he'd ever known. Nobody could be more unselfish or more generous than Mary. She was all that any man could ask for in a wife. Why hadn't she accepted him? Because she was unselfish. She'd been willing to tie herself up with the worthless Fortescue because he had meant nothing to her. Now Rory could see that she had not been willing to marry him because she had loved him too much. Dear Mary! Dear, dear girl! It was too late now to tell her how much he loved her, but perhaps she knew. Perhaps she understood now and it was no longer necessary for words. Perhaps she'd always be there, right beside him to help him as she had in the past. He hoped so. God knows, he needed her. He could no longer control his tears. His sobbing embarrassed him but he did not care who saw him; he did not mind even when Timmy and the boy Peter came back to say that Maria was not hidden in the closet, nor was she in the barns or any of the hiding places that Peter knew. Would Peter tell them if he did know? Indeed he would. He loved Mr. Tim and he loved Mr. Rory too. As for Maria, Peter spat on the ground. Even if she was his sister, he hated her. She was always trying to make him do nasty things with her—things he couldn't do and wouldn't want to do if he could.

And now, Rory was faced with something he didn't want to do either. Bury Mary. Put that glorious body into the ground. Say farewell to it forever. He sat down disconsolately on a bench at the far end of the patio where a mass of bougainvillea cast an even darker shadow over him. Tim sat beside him, sharing his silence, while K'tu came to squat cross-legged on the floor less than an arm's length away. After a time Ganimedes came from the kitchen with a mug of steaming coffee and when Rory tasted it he silently thanked the boy for the strong, lacing of Jamaica rum.

The door to Mary's room remained closed, although once Penny had come out and gone to the kitchen to return with another pan of hot water. At length, after what seemed hours, Mama Phoebe and Penny both emerged. Penny was crying and Tim advanced to put comforting arms around her. Mama Phoebe, seeing the empty cup on the bench beside Rory, scolded him for not having eaten anything and went to fetch something more substantial than rum-laced coffee. When she brought bread and eggs, he devoured them without tasting them. The fire had not entirely disappeared form his stomach but the food seemed to quench that which remained. He was no longer engorged with desire. Tragedy had dulled his seemingly unconquerable passion.

He did not know how long he sat there with K'tu at his feet. Occasionally one of the others would pass him: Mama Phoebe on an errand of some kind; Tim comforting Penny; old Tio Carlo shambling along in his greasy rags; Ganimedes and Peter arm in arm, giggling between themselves as they continued to seek other hiding places where Maria might possibly be but where they hoped to have moments alone in the darkness.

Rory sat there for hours before he noticed a flush of pale light in the east, then a gradual lightening of the sky. A new day was about to dawn. He stood, then sat down again. There was nothing for him to do right now; he could not start for town until it grew lighter. His head started to nod drowsily. He napped, still conscious of whatever small movements went on about him, but erasing some of his grief in numbness of sleep.

A commotion outside the patio gate awoke him to broad daylight and brilliant sun. He heard shouts, the stomping and whinnying of horses, the jangle of bits and the whine of leather upon leather, interspersed with the shouts of men demanding admittance. He lifted his head to see Mama Phoebe lumbering past him, strained his ears to hear the distant conversation, then saw her slip back the big bolts and open the gate. Several men entered, and one, who appeared to be in command and wore a black sash embroidered with silver lace, walked toward Rory. He was a tall man dressed in shabby black, and his tricorne hat also sported some tarnished lace and a cockade of red and scarlet feathers. He advanced to where Rory was sitting.

"You are Sir Roderick Mahound." The peremptory statement was not a question.

Rory glanced up at him. Then he stood up slowly, scanning the man's face carefully. "And you, sir? Who might you be?"

"John Fredericks, Aguacil of the Illustrious Cabildo."

"Whatever that may be."

"We still use the Spanish terms here." The man's voice dropped a little as though apologizing for something so entirely un-English. "We've not changed the office as yet. You might say I'm the constable of the town council."*

"Then you have saved me a trip, sir. I was waiting until daylight to ride into town and report to you."

"To report a murder and give yourself up?"

"To report a murder, but by no means to give myself up. What do you mean by that?"

"That you are the murderer and that I am here to arrest you, Sir Roderick Mahound. I formally arrest you in the name of His Britannic Majesty for the murder of Mrs. Mary Fortescue of Port of Spain."

"You'll do nothing of the sort!"

"I'll do it and be damned to you. You'll either go along with me peaceably or we'll carry you over the saddle like a sack of corn. As to whether you're innocent or not, that's for the governor to decide. He's judge and jury right now until we get a full court of English law set up. Are you coming or," he pointed to the several men who had followed him, "do we take you with us by force?"

"This is ridiculous." Anger was overcoming sorrow in Rory's mind just as sorrow had overcome passion. "I'm Sir Roderick Mahound, Baron of Sax and Prince of Sa'aqs. I'm here to sell an important cargo of slaves. Mrs.

* For many years after Trinidad had been taken over by the English, the Spanish form of government persisted in the Cabildo, the town council.

414

Fortescue was my best and oldest friend. Why should I murder her? I know who killed her. It was a mulatto wench, a slave of Mrs. Fortescue's by the name of Maria."

"You have witnesses to the fact?"

"No, but we all know it was she who did it."

Fredericks shifted his tricorne onto the back of his head and stared at Rory, his lips curling. "Now aren't you getting things twisted around? She's the one who's accusing you. Said she saw you do it with her own eyes. She rode into Port of Spain, roused up a notary from his bed, and gave him her sworn statement under oath with all the details; and those details sound pretty damaging against you. It's a likely story; sufficient to warrant your arrest. Now are you going to come with us or do I again have to threaten you with force?"

Rory paced up and down, taking short, contemplative steps before the constable. He looked to Tim, mutely seeking advice, then to Mama Phoebe.

"Might's well go 'long with 'em, son." She nodded her head gravely, glancing from him to the constable and back again. "Might jes' as well. They fin' out yo' innocent. Then they cotch up wid dat Maria and jail her. She done it. We all knows 'at." She emphasized her words with a waggle of her sausage-fat forefinger at the constable.

"I'll go." Rory had resigned himself. "I'll have my servant harness horses for us and"—he turned to Tim—"you'll ride along with me, Timmy?"

"That I will."

"'Twill not be necessary—nor permitted." The constable's words were spoken with the finality of authority. "You'll not need a servant where you're going. We're taking no chances. You'll go with us alone." The other men with him nodded their heads in agreement. It was not entirely to their liking to arrest a white man—an Englishman—on the word of a mulatto slave, but it was true that Mrs. Fortescue was dead and evidence did most certainly point to Rory. Mary Fortescue's death spelled only misfortune and inconvenience for them; all of them had, at one time or another, been her customers and felt friendly

415

toward her. Mary had been popular and well liked in Port of Spain; she was almost a civic figure.

Rory resented the manacles that were put on his wrists when he mounted his horse for the ride into Port of Spain. He was no ordinary criminal and they could have taken his word that he would not esape but neither his assurances nor, in the end, his abject pleading were able to sway them. He was ignominiously handcuffed, and the reins of his horse were taken by the rider in front of him. He could do nothing but follow along with another rider behind him. He calmed K'tu who had to be restrained when he saw his master thus treated, and he reassured both Tim and Mama Phoebe that everything would come out all right.

But he was not so sure himself that it would. He already sensed a change in the attitude of the men toward him. From the moment they left Melrose they were no longer respectfully subservient as they had been at first because of his title. He realized that they were envious of him and that their own importance had been magnified by the fact that they were now superior to that well-nigh sacrosanct personage—an English baron. Consciously or unconsciously they were reacting to it; a bloody toff, his hands manacled, under arrest! It was a new experience for them and they were quick to take advantage of it with curt commands, and once, even though it was done so as to seem inadvertent and an accident, he felt the sting of a man's riding crop on his arm.

It was midmorning when they entered Port of Spain. As their little procession progressed down Charlotte Street, it attracted quite a following of whites, free Negroes, and slaves who were all curious about the well-dressed man with the long yellow hair, being led a prisoner through the streets.

However, an even greater ignominy awaited him. The procession, now augmented by the rabble that followed it, continued on to Brunswick Square which was, despite its grand name, just a treeless, dusty savannah in the center of the town. They crossed it, accompanied by the hoots and jeers of the crowd, to the iron cage which had recently been erected there for the incarceration of criminals. Bare

416

and gaunt it stood, virtually roofless: a nine-foot cube of solid iron bars, entirely open on all sides, affording not even a modicum of privacy to the hapless individual who might be imprisoned there. Rory was prodded down off his horse and forced to stand waiting before the door of the cage while one of the men rode to the house of the *alcalde*—one of the two magistrates in the town—to get the key. After what seemed hours, although they were actually only minutes, the man returned, the key grated in the lock, the iron-barred door swung open on rusty hinges, and Rory was pushed inside. The door closed with a metallic clang which caused the whole cage to quiver. The lock grated again and the constable and his aides left. There was no reason for them to remain because no guard was necessary; there was no possible way that Rory could escape.

Although the Aguacil and his men had departed, most of the motley mob remained, pressing close against the iron bars of the cage. Rory was discussed in Spanish, French, Italian, and Hausa. White, brown, and black fingers pointed at him, and hands extended through the bars to pluck and tear at his clothing until he found safety in the exact center of the cage. Then the pelting began. A youngster with an overripe mango was the first and his aim, although hampered by the iron bars, was sufficiently good so that the fruit caught Rory on the side of the head. The guffaws of laughter that greeted this juvenile trick inspired a search by even the more mature members of the crowd, and soon Rory was the butt of a barrage of rotted fruit—plantains, mangoes, avocados, guavas—which was augmented by an assortment of overripe eggs, cabbages, and a variety of decomposing vegetables. He stood facing his tormentors first on one side and then the other, trying unsuccessfully to dodge their missiles but to no avail. Finally admitting defeat, he slumped down in one corner of the cage, and covered his head with his arms. A trickle of warm liquid seeped through the material of his coat, running down over his skin, and he turned to see a grinning Negro leaning against the cage, his pantaloons open, urinating on him. Cheers greeted this essay and others lined up to bespatter him. Like an animal, he

417

crawled to the center of the cage and slumped there, deaf and blind to the jeering mob. The sun beat down upon him, the choking dust swirled about him, the juices of the rotted fruits congealed on his skin, and the stench of urine clung to his clothing. He was perishing of thirst, exhausted from the sleepless night and the torturing ministrations of Tio Carlo. Frustrated in his desires for Mary; plunged into grief by her death; utterly hopeless, tormented, filthy, and abandoned, he was ready to welcome death.

Clouds—towering white cumulus clouds—built up in the clear blue of the sky, sailing across it like elephantine white-sailed galleons. In their stately progress they mercifully blotted out the sun. Their white freshness changed to an ugly gray and presaged rain, which was enough to disperse Rory's tormentors. The first raindrops, big and fat, fell, and he was abandoned in a graying world, hearing only the beat of the rain and the lashing of the palm fronds. It drove down upon him and its wet freshness provided some relief. He opened his mouth, trying to get enough of the moisture to swallow, then caught it in his hands and gulped it greedily. It washed the scum of filth from his face and clothes and cooled the fever of his body.

But, as the storm increased in its driving furor, the rain slashed across his face like the rawhide thongs of a whip. His clothes became a sodden mass and where before he had been suffering from the heat, he was now cold and shaking with a sudden ague. But there was at least water for his parched throat. He removed his coat and wrung it out, holding it before his upturned mouth so that a trickle could run down his throat. Without his coat the rain beat through the thin cambric of his shirt. Unable to stand any longer, he sank to his knees on the iron bars and the slippery mud that floored his cage; then, with the torrent belting down on him, he collapsed on his belly, his arms outstretched. Gradually the steaming torrent subsided to only occasional spatterings; then these too ceased and he felt a warmth on his back. The sun was out again and his clothes began to steam so that he longed to shiver once again in the rain. Hours passed.

The silence was broken by the clop-clop of horses'

hooves and the grinding of carriage wheels as they came to a stop. He heard voices. One of them was a woman's and had a cultured twang that seemed familiar. The other was a man's, high-pitched, weary, and querulous. They seemed to be arguing.

"But I tell you he's a murderer, my dear." It was the voice of the man.

"Lud, lud, is he, Sir Basil?" The woman's voice questioned. "Where's our much-touted English justice which claims that a man is innocent until he be proven guilty? Bah! This man may be a murderer, as you say, but it's not yet been proved against him. Furthermore he's an Englishman, and if I'm not mistaken, one of title. What an example you're setting for the niggers, allowing him to be treated as an animal before their very eyes."

Rory peered between the bars in the direction of the voices. Lady Mary and a man who must have been the governor were seated in a coach which was painted and decorated, albeit crudely, to simulate a state coach. Lady Mary's white hand pointed to him through the opened window of the coach.

"Let them pelt one white man with garbage, sir, and they'll get the idea that they can throw rotten eggs at you or me. You've got to keep them in their place. You can't allow a white man, an Englishman, to be treated with disrespect like this. They'll lose their awe for us and we'll all end up with our throats slit just like the French in Haiti if you allow a thing like this to go on."

The man's voice was patient as though he were well accustomed to listening to her tirades. "But we've no gaol, my dear. We gave it up when you complained of the stench from the cells under Government House."

"That I did and stink they did, but they're still there and my advice to you is to put one of them to use. Have this man taken there, unless you want to lose what little respect these idiots in Trinidad have for you."

Sir Basil raised a gold lorgnette attached to a black silk ribbon and gave Rory the benefit of a long and searching stare.

"You may be right, my dear. You just may be right."

"Of course I am." Catching Rory's eye, she touched her lips as a caution to him not to indicate he knew her.

Sir Basil patted her arm with a gesture that let his fingers slide hopefully along her flesh. She edged away from his hand. "How very right you are, sir, to agree with me. No wonder you make such an able administrator." Lady Mary settled back in her seat as the coach drove away.

Later that evening, after it was fully dark, a sergeant in command of a platoon of soldiers came to the cage and unlocked the door. With gruff but not unpleasant words, he bade Rory come out. The platoon closed about him and he marched with them, alone in a hollow square, the short distance to Government House. They took him around in back where a flight of stone steps led down to an iron-barred door. It opened with a grating of hinges and Rory was brought inside. At the end of a narrow corridor, he entered an iron-grated cell. Against the wall a plank bed was suspended by chains and Rory noticed that it had a mattress and had been spread with a clean sheet. A candle burned in a pewter candlestick on a rough table. A pair of clean cotton pantaloons and a shirt were hung over the back of the single straight chair. There was a plate on the table with an earthen bowl over it to keep the contents hot. The sergeant left after locking the barred door, not forgetting to doff his cap and make a respectful nod of his head.

Slipping off his filthy clothes, Rory donned the clean dry ones. He discovered a comb on a shelf under a cracked mirror and saw that there was also a razor. But before he used them, he turned to the table, lifted the bowl and attacked the plate of hot spiced meat and vegetables. He stuffed himself voraciously and the food settled in his stomach with a warm and comfortable glow. Stumbling to the bed, he threw himself upon it and slept, ignoring Old Harry who, despite all Rory's tribulations, was once again demanding recognition.

CHAPTER XXXIX

THROUGHOUT THE NIGHT RORY NEVER dreamed but slept the heavy, drugged sleep of exhaustion. How long he slept he did not know, but when he finally awoke he opened his eyes to a brightness in the cell which filtered through a matted thatching of vines that covered the one small grated window high in the thick masonry. Almost unconsciously his hand sought the pulsating turgescence of his body and grasped it with a sigh of relief and contentment. At least that problem was solved, and the warmth of his clutching hand provoked such a series of delightful fantasies that he could not resist moving it, at first slowly and then with a frenzied tempo which proved, almost at once, that he was in all ways fully recovered. He stretched out lazily, satiated for the moment, letting his feet hang over the edge of the thin mattress until his breathing became regular again, and then, opening his eyes once more, he oriented himself in his cell, recalling but dimly how it had looked through his tired eyes the night before.

It was as he had remembered it except now, in the heat of the day, there was a cool dampness which smelled of masonry and decaying of leaves. Pushing himself up, he sat still for a moment, then swung his legs over the edge and stood, stretching his muscles, his arms high over his head; he looked up to the crumbling plaster of the ceiling. The walls were of stone, glistening with damp and the iridescent slime of snails' meandering pathways. The bed, the table, the chair, the iron bars for a door, and the huge padlock were all as they had been the night before. There was only one small thing which had changed. A tray covered with a clean white napkin had been placed on the table and the bowl that had contained the stew which he had fallen upon so ravenously last night had disappeared.

He found himself again so hungry that he did not even bother to wash his face in the bucket of water that stood on the floor just inside the grilled door. He sat down at the table, pulled off the napkin and saw a compote of fresh fruit—ripe bananas, pineapples, and mango, cut up and sprinkled with grated coconut and sugar; a loaf of crusty bread, and an earthenware pot, still warm, of coffee. But more than the food, more than the tantalizing aroma of fresh bread or the desire to slake his dry throat with coffee, his interest centered on the thin hoop of gold wire with pendent decorations that was on the plate beside the bread. It was one of Almera's earrings—a trifle he had bought for her one day in the bazaar of Sa'aqs. He remembered the day and waves of nostalgia swept over him. He was homesick for Baba, for the mud palace of Sa'aqs, for another of those scented nights in his hareem with any one of his beauties, but most especially—he picked up the earring, listening to the faint jingle of the dangles—with Almera.

So . . . Almera had access to his cell. She had come in while he was sleeping and left the tray with his breakfast. He wondered if she had looked down at him, sleeping there on the hard planking and if her eyes had gloried in what they had seen. Would that she had tarried to wake him. Even the ministrations of her hand would have been more acceptable than the sterility of his own. The one thing in life he was certain he could depend on was Almera's devotion. His fingers toyed with the earring. Surely if Almera had the keys to his dungeon, he could escape? Yet, as he chewed the crusty bread and drank the strong coffee, he realized how stupid that would be. Escape from what? He was not guilty of Mary's murder; it was only a matter of hours before he would go free. Certainly he had friends in Trinidad who were already trying to establish his innocence. Jehu and Elphinstone would by now be apprised of his dilemma and would be working for him. And there was Tim. And Lady Mary! Was she a friend? That was doubtful, and yet were it not for her he would still be caged in that devilish contraption, like some wild animal snared alive. Lady Mary must be his friend in spite of everything. The meager comforts of his cell, the breakfast, and the earring that Almera had left all testified to her influence over the piddling Sir Basil.

Now that he had wolfed the food he felt better, with all his bodily needs satisfied for the instant. He stripped off the trousers and shirt which had been provided for him and scrubbed himself with the water and the small bar of soap which he found, combed his dripping locks with the wooden comb, and then, for lack of anything else to do, paced the length and breadth of his cell, counting the ten steps in one direction and the six in the other until he had reached a figure that ran up into the hundreds. Tiring of this activity, although he had needed the exercise after yesterday's crouching and cringing in the cage, he went to the door of his cell, rested his elbows on one of the crosswise iron bars, and clung with his hands to the uprights. The space between the bars was too small for him to stick his head through, but he was able to get a slanting view of a long, grim, stone-lined corridor with a series of barred doors like his own and an open door at one end which let in the light; a door at the other end, also open, gave a glimpse of ascending stairs. There was neither movement nor sound in the corridor, and he was, he felt sure, the only prisoner. He could have wished for others; even the sound of another man's breathing would have been welcome. The quiet of his cell pressed down on him like a weight. What could he do? He had indulged himself before getting up; he had eaten his breakfast; he had washed himself and combed his hair; he had paced his cell and he had leaned, peering out like a caged panther; now there was nothing else to do and he was thoroughly bored.

Rory had never been one to enjoy being alone; he had always depended on the excitement of companionship with others. He was a purely physical person and the nearness of another, be it male or female, was necessary to him. Now he was alone, dependent on his own thoughts with nobody to share them with. Damn! He couldn't stand it. He had to talk with somebody or at least be aware of their presence. He made a quick circuit of his cell, then threw himself down on the bed, propped his head up on his hands and stared out into space, alone with his thoughts, trying to control the restlessness of his muscles which demanded action. He wished he could go back to sleep, but he was much too wide awake. Damn! Something would have to happen. He'd have to get out of this place; the walls were closing in on him. A wild howl of senseless protest rose in his throat, but he strangled it. That would be stupid. If he were to make his presence here obnoxious, he'd find himself out in the cage again and no matter how confining the cell might be and how he missed companionship, it was a lot better than the crowds of yesterday, with the curious eyes staring at him and enemy hands pelting him with garbage. He tried to resign himself, but each minute dragged on like an hour.

And it must have been several hours before he heard a welcome sound, a scraping of feet on the stairs at the end of the corridor. With a bound he was off the bed, his neck craning as far as possible to get the widest view of the stairs. It was not Almera. The high-heeled satin slippers with the buckles of brilliants and the hem of a sprigged taffeta gown which covered a froth of beribboned white lace petticoats could never have belonged to Almera. He waited for the feet to descend, saw the voluminous belled skirt followed by a slender waist and then the fullness of breasts in a precariously confining bodice and the milky whiteness of arms. Finally the pink paleness of the face and the gold pile of ringlets identified her. He wondered what the result of this interview might be.

At the bottom of the steps, Lady Mary glanced furtively around as if to make sure that she had not been followed. Spying Rory's arms through the grating, she raised both hands, palm up, waving her fingers, then covered her mouth with one hand to enjoin silence. Her little slippers made no noise as she ran along the corridor and when she arrived at the grating of his cell, she clung to the bars for support and then to his hands.

"Damn you for a vile rogue, Mahound." The sharpness of her words did not lessen her grip on his hands. "So you slit your fancy woman's throat, did you? Well, 'twas only

424

what the strumpet deserved. A common whore she was, and she ended like one at the hands of one of her lovers."

He tried to free himself from her grip, but she clung to him desperately. At that moment he would have slapped her, forgetting in his anger how much depended on her good will. He choked back his choler.

"Mary's death was not at my hands, milady. She was by far the finest woman I ever met, whoremistress though she was, but withal a lady, even a great lady. That's what she was. Believe me, I'm innocent of her death or any other woman's. And believe me in another thing, I'm grateful to you for taking me out of that cage. 'Tis far more comfortable here."

"And safe, too." The venom was disappearing from her words. "There's a wild and vengeful hue and cry against you, my lad. Half the men of Port of Spain are talking about hanging you, and you'd not have been safe in the cage another day. They'd have killed you." Her arms entered through the bars to clasp around his neck. "Oh, Rory, you despicable low-down scoundrel, I love you so much. I've tried to kill that love in every way possible. I've damned you to the floor of hell and then prayed that I'd get you back again. I've wanted you so much that I consorted with that nigger stud of Mrs. Fortescue's, just pretending that he was you. Rory, Rory, Rory, what have you done to me?"

"Nothing, except to rape you once, which I've always regretted. Frankly, you were a damned poor fuck, milady. Probably the worst I ever had. That's why I regretted it."

"But *I* haven't. Never. Oh, Rory, my very darling, had I the key, I'd enter your cell now and this time, if you would not rape me, I'd rape you. But could I? I must remember how miserably you failed me recently."

"Through no fault of my own." He could boast again. "A yellow wench at Melrose decided that she wanted me all to herself and put a spell on me—some African mumbojumbo—which made me useless to all other women except herself."

"As if I'd believe that!"

"You'll have to, because it's true, though I'd not have believed it myself if I'd not experienced it. Well, in matters like this one fights fire with fire—obeah with obeah. I went through a blazing furnace in my guts to get Old Harry to stand up again. That's why poor Mary Fortescue was killed. The wench who'd put the evil spell on me did away with her. 'Twas Mary who'd arranged to have me cured and the wench knew it. So she stabbed her with a kitchen knife and ran into town and spread the news that I'd done poor Mary in. 'Twas her revenge on me." He reached out through the bars and drew her to him. Their lips met through the bars. His tongue forced its way between her teeth while they clung to each other with wordless little moans and half-audible mutterings of endearment.

"You've not the key, Yasmin?" His voice was hoarse as he moved his mouth an inch away for hers.

"You think of keys at a moment like this?" Her anger rose quickly.

"Hush! Why must you always take me wrong? I was thinking only of removing these iron bars from between us."

"Oh, darling," she was properly contrite, "why must I always jump down your throat? My nature, I guess. I'm nothing but a vixen, a spitfire, a . . . "

"Darling." His hands had crept under her bodice.

She gave herself to him for a long moment, lost in the fervor of his lovemaking.

"The key, darling? Alas, I do not have it. Spiggott, he's the sergeant in charge of the guards, he has it. This morning I had Almera prepare your breakfast and bring it down to you. Spiggott accompanied her and opened the door for her."

"I knew that she had been here."

"But how? She said you were sleeping soundly when she left the tray."

He released her to fumble in his pocket and draw out the earring. She nodded in recognition.

"The girl worships you, Rory."

"Yes, I know. She has always loved me and I must confess I've loved her, too, but not. . . . Oh, Mary, Mary, Mary, oh, Yasmin, what have you done to me to change all my feelings so suddenly?"

"I said she worshipped you, Rory, but I did not say that she loved you. There's a difference, you know."

"No. That girl would give her life for me."

"Granted. She has that peculiar loyalty which only Moorish girls have. You're her master. She'd do anything you ask, even pretend she loves you, and you'd never know the difference, but I happen to know differently. She's in love with another."

"I don't believe it."

"You'll probably never believe that any woman could care more for another than she could for you. You're vain, pompous, and conceited, Rory. You see, I know all your faults and yet I still love you. And I can tell them to you because I'm not afraid of you. But, as much as it hurts your vanity, I'll tell you one thing more; Almera is madly in love with Fayal."

"With Fayal? With that prick that walks like a man?"

"But remember that he is a man and that Almera is a woman. There's no accounting for love, Rory. Look around you. Did you ever stop to think what some particular woman might see in some particular man or what he might see in her? No, we cannot question what Almera and Fayal see in each other. She would never have told you because she worships you with the dumb and docile love of a dog for a master—or of a devoted slave for a master. And, I must confess, that is the way I love you, too. I'd willingly be your slave and worship you as my master, but remember this, I'm not docile."

"Nobody could ever accuse you of that." He grinned.

"And I never intend to be. You may think that's what you want, but docility and meek obedience is not what you are looking for in a woman. You've been spoiled by all those fawning creatures in your hareem who were so anxious for a real man after fooling around with stupid eunuchs that they cozened you into thinking they were all mad about you. We're evenly matched, Rory. I'm no doormat for you to wipe your feet on. I'll not cringe and bow to you and follow you about with downcast eyes, waiting patiently for that crumb of love whenever you want to cast it in my direction. Never! And yet I'll say this

427

and you had better believe me. No woman could love you more than I do and can. I'll prove it to you now."

"Hush, it's no time for talking, Yasmin." His hand returned the earring to his pocket and then came through the bars to clasp hers. Slowly he pulled her hand down through the bars, a captive willing to be led; it progressed over the flatness of his belly, halting while he undid the one button that held together his waistband, then a little way further through the mat of tight, curled hair, to grasp, to clasp, and to marvel.

"The treatment was most evidently efficacious." She smiled at him before her lips sought him.

"As you can see." His arms pulled her toward him, crushing her body against the unyielding iron. "Damn these bars!" His body was reacting to the slow movements of her hand.

"And double damn them!" She seemed no longer able to support herself and slid down through his arms to her knees while he surrendered to her. He looked down at her in disbelief. Could this be Mary? Was this the haughty wench who had fought off sultans and beys and was now on her knees before him, humiliating herself in this most abject and groveling form of love? Could this possibly be she—this slave, slobbering over him willingly, unmindful of the iron bars that separated them? Was this the pink and gold loveliness of that English spitfire who had damned and cursed him and was now demeaning herself out of love for him? She had said that she would prove her love for him, and yet, despite his very eyes and the evidence which could not be denied, it was hard to believe it was she—Lady Mary, Yasmin. He gazed down at her, slack mouthed, until he felt for the second time that morning the fluids rising in him and his knees buckled under him. His hands clung to the bars for support and he sucked in huge lungfuls of air until he was forced to expel them and flatten himself weakly against the bars, gasping for breath. Even then she was unwilling to release him, and he was forced to pull himself away from her.

She stood up smiling. "There's an old saying, Rory, that love laughs at locksmiths. I've found it to be true, but not altogether satisfactory. Look, darling, I've a fertile mind, as you may well know. . . ."

"As I have just found out," he said, readjusting his trousers. He was able to talk once more although he could still not believe what had happened.

"And I'll think of something. I'm sure to." She brushed the dust of the floor from the sprigged taffeta and retreated a few steps, holding up a warning finger. They both listened. Somewhere up above a door opened and there were heavy footsteps on the stairs. In another moment, they could see the thick-soled boots of a man descending the steps. The boots became a pair of soiled white breeches and a blue jacket and then were followed by a florid face with a cockaded leather shako above it.

"Milady!" The soldier clicked his heels in sudden surprise and saluted. Realizing that this was hardly the correct form of address, he shot one leg behind him and bowed. "Milady Cleverden." He was thoroughly shocked at her presence there.

"Dear Sergeant Spiggott," she was all fluttery apologies and blushing confusion, "you've discovered my little escapade. Curiosity, Sergeant, just female curiosity, nothing more. I felt I just must lay eyes on this bloodthirsty ruffian who goes about the country murdering women, or so 'tis said. I thought it far more interesting to see him alive and breathing than dancing on the end of a rope."

"And that's where he's going to end up, milady. Believe me. The whole town's up in arms. Seems that Mrs. Fortescue was a prime favorite here, beggin' your pardon, and there's not a man in the whole town but what's wanting to blast this rogue to hell, begging your pardon, with a shot of ball. Lucky he'll be to live till his trial. But Sir Basil says that justice must be done and that the man must stand trial to determine whether or not he's guilty, even though we all know he's guilty as hell."

She batted her lashes at the red-faced sergeant and sidled almost up to him. "So in the meatime you'll have to protect him, Sergeant, and also, he'll have to eat. I'll have my woman prepare him something for midday. We can't starve him to death if he's going to swing from the end of a rope."

"That we can't, but if I had my way it would be bread and water for a scoundrel the likes of him."

"Agreed, Sergeant, yet we must not forget that he's an English peer, must we? And even in the Tower of London, an English peer has certain considerations in the way of food and lodging. He's entitled to it."

"Them's his Excellency's orders, milady. Food for him from his own kitchen, he says, and a sheet for his bed and a chair to sit in and these." He held out a small box which he had been carrying behind his back. As he lowered it for Lady Mary to see its contents, Rory could see that it contained some sheets of paper, a couple of quills, an inkwell, and a shaker of sand. "So's he can write out his own defense if he so wishes, or communicate with his solicitor, although I doubt if there's one in all Trinidad who'd take over the case of such a murdering scoundrel."

Lady Mary looked first at the sergeant and then inventoried Rory from head to foot.

"Yet he scarcely looks like a murderer, does he, Sergeant?"

"It's them handsome ones who look as if butter wouldn't melt in their mouths that's always the worst. Innocent-lookin' they are, but ready to slip a knife into you at a moment's notice. 'Twas dangerous for you to be here with him alone."

She waved her hand in a deprecatory gesture. "He can't hurt me, locked up as he is. I just wanted a glimpse of him, that's all. But now I see it was ill advised on my part. We'll not say anything about it, will we, Sergeant? It will remain a little secret between us."

"That it will, milady. His Excellency would be stark raving mad if he knew about it."

"It won't happen again, I promise you. My curiosity is satisfied. And now I'll go upstairs and have my woman bring down his meal. Will you be here to unlock the door for her?"

"That I will, milady. I'll wait here." He opened the barred door of another cell and dragged out a chair which he stood against the wall opposite Rory's cell. With a sweep of her taffeta skirts and a lowering of her eyelid,

430

which was accompanied by a winning and conspiratorial smile to the sergeant, she was off and up the stairs.

The sergeant sat down, hitching his chair away from the wall so that he could tilt back comfortably in it. He leisurely twirled the ends of his huge moustache while he regarded Rory.

"You can thank your lucky stars you're a big brute," he sniggered and spat on the floor. "Big blokes like you hang easy. It's the little ones that don't weigh much that take a long time a-dying. Sometimes we have to pull on their legs to crack their neck. But you, you'll go easy. Just one swing on the rope and you'll be seeing them pearly gates opening wide for you—or that fiery furnace."

There was nothing Rory could say, no answer that he felt like giving. The iron bars which had at first seemed so temporary now were closing in on him. Secure in his innocence, he had not felt afraid. Now fear like a long obscene black worm crawled into his head and dominated his thoughts. Could they hang him? Would they? They just might. Turning his back on the grinning Sergeant, who seemed to be mentally measuring him for a coffin, Rory sat down to the table, and with fingers which he noticed were trembling, he spread his writing materials before him.

A note to Tim! No, to Jehu! No, not to either of them. He would have to write to them in English and it might fall into the wrong hands. Almera could speak but not read Arabic. Fayal could do both. He started to write. The cursive Arabic characters flowed from his pen.

FAYAL, MY FRIEND,

Almera will explain what has happened to me if you do not already know. Get a horse and ride out to Melrose and tell the red-haired man Tim to come to town and bring my man K'tu with him. Tell them to go to the ship to see Captain Jehu. Tell Captain Jehu to get the ship ready to sail, well watered and stocked with provisions. Never mind a return cargo. I do not know what may happen, but it is well to be prepared. You stay aboard the ship and tell Tim to come here to see me tomorrow. Have him say he is

431

my solicitor. I understand Almera loves you and you return her love. My blessing on you both. *El mektub mektub,* my friend.

He spilled sand over the sheet of paper, brushed it off, doubled it over and over until it was a tiny square. He turned his chair to face the door of his cell and noticed that Spiggott was dozing, his head on his chest. Again he heard the upper door open and this time he could see by the soft leather sandals and the flowing veils that it was Almera bringing him his meal. She glided through the hall, a veil covering her face, the tray held aloft, passing Spiggott who opened one eye, then came over to unlock the door; as Almera passed Rory his tray, he slipped the folded note into her hand.

"Take this to Fayal quickly," he whispered in Arabic.

"To Fayal?" she looked up at him in surprise.

"Yes, to Fayal."

Her eyes, above the veil, looked at him with a strange expression.

"You are free to love him, Almera."

"My lord and master," she answered and would have kissed his hand had he not drawn it away quickly before Spiggott could notice.

"Hey, what's all this talk going on?" Spiggott pulled Almera from the cell and slammed the door shut. "If you're going to talk, talk the king's English so I can understand it."

"Merely thanking her, that's all." Rory heard the padlock snap shut, but he knew he was not alone. Both Almera and Lady Mary were on his side. Suddenly the bars did not seem quite so solid as they had before.

CHAPTER XL

IT MIGHT HAVE BEEN BECAUSE HE HAD SLEPT so soundly the night before; it might have been that he was not physically tired because he had had no exercise that day; it might have been because he was not accustomed to sleeping alone without the soft pliancy of a woman's body touching his own; or it might have been that his nerves were too frazzled to let him forget his predicament. Whatever it was, he was unable to sleep, but tossed and turned on the narrow pallet, finding no comfort in its meager softness. He could keep track of time by the booming of a bell somewhere in the town which tolled off the interminable passing of the hours in dull, metallic thuddings which he counted. He had counted nine strokes, then ten, and now it was starting on eleven.

The supper Spiggott had brought him—Almera was absent that evening and he wondered if she had been out searching for Fayal—had been plentiful, but now once again he felt hungry and he pulled himself up off the bed, remembering a crust of bread which he had not eaten. His groping hands searched for it in the darkness and found it. Momentarily he was grateful that it was a larger crust than he had thought and he took it back to his bed, sitting on the edge of the planking and munching on the dry crust.

So Almera was really in love with Fayal. At least that was what Lady Mary had said, and her looks had confirmed it. In love with Fayal and not with himself? Impossible! How could any woman prefer Fayal to himself? He smiled grimly in the darkness. Yes, he'd have to be honest with himself, many women might fall in love with Fayal. Most certainly. But not Almera! Never! She was his own; she always had been; she always would be. Why, she was even the mother of his son, so how could she love Fayal? He never doubted her loyalty to him, and what was loyalty but another word for love?

Yes, he desired her. Yet, as he commenced to weave his colorful fantasies around her, he realized that the white and gold loveliness of Lady Mary had a way of intruding itself to blot out completely Almera's darker beauty. Mary on her knees before him, separated from him by the iron grating of the door, debasing herself before him in absolute and utter love. Lost in his reminiscences, he almost forgot where he was. The darkness hid the walls of his cell and only a faint light silhouetted the iron bars at the door. How long he sat there, lost in his thoughts, he did not know, but slowly he returned to the world of reality.

It was a clamor of shouting that brought him back. It had started far off, scarcely perceptible, but had gradually come nearer until now it rose outside the residence itself. Demanding shouts of angry men filtered down through the thatch of vines outside the window of his cell. He heard his own name shouted in bitter wrath and high-pitched anger. He heard demands for his life that sent him quivering from his perch on the plank bed to crouch in a corner of the cell, doubled up in embryonic protection against the screaming world outside his cell. His cell? What protection would that be against the howling mob outside? He thanked some far-off god, whether it was Allah or Christ he did not know, that he was not exposed to this wrath in that open vulnerable cage. Here at least there were solid walls, and for the first time he was thankful for the iron bars of his cell.

The clamor was interrupted by a volley of musketry, and then the shouts were renewed with intensity. He held his breath after the shots, waiting to hear the moans of pain, and when there were none, he figured the soldiers had fired over the mob's heads to frighten rather than to injure. Above the roar and the confusion, he could hear his name again and again, coupled with epithets so vile that he instinctively crouched even lower, longing for something to cover his face as he cringed in the cell. There was no doubt; the mob was out for his blood. Every man in that unseen horde was stridently accusing him of the murder of Mary Fortescue, and not one among them would be unwilling to tear him limb from limb to avenge her death.

A light appeared in the long corridor, and he heard the staccato hammering of a pair of heavy boots. Raising his head, he saw Spiggot running and heard the clang of the heavy grating as he slammed shut the door at the end of the corridor. Rory had a quick feeling of relief. It was one more barrier between him and the mob. Evidently Spiggot had been none to soon, for the shouts were now close at hand, strained through the grating itself.

"Let us at the murdering bastard!"

"Hanging's too good for him!"

"We'll plug his ass with gunpowder and blow the bloody bounder to hell."

"Cut off his balls and stuff 'em in his mouth."

"Cut off his prick, too, and make the whoremonger bastard eat it."

"What he did to Mrs. Fortescue! No woman will ever be safe with him a-whorin' round."

"Come on, Spiggott, let us at him or we'll blow you to hell too."

A shot rang out, fired by some careless hand outside, and the blast was followed by the ping of a bullet as it ricocheted from one wall of the corridor to the other.

Spiggott threw down the candle and stepped on the flame, plunging them into darkness. Rory could hear his running footsteps as he retreated along the corridor. He had felt a momentary safety with the sergeant there. Now there was nothing left—nothing between him and the shouting, threatening mob outside except the two iron-barred doors, and he knew, with the frenzy mounting, that these would prove no protection.

"Get a log, men, a good strong one." Some self-appointed commander was demonstrating his leadership.

"We'll batter down the dooor."

"Come on, men, all together. Those goddamned iron bars can't stop us."

"But they will." Where the voice came from Rory could

435

not tell, but it was near him, right outside his cell. It spoke with authority and the cultured diction of a Mayfair salon. Somewhere in his frightened memories, he knew he had heard it before. It continued.

"Disperse! We'll have no taking of the law into common hands such as yours. This is a part of England, lads, and we'll do things in the right way. The man will be tried before a jury of his peers. If he is guilty, he'll be punished. You've my word on it. Now disperse, go to your homes. Leave these matters to me. Justice will be done."

Rory identified the voice. It was Sir Basil, standing in the darkness just outside his cell. Rory crawled across the floor, abjectly groping through the bars. His searching hand encountered a buckled shoe and crept up to a thin, silk-shod ankle. He clung to it; the mere touching of flesh gave him confidence even though the howls from the doorway had not subsided.

Another shot.

This one did not richochet from wall to wall. Rory felt the foot he was clasping move, then it was wrenched from his grasp, and he heard the dull thud of a body as it fell to the floor and the rattle of lungs bubbling for breath.

For the second time a light appeared and a thunder of heavy-shod footsteps was heard on the stairs. This time Spiggott held aloft a lantern and there were soldiers behind him, the light splintering on their bayonets. Spiggott advanced down the corridor, his musket aimed in readiness. He stopped momentarily before the prone figure of Sir Basil. In the smoky light, Rory could see a stain of bright blood on the ruffled cambric of the old man's shirt and the stain was fast seeping into the shiny black satin of his coat.

"You've shot the governor, men, and heaven help that bastard that done it!" Spiggott aimed his gun and was about to fire point-blank into the mob outside but he hesitated, then lowered the musket. "Might kill an innocent man—begone, you ill-begotten, hell-and-be-damned cullies. Get yourselves to your homes. An English governor is dead. Why, it's as bad as killing the king himself. The one what fired the shot will be found and he'll dance at rope's end on thin air, like you've been thinking of hanging this 'un here. Get gone!"

"The old duffer's dead," someone yelled, "but we're after the bloody bastard what killed Mrs. Fortescue."

"And you'll not get him," Spiggott roared back, drowning out the clamor. "You'll not lay one of your dirty fingers on him. I'll blast you all to hell if you don't get away from here!" Again he brought up his musket, and the soldiers behind him, without any spoken order, leveled their muskets at the doorway. Rory, by craning his head, could see the shouting faces and the gesticulating arms through the bars at the end of the hall.

There was no mistaking Spiggott's words and the fact that he meant business. Gradually the clenched fists around the bars loosened their hold; slowly the arms were pulled back and the shouting mouths retreated into the darkness; but the mouths were not stilled and the threats continued.

"We'll be gitting him, Spiggott, spite of all you can do."

"He killed her. Blood for blood."

"Blood's already been shed. More'n enough for tonight." Spiggott signaled to the soldiers behind him to keep the doorway covered and laid down his own musket as he knelt on the floor beside Sir Basil.

"Wasn't a bad man in his way." He turned to look up at Rory. "A bloody murderer you may be, lad. God knows if you're guilty or not, but according to him, you get a chance to prove that you're innocent. Isn't safe to leave you here, nor safe to put you out in that cage neither. What am I going to do with you?"

"With whom?" Lady Mary, her dress changed to one of somber, lusterless black, stalked into the circle of light. "With him?" she pointed down to Sir Basil's body.

"Dead he is, milady." Spiggott removed his battered leather shako and clambered to his feet. "Shot he was, by them outside. They've gone now, skulkin' out like dogs with their tails 'twixt their legs, but methinks they'll come back again this night. There's nothing we can do for him now." He pointed down to Sir Basil.

"Have him taken upstairs and lay him out on our bed."

437

She pondered a moment. "There must be someone in this godforsaken town who lays out the dead."

"Grammy Withers."

"Then go for her. And order a coffin for him."

"Yes, milady." Spiggott was so indoctrinated to taking orders from his superiors that he did not question her, yet he did have a moment of indecision. "But what about him?" He nodded in Rory's direction.

"We've got to hide him. I'll take full responsibility for him while you are gone. Have you any manacles?"

"That we have, ma'am. Leg irons, too."

She pondered for a moment, avoiding Rory's eyes.

"Take him upstairs. He'll not escape with your men around. Then fetch the manacles and leg irons. Put them on him and give me the key. I've a pistol upstairs and I'll stand guard over him. I'll make it my responsibility to see that the rogue does not escape. From now on, at least for the time being, sergeant, you're taking orders from me."

"Yes, milady."

"Then hurry. Get the door of his cell unlocked and take him upstairs. I can hide him in the buttery—the windows there are high and barred and he'll be more secure if they come back."

"As they will, as they most surely will, milady."

Spiggott circled the body of Sir Basil on the floor and came over to the door of Rory's cell. The key grated in the padlock and his fingers encircled Rory's wrist with a grip of iron. "One move out of ye, my lad, and it's a slug of lead in your heart." Rory felt the cold muzzle of the gun through his thin shirt. Spiggott yanked him out of the cell and stood him up facing the wall while he directed the soldiers to pick up Sir Basil's body and carry it upstairs. They led the procession up the narrow stairs, followed by Lady Mary, who had finally decided it might be well to show a little grief and carried a square of lace and linen before her face. Rory, with Spiggott's gun still at his back, brought up the rear.

In the courtyard above, the procession divided, those carrying the corpse going on to ascend another flight of stairs, while Lady Mary led the way to the kitchen. They stopped momentarily at a large armoire at the further end of the patio. Spiggott opened one of the tall doors and after some metallic fumbling, drew out a pair of manacles and another pair of leg irons. These he snapped around Rory's wrists and ankles. He was about to put the keys in his pocket when Lady Mary, her little pretense of grief over, held out her hand.

"I'll take the keys, Spiggott." She placed them inside the white ruching that bordered the bodice of her dress, wincing a little as the cold metal touched her. "Now the pistol. It's on Sir Basil's desk in the office. I well know how to use it and if he moves, I'll give him that slug of lead you promised him a few moments ago."

Spiggott was gone for the briefest of moments, but while he was away, Mary leaned over and whispered in Rory's ear, "Trust me, darling."

Spiggott returned and handed the pistol to her. One look at the fire in her eyes convinced him that Rory would be in safe hands. He opened the door at the end of the hall which led to the kitchen. One candle burned feebly on the long, scrubbed trencher table.

Mary indicated a chair for Rory to sit in. "No need to lock him in the buttery," she said. "Better for him to be here where I can keep an eye on him until you return. If I hear any disturbance outside, I'll hide him in there."

"Better if I chain him to the table, milady?"

"No, he'll be safe here without it." She sat down opposite Rory, her pistol aimed at him. "Now, Spiggott, there are a lot of things I want you to do and there's nobody else around here I trust like you."

"Thank you, milady." He pulled at his forelock and bobbed his head in acknowledgment.

"First, you know where my woman, Almera, sleeps."

He nodded.

"Go there and rouse her. I want to give her instructions about what clothes to lay out for poor Sir Basil."

Again he bobbed his head.

"Then go and fetch this Grammy What's-Her-Name. Tell her to come right over and attend to my husband."

Another bob of his head.

"Bring her back yourself so that you'll know she gets

439

here. Perhaps the old beldame would be frightened to go out alone at night."

"That she would and that I will."

"Then when you have brought her back here . . ." Lady Mary stopped suddenly and looked up searchingly at Spiggott. "By the way, how far away does she live?"

"About half an hour by horse, milady, but if I bring her back twill take longer 'cause she'll have to walk."

"Very well. Take what time you need but be sure she gets here. We'll have to bury him today or he'll stink. After you bring her back, I want you to go to the Aguacil. Tell him about Sir Basil's death and say that the Illustrious Cabildo will have to take over the government of the town. Until they do you can consider me in command. Right?"

"Right, milady."

"And deploy all your soldiers at the gate that leads into the cells below. Outside. They can be seen there and the mob will think this man is still there if they decide to return."

He nodded.

"Then go!"

She waited until she heard his footsteps diminishing down the tiles of the patio. Laying the pistol on the table, she came to where Rory was sitting. She took his face in her hands and pushed his head back and her lips sought his hungrily. Those same hands, seeking under his shirt, molded the muscles of his chest, and her fingers toyed with his hardening paps. A door opened and she released him quickly, fearful that it might be Spiggott returning; but it was only Almera, who stepped inside and closed the door behind her.

"You sent for me, milady?"

She put her fingers to her lips, hushing her, and beckoned to her to come over to them.

"Fayal? Where is he?"

"With all that has been going on, milady, he has been with me in my room."

Mary smiled. "One excuse is as good as another, but at least he's here. Now listen carefully. We have little time. Go to your room and fetch Fayal. Fetch me also the black

440

robe that you have and the black veil that covers your face. And the baby. You and Fayal get back here as soon as possible."

Almera glided out the door, but not before casting a frightened look at Rory in his chains and at the ominous pistol on the table. Mary reached down into the white lace of her bodice and extracted the two keys. It took her only a moment to unlock the manacles and the leg irons. Rory stood up and clasped her briefly in his arms.

"Your ship?"

"If Fayal delivered the message, she's ready to sail."

"Then trust me. Let me be the general who gives the orders for the time being. You'll have plenty of time to be my lord and master afterwards. Hark!"

Again the door opened and Fayal entered with Almera, who had the baby in her arms. Over Fayal's arm was draped a long length of dull black cloth.

Without speaking, Mary took the cloth and shook it out until it formed a voluminous robe. She gathered it up and put it over Rory's head. It came only a little below his knees, but she disregarded its shortness. Throwing back the hood, she tied the black veil over his face. "It's better that we walk. We will not be noticed as much as in that damned state carriage. Fayal, you know where the ship is. It's best that we do not all go together, so start now and take Almera and the baby," she pushed them toward the outside door. "We'll follow in a few minutes. If anyone asks where you are going, say that you are going to fetch the old lady that lays out the dead. Do you understand?"

"Yes, milady. Shall we go aboard the ship?"

She nodded. "Now go!"

They slipped out the back door silently. Mary came closer to Rory. "Do I dare chance it?"

"What, darling?"

"My jewels. They're upstairs."

"You'll have more jewels in Sa'aqs than you ever saw before. Let's get out of here now."

"Yes," she assented, reaching her hand down to nestle for a second in the warmth of his crotch, "there's only one jewel that matters from now on—this one—and that's mine now and forever."

441

"It is, Mary, it is."

"Then we go. Remember, Rory, if we are stopped on the streets, let me do the talking." She opened the back door slowly and peered out into the darkness, beckoning for him to follow. The soldiers had lighted a small fire below at the dungeon entrance and were gathered around it. They skirted it and the shadows of the house and hid themselves in the deeper shadows of the trees that bordered the driveway. Once out on the street, they kept to the darker side, their black clothes blending into the shadows.

Twice they passed taverns, lighted far beyond their usual closing hours, from which issued strident and drunken roisterings. They skirted them in wide circles, Rory making himself as small as possible and walking with a mincing gait. Both were passed without any incident. Those inside were too preoccupied even to look out. Finally they came to the deserted road that led to the port. It was a long walk and took them over an hour. Only once did they meet anyone and the group coming toward them had signaled their approach by drunken singing. A clump of plantains offered them security within its broad leaves and deep shadows, and Mary clung closer to Rory as they heard his name bedamned and threatened, but the roisterers passed and they were safe.

Finally, after so long a period of suspenseful walking, they glimpsed the lights of the *Shaitan* and Rory noted gratefully that there were more lights than were ordinarily used at night, which denoted activity aboard. As they arrived at the gangplank, Rory made out Tim's figure silhouetted against a lantern.

"Timmy!" Rory steadied Mary across the gangplank and jumped down to the deck in a parachuting billow of black robes.

"Rory!" Tim welcomed him with open arms while Rory tore the stifling veil from his face.

"Jehu?"

"Ready to sail at a moment's notice. The tide is going out. You arrived in the nick of time."

"Almera and Fayal?"

"Here with the child."

442

"Then, Timmy, hop ashore, we're sailing."

"But . . ."

"But me no buts, Timmy. Do it for me, for the love that's between us, Timmy lad. I've come nigh to hanging tonight. It's only by the grace of God and Lady Mary that I'm here."

Tim stepped closer to Mary, leading her out of the shadow into the circle of light from the ship's lantern.

"My God! Yasmin!" He hesitated a moment. "I'll go, Rory. I'll go and settle everything up for you. Sell the slaves and all for you."

"For us, Timmy."

"Your hand, Rory." There were tears in his eyes.

"You have it, Tim, and my heart, too. Get Ephinstone to help you. God bless you. Now go."

Tim sped over the gangplank. When he was halfway across, Rory's voice halted him. "And Tim . . ."

"Yes, Rory."

"If Mama wants to come back to Africa with you, bring her, too."

"And Penny?"

"You'll have a hareem in Africa and a king that's a queen waiting for you."

Tim disappeared into the darkness just as Jehu came down the ladder from the quarterdeck.

"I thought I heard your voice, Rory. You're really here! I've been worried about you."

"Then keep right on worrying, Jehu, until we reach the open sea. Let's get out of here quick."

"Cast off!" Jehu didn't wait for the bosun to pipe the orders. "Cast off, men. Twenty pounds sterling to every man jack of you when we reach Africa, and a free passage back to wherever you want to go."

"Aye, aye, sir!" they bellowed.

The strip of black water was already widening, and with each additional foot, Rory felt a new surge of freedom. The sails came down with a clatter and filled, billowing out in the soft night breeze. The ship turned and water churned beneath her keel. Rory took Lady Mary in his arms. Already the dim lights were beginning to be swallowed up in the darkness.

"Yasmin." His voice was muffled in her hair.

"My lord and master," she answered.

"My darling, very dear." He pulled off the black robe which the breeze was whipping around his body.

"But I'm even more than your darling and your very dear." The scudding clouds parted for a moment and the moon highlighted her eyes with a dancing light.

"What could ever be more than our loving each other, Mary?"

"Our son, Rory."

He held her at arms' length, his lips compressed into a thin line. "What are you talking about, *our son?*"

"Just that. The child with Almera is not hers; it's mine—ours."

"But how?"

"How? In truth, Rory, it was not a very complicated matter. You planted the seed, I bore the child. Planting the seed was the least difficult of all. Bearing him, too, was comparatively simple, but oh, those days and days of tight lacing so that nobody would know. Ay, Rory, that was the complicated part. But nobody did know. Almera's child, which you also planted and which would have been a daughter, was stillborn, strangled on the cord. Mine followed almost immediately with only Almera to help me. So, were I ever to hold up my head again in England, it had to be Almera's child despite its yellow hair and white skin. Now I can tell you that it is all ours. Almera will bear me out; and now, for the first time, I can give our son the love he really deserves."

He gathered her into his arms, softly and tenderly and without passion, pressing her cheek to his own. There were tears, but whether they were his or hers it was impossible to tell.

"Another Baron of Sax," he whispered.

"My darling, let us say a Prince of Sa'aqs, for that is where I want our home to be."

"Inshallah!" Rory led her gently toward his cabin.

CHAPTER XLI

THE GREAT RED ORB OF THE SUN, SINKING into the western horizon, silhouetted the squat, phallic minaret and cast a long black shadow over the palace of Sa'aqs. It was now a palace of glistening marble and the sentries who guarded it were spruce in their baggy white trousers, their gold-laced black jackets, and their red fezzes. It was quite a change from the old sunbaked mud palace with its tatterdemalion soldiers slouching at the gates. A little wind that had sprung up with the setting of the sun rattled the fronds of the date palms, brushing them against each other with a metallic rasping. A white racing camel, its unmelodious bell clanking from a string of blue beads around its neck, picked its way daintily through the dust to the prods of the camel boy on its back. The boy pulled the beast up sharply, edging it over to one side of the narrow street, making way for two horsemen who galloped up to the big iron entrance gates of the palace. Waiting grooms took their horses and the men disappeared between the guns of the sentries into the darkening interior.

One of the men, the huge black, clasped the other man about his shoulders. The second removed the wound turban of white muslin, shaking loose his yellow hair until it fell down around his shoulders.

"A good ride, Baba."

"And there'll be another tomorrow, Rory."

"And for all our tomorrows, I hope, my brother."

"As Allah wills."

Slipping out of their heavy woolen djellabahs, which they tossed to the huge black woman, voluminously aproned and skirted in white, who grinned back at them

445

with Mama Phoebe's comfortable affability, they passed into a large courtyard where a curtain of vines screened out the last few rays of the sun. A fountain tinkled into a basin of azure tiles and a cloying scent of roses and jasmine hung heavy in the air. A boy of about five, his flaxen blond hair matching the pale citrine of his silk kaftan, ran up and clasped his arms about Rory's knees and a woman, unveiled but dressed in Moorish robes, followed him. She bowed with a perfunctory but respectful obeisance to Baba; then linked her arm in Rory's, drawing him close to her.

"My lord and master," she smiled up at him, sharing the smile with Baba.

He looked down at her and laughed. "Listen to her, Baba. Just like a Moorish wife she flatters me with 'lord and master' although I am, in truth, no longer lord and master of my own hareem, nay, not even of my own person, for the Princess Yasmin controls even that, down to the paring of my fingernails. I've become nothing but her slave."

"And what a day that will be! Rory Mahound a slave to a woman." She linked her other arm in Baba's. "Imagine *him* being a slave to any woman."

"Something tells me he always has been. But according to palace gossip, my sister, there have been complaints about him. The girls in his hareem are languishing for want of attention." Baba patted her white hand.

She laughed, propelling them toward the marble stairs which led to the upper apartments. "I've a mind to appoint Fayal as chief eunuch to my husband's *hareem*, although Fayal is about as far removed from being a eunuch as it is possible to be. Still, with him to service them, I'm sure they would no longer languish. And, speaking of Fayal, he's waiting for you in your rooms, Rory. I've had him lay out your sea-green caftan with the broidery of emeralds and pearls. For you, Baba, I ordered K'tu to lay out your white ribbed silk, and you're to wear your diamond egret in your turban."

"You see, Baba, we're no longer our own masters." Rory picked up the boy in his arms and slung his legs around his neck, jouncing him like an unruly horse, which

446

caused the boy to grab at Rory's hair and shrill with happiness.

"But why all this splendor tonight, my sister?" Baba lifted the boy from Rory's shoulders and placed him on his own. "For a simple dinner must we rival Suleiman the Magnificent?"

Mary pulled them both closer to her. "You see, my husband and my brother, how very necessary it is for you to have me around. You have already forgotten."

"Forgotten what?"

"That this is a most important day! That even now His Half-Majesty the King of Basampo along with His Entire Majesty the King of Basampo are upstairs in their bath."

"Tim's arrived?" Rory broke away and started to run up the stairs, but she held him back.

"I doubt if the little King of Basampo would appreciate your bursting into his bath. To my way of thinking that young king has something to hide, and you'd better not try to discover what it is. Yes, they are here. Their caravan came while you were out riding, and you can be glad that I was here to do the official honors. I even remembered to have a salute of twenty-one guns fired for His Majesty and another of eleven guns for Timmy."

"Their caravan? Was it a large one?" Baba asked anxiously.

"Timmy said something about three hundred prime slaves."

"Good, we'll be able to include them in our next shipment and Basampo slaves always bring top prices." For a moment Rory was all business.

"Thank God you're not going back to Trinidad or San Domingo or Cuba or any other place with them." Mary clutched him a little closer.

"No, Mary, that's for Timmy or Mansour. Baba and I will stay here and grow old together while the others turn our black ivory into sparkling gold. It will be good to see Timmy again. We've all come a long way together."

They paused a moment at the foot of the stairs, then started slowly to ascend. When they reached the top, Baba took the boy from his shoulders and placed him on the floor. Mary took her arms from the men, kissed Rory

447

lightly on the mouth and Baba on the cheek and with an admonishment to them not to be late when the big gong sounded for dinner, started to leave them, going in the opposite direction from that in which they were facing. "Almera is helping me to dress. Remember, we meet in an hour." She took the boy by the hand.

"A long hour, my darling, without you." Rory's hand rumpled the boy's hair.

Her fluttering veils, her soft footsteps, and the waving farewells of the boy faded off down the long corridor. Baba linked his arm in Rory's, and they walked slowly down the dim hall to their apartments. At his door Rory stopped and took Baba's hand in his own.

"Ours is a happy life, Baba."

"Allah has so willed it, Rory."

"And may He always so will it."

"If it is written on our foreheads and in the Book of Fate, Rory."

"Baba, my brother."

"And you, Rory, mine."

THE MAHOUND, 1968–1969:
Albany, New York; Athens, Greece;
Tulsa, Oklahoma; Nairobi, Kenya;
and Acapulco, Mexico.